I0594068

Mob Knight

The O'Rourke Brotherhood

Sabine Barclay

OLIVERHEBERBOOKS

All rights reserved.

No part of this publication may be sold, copied, distributed, reproduced or transmitted in any form or by any means, mechanical or digital, including photocopying and recording or by any information storage and retrieval system without the prior written permission of both the publisher, Oliver Heber Books and the author, Sabine Barclay, except in the case of brief quotations embodied in critical articles and reviews.

PUBLISHER'S NOTE: This is a work of fiction. Names, characters, places, and incidents either are the product of the author's imagination or are used fictitiously. Any resemblance to actual persons, living or dead, business establishments, events, or locales is entirely coincidental.

Mob Knight Copyright © 2024 by Sabine Barclay

Cover art by Dar Albert at Wicked Smart Designs

Published by Oliver Heber Books

0 9 8 7 6 5 4 3 2 1

As one door closes, a window opens.

We've come to the end of The O'Rourke Brotherhood. Thank you for reading and loving these bad boys.

Never fear!
The Syndicate Wars world isn't over.
The Cartel Brotherhood will capture your heart.

Find me writing Historical Romance as Celeste Barclay.

Happy reading,
Sabine

Subscribe to Sabine's Newsletter

Subscribe to Sabine's bimonthly newsletter to receive exclusive insider perks.

Have you read *The Syndicate Wars?* This FREE origin story novella is available to all new subscribers to Sabine's monthly newsletter. Subscribe on her website.
www.sabinebarclay.com

The O'Rourke Brotherhood

Chapter One

Joey

"Just let me know if you need anything, Mrs. Ramirez. You know I'm here to support you and Armando. All you have to do is call me."

"Thank you, Ms. Bracero."

"You've done so much for your grandson, but I know there's more you want to do. If he needs another trip to the doctor, let me know, and I will come with you."

I look at the older woman as we converse in Spanish, and my heart breaks for her as I think about her six-year-old grandson. He's the most adorable kid in the world. As a social worker, I see the best and worst. Armando's one of the lucky ones.

I spin around at a pop-pop-pop noise.

I know what it is. I'm halfway down the steps leading to the Ramirezes' apartment building. The little boy's still tucked away in bed in his grandmother's apartment. Mrs. Ramirez calls out to me as my gaze sweeps the surrounding area. I immediately spot the men standing outside the bodega across the street. I look to my right and spot a man with a shock of strawberry blond hair and freckles standing just beside the entrance to the pawn shop next door. I get what's happening in an instant, and I know the men across the street won't stop until they've hit their target.

"Go inside, Mrs. Ramirez. *Now!*"

I bolt down the last couple of steps and move to my right, shoving the man as hard as I can. He staggers backwards, even though he must be nearly twice my size. His hand shoots out to grab my shirt as he looks toward me. Shock registers on his face as he realizes I'm not attacking him. He tries to regain his balance as his arm windmills, but it's holding his gun. I watch in slow motion as he points toward the sky to keep it away from me.

Then we're falling.

He's doing his best to shield me as we tumble down the stairs toward a basement apartment. But we go head over toes, rolling side to side. His arm is around me, and he's gripping me, still trying to curve his body around mine to take most of the impact. When we reach the bottom of the stairs, I already hurt everywhere. Now that we've come to a stop, my shoulder screams at me since that's what I landed most of my weight on when I hit the first step.

"Are you okay?" There's no sympathy in his voice with that demand.

He looks me over, and I can practically read his thoughts. He wants to make sure I'm fine, so he can get up, walk away, and go back to the shootout that's about to take place if he shows his face again.

"I am, but you won't be. Stay down. Don't move." I scramble to get back onto my feet, but he grabs hold of my shirt, this time from the back, and yanks me toward him.

"What the devil do you think you're doing?"

"I'm going to make sure you don't get shot. You or anybody else on this street."

"You are not getting in the middle of this. You are going to stay right where you are."

"I don't know who you are, but I know who those men are, and I know what they're capable of."

There's an aura of menace that surrounds him, and I should be terrified, but he doesn't seem to direct that toward me. Irritation perhaps, but I'm not scared of him. However, I am scared of the men across the street. The glower he shoots me as he speaks tells he doesn't believe I can do anything for him.

"I don't care if you don't know who I am. I know who those men are too, and there's no way in hell I'm letting you stick your head out where it can become their next target."

"The difference between you and me, though, is that I'm not the one they obviously wish to kill."

"But you are the one who'll get killed if you keep arguing with me and go up there. The moment they see movement they'll shoot. They won't wait to see who it is."

I point to his red hair, then mine. "There's no way they can confuse the two of us."

"It doesn't matter about confusing my red hair for your brown hair. It's about a single bit of movement. They won't wait. I've said that twice. Don't make me say it a third time."

I don't bother waiting as he suggests—commands—me to stop. Instead, I push against his chest and scramble again for the stairs.

"Ronaldo, Jesus, stop. It's me, Jocelyn."

I call out to the men across the street. I know I have a voice that projects. There's no way they don't hear me. I raise my hands slowly and put them above my head where I know they can see them without seeing the rest of me.

"I'm coming up the steps alone. Don't shoot."

3

"*Señorita*, you helped him. Why should we leave you alone?"

Those are *not* the words the redheaded man wants to hear as he reaches for me a third time. I skirt away from him.

"I'm the voice of reason here, just like I have been since you were in grade school, Ronaldo. There are too many people here on the street. I don't care who knows who you are and what you are. You're going to kill somebody other than this man you're aiming for. Do you want that on your conscience? Do you want people to know you shot a little kid because you couldn't shoot straight? You had your chance. He's a big guy with bright hair, and you couldn't hit him. I'm not giving you a chance to miss again and take out somebody we care about."

"*Señorita* Jocelyn, you always need to be in the middle of everything. Haven't you heard curiosity killed the cat?"

"Well, this cat's got claws, Ronaldo, and you know that. I'll sink them in deep. Put the gun away, and you three deal with whatever business you have going on, but you do it somewhere else. You don't do it on the street. You know the rules just as well as I do, and you know how I feel about having the kids see this around them."

"Fine, tell the *hijo de la chingada* he can come out, and I won't shoot him." Motherfucker.

"Language, Ronaldo. Do you want me to tell your *abuelita* how you speak?"

There's a pause, and I know that single threat is more intimidating than anything else. I've met the woman several times, and she scares the ever-loving shit out of me. She wields a *chancla* like she's some samurai warrior. Her flip flop with a wood sole is nothing to underestimate.

I know she paddled Ronaldo's ass more than once when he was a child. She probably should have done it a few more times, considering how he turned out. I'm not a proponent of corporal punishment, but...Lord. I can only imagine how he would've been if she hadn't been such a strict disciplinarian.

"My *abuelita's* visiting my dad upstate."

"I have her number in my phone. I could call her right now. She can have a message waiting for when she leaves. Or maybe I'll catch her before she even sees your *papi*. She can tell him all about what you're getting up to these days. I'm sure it's exactly what he wished for when he went away."

There's enough snarkiness to fill a cup when I call his father Daddy. I was walking up the steps as I spoke, and now I'm on the sidewalk once again. My tone tells him his grandmother visiting her son in prison won't deter me from telling her. I lower my hands, but I keep them out to my sides.

"You're just as guilty as Ronaldo, Jesus. Just because you haven't said anything doesn't mean I forgot you're there. Really, you're going to do this right outside your mother's window?"

I twist and look up. I see a woman half hanging out of her window, and I can see the fear on her face. I look back across the street and point up.

"You really want to have your mom watch what happens? Do you really think you're going to win? From the way this man's snarling at me down here, I'm pretty sure he's the one who will put up a bigger fight. Whatever this is, take it inside. I don't care what you do to each other as long as you don't do it where any of the kids can see."

"This is all about you protecting the kids, *señorita* Jocelyn? What? Now that I'm nineteen, you don't care about me anymore?"

I snort as I listen to Jesus. "If I didn't care about you, do you think I'd even be having this conversation? But you wanted to be treated like an adult. You wanted to tell me how much of a man you were when you turned eighteen last year. Well, now you can show you're man enough to know when you're wrong and to know this isn't just about you and whatever this guy did to piss you off."

I hear a huff coming from down the steps, but I don't dare shift my attention away from the men who still have guns drawn. They may not be pointing them across the street anymore—they're pointing them at the sidewalk—but I wouldn't put it past them to lose their shit and turn their guns on me. One wrong word is all it'll take if I test their machismo too much. There's a fine line between reminding them of promises they made to me and shaming and humiliating them. I don't need them thinking they have to prove their *huevos* have dropped.

"*Señorita*, go inside and leave this alone. We'll take it back into the bodega. He can come inside, and we won't do anything to him until he's through the door."

"Yeah, and how many people are still in that bodega? Hmm? I doubt it's empty. I'm guessing that's why he isn't in there with you. He isn't the one pointing a gun where it could fire and hit somebody."

"No, he's hiding behind you like a little bitch."

"You really think a man his size is hiding? No, he won't show himself in front of you because he doesn't trust you not to shoot me. Is he wrong?"

I can't hear the swearing because they're not yelling them across the street, but I can read their lips well enough to know there's a whole slew of Spanish and English curse words dropping out of their mouths.

They don't like me putting them on the spot like that. Asking them the one question they absolutely don't want to answer. They don't want to admit any fear of shooting me, but they also don't want to admit they would shoot a woman.

Their boss wouldn't agree to that, but they're still young enough to not understand the consequences of what they're risking right now. I've known these two guys since they were in eighth grade, and I started working in this neighborhood. I know the things they've done because I was their social worker while they were in high school. They're not horrible kids, but they make shit decisions. People they work for take advantage of that. They didn't come recruiting these two. These shitheads went knocking on doors, thinking they could be more man than boy.

They've done odd jobs. Knocked off some shops, stolen some cars, but they haven't killed anybody. Yet. I know nobody's shot either of them. I'd like to keep it that way. But the man who's still standing just a couple steps below me doesn't give me the impression this is the first time he's been in a situation like this.

It wouldn't surprise me if the man would shoot to kill and wouldn't miss. I'm pretty positive the only reason he's still standing is because Ronaldo and Jesus aren't half the marksmen he probably is. I don't care to test my theory that he's a better shot than I expected or that Jesus and Ronaldo are even worse and will hit somebody else.

The street's pretty cleared out around us, but there are still folks farther down the block in each direction who don't know what's going on and are approaching.

"Leave before somebody calls the police. Do you really want to be here when they arrive? Do you want to explain what's going on?"

Those questions are as much for Ronaldo and Jesus as they are for the redheaded stranger. I can feel his eyes boring into me, and I'm certain he's going to be pissed when he finally gets to move. But I don't want any dead bodies on my hands. I've seen a few, and that's been more than enough for me.

"*Señorita*, you don't get to decide this one. We have business to finish, and that gringo has some explaining to do."

I glance over at the man just as he rolls his eyes. I look back at the two teenagers and barely stifle my laugh.

"Ronaldo, you talk shit, my friend. I don't think you can get him to do anything he doesn't want to do."

"But you can." Ronaldo darts his gaze to my left as though he can see the guy through the sidewalk. "You're the one who should go inside instead of letting him hide behind you like a little bitch."

"He's listening to you, and he hasn't come out. You really think this is about him fearing you? He knows you're too damn trigger-happy and that if he moves your aim's going to be crap, and you're more likely to hit me than him."

"No, he's a much bigger target than you. And with that red hair, it'll be easy to hit."

I hear the guy next to me mutter in disgust. "If that were the case, one of those three shots would have hit me."

I keep my voice down, so it's barely more than a whisper. "Do you really think you should test that?"

I think I get more of a grunt than an answer, but I'll take it.

"Ronaldo, Jesus, this is your last opportunity before I reach in my purse and pull out my phone. Do you want me to make that call? Or would you rather explain this on your own later, when you're not likely to die before you get to?"

He definitely doesn't want me to call Enrique Diaz, the Colombian Cartel *jefe* and *el padrino*—Godfather—in this neighborhood.

I watch Jesus holster his gun first. He grabs Ronaldo's left forearm and yanks. He tilts his head back toward the bodega.

"I'm going to follow you inside, so I'm sure you don't come back out the moment you think you can hit him. You don't solve whatever problems you have on the streets. You know the rules."

"He started it!" Jesus calls out, and he sounds like the middle schooler I once knew.

"Yeah well, I'm ending it."

"Why do you have to sound like a mom?"

"If you stopped acting like you needed one, then I'd stop sounding like one. I'm crossing the street."

"Oh, no you're not."

Those are the first intelligible words the stranger's said since I walked up the steps. I ignore him and step away from the railing and move around to cross the street. I sense him walking up behind me. The moment Jesus and Ronaldo disappear through the door, he wraps his arm back around my waist like he did earlier and hauls me down the steps.

I have my back to his chest, and it's a solid wall of muscle. I could fight, but I'm more likely to wind up with us both falling down the stairs again. As much as my shoulder hurt when I landed, now it's my elbow. It's burning and throbbing at the same time. I'm happy to have my hands back down at my sides. It was near agony holding them out so the guys could see me.

They know I'm fully able to defend myself in a neighborhood like this. I didn't want them thinking I was taking anything out of my purse other than maybe my phone.

"What the hell did you think you were doing? You make it sound like you know what those guys are capable of. So, if you know, and you know they're shite shots, then why would you put yourself in danger like that?

"Because whether you get shot isn't my problem. My problem is if somebody in this neighborhood does. You saw the kids on the street playing. I'm certain of it. I'm certain you know every single person who was around. You could tell me a detailed description of each of them. You're more situationally aware than either of those *idiotas* are. I'm not interested in having to explain to parents or grandparents or aunts and uncles why their kid isn't coming home simply because he was playing outside in his neighborhood. I'm not letting you or them put me in that position. I'm not in the mood, and I don't have time. I'm already running late for my next appointment."

"Who are you?"

The question isn't a surprise to me, but I'm still unsure how I want to answer it. Should I stick out my hand to shake it? It's my right elbow that hurts like a motherfucker, so it wouldn't be that hand. How ridiculous would that be?

Hola, señor hottie. Nice to meet you.

I look him up and down, and I can admit what I thought in the seconds before we were tumbling down the stairs. He is the hottest man I have ever seen in my entire life, whether it's a living man or somebody in a picture or in a movie or on TV. He's breathtaking and huge. I'm surprised he didn't squash me like a bug by the time we made it to the bottom of the steps.

"I'm Jocelyn."

He waits to see if I give a last name. He cocks an eyebrow, but I say nothing else. He shakes his head and just grins.

"You know I can find out, so why not just tell me?"

"I'm Jocelyn Bracero."

"You made it sound like you're a social worker or something when you said he knows how you feel about situations like this and that you'd call his grandmother."

"I am. I've been assigned to this neighborhood for the past five years. I told you my name. Now you tell me yours."

"I'm Cormac O'Rourke. It's nice to meet you."

Chapter Two

Cormac

I stare at the irritated woman before me, and I don't know what to make of her. Part of me thinks she's the most foolish woman I've ever met, and part of me thinks she's braver than most men I know all put together. She looks at my hand when I reach out to shake hers. She hesitates, but when she lifts her arm to take my hand, I watch her wince.

"What's the matter?" Maybe I could have sounded nicer than that, a little less demanding.

"It's nothing."

"People don't flinch when it's nothing."

"I banged my shoulder a little, and my elbow's a bit sore."

I don't ask for permission when I reach out and tenderly touch her arm. I look at her elbow, and it's obvious she's injured.

"You need to have this looked at."

I feel badly because I already know the only thing that went wrong for me is I tore the sleeve of my suit coat at the

11

shoulder. My back is already broad, and the coat pulled too tight across it while we fell, but this could be serious for her.

"No, I'm fine. Like I said, I have other appointments today."

"They can wait. You're obviously hurt. If you don't get this looked at today, then you're going to end up being out of work for more than just an afternoon."

"I told you, I'm fine."

"Are you always this stubborn?"

"Yes." Her answer is decisive, and it makes me chuckle.

"At least you're honest."

She jerks her chin toward the bodega. "You need to deal with whatever that's about."

"You need to deal with your arm. I'm not leaving until you do."

"Are you always this bossy?"

"Yes."

Her chuckle matches mine. "At least you're honest, too."

There aren't many people or many times someone would say that about a mobster. I'm the least honest person most people could meet, unless they're talking to some other syndicate man. I lie for a living. At least that's what it feels like. It's more like I lie for survival.

We stand, staring at each other at an impasse. I let go of her arm as gently as I can, but she winces again.

"You are going to see a doctor about that."

She glares at me, and I can tell she doesn't appreciate the finality in my tone. But I'm not giving in to her. She's about to meet her match in stubbornness.

"I'm not leaving here until you promise to see a doctor. And if I don't believe you, then I'll take you to the emergency room myself."

"I'm not wasting time with something they're probably going to say is just nursemaid's elbow and that it'll heal on its own. I just shouldn't use that arm very much. Fortunately, I'm left-handed."

I shake my head. I still don't believe that's all it is. At best, it's partial dislocation like she said. But at worst, it could be far more. And I feel guilty that the only reason she's injured is because she tried to save me and fell down the steps. An average-sized man wouldn't have crushed her like I almost did.

"You're being as awkward as those two boys were. Why can't you admit you need help?"

"Because I don't. Like I said, a doctor will just tell me it's nursemaid's elbow, and I need to rest. Why are you being so demanding?"

"Because I feel guilty."

I rarely blurt things like that. And I rarely feel that emotion toward anybody who isn't part of my family. Not even the men I command. When I make a mistake, I might regret it, but rarely do I feel guilty. It's not that this is an emotion I'm unaccustomed to. It's just one I don't care for.

"I absolve you of any guilt you feel because I pushed you down the stairs, not the other way around."

"I was part of the situation that led you to believe you needed to protect me. Or rather, the kids in the neighborhood."

I flash her a grin that usually makes most people relax. I've been told it's charming when you pair it with my baby face. I'm not the youngest in the family. That would be my cousin, Sean, who's three minutes younger than his twin brother, Shane. Yes, Shane, Sean, and Cormac. Couldn't get much more Irish than those names. Unless you toss in Seamus, my brother, and Finn and Dillan, my cousins. Good Irish names for good Irish mobsters.

"I protected you because it was the right thing to do." She pauses before she smiles. "For the neighborhood."

She shifts her gaze to the bodega Frick and Frack just went into before she looks back at me again.

"Are you going to deal with them in there?"

When she furrows her brow, I know what she assumes that means. Had she not intervened, that's likely what would've already happened. She's right about not involving people in the neighborhood. I didn't draw my gun first, and I didn't shoot, but I would've if I needed to. I believe she knows that, or at least the latter part. I don't know if she realized I wasn't the one who fired my weapon.

Now, cooler heads prevail. They're off the street, and I didn't have to fire a shot. I check the safety, even though I know it's on, then tuck the gun into my lower back holster. She notices the rip in my sleeve when I move. Her gaze locks with mine, but only for a second, knowing it reminded me of her elbow.

"You still haven't agreed to go to the doctor."

"I won't. It's unnecessary."

"You basically told those boys to act like men. And now you're the one who's being stubborn instead of being an adult. Maybe you ought to get a spanking instead of them."

Her eyebrows shoot straight to her hairline, or at least close to it. My palm itches to do just that. I didn't miss how soft she is in all the right places, and how she felt in my arms. She's definitely got an athletic build, but her tits pressed against my chest were unquestionably natural. And the feel of her arse when my hand thumped against it was plush. I don't think I've ever used that word before, but it's one that best describes what filled my hand for too brief a moment.

"Do you have a *chancla* holstered back there? Is that your actual weapon of choice?"

I'm not sure how to answer that, but my hand seems to have

an idea. I lift it and look at it before twisting my wrist toward her, then back to me.

"Do I really look like I need a *chancla*?"

Something flashes in her eyes, and it's not fear or revulsion. It makes me want to do wicked things to her to see if I can make her scream my name as she comes. This is *not* the time to be fantasizing about fucking a woman who I'm trying to convince to go to the emergency room.

An SUV I recognize pulls up along the street near where we stand, cutting our conversation short. This fucknut is the last person I need to see right now since I'll just wind up in an argument with him. When Jocelyn turns to look at the man getting out of the SUV, I watch her freeze, then her head whips back around to stare at me. She takes two steps backward as she shakes her head.

"No. You—I—I gotta go."

Her declaration definitely isn't something she's willing to compromise on. I'm certain she just figured out who I am since she recognized Pablo Diaz. She shifts so Pablo can't see her since I block his view of her. She's not just avoiding him; she's hiding from him. What the fuck did that motherfucker do to make a woman who's just gone toe-to-toe with me hide? I want answers now, but if I demand them from her, Pablo will see me talking and wonder who I'm speaking to. If I go to him and ask, then I just expose her. I keep my voice low, my lips barely moving.

"Stay where you are until I tell you to go back down the steps. You can wait there until I get him into the bodega."

"No, you can't go in there now. It would've been bad enough if you were going to return with just Ronaldo and Jesus inside, but Pablo Diaz is not a man you want to be in an enclosed space with."

She doesn't sound like she's speculating. She sounds like

she knows from experience. That pisses me off even more. What did he do to her? I will find out, even if it's not today. I watch Pablo walk toward the bodega, but I'm certain he's already seen me. He confirms that when he pauses at the door and looks over his shoulder at me.

He raises his eyebrows, and I shrug. It tempts me to swear at him, but I remember how Joey didn't like that punk-arse kid swearing on the street where anybody could hear him.

"You coming or what?"

Pablo calls out to me, and I cross my arms and adopt a smug expression.

"When I'm good and ready, which means those little boys go home to their mamas. I'm not getting shot today."

"Unless it's by me.

Pablo grins, but there hasn't been humor in that guy's voice in at least a decade. Not since he became his family's chief enforcer. My brother—Seamus—and I are the top enforcers in my family. However, we divvy up the unsavory stuff we must do amongst all the brothers and cousins. We all know Pablo is the only one who deals with that shite in his family. It's killed his soul.

"You wouldn't dare mess up my pretty face."

I grin, and it's about as humorless as his. We've had plenty of trouble with the Diazes over the years, so we exist in a perpetual stalemate. That's our version of homeostasis. If we're in a shootout, like I nearly was, then everyone is fair game. It's shoot or be shot. But in situations like this, we're supposed to use our words.

I bet Joey's used that phrase with some of her younger— what do I call them? Clients? Patients? I don't know what social workers call the people they work with. I've never given it any thought. But now that I do, it reminds me Joey's hiding behind me. Her shoulder has brushed between my shoulder blades twice as she tries to stay tucked behind me. My feet are close together to hide her legs.

"Pablo, go in there. Make sure your *niños* went home. And then we'll sort this out." Little boys.

"Fine."

"Just don't take too long. I have other shite to do today."

"You think this little distraction was on my calendar? I have better things to do than this." He opens his mouth to say something else, but there are kids approaching, and neither of us wants to make this situation worse.

I'll wait until one of his guys gives the "all clear" sign before I go in. I watch Pablo duck inside, then count to twenty before I speak to Joey. I don't dare turn around since I'm certain Pablo's watching me through the window, even if I can't see him. When she descends the steps, I keep my voice low, but I'm certain she can hear me since she stops once her head disappears.

"Why are you hiding from him?"

I turn my head just enough, so I can see her out of the corner of my eye. I lean against the railing as though I don't have a care in the world as I wait to cross the street. It helps block where Joey now hides again.

"I had a run-in with him several years ago in a neighborhood like this."

"Let me guess, Jackson Heights."

There's a moment before she says anything. "Yeah."

I'm certain the fact that I know where she met Pablo, and she obviously knows he's Colombian Cartel only reconfirms what she's guessed about me.

"What happened when you met him?"

There's an edge to my tone I didn't intend. There's nothing good about this story if this is how she reacts years later.

"I didn't know who he was back then, but it was a situation

sort of like this one. I called the police, and they came. I guess they didn't realize who was involved, either. They wound up making a big deal out of it, in spite of how no one in the neighborhood wanted to give statements. I guess his younger brother is a cop because he made it all disappear. I'm lucky his family didn't make me disappear."

I don't respond aloud, but Juan *was* a cop. He's no longer anything. Probably not even ash or acidic sludge in the Flushing River. He crossed the bratva one too many times, and he learned his lesson. It was probably one of the last cases he worked if it was five or six years ago.

"You fear Pablo will remember you and go after you this many years later."

"I've heard you guys have long memories for things like that."

It happens all too often that I'm lumped in with other syndicates from people who don't understand the difference. I'm most certainly not a Cartel member.

I'm a mobster. But now isn't the time to correct her.

Chapter Three

Joey

I insulted him by saying you guys. I suppose the red hair and freckles could've told me he's Irish mob, even if his name didn't make me realize it. If that's the case, then he shouldn't be anywhere near this neighborhood unless it's to stir up trouble. I don't like that.

This kind of trouble usually winds up with innocent people getting hurt. I want nothing to do with that. I'm protective of this neighborhood. It's not like I have every family on my caseload, but I get to know the kids here. Some of them call me *señorita*, but a few even call me *tía*. I consider being called "aunt" among the highest praise, so I look out for everyone here.

I have nothing to say now that I've figured out the truth. Cormac turns his head as though he's looking down the street, but our gazes meet for an instant before he looks away.

"You've put it all together, haven't you?"

I'm pretty sure I have.

"And you've decided I'm just as bad as Pablo, right?"

He hesitates for a moment, and I wonder how he intends to deny that statement.

"We're similar, but not the same."

"Isn't that just semantics?"

"Not in my world."

There's an edge to his voice that tells me I risk genuinely insulting him if I keep pushing, and that actually bothers me. I don't feel like he deserves me being rude to him when he was so concerned about me earlier. But it doesn't mean I have to agree with him or approve of what he does.

If I know the man he is, then I should be just as petrified of him as I am Pablo. But even though I just watched them together, he comes across very different. I actually feel safe with him. It's why I didn't run when he told me to stay behind him. I could've taken my chances and ducked down these steps again, but I didn't. I don't know if it was how insistent he remained about me getting my elbow checked out or that he told me to hide behind him. But he is more reassuring than he should be.

I'm a fool to believe he's anything other than the monster I know Pablo is. He remains silent while I consider what's happened over the past forty-five minutes. When he pushes away from the fence, he issues another command.

"Get your arm checked, *cailín*. I'll know if you don't."

Before I can respond, he's stepping away. I watch him cross the street, his long strides at least twice as wide as mine. I watch him yank open the door to the bodega and stand just within it. His shoulders aren't quite broad enough to span the width, but they're pretty damn close. I always thought Pablo was intimidatingly large, but I can see Cormac is even bigger than him, which just reconfirms it's a false sense of security to trust I'm safe with Cormac.

I can't hear the conversation, but I remain hidden, even though I should seize this opportunity to get to my car. However, I rationalize to myself that somebody could spy me through the window and recognize me, then tell Pablo I'm here. Then again, I don't believe he would do anything while Cormac's here.

However, he'd know Cormac shielded me, and I don't want to be the reason those two Titans clash. It takes another ten minutes—I know because I keep glancing at my watch—before Cormac steps out of the doorway. I've kept my head down, so I don't know everything that happened. I only peeked a few times, and I didn't see him shift from where he was. I know it was so he could make a hasty getaway if need be.

He steps back and lets Pablo walk past. I can't see all of Pablo's expression because he has sunglasses on, but it looks pretty grim from here. Then again, if a guy can have a resting bitch face, it would be Pablo Diaz.

I keep my head just high enough to watch what's happening across the street as Pablo stalks to his SUV. I see Cormac wave to him as Pablo climbs in. It's patronizing as fuck. Once the Colombians drive away, Cormac's attention rivets back to me.

I'm certain he doesn't see me because I ducked my head down the moment Pablo got in the vehicle. But Cormac is definitely staring at me. I can feel it even if I can't see him now. I wonder what's going through his mind because I'm positive I'm about to hear it. It only takes a moment longer before he appears at the top of the steps. I see he's fighting the urge to put his hands on his hips, instead of fisting and unfisting his fingers.

"I made sure you had a chance to leave. Why are you still here?"

"Because somebody might have seen me through the window and recognized me."

He stares at me for a moment before he nods. "They're gone now. Ronaldo and Jesus slipped out the back the moment they saw Pablo arrive. They were no more interested in talking to him than you are. Things smoothed over pretty quickly."

Smoothed over? Is that what they call not shooting each other?

I have a lot to learn about how New York syndicates work.

I shouldn't think that.

It's not like I'm curious about Cormac O'Rourke at all. That would be foolish and ridiculous. But he's the sexiest man I've ever seen with the sun on his strawberry blond hair. It appears to glow like a halo. But he is the furthest thing from an angel you can get. Then again, he became my self-appointed guardian after I did the same thing for him. I'd hardly call myself angelic either.

I take the steps up to the sidewalk where he once more lifts my elbow with such care I barely feel his fingers on my arm. But I still can't help but wince. His expression hardens in an instant.

"I see the bruising, and you're still in pain. You're seeing a doctor."

"I'm telling you I just need some ice and to rest it. I'll be fine, Cormac. I promise you. It's all right."

"Are you a doctor and a social worker?"

His arrogance could annoy me if I didn't believe it was out of genuine concern.

"I've had this before. I know this feeling."

His expression turns into a thundercloud, and I want to swallow my words, but I don't know why he's reacting this way.

"You called it nursemaid's elbow. That's usually something that only happens to kids when they refuse to follow whoever's holding their arm, and they drop their weight. Yanking the kid's arm usually isn't intentional, but it can be. It's also something most kids don't remember. Are you telling me you know what it is from seeing your—" his hand gestures into the air— "clients, patients, whatever they are? Because that's not how it sounds. It sounds like this has happened to you since you've been an adult."

He's digging a little too close to the truth, and I don't like it. I need to get out of here before he pushes too hard, and I end up saying something I shouldn't. Because as much as I want to resist, something about him compels me to tell the truth.

"Cormac, you're making a bigger deal out of this than it should be. I can remember it from when I was a kid, and yeah, I have seen it in clients. It'll heal. There's not much to be done for it. How do you know what it is?"

I turn the tables on him, but the moment the words are out of my mouth, I wish I hadn't. I don't want to know what he does to people who cross him or his family.

"When I was six, I got into an argument with my cousin when I refused to give back a toy he wanted. We were yelling over each other, thinking the loudest would win. My mom tugged at my arm just like my aunt tugged at his. We both did the same thing, which was drop all our body weight to sit because neither of us wanted to give in about the Lego set we were playing with. He and I both wound up with the same injury. I was old enough to remember."

I watch him, and I have no reason to think he's lying, but he could be. I bet he's avoiding telling me the whole truth, which is he's probably caused this in other people. I don't want to imagine the things he's probably done, but I can't help it after seeing him pointing a gun at two guys who are barely more than kids.

As I watch him, I'm certain that's what kept him from shooting them. If they'd been much older than they are now, he probably would have, and I doubt he would've aimed to miss.

He was giving them a chance. I suppose that's pretty honorable all things considering.

"Joey, just have it looked at on the off chance it's worse than you think. If it's not that bad, then no big deal. But if it is, then you'll just end up making it worse if it needs something more than ice and rest."

The last thing I want is an emergency room co-pay. All I hear in my head is cha-ching, cha-ching, cha-ching. That's not worth it to me, but I can't tell him that. He nods. I think he's giving up. More fool am I.

"If you think the emergency room will be a waste of time —" He cocks an eyebrow, and I know he knew what I was thinking. He just doesn't want to embarrass me by saying money— "then let me refer you to a woman I know who won't bill you if you say I sent you."

My brow furrows, and I wonder what kind of arrangement he has with a woman who'd examine me at no charge. My gaze darts to his left hand, but I don't see a ring.

"She's not my wife or my girlfriend. I don't have either of those."

My cheeks radiate heat, completely embarrassed he knew what I was thinking—I don't want to think he's taken. Then again, maybe he could believe I'm worried she'd get the wrong idea if he sent a woman to her. But if she were his wife or girl-friend, and he did, then she would probably understand I mean nothing to him beyond a sense of guilt. I'm certain that's why he's insisting. He already admitted he feels guilty. That's why he wants this off his conscience.

"I do feel responsible, and I do feel guilty."

I take the last step up and stand before him as he admits his reasons. I moved slowly because I was still scanning the area to ensure the wrong person wouldn't see me coming up the stairs and even worse, speaking to a mobster in a cartel-owned neighborhood.

"But it's not just those things that make me insist you get it looked at. You work in a rough neighborhood and likely help kids whose families either don't have the means to do all the things they wish they could for their kids, or families where you're a lifeline for the children. You being out of commission means more than just you being hurt. It means those kids won't get the support they need. I don't want that either."

"Does your conscience usually speak this loudly?"

"No."

I didn't think about the question before I spat it out, but he doesn't think about his answer either. It's immediate, and it confirms what I already knew: I should have nothing to do with a man like Cormac O'Rourke. Yet here I am, in no hurry to leave. I could have bolted. Instead, I'm dragging out this conversation.

One part of my mind screams I'm an idiot, and the other can barely keep my tongue from hanging out and drooling over him.

"I won't insist you get into a car with me. I can tell you don't trust me that much, and that's fine. But let me give you this woman's number, and you can call her when I'm not around. I won't ask her if you do, so you won't have to admit to giving in."

He flashes me a smile as he sticks out his hand. I take a second to realize he's waiting for me to give him my phone. I hesitate. I'm not sure I should hand it over.

"You can watch everything I type on the screen. I'm just going to put a phone number in your contacts."

"All right."

I peer down at the screen as he types in the name Meredith and then a phone number. I shift my gaze up to his face, but he's still looking down. He doesn't put a last name in, and it makes me suspicious, or rather, it confirms my suspicions. This is a mob doctor who would see me off the books. That would only suck me deeper into a world I've been hiding from ever since my first encounter with Pablo Diaz.

Guys like Ronaldo and Jesus are all over this neighborhood, but men like Pablo—and clearly like Cormac—aren't some low-level hustlers. If he has the last name O'Rourke, and he wears custom-tailored suits like he has on now, then he has to be a pretty senior member of that family.

He hands back my phone, and I lock it before dropping it in my pocket.

"Are you headed to your car?"

I nod. I'm certain he's not taking a bus or a subway.

"Is it close, or should I walk you there?"

My eyes widen, and I shake my head no. Understanding registers on his face. He knows I don't want to be seen with him, and it makes me feel horrible because it's not that I'm embarrassed or that I'm judging him for who he is—what he is. It's purely about my safety.

"All right. You go, and I'll follow behind. I'm not letting you walk alone to your car after what just happened."

I point three cars down the road. "I'm right there."

When I head toward it, he walks two steps behind me. I want to turn around and tell him I'm fine since it's so nearby, but people have already witnessed us talking on the street for a long time. It's inevitable it'll get back to Pablo, and that means all of that time spent hiding was worthless. I unlock my car with a fob and open the door as Cormac reaches into his pocket and pulls out his phone. I see the screen flash. I get no chance to say anything before he answers the call. He glances at me as he walks by.

"Have a good day, Joey."

"Wait! Why do you call me that?"

Chapter Four

Cormac

Why do I call her that?

It popped into my mind, and it won't pop back out. I think Jocelyn is a pretty name, but there's something about Joey that works for me. She's clearly not easily intimidated if she works in this neighborhood, and she was willing to literally stick her neck out for me to protect me. I can tell she has a sense of humor that leans toward dry, which I appreciate. She's got an athletic build her professional attire hides, but I felt as we rolled down the stairs. I'd rather go for a roll in the hay with her than down steps again. I get the sense she was a tomboy growing up, so I guess that's why Joey comes to mind.

I didn't mean to say it aloud.

But I know I said it more than once, which is never a good sign in my family. Giving a woman a nickname is essentially a marriage proposal. I am not looking to get married. I'm not looking to date. I'm not even looking to fuck these days. I just got out of a three year "relationship."

I had a sub for three years, but I ended things recently. It was a splendid arrangement I didn't foresee ending. But her best friend was my brother's former sub. We met the women the same weekend at a BDSM club Seamus and I are silent part owners of. He hit it off with Makayla, and I hit it off with Deirdre. But things got ugly a month ago when Makayla tried to get in touch with Seamus after he ended things to date his now-wife. She texted twice, and he didn't read them. He blocked her instead. She didn't take that well.

She didn't go all *Fatal Attraction* or *Single White Female* on him, but she tried to out our family business. When you're with someone for three years, and your family's name's been splashed in the news over the last five years—thanks to shitty dead relatives—it's difficult to hide who and what we are, even if we never admitted it.

Makayla went so far as to have Deirdre suggest to me that Makayla have a threesome with Tiernan and Seamus. They thought I'd pass the idea along to Seamus. He about lost his ever-loving shite. I didn't tell him as an endorsement. I told him as a warning because Makayla also threatened to tell people she'd been a mobster's submissive for three years and repeat organized crime things she supposedly learned while with him.

It's why Tiernan dealt with it. Seamus was too pissed off. My sister-in-law made sure Makayla understood there isn't a fucking chance in any universe they'd be interested in her having any contact with Seamus.

I told Deirdre not to get either of us involved, but she claimed she was trying to help her friend who's in love with Seamus. I stared at her as though she were an idiot. I really thought she was. How would suggesting a woman who's in love with my brother join a threesome with him and his wife be a good idea?

Deirdre overstepped just by suggesting it, but the way she

spoke didn't fit our D/s dynamics. I warned her, but she persisted. Even after two punishments, she wouldn't chill the fuck out about it, so I ended the contract.

So, I'm not looking for anything remotely committed right now. I don't even want a situationship after that, so I have no clue what I was thinking when I gave Jocelyn a nickname.

I'm not marrying her.

I'm not dating her.

Though I wouldn't mind fucking her.

But that isn't happening, and that's the last thing I need right now. I'm trying to uncomplicate my private life. She would be nothing but a complication, considering how we met and how our occupations couldn't be more opposite even if we tried. Her job is to help keep families together. My job—in part —very frequently—is to rip them apart.

One thing I can say about kids and protecting them is that my family stopped recruiting when my cousin Dillan became the boss. None of us are interested in drawing kids who are barely out of elementary school into this world. We don't go scouting high schools like college coaches. If someone comes to us, and they're over eighteen, then we might consider it. If Dillan accepts someone, it's usually a legacy guy. That sorta makes it sound like the guy's being admitted to an Ivy League. The mob isn't officially hereditary, but yeah, it is.

It's not automatically handed down generationally unless you're born into the boss's family. I was, so there was never a choice. We've been in the mob for three generations on one side of the family and four on the other. When your great-grandfather, grandfather, uncle, and cousin once removed have been bosses, and your cousin is the current one, there's no declining the calling.

"Are you still there?"

"Yeah." Whoops. I have no idea what Dillan just told me.

My mind completely wandered as I walked to my car and for the last four blocks as I head home. I'm never unfocused.

"Do you have bad reception or something?"

"I guess so." Not at all.

"Did you hear what I said?" He's getting testy, so he's said whatever it was more than once.

"Parts." Not at all. "I can hear you now, so can you give me the gist of it?"

"The gist is what the feck happened today?"

Feck.

Our parents would crucify us if we ever truly swore at each other. It's the eleventh commandment. No—twelfth. The eleventh is never go a full day without telling everyone you love them.

"I went to collect from Ignacio, and his dumb-arse nephews were there. Rather than being men and staying the feck out of it, they thought their balls dropped today. They thought they could stand up to me."

"Okay. But how did it get to them shooting at you and some woman pushing you down a flight of steps?"

Fucking city cameras. Our mutual cousins Sean and Finn—who are brothers—are skilled hackers. They keep a running feed of the city cameras in all five boroughs in case we need to track someone down or find out where they've been. Word got back to someone, and at least one cousin went to work.

"She's a social worker and was in the neighborhood. I guess she's known Ronaldo and Jesus since they were kids. She recognized them and was on my side of the street. What the hell possessed her? I don't have a clue. But she shoved me out of the way. We wound up losing our balance and falling. She talked the guys into going back into their uncle's bodega."

Ronaldo and Jesus are cousins who try to one up each other all the time. They don't get what my cousins and I understand

—you don't battle each other when you're at war with everyone else. They wanted to prove who had the bigger pair today, and I didn't want to shoot a couple dumb-arse kids.

"Why'd she hide when Pablo showed up?"

Something doesn't feel right about divulging more. It's not that what Joey—there I go again—told me is some massive state secret, but it doesn't feel like my place to say. She confided in me, and she trusts me not to tell anyone, in case it gets back to Pablo. I know my family won't say shite, but it's the principle.

"She fears him."

"Smart woman. But why?"

"I didn't get her entire life story, Dill."

"But you stood talking to her for quite a while."

"Yeah. She got hurt when she fell and landed on her elbow. We were arguing about her seeing a doctor. I even offered Meredith if she didn't want to go to the ER."

There's a long pause before he speaks again. I know it doesn't thrill him I gave Meredith's name to anyone. She's been our family's private physician—private surgeon—since my grandda led the organization. Things got messy when my cousin Shane fell in love with her daughter. That shite was complicated, but the long and the short of it is, she was nearly outed to the NYPD and DEA. They almost found out her connections to us. I should help her keep a low profile, but I trust her nearly as much as I do my mom and aunts. That's about the highest form of praise from me.

"Do you think she'll call Meredith?"

"No."

"Then why'd—"

"It felt like the right thing to do. She wouldn't have gotten hurt if she hadn't protected me. I tried to shield her, but I probably did more harm than good since I'm so much bigger than her."

"Okay. What'd Pablo have to say?"

"Same shite, different day. He's pissed we're encroaching on their territory. Enrique's embarrassed that we've been there for nearly a year, and Ignacio never went to him for protection. Not that he could afford it after paying us to protect him from Enrique."

Dillan chuckles. We have a few business owners on that street believing we're keeping Enrique Diaz, the Colombian Cartel *jefe*, away from them. They're too scared of that old motherfucker to ask many questions. He didn't give a fuck about them until today. He only gives a fuck because we're extorting those people, and he didn't think to do it himself. It makes him look like a pussy to have another syndicate slip into one of his neighborhoods and start collecting money he could be strong-arming from his own people.

Oops. Oh, well. Too bad, so sad.

"Was it Ignacio who called Pablo or one of those dumb-arses?"

"Neither. Ronaldo's or Jesus's mother—I don't remember which since they're both Ignacio's sisters—was looking out the window of their apartment across the street and saw the eejits come out and shoot at me. Rather than try to get her son and nephew to stop, she called Pablo."

"What's he want in exchange?"

"Obviously, he *wants* us to leave without giving anything up to us. But he's *willing* to way outbid Maks for that textile factory in Bangladesh if we get out of the neighborhood altogether."

We were going to make an offer on it just to fuck the bratva over. We don't really want another overseas factory, but the Kutsenkos do. Helping us fuck over the bratva at the Cartel's expense works for us. Our racket was going to end eventually, so the money wouldn't come in forever from that neighborhood.

Losing future income there is less than what it'll cost Enrique to get that factory.

But for him, it's more about saving face and hiding that a rival swooped in and took over one of his neighborhoods. He'll pay out the arse to keep that quiet. He'll also make sure the shop owners know they erred not going to him. He'll make sure they pay him back for what they should have tithed to him, and he'll make sure they understand silence is golden.

"When's he going to put in the offer?"

"Tonight, at eleven. It'll be nine tomorrow morning there."

"Maks should be having a hissy fit to rival his twins by nine-ten. If only I could watch." Dillan chuckles, and I laugh along with him.

"I'd bring the popcorn if you'd bring the Twizzlers." We've been doing that since we made up over the Lego set that wound up with us both getting nursemaid's elbow.

"Tell your brother to bring the grape soda. And none of that organic popcorn shite you tried to slip in last week during the rugby match. Tasted like newspaper soaked in misery."

"Woe is you. You wouldn't have known if you hadn't seen the bag when I popped it."

"As though the popcorn weren't bad enough. You insist on that vegan imitation butter shite. Nana and Granny are crying in heaven. Irish men eat Irish butter."

"Feck off. Tell Sean to keep an eye on the Cartel's accounts and Maks's emails."

We all hack one another's bank accounts and emails, but having a cousin with a graduate degree in national security comes in handy since we hide our shite the best. We spread so much misinformation, the other syndicates think we're the impoverished ones when we have more than all three—the Mafia, the bratva, and the Cartel—have all together.

And that's saying something, considering Enrique Diaz is

one of the most powerful men in the world. No drugs move in the Western Hemisphere without him knowing about them. It's not worth his time, effort, and money to stop the other three syndicates here in NYC.

But just about every other syndicate on this side of the world pays a tariff to him for the privilege of doing business. He insists everyone knows his family is the Cartel with a capital C, not to be confused with low-level competitors like the Mexicans or Guatemalans.

He's as bad as the *Cosa Nostra*, who lose their shite whenever someone who isn't Sicilian is called Mafia. They like to make sure *everyone* knows they're the "real" Mafia, so they get a capital letter too. The Ivankov branch, run by the Kutsenkos, couldn't give two shites if Americans capitalize bratva or not. It should be, but that's not the hill they're dying on.

And we don't give a rat's fart whether we have a capital M for mob because everyone knows the O'Rourkes are *the* mob pretty much any and everywhere. Some of the other syndicates —like the Poles—want the recognition, so they call themselves the Mob. If they cared less about proving they're big bad mobsters and spent more time actually being mobsters, they might be relevant.

"Do—" Dillan hesitates. He never hesitates. "Do you want Sean to let you know if Jocelyn talks to any witnesses tomorrow?"

"She's a social worker in that community. She's bound to be there tomorrow or another day this week or next. We can't assume she's there for any other reason than her job. If her name comes up, let me know. But I don't want Sean invading her privacy or her clients' when there's no reason to."

That feels worse than telling Dillan why Pablo terrifies Joey. If she found out, she'd never forgive me. That might crush me.

What the fuck is wrong with me? Why does this matter to me?

I'm acting like I'm going to see her again. I'm acting like she'd care whether she sees me again.

"All right. Do you think she knows anything useful?"

I'm sitting in traffic—shocker in New York—which irritates me. Now this conversation is too. I try to keep the frustration out of my tone.

"I'm certain she knows plenty of useful things, but I doubt any of it matters to us."

I failed at that. I sound like a dick.

"What's the deal with you?"

Dillan could sound accusatory, but he's being patient with me. That's almost worse. I'm not looking to pick a fight, but it makes me feel shitty that he's patient when I'm testy.

"It's been a long day, and that was before getting shot at. I ripped my suit, and my ribs hurt like a mother. I nearly crushed a woman today who felt she needed to protect me. And I had to deal with Pablo. As though that last one isn't bad enough, I'm stuck in traffic on the bridge."

"You've been shot at before. Hell, you've been shot."

"And I've ripped suits before and bruised my ribs before. But I usually don't get stuck in traffic right afterward."

Yeah. Let's blame it on traffic. Dillan and I both know that's bullshit, but he backs off.

"Sean'll let you know what comes of the Bangladesh deal. Banged up ribs or not, maybe a night at your club will do you some good."

I respond with a noncommittal grunt. Tying a woman up, spanking her, then fucking her into next week is usually the best solution to a fucked-up day. Even though things are over with Deirdre, I can still go to my club. Our contract included a monogamy clause, which I'm certain she broke now that I know

Makayla broke that clause with Seamus. I had women I'd scene with before Deirdre, and we sometimes went together and included another woman. So, I'm not without options, and I don't need to fuck some random woman either.

But it holds no appeal. My dick doesn't even twitch at the idea. I'm too fucking tired.

"Nah. I'm going home, soaking in the bath, and going to bed early. I'm wiped."

"Talk to you tomorrow. Love you."

"Love you, too. Bye."

If we were the only family that was affectionate and demonstrative, then people would call us weak. But all Four Families—the Mancinellis, the Kutsenkos, the Diazes, and us—are all the same. No one hides our devotion to our family, and no one doubts we'll each put our family ahead of absolutely everything in this life and the next. We're stronger for it, which is a pain in the arse because it means the balance of power is constantly shifting. No one family is on top, or at least not for long.

It takes me another thirty minutes before I pull into my garage in Boerum Hills in Brooklyn. I nodded to my security detail parked around my block as I drove by. I live in a quiet area, and I like it that way. Only Finn got a place in the city—SoHo—and that was only to make life easier since he owns several restaurants, bars, and nightclubs mostly in Manhattan.

The rest of us preferred not to be in Manhattan like the other bachelors our ages. We prefer hiding in plain sight as opposed to the flashy penthouses. The other families think we can't afford them. We can afford them twenty times over because we don't waste our money on stupid shite like that. We like our privacy, and there's no such thing in Manhattan.

Once I'm in my place, I make a beeline to the kitchen. My latest batch of kombucha is ready, so I pour myself a glass. It tastes like straight up arse, but I swear it's why I'm the only one in my family who never gets colds. Like never. The moment I feel a tickle, I kill it with this vinegar-flavored shite. I was feeling under the weather this morning, and now I feel like arse. I beg my tastebuds for forgiveness and down the brew.

My phone vibrates in my pocket as I walk away from the dishwasher and head to my bedroom.

MP

Meredith Prichard. My chest tightens. Is this about Joey?

"Hello."

"Good evening, Cor."

Fuck. She's pissed I gave her number out.

"What's up?"

"I spoke to a delightful young woman about an hour ago. Imagine my surprise."

"Is Jocelyn all right?"

"Her elbow wasn't as bad as she suspected. She tweaked it but didn't dislocate it. She also has a mildly sprained wrist. She felt a migraine coming on from a bump on her head."

"What? She said nothing about hitting her head." That pisses me off.

"With the fuss you made about her elbow, she said she didn't trust you not to drag her to the ER and demand an MRI on the spot. I made a house call and checked her out. No signs of a concussion, but I gave her the protocol and instructions to follow up with her doctor in the morning."

"Does she know you're telling me all of this?"

Doctor-patient confidentiality is a little murky in our world.

"Yes. She assumed I'd call you to tell you she'd called me. She said I could share all of that."

"Anything else? Anything more serious?"

I don't want to admit how anxious I am. I'm in my room, stripping off my ruined suit. I examine my ribs in the mirror as I listen to Meredith. They need wrapping, but I don't need a doctor to do that. I have plenty of experience doing it for myself.

"No. Cormac, why did you send her to me?"

"She didn't want to go to the ER."

There's silence while Meredith expects me to fill her in more, but there's nothing more to say.

"Couldn't you have suggested urgent care if she didn't want to go to the ER?"

"I didn't think she'd go anywhere, but I thought she might see you if it didn't feel like a big deal."

"She wasn't forthcoming about how she got injured. She said she tripped. Cormac, did someone hurt her?"

"No. She was somewhere she should have been safe when something dangerous happened. She protected me, but we fell in the process."

"The way she answered—it was too rehearsed. She's given the 'I tripped' excuse before. It almost sounded plausible except I've heard it too many times to fall for it."

My hand grips my phone so tightly I fear I could crack it. My other hand fists. I tell myself not to overreact.

"Were there any signs she's being abused now?"

"No. But that doesn't mean it isn't happening."

"Do you think I need to check on her? Intervene?"

"I don't know. Something felt off."

"I thought maybe the hospital fees kept her from wanting to get checked out. Now I wonder if she feared someone would push for a full examination and find things she doesn't want shared."

"That thought crossed my mind, too. Cor, it could just be a trauma response she developed years ago and is still her instinctive response."

"But it could be something more."

"I trust your discretion, and she relaxed once she found out I've known you since you were twelve. Learning that didn't make her more comfortable with me. It made her more comfortable about you. It was like she feared trusting you. But once she knew I've been around you for most of your life, and I spoke fondly of you, she stopped doubting herself. I think she would listen to you if you spoke to her. Just go easy on her."

"Do you know where I could find her tomorrow?"

"She said she had appointments in Port Richmond."

That's the part of Staten Island we were in today. Do I just camp out there all day? That's a great way to guarantee getting shot. Pablo's going to have his goons patrolling the streets, looking for anyone with red hair. I could have Finn check the DMV records, so I can find out her address or license plates. I'm not hanging outside her front door like a stalker. But the license plates would make it easier for Finn or Sean to track her once she's in the neighborhood.

All of this feels super stalkery. Nothing about this strikes me as something she'd be okay with. But she might have to suck up being angry to give me some peace of mind. How fucking fucked-up is that? Talk about selfish. But it's true. I'll risk her ire to reassure myself she's safe. That means I have to find her somewhere outside Port Richmond because it won't be safe if anyone sees her with me again.

My mind's whirring a mile a minute. I'm assessing every-thing. I'm used to making life-altering decisions with no room for error in a matter of seconds. It's why I'm alive and in my early thirties instead of being worm food in my teens.

"Did she mention her office?"

"She splits her time between Port Richmond and Manor Heights. I don't know which one she'll be at tomorrow. I don't know if she's going there or just straight to whatever appointments she has in Port Richmond. She said she works in schools, too."

I rack my brain for the schools in the area. She made it sound like she's known Ronaldo and Jesus a while, and they both graduated from high school a year ago. There are high schools in both neighborhoods and a few P.S. whatever elementary and middle schools. I don't remember the numbers in that area. My guess is she's assigned to a middle school. Then again, they could have assigned her to like ten, given the perpetual shortage of social workers.

"All right. I'll figure something out and check on her tomorrow. Thank you, Meredith."

"You're a good lad." Every once in a while, her Welsh accent gets extra strong.

She's a retired British Royal Navy surgeon and salty as the day is long. She's heard every excuse, so nothing impresses her. But she's kind and been like a third aunt for nearly two-thirds of my life.

We hang up, and I'm left looking in the mirror at my bruised ribs. Could Joey's clothes have hidden more than just the hottest body I've ever felt?

Fucking hell.

What kind of perve am I if she's being abused, and I'm thinking about feeling her up?

I spend way too much time in my head. Introspective is what my mom calls it. Morose is what Seamus calls it. Prone to overanalyzing and being too self-critical is what everyone— including me—knows it is.

I don't have a plan for tomorrow—completely unusual, utterly stupid, and unnecessarily reckless, so I better wake up with something, or I'll find myself fucked in more than one way. But not the kind where I tie a woman up, spank her, and get my rocks off.

Chapter Five

Joey

There isn't enough arnica or Epson salt to make my body ache less. My entire right arm is a massive bruise I slathered arnica on this morning. I soaked in a tub of Epson salt for nearly two hours last night. I kept letting out cold water and refilling the tub with warm water and more salts.

I don't regret my Good Samaritan intentions, but I wish Cormac O'Rourke weren't a giant. He tried his best not to crush me and to cushion my fall, but the man is one massive muscle with some bones poking out here and there. It was like slamming into a brick wall over and over. An exceedingly masculine brick wall who smelled divine.

I'm short. Like really short at five-foot-two on my best day. He's easily six-four. I'm pretty proportionate for my height, so I tip the scale at one-twenty. He has to be double that. My guess is two-forty. So yeah, it hurt having him land on me. Being tucked against him didn't help much either, since he's the real man of steel. Forget Superman. It wouldn't surprise me if under that custom-tailored suit, Cormac O'Rourke's body is a work of art.

In any other situation, I would appreciate it and even wish I'd been pressed against him longer. I appreciated he did his best to shelter me, and despite why we were clinging to each other, I liked the way he felt. Because I could tell he was doing his best to shield me, I felt safe.

I'm not scared of the neighborhoods I go to, but I'd be a fool not to be vigilant. I'm wary of strangers, and I always park under streetlights in case I'm leaving home visits after dark. I've faced irate parents and guardians who've done their best to intimidate me. I've had children melt down in front of me, throwing, kicking, biting, and hitting out of fear, frustration, anger, and desperation. I do my best not to let my fear show, but there are times when I'm reminded I chose a dangerous career because of the homes I enter. I get a lot of the cases other social workers can't face. That gets heavy. Like really, really fucking heavy.

Cormac made me feel protected and safe for those excruciatingly long and disorienting seconds. He made me feel the same way times ten over when I hid behind him. I wound up using him as a human shield and endangering him, but he hesitated no more than I did. I can't explain what compelled me to put myself in the line of fire, but I get the distinct impression Cormac will protect those who can't protect themselves. That feels entirely contradictory to the notion that he's a mobster. But—I don't know—I just got honorable vibes from him.

"Jocelyn?"

"Hi, Estella. ¿*Como estás?*" How're you?

"I'm all right. How about you? I heard you were near a shooting."

We continue our conversation in Spanish, lapsing into it as often as we speak in English. Almost all of us are like that in this office since most of the people who work here—social workers and support staff—are bilingual.

"A couple of guys fired some shots, but they didn't hit anyone."

"Something about the Cartel and some kids you know."

"They aren't kids anymore. Ronaldo and Jesus think they're men and wanted to prove it. Instead, they came close to dying. They're lucky they didn't hit a bystander because neither of them can aim for a damn."

"Who were they shooting at?"

I hesitate. It feels wrong to say Cormac's name. It's not a secret since there aren't too many redheaded men with freckles in that neighborhood, and certainly not ones encountering Cartel members.

"*Un catire.*"

Estella's brow furrows. Her Puerto Rican Spanish and my Mexican Spanish don't always match. It doesn't help when I toss in Colombian words or phrases I learn from my clients like that one.

"It means a fair-skinned or fair-haired man. He wasn't from the neighborhood. I intervened and de-escalated things. I reminded them Enrique will put up with fist fights but nothing that endangers unaffiliated people." I grin. "And I might have threatened to speak to Ronaldo's grandmother."

Estella pretends to shiver. "*Señora* Castillo's been scaring kids into behaving on that block for the past forty years. If Humberto Diaz hadn't sucked her son into the Cartel, he would have been a model citizen. Back then, Humberto was the only person scarier than *señora* Castillo."

Enrique Diaz's uncle. He was back in Colombia long before I knew what I wanted to be when I grew up. There are plenty of rumors about the man, and best I can tell, every one of them is more truth than lie.

I gather a stack of papers on my desk and put them in my bag as I speak. "Hopefully, she deals with Ronaldo, and he keeps Jesus in check. Ignacio needs to rein them in, too. Their mothers give in to them too easily. No matter how much trouble they get in, they can do no wrong according to those two women. They cater to their sons' whims."

"Are you headed back over there today?"

"Maybe. It depends on whether I get everything done over in Manor Heights. I have sessions at the elementary school until noon, then I have two at the middle school. Then there are some home health follow-ups."

Not only do I provide clinic hours at the schools, I also check on kids who are out of school for health reasons. They have teachers who work with them throughout the week, but I make sure everything is all right with their home life and that they're getting the medical treatment they need to recover.

"Be careful."

"*Gracias. Hasta luego.*" Thank you. Until later.

I gather my purse, work bag, and coat before I head back to my car. Even in broad daylight, I carry my keys in my hand. I'm ready to bolt for my vehicle when an enormous shadow shifts and a man steps in front of me.

"Cormac." I put my hand on my chest. "You scared the bejesus out of me. What are you doing here?"

He glances around, far less imposing than yesterday. He's not any smaller than he was when we met, but the air of controlled anger is gone. He appears reluctant to speak now that he's in front of me.

"I was worried about—about what happened yesterday."

Was he going to say he was worried about me? Is he blushing? Oh my God. I think he is.

"How'd you find me?" It's not an accusation so much as shock.

"I figured you'd be at the Port Richmond CPS office or here. I thought you might not be rushing to head back into the area where we met, so I tried here first. If I was wrong, I would have gone there next."

Bashful. Like one of the Seven Dwarfs. That's how I'd describe the Cormac in front of me right now. That makes my lips want to twitch. That might be stretching it a bit far. He doesn't come across as anything but a ruggedly handsome man. Except I think he's shy now that we're not in a situation he feels he must control.

Control.

That's what radiated from him yesterday. He might have been the target, but even with me butting in, he came across as very much in control. It certainly appeared that way when Pablo showed up. But now that his life isn't in danger, his presence isn't as—as—it doesn't—I don't know how to articulate it. It's everything he was yesterday, just less, I suppose. Like a tamer version. Like the difference between a lion in the wild and one at a safari park. Don't underestimate him in either place, but at least now he's approachable.

"Do you need something?"

He's just staring at me, as though the ball's in my court, but he came to me.

"I wanted to make sure you're okay. I know how sore I am. It must be ten times worse for you. And I want to say thank you. I don't believe I did yesterday, and I should have."

I can't remember if he did. Maybe. I really don't know since a lot happened, and I vacillated between trying not to wince in pain and trying not to drool.

"It's all right."

"All the same, thank you for pushing me out of the way and for calming those boys down."

Now my lips twitch, and I don't hide it.

"I heard calling them boys set everything in motion. You hurt their pride."

"Pride goeth before a fall."

I'm pretty sure that's scripture, and that's the last thing I expected a mobster to quote.

"True."

I wait for him to say something—anything—else, but he remains quiet. The silence draws out and threatens to get awkward. Um...

"You said you were sore today. Did you get hurt?"

"Just my ribs."

My fingertips itch to feather them over his abs and pecs, which are hidden by his button down and his suit coat. But I felt them yesterday when they pressed against my tits and belly.

Washboard.

Eight pack.

I bet he has that sexy as all get out V over his hip bones, and I bet his chiseled ass has those grooves on his hips meant for someone to slip their hands over and hold on. I bet he has those dimples at the base of his spine. I've practically stripped him buck naked in my mind, ready to fuck him right here, right now in the parking lot outside my office.

"I think that was probably my elbow that did that as much as the steps. Sorry about that."

"I can hardly complain, considering you saved my life and got hurt in the process. How is your elbow?"

Does he genuinely want to know? Or is he fishing for whether I called Meredith?

"Just like I told you, it needs ice and rest."

"That's good. I'm glad it's nothing too serious."

I stare at him, but he says nothing more. I tilt my head and cock an eyebrow. This expression usually gets kids to confess everything—even if they know they didn't do anything wrong. They'll admit to something just in case they should apologize. It shouldn't surprise me he's impervious, but I'd hoped he'd admit he probably called Meredith to see if I gave in.

"I took you up on your offer and called your doctor. She made a house call."

"I'm glad you did. She can be a bit unsympathetic, but she's gentle, and she knows what she's doing."

"She was super sympathetic." I grin, which turns into a laugh when he playfully scowls.

"She usually tells my brother, cousins, and me we got what we deserved. She's been doing it since we were kids and played sports like we were on our way to the pros. We were all in, and we all got injured at one point or another. She set bones and stitched up cuts, so they barely hurt. But she'd tell us we should have paid more attention or moved faster, then she wouldn't be making those house calls."

I wonder if all their injuries were sports related. I doubt they were. I'm certain some of Meredith's patching up came from war wounds that go along with being a mobster.

"I could see that. I didn't expect her to be British."

"Yeah. She grew up in Wales, served as a navy surgeon, then came to America after she retired."

"Wow. That's a major move to make on her own."

He hesitates for a heartbeat before he responds. "Her husband is Welsh too and a retired British Royal Marine. Their daughter just married my cousin a month ago."

"Wow. Were they childhood sweethearts or something?"

This hesitation is a moment longer. He's weighing what he should say. Is he nervous I'll repeat what he tells me?

"No. They didn't know the connection when they first met a few months ago."

"A few months? Was it a whirlwind romance?" I'm honestly curious. It's equal parts romantic and nosey.

"Pretty much."

I wait for more, but it's not forthcoming. I look around as more people pull into the parking lot. We're off to the side, so we're not that noticeable. But people have seen us. I'm on the clock. I'm not supposed to be shooting the shit.

"Do your colleagues know what happened?" He blurts the question just as I'm about to excuse myself.

"A colleague heard about the incident, but she didn't have specifics."

"Do you think other people will know what happened? Will they question you about getting involved in syndicate business?"

"Maybe. As long as Martha, my boss, knows at least part of the truth, then I won't worry about everyone else."

"It'll take your elbow a while to heal. You should take it easy, so you don't make it worse. But people might notice."

"They probably will. I'll just tell them I tripped. Everyone knows I'm accident prone."

His brow furrows in the most unusual way. It's like he's concentrating, so his brow creases. But his eyebrows go up in question.

"You don't strike me as clumsy."

"I'm not. I'm accident prone. Usually, it's from trying to do too much all at once."

"Do you trip often?"

Is there an edge to his tone? Or am I imagining it?

"No. I bump into stuff, though."

He steps closer until I have to look up to keep seeing his face. He towers over me, and anyone else his size would likely intimidate me. I want to climb him like I'm a fucking koala and hold on.

"Joey, that's what women, in particular, say when they're covering up the real reason they get injured."

I have nothing to say. I just look at him and blink. Words escape me until they come rushing back.

"Did Meredith suggest that? Are you here because you're curious? Or are you trying to catch me in a lie? I'm certain you discussed me with Meredith."

"She let me know you agreed to see her and that I didn't need to push you about going to the ER or Urgent Care."

"Then you discussed things that should have remained private between her and me. So much for HIPPA."

"I don't know the entirety of what you told her, but it was enough to worry her. Enough to make her ask me to check on you. Meredith doesn't catastrophize. She doesn't exaggerate either. If she's concerned enough to say something, then the situation warrants it. I trust her."

I know those three words are among the highest praise he probably gives based on his expression. We're holding a pretty steady conversation, but I wouldn't call him chatty. A man of few words would best describe him right now.

Now that I think about it, he didn't even say that much to me yesterday. At least, not besides commanding me to hide and to go to the emergency room. I definitely feel like it's still waters run deep. He may not be the most talkative man, but he's clearly very observant, and I feel like he's extremely astute. He reads people better than we want to be read.

As he watches me, it's as though he can see into me, and I feel far too exposed by that. He's gotten a little too close to the truth a few times already, but I don't want to end the conversation either, which makes no sense since we have little to talk about. I wait to see if he will take the lead again, but he remains quiet until I look toward my car.

I think he realizes we're running out of time to chat since

the parking lot just keeps filling up more, and people are noticing us talking together.

"You said you called the police on Pablo all those years ago, but his brother took care of it. Why are you still concerned about Pablo seeing you around?"

My gaze locks with his as my mind scrambles for an explanation, but it's not one I wish to give. It's one I doubt Cormac would appreciate.

"Joey, I won't get angry because of what you say. You can tell me. I just don't get why you'd still be on his radar."

I don't know how to navigate this conversation. Most people don't know how steadfastly I avoid being around Pablo. I make excuses if I know he's coming or if he's already somewhere. I don't want to explain there's more to it than accidentally calling the police.

"Joey, the longer you remain quiet, the longer you have to devise some story to try to appease me. But all it does is make me trust you less, which is the last thing I want. So, either tell me the truth, or tell me it's none of my business, but I don't want to hear excuses or lies."

He is painfully blunt as he speaks. He's not unkind. There's no harshness to his tone, but he certainly isn't interested in giving an inch because he fears I'll take a mile.

"It's just a feeling I get. Why do you call me Joey?"

"It just seems to fit."

He watches me while I wait for him to say more. When I remain quiet, he shrugs. If I was being tightlipped, then he's being taciturn.

"I know you have appointments to get to, so I don't want to keep you. I wanted to check on you and make sure you don't need anything else."

"You wanted to know if I would admit I asked Meredith for help."

He shrugs again. "If I didn't think she could, I wouldn't have given you her name. I'm glad she checked you out."

We seem to spend most of this conversation staring at each other. I adjust my bag on my good shoulder and shift my gaze toward my car.

"It was nice meeting you, Jocelyn."

Wait. Did he think I didn't like the nickname?

"It's Joey, and it was nice meeting you too—Cor."

Estar hasta las narices. Up to the nostrils loses something in translation, but this is fucking overwhelming.

He's the most alluring man I've ever seen, and when he grins. Fuck. I'm tempted to look at the ground to see if my panties are at my ankles. I'm definitely wet. I guess he liked me using a nickname for him.

I don't want to leave, but I need to escape since I feel my cheeks burning. I head to my car, but I look back as I open the door. He's not there anymore. I sweep my gaze over the parking lot. He couldn't just vanish. I glimpse red hair before it disappears into what I think is a sedan. I plug my phone in and set my GPS to avoid roadwork. I wind up pulling out of the parking lot behind him. I don't know tons about cars, but I'm certain the Audi Cormac drives costs about as much as I earn in two years.

He's on my mind the entire way to the middle school. I struggle to focus on my counseling sessions throughout the day. The man's an utter distraction, but my mind snaps to attention as I get out of my car in the neighborhood I was in yesterday. The hair goes up on the back of my neck. I aim for subtle as I look around. Someone's watching me, but I can't figure out who or where. It's unnerving.

My ego wants to think it's Cormac. That maybe he's still worrying about me and wants to keep checking on me. That maybe he thinks I need protecting—or at least, will indulge me since I still fear Pablo being around. But I never see a hint of him. I know it's an overactive imagination, since I can't find anyone staring at me, but I can't stop wondering if Pablo saw me with Cormac yesterday. Maybe he's forgotten about me and didn't even recognize me. Or maybe seeing me with Cormac reminded him of the trouble I caused and made him suspicious since I was with a rival.

So many maybes.

But it's easier to imagine a danger I know than a danger I don't. If it's someone other than Pablo, and it's not Cormac guarding me, then who the fuck is giving me the heebie-jeebies?

Chapter Six

Cormac

I've kept myself busy for the past two days since my insane decision to meet Joey at her office. I rarely have extra time, but when I do, I have some favorite spots to hang out. They're not where anyone expects, but they're places where I can just be Cormac. I'm not a mobster. I'm not a billionaire. I'm not anyone but myself, and the people there appreciate me volunteering. It's probably because most of them aren't old enough to be jaded.

I'm glad I saw Joey and saw for myself she wasn't too seriously injured. But despite work and my time at the community centers keeping me occupied, my mind keeps slipping to her. Her and Pablo. It makes no sense to me why she still fears Pablo all these years later. I can understand a wish to avoid him to avoid an uncomfortable situation. I can understand a wish to avoid him because he's an arsehole. But her feelings are genuine. That or she's a better actress than anyone I've seen on TV.

"Cor?"

"I'm in my office."

My brother knows he can still come and go from my place whenever he wants because I'm the last bachelor. We all used to have an open-door policy when everyone was single. None of us brought women home with us. Home is for family. Home is our sanctuary. There was never a fear we'd interrupt someone doing something we shouldn't see. Now that everyone else is married, that's a reasonable concern. We text when we turn onto a couple's street and again when we're pulling through their gate. Even then, sometimes it's a close call.

"Do you have the briefs?"

"Yeah. I just finished reviewing them. I made my notes, but they look good."

Because of our family's line of work, Seamus and I don't have a slew of paralegals to help us with our legal endeavors. We don't bring anyone that close since many times, the lines blur behind the scenes. That means Seamus and I review cases for each other and together, even though he specializes in criminal law, and I specialize in corporate.

"You've been holed up here since yesterday afternoon. I thought you were going to meet us to work out this morning."

"I wanted to get your briefs back to you when I said I would. But I have that merger I want to finalize."

"You always have a merger to finalize. That doesn't mean you stop working out."

"I missed a morning. I don't think I'm going to wither away."

My brother and I are the biggest men in our family, just like our dad is the biggest of the brothers. It's not like there's a massive difference in our size from our cousins. We can still wear each other's clothes, but Seamus and I are a little broader across the back and chest than the others, and our legs are more like tree trunks. We're just denser—many have said that about our intellect too. Sometimes it pays to come across as the muscular oaf. People talk more when they think you're too much of a meathead to understand.

"Okay. How're your ribs?"

"Sore but fine."

"So, neither work nor your ribs are the reason for you to bail. You didn't want to come over for dinner last night either."

"Did I hurt Tiernan's feelings? Was I rude?"

"No."

Seamus and I are known for the best manners in our family.

"Then why're you making a big deal over nothing? We're all homebodies. I didn't feel like going out, so I decided my time was best suited getting work done."

I know he doesn't believe me. However, I'm not ready to admit I wanted to work to stay distracted from Joey. And I didn't want anyone in my family asking why I was mooning around, thinking about her. I know they'd guess, and I'm not ready to discuss it. From Seamus's expression, I know he's in two minds whether to press the issue. He holds up the folder I passed him.

"Thanks. I'll send them back for a last review when I finish."

He's going to let it go. For now. Seamus gives me one last long look before he nods. We speak at the same time, trained since the moment we could talk.

"Love you."

That's a requirement our parents set up for us when we were learning to talk. We never swear at each other, and we never go a day without telling each other we love them. Since I talk to almost everybody in my family every day, that's easy to do.

We understand how temporary life is since we're always on death's doorstep. Our parents taught us the last thing you say to somebody should never be harsh words since you might never get to take them back. In their minds, we should say it every single time we talk to each other. That doesn't always happen since we usually talk to each other multiple times a day either by text, call, or seeing each other. But it always happens at least once.

Our parents usually insist we only speak Irish when we're with them. We normally do in front of them, but their fear we'll forget the language is wasted since we all lapse into Irish and switch between that and English as naturally as we breathe. By the time we each started kindergarten, we were fluent in both languages; reading, writing, and speaking, even if it was just simple stuff.

A set of sisters married a set of brothers. All six of them learned English only just before they went to kindergarten. It's not because they were new arrivals. Our families have been in the U.S. for generations, but we want to preserve that family tradition, and it's best for business.

It often pays to speak a language whomever we're negotiating with can't. When we're on missions, we try not to speak at all. But if we have to, it's in Irish. No point in giving away what we're going to do next just so the enemy can find us. We're all big enough and with bright red hair to stand out. We don't need to make being a target any easier.

Seamus takes off, and I turn my attention back to my computer. My mind once again goes back to Pablo and wondering if there's more between him and Joey than she'll admit.

I considered following her yesterday, but I drew the limit at that. I wonder where she is now. I wonder where Pablo went yesterday since I'm certain he went back to see Ignacio to reinforce the message he left with the bodega owner. Supposedly, anybody in that neighborhood is off limits, but I don't think Pablo knows everyone we're doing business with.

I'll have to go back soon to collect on more protection payments. It's not like people do a direct deposit to us or PayPal or Venmo it. There's no digital payment set up for something like that because the last thing we need is anybody tracking that money. We're certainly disinclined to pay taxes on it.

I look at my calendar to see when I'll have time for that tomorrow since I have several client meetings already lined up. We're always in the midst of some merger or acquisition or sale. We flip corporations much like some people flip houses. Some we buy and hold on to, but many we buy, make sure they appreciate, then sell at a profit.

Others we break down into smaller parts and sell those off or turn them into shell corporations too. We're careful not to commit excessive tax evasion because we're not going down like Al Capone. A little humility goes a long way, so we ensure we look on the up and up as much as possible.

Joey's still on my mind when I turn in for the night. I don't wake up thinking about her, but as I conclude my last client meeting and head over to Port Richmond, once again, I'm thinking of her. As I find a parking spot, I look around and wonder if she's here too or if she's in a different neighborhood. Unfortunately, she's not the one I recognize.

Dios mio, that *hijo de puta* is here again.

I release a beleaguered sigh as I lock my car. None of our cars are straight off the factory line. They all have customization. Not just my family's, but the vehicles belonging to all the

Four Families are like that. They don't beep when we lock or unlock them. The headlights don't flash when we lock or unlock them. And the dome light goes on if there's a bomb underneath our car. Normally, they don't turn on because we don't need the interior being illuminated when we're trying to be inconspicuous.

Pablo spots me at the same moment I spot him. His scowl is going to stick one of these days. Maybe I should slap him upside the back of the head and see if that old wives' tale is true. Lord knows I've slapped him across the face and knocked that smirk off it more than once.

He's grinning at me by the time I cross the road. I'm willing to meet him on his side of the street rather than being stubborn and thinking he'll come to me. I want this conversation over as soon as possible. He is not who I want to waste my time with today.

"I thought you understood you aren't welcome back here."

"I have memory problems."

"The hell you do. You have a memory like a fucking steel trap. I'm positive you remember the conversation we had two days ago."

"Maybe."

I shrug and return his grin. It's patronizing as fuck, and I know it irritates him, but I'm just fine with that. We've never been friends, and I'm not looking to make friends with him now.

"Look, Cor, you know this is our neighborhood. Just butt out. Go somewhere else. Go find a Russian one and fuck with the Kutsenkos instead of us."

"What, and forget to return the favor for all the trouble you've caused my family lately? No, I think not. I think one good deed begets another and shouldn't go unpunished."

He doesn't care for my mixed idioms. I'm pretty sure he

would snarl at me if there weren't people around. I should give him a hard time about how he sounds like a baby walrus when he does.

"Maybe I'll take you up on your suggestion and find a new neighborhood to take from the Kutsenkos. But we're not going anywhere until we collect the last of what's due here. So, either you pay up for your *amigos* or they pay up. One way or another, we're getting our money. I've got a baseball bat in the back of the car. I'm happy to use it, whether it's against your kneecaps or against some windows."

"You're not doing shit. You've always talked a big game, Cormac, but there's nothing you're going to do while my men and I are here."

"Yeah, but you won't sleep in a neighborhood like this. You're going home at some point. I've always been able to wait you out. Nothing's changed about that."

"I bet you're waiting for Jocelyn Bracero."

It shocks me to hear Joey's name from Pablo. I've been worrying they might be connected. Now, it's confirmed. I don't know why it surprises me so much, but my expression gives nothing away. I've always had a poker face.

The other guys in the Four Families had to learn not to give their thoughts and emotions away, but it came naturally to me. I'm the most stoic in our family. I was the kid who would have the hundred-and-four fever and tell my parents that I felt a little off.

Seamus was the one who would point to wherever he didn't feel well and say, "it hurts right here." I'd be nearly on death's doorstep before I would go to my parents and say something was wrong. I just have a higher pain tolerance than most, and that's always terrified my parents because they fear one of these days, I'm going to be injured worse than I realize. They fear I won't admit I need help until it's too late, but I've learned my lesson about that. If somebody else in the family insists I need to get checked out, even if I don't agree, I do.

"You can pretend like hearing her name doesn't bother you, but I saw you together the other day. I saw you chatting on the sidewalk, and I know she's the one who pushed you out of the way, so you wouldn't look like a piece of moldy Swiss cheese today."

"I thanked her for making sure there wasn't a shootout here on the streets while kids were out playing and coming home from school."

"Yeah, I heard she tackled you and knocked you down the stairs. I thought you were more solid than that. Maybe you're getting flabby in your old age."

This fucknut is older than me, but it's obvious there's nothing flabby about either of us. I cock an eyebrow and roll my eyes.

"What's it matter to you whether I spoke to her?"

Pablo assesses me for way too long, and I'm uncertain if his mind is as blank as it usually is, and he's trying to unnerve me, or if he's really thinking about how to answer that question.

"She's not who you think she is, Cormac. I'd stay away."

"Really?"

"Yeah. Consider that a neighborly tip."

"There's nothing neighborly about you. What's it matter to you whether I know Jocelyn?"

I've asked twice. I won't ask a third.

"It doesn't matter to me, but it will matter to you. I'm telling you it's a mistake to have her anywhere near you."

"If I didn't know better, Pablo, I'd think you sound possessive."

He laughs at that, but the man hasn't given an actual laugh in at least twenty years, so it sounds rusty at best. It's more like a cackle.

"I'm just giving you a warning. Don't come to me later and make me tell you I told you so."

"You've got to give me a better reason than that. But it's not like I'm going to see her again soon."

He juts his chin to the left, and I look over my shoulder. Sure as shittin'. Joey's walking out of an apartment building. It's the nicest one on the block, far nicer than the one she left just before we met.

Her shock isn't a surprise, but her dismay hurts. I watch as her head turns each direction, and her gaze sweeps the street. She pauses as she spots Pablo's SUV and his men standing near the vehicle. She turns her attention back to Pablo and me, and it's as though I can hear her thoughts from here. She looks like a rabbit ready to flee, trying to decide which is the fastest way to get back into her warren. She opts for spinning on her heels and rushing into the building she came out of.

"Doesn't look like she's so pleased to see you, *amigo*."

Pablo's voice is nothing short of a sneer. I resist the urge to slap it off him.

"She didn't mind talking to me the other day. Maybe she doesn't mind seeing me, and it's your ugly arse she's avoiding."

"I don't know. The last time I spoke to her, she didn't seem to think I was so ugly. At least not the way her eyes kept skimming over me."

He's trying to goad me, and it's working.

Thank God for my stoicism.

"When was that? Six years ago? Wasn't that the last time you spoke to her?"

"Hardly. It was yesterday."

That's a gut punch, and he knows it. I look back across the street and shrug.

"Well, then she's all yours."

No, she's not!

My brain screams to me, but I want to see Pablo's reaction. The smug bastard grins again. I've never wanted to punch him so much. But if Joey's lied to me or changed her mind about Pablo, then I'm barking up the wrong tree. I'm not interested in pursuing somebody—period—let alone someone who's not interested in me.

I just want to make sure she's safe. And I guess she is, if she and Pablo are talking.

"That really chaps your ass, doesn't it?"

I haven't looked away from Pablo since I turned my attention back to him after Joey walked back inside.

"What chaps my arse? It turns out she doesn't have as good taste as I thought she did. What's it to you, Pablo?"

"Wouldn't you like to know?"

I shrug and look past him to Ignacio, who's standing in the doorway now. I cock an eyebrow, and Pablo twists to look over his shoulder. I don't know how he isn't already sure it's Ignacio since there's no one else who'd be standing there. But he double checks because just like any of us, no one's fond of people standing behind us who aren't family or our men.

It leaves us too exposed, and that's just asking for trouble. Pablo's grin drops, and his face morphs back into the scowl. It's the one I expect from him. He looks back at me, and now it's my turn to grin.

Ignacio dropped off an envelope at one of our strip clubs last night. It's the last part of what inevitably became his last payment. At least it's better than a swift kick up the backside, as my granny used to say. She wasn't as full of expressions like that as my nana, but she definitely had a few.

"What do you want, Ignacio?"

Pablo speaks to the bodega owner, but his gaze remains locked on me. That just makes my smile even broader. He wanted to goad me earlier. Now I'm returning the favor.

"I thought I'd offer you horchata, *el tigre.*"

The tiger. It's one of Pablo's titles because of his seniority. There're a few others he could go by, but it's the one he favors. People sucking up to him usually call him that. I prefer the title of arsehole. I find that the most fitting.

"Not right now—but thank you." He tacks on that last bit as an afterthought.

I look at Ignacio and shake my head, still giving him a smile. The man's brow furrows in confusion because I know he wasn't offering anything to me, but Pablo doesn't need to know that. Let him think his little bodega owner still fears me or believes we might do business, so he's offering his hospitality to me, too.

"Pablo, I got shite to do that isn't getting done standing here with you."

"Then you should go finish whatever crap you have. Wherever it is, it isn't here. We both know that."

"The sooner you let me collect the outstanding balances, the sooner I'll leave the neighborhood, and I won't come back."

"What? You don't want to see me with Jocelyn?"

"I already told you. You can have her. If she's interested in you, then who am I to stand in the way?"

"How very altruistic of you, Cor. I've never known you to be that way."

"I am with people who're worth my time. I can spare a minute for you today."

I am not eager to turn my back on him like I did the other day as I crossed the street to tell Joey it was safe for her to leave. But it looks like I'll be doing that again. I turn to my right, ready to head to the first business on my list.

"Did you know she has this little quirk where she squirms when—"

Dramatic much? Pablo stops before he says whatever it is he thinks will piss me off. Hell. There might not even be anything at all he plans to say. He leaves the thought dangling to make me curious—or suspicious.

It works, but I won't let that bother me. I noticed Joey came back outside again when I turned away from Pablo. She's trying to sneak away while we're focused on each other, but I'm certain Pablo notices her just as easily as I do, and he proves it.

"*Hola*, Jocelyn."

I turn to face her as she stops dead in her tracks. She's not thrilled to see him either. She doesn't seem to appreciate his attention in public. Are they more than what she said, and they've been keeping it a secret? She doesn't look fearful. She looks annoyed. It doesn't match what she was doing the day I met her.

Did they work things out between then and now? Did the piece of shite charm her?

I watch her. Then I notice Pablo's shadow shifts. I turn back to where he stood, but I'm forced to watch him cross the street toward Jocelyn. She looks more than uncomfortable.

Her gaze darts to me, then she pivots a second time and dashes back into the building. Now I'm pissed.

"What the feck, Pablo?" We often use feck just to irritate others. "Why is she running from you if she's supposedly into you?"

I hate that I'm following him anywhere like I'm a little bitch, but my ego's more interested in what's between Pablo and Joey than it's concerned about appearances.

"She's not running from me. She knows I'll be up when I'm done with my conversation with you."

"She really believes you and I are going to discuss business out here in the open?"

"We've just been chit-chatting so far."

"So why does she feel like she can't be here for that?"

"Because she's got better things to do up there. You know who owns that building, right?"

I do.

It's his bag of arse cousin, Javier. That shouldn't matter, but it does the moment he speaks.

"Did you know he keeps an apartment there he doesn't rent?"

I did know that. It's where he tucks away his subs since we're all into a kinky lifestyle. It's not that this is a horrible neighborhood that's unsafe. It's just an unlikely place. He believes his relationships are private. Amongst all of us, there's nothing private about the Four Families' sex lives. We know far too much about each other.

"She might have been looking me up and down yesterday, but who do you think she's going to up there? Who do you think she's been with each time she goes back inside?"

"If it's Javier, then her taste is even worse than I thought when it was just you. She went from wanting a sociopath to a psychopath. I wouldn't say she's making any improvement in taste if that's who she wants."

I hate speaking about her like that. But if it is true, then I'm not lying.

"You went to see her at her office. You were very chummy together."

That makes me go rigid as I square my shoulders. "Are you following her?"

"I could ask you the same question."

"You could, but I've already asked you. What's the deal? Are you following her? If she's with Javier, then why are you getting in the middle of things?"

"I'm not the one who followed her. But that doesn't mean we don't know what she gets up to."

"Is that how little Javier trusts her? Is he following her? Has he finally gone full-blown psychopath and is a stalker? Worried he can't keep her satisfied? That she might run off with someone else?"

"Fuck off, dude."

"Dude? You're getting soft in your old age. *Pudrete*. You and your *patético primo*."

I've been telling him and his pathetic cousin to go fuck themselves for twenty years. I grin and waggle my eyebrows at him.

"None of us are worried any woman would pick you over one of us." Pablo attempts to appear disinterested, but he's the one who started this.

"That's because there's no point in worrying about something you can't change. But whatever. If she wants to be with somebody in your family, then that's on her. I have shite to get done, Pablo. All you're doing is delaying me, so the men I'm here to see today have time to run like little bitches. That's fine by me. It means they keep their stores unguarded. I'll just get what I need and be on my way."

"You're not taking shit from this neighborhood, Cormac. I'm warning you. This neighborhood's off limits."

He steps up in front of me, and we're almost equal in size. Except I have about ten pounds and a quarter inch on him. I know I'm still stronger than him from the last time we got in a fight, which was three weeks ago today, actually. I push my shoulders back even more, and I make it obvious just how big I am.

But I see no fear flash in his eyes. Not that I expected it since we've known each other nearly our whole lives.

"What're you going to do to stop me, Pablo? Get your arse beaten in front of your men and half the neighborhood? Seems like that's what always happens when you challenge me. Certainly, what happened last month."

"You'd really risk a fight here in the middle of the street?"

"I'm not the one who's getting too close. Back off, and there won't be any reason for a fight."

He doesn't move, and I didn't expect him to. It's been at least a decade, if not more than that, since I fought over a woman. The last time—now that I think about it—was a melee during high school, when Javier and his two shithead brothers insulted Maria Mancinelli. My brother and cousins and I taunted the Mancinellis about not being able to protect Maria since the Kutsenkos stepped in. And we taunted the Kutsenkos about how they couldn't stop the Diazes. That was the first, last, and only time I fought over a girl.

When he leans in, I tell him a second time. "I'm not doing this here, Pablo. So, back off."

I move to step around him, and he moves to block me.

"Why don't you go up and say hi to your new friend? I'm sure Javier wouldn't mind."

I make to step around him again, but this time he gets closer than he realized. The tip of his shoe bumps into my foot. In our world, that's as good as a declaration of war. I put my hands on his chest and shove him hard.

"Personal space, *dude*. You're in my bubble."

He doesn't have to look around to know people are watching. He has the same sixth sense I do. Plus, it's just obvious two opposing syndicate men squaring off in the street won't end well for anyone. But it'll give all the *chismosos*—gossips—in the neighborhood shite to talk about for days.

"You shouldn't have done that, Cormac.

"What? Tell you more than once to move the feck out of the way, and when you didn't, I made you? You gonna run and tattle to your *tío*? You need Enrique to solve all your problems, don't you? He's had to get you out of a lot of shite lately. I believe it was my sister-in-law who made all of you—including

Enrique—apologize. I know your uncle didn't appreciate being lumped in with you for that major feck-up."

Nothing.

"You really got nothing else to say?"

I pause for a moment, giving him a chance to respond or get out of my face. Instead, I see him make a fist. I'm ready to duck, then plow my fist into his gut when he decides punching me is the response he wants to give.

He "oofs," but that's it. He's got washboard abs just like the rest of us. It doesn't hurt my hand, and it's only a momentary distraction for him. It's enough for me to plow my other fist into his temple. He staggers back a step before he launches himself at me, swinging one fist after another.

He gets a glancing blow off my chin with his third or fourth attempt, but it does nothing to me. As my mother loves to remind me, I have a hard head. He tries again, but I lean forward, putting my shoulder into his sternum and pushing. We both go sailing, landing hard. This time, I don't care that I land on top of the person I fell with, but I don't stay on top long. He rolls and shoves me, so I wind up on my back, but only for as long as he did. I push him off, and we both scramble to our feet.

It's rare you see two men in fifteen-thousand-dollar suits grappling with each other in the street. We come back together like a clash of angry lions. Or—oh wait—tigers. That's right. Well, I'm about to show him who the leader of this pack is.

I drive my fist in an uppercut that lands below his chin, snapping his head back. I draw my fist again for a jab, but his men intervene. We weren't fighting long because it wasn't that far for his men to get to us. They pull us apart, but he and I try to launch ourselves at each other again.

It's only when I see Joey's horrified expression as she stands beside her car that I stop. I shake off Pablo's men, and they let go when it's obvious neither he nor I will try for another round. We both straighten our ties and shirt cuffs beneath our jacket sleeves.

"Pablo, let me finish my business, then you don't have to see hide nor hair of me. But keep me from finishing business here today, and it'll be a lot more than extorting some piddly store owners that I go for next."

I notice movement across the street as Luke, one of our most trusted men and something like a third cousin twice removed or some shite, nods to me before he slips into one of our SUVs that just pulled up.

Pablo's head whips around in time to see Luke hold up manila envelopes and duck into the SUV. I run my hand through my hair and smirk at Pablo as pure rage settles over his face. I step onto the street and walk around him.

We're both carrying guns; I'm certain he felt mine holstered under my arm just like I felt his at his lower back. The cardinal rule Ronaldo and Jesus broke is that you don't shoot where anybody can not only get hurt but be a witness. Pablo and I understand that way better than those *niños*.

I get in my car and watch through my rearview mirror as Pablo gets in his vehicle with his men and heads off in the opposite direction. I keep glancing at him when I stop at the end of the block. I shift my gaze forward as the light changes, but I slam on my brakes before I go more than a foot because a kid steps off the curb, waving his hands. He comes over to my window, his hands where I can see him. The boy couldn't be more than ten or twelve years old. I roll down the window halfway.

"You can't tell anybody I told you this." He darts his gaze around, clearly having second thoughts.

"What can't I tell anybody?" I keep my tone light, trying not to scare the shite out of the boy.

"Those things *señor* Pablo said about *señorita* Bracero weren't true. *Señor* Javier owns the building, and he has a friend who lives in his apartment, but it's not *señorita* Bracero. She was there to see my cousin. He caught whatever I had. I just got better enough to come outside to play today. My *abuelita* didn't want me to, but I was bored. I can't stay long because she'll be back from the grocery store soon. But I went to see how my cousin was doing, and she was there. I saw her. I watched through the window when she went down the first time. Then she came back inside just as I came downstairs to leave. She told me to stay inside. I listened to her, but the front door was open."

He points back toward the building.

"You were close enough for us to hear your conversation. She didn't like what *señor* Pablo said because it isn't true. *Señor* Javier hasn't been here in like two months, maybe three. His friend who lives here is always angry these days. I think she misses him."

I offer him a more genuine smile than I did Pablo. Trouble in paradise between Javier and his sub. That's a little nugget to tuck away for later. Not because I would do anything to the woman, nor would anybody else in my family, despite what's gone down in recent years. However, it is a nice little nugget for when I want to piss him off even more than I did Pablo.

"Thank you for telling me this. Was *señorita* Bracero angry when she left?"

"Yes, extremely."

"At *señor* Pablo or at me?"

"Both of you. But I think more at *señor* Pablo because of what he told you. She wasn't pleased when you got in a fight. That's when she left for good."

"Thank you for telling me this."

"Please don't tell her I did. I'm supposed to be going home.

She made me swear I wouldn't waste any time. But I don't think this is a waste. I don't like people who lie."

A shiver runs through him, and it makes me wonder who's lied during his brief life.

"And *señorita* Bracero is always kind to all of us. And she's so patient. I wanted to help her because she always helps me and my *abuelita*."

"I'm glad to hear she does that for you. I won't say anything to her about you. But I'm happy to know she has such a brave and loyal friend as you."

The boy beams at me as he steps back and turns around. He starts to run but stops and coughs for a moment. I'm ready to get out and help him, but now he walks quickly instead. He seems fine, but I follow him to make sure he gets into the building I saw Joey come out of the other day. I wait to see if any of Pablo's men or anyone else follow him in.

It's fifteen minutes before anyone does. And it's an older woman who looks a lot like the boy, so I'm confident Pablo didn't see him talking to me. Or if he did, he's not lashing out to punish the boy. I don't think he would, but I put nothing past the Diazes.

I wonder if everything Pablo said was a lie. Most likely it was. But now there're more thoughts jumbled around in my head. I'm considering the possibility that maybe Jocelyn lied about how things stand with Pablo. Or maybe he spoke to her yesterday and charmed her. That stirs an emotion in me I have rarely felt. I grew up with five other boys and Dillan's little sister, Colleen, before she died.

I think I've shared everything for the most part, and I've always been glad to do it. Seamus was two months premature, so I was only seven and a half months old when he was born. We're practically twins, so we've always acted more like we are than not. We don't have the same genetic intuition Sean and

Shane have. But we're pretty damn close. I've always shared everything with him until Tiernan came along. I would never ask, and he would never offer.

But the thought that Pablo might have something I don't— that he might have someone I want—makes me want to punch him all over again. Preferably with a knife in my hand. I head back to my place, but a call from Dillan makes me turn around.

Chapter Seven

Joey

What the fuck did I just watch? I keep asking myself that over and over on a constant loop as I drive home from the office. I kept myself distracted with a couple of calls on my way from the neighborhood to my office. But now that I'm walking in the front door of my apartment, I can't get it out of my mind. I just keep replaying the sight of those two colossi going at each other. It was like something out of the Roman gladiators.

I don't know what happened by the end. I didn't stick around to see. I think they were ready to talk again by the time I turned off that street. But it terrified me to see them going at each other. I don't know who I worried for more: that Pablo might do something to Cormac and kill him, or that if Cormac killed Pablo, the retribution that would rain down on his family. I want to think it wouldn't come to that, but I know it very well could if pushed too far. All it takes is one wrong word to go from an acrimonious conversation to a full-on street war.

I don't know what they were arguing about. I tell myself not to have such an ego that I might believe it's about me, especially since the reason Cormac was in the neighborhood was to collect more money. At least, I assume that's what it was about since that was why he was there the day we met. If it was about me, then I definitely don't want to show my face anywhere Pablo might see it. But it couldn't possibly be about me. I'm not that important to either of them unless I was just an excuse for them to argue.

Maybe that's all they wanted. Justification for another battle in whatever war of attrition these families have going on with each other. If that's the case, I don't want to be the excuse. I want nothing to do with either of them if I'm going to be put in the middle or used. I don't need anyone blaming me for shit that goes down between the two of them because I'm their scapegoat.

But there I go again. I have way too high an opinion of myself to think I'm even a blip on either man's radar while they're doing business with each protection racket target or their family rivalry.

I make myself dinner and flip on my TV. I've got some reality TV shows to get caught up on and a couple of historical dramas that just started their new season. I have every intention of bingeing those over the next three weekends. They keep my mind occupied until my eyes are fighting to stay open. It's not that late, but I can say watching the WWE match right in front of me today wore me out. However, once I'm in bed, my eyes suddenly find toothpicks to prop them open.

My brain is back on its hamster wheel, memories whirling through my mind. My interactions with Cormac and mine with Pablo. I remember back to that day six years ago when I made the mistake of calling the police. I had no idea it was Pablo's men beating the shit out of a middle-aged man. I thought he was being mugged because it was after dark.

I'd been running late all day after having to make two trips to the hospital and call Child Protective Services on a family. I didn't leave as early as I wanted, and it was winter, so the sun set early. All I'd heard were somebody's screams and the sound of fists hitting their target. I saw a man run out of an alleyway with two guys coming after him with their guns pointing at him. Then a giant—Pablo—stepped out of a shop, his arms crossed, as he watched.

I'd hidden in my car with my headlights off, slouched in my seat as I called the police. To my great misfortune, there was a cruiser only a couple streets over. Not in a Cartel-run neighborhood here on Staten Island, but one in Jackson Heights in Queens. I foolishly gave my name. I won't ever do that again. If I ever have to call the police on anything to do with men in these neighborhoods who aren't connected to my clients, I'll always do it anonymously.

I waited around until the cops came because I was too scared to pull out of my parking spot and have any of them see me. It didn't take long for the cops to discover what was going on, and a young man dressed in plain clothes arrived and talked to the officers. He obviously knew the men involved—all four of them—and he stuck around to talk to the guys after the uniformed cops left.

Nothing prepared me for the detective to pull his gun on the guy who was being chased. He put the weapon to the man's forehead, right between his eyebrows. I fully expected to watch the man die. That wouldn't have been the first time I saw something like that, but I thought those days were long over and far, far in my past. It reminded me way too much of my life in Mexico when I was a kid.

Today brought all of that back to me, even though there weren't any guns drawn.

It wasn't until after I got home that night that I discovered what was going on with the man they chased. I made some discreet calls to other social workers I know who'd worked that area before, and none of them reassured me I'd made the right decision calling the cops. That's when I learned it wasn't just a Latino neighborhood.

It was where the Colombian Cartel runs everything.

As soon as I found that out, everything went downhill, even though it all made more sense. When I described the young man who arrived, I discovered he was most likely Juan Diaz, the *jefe's* nephew.

I still don't know how a *jefe's* nephew ever got a job on the NYPD, but corrupter things have happened. I know he died a few years ago after fucking around and finding out with one syndicate. I've studiously avoided finding out the details, but it was inevitable that I learned at least a bit of what happened. He'd gone after a Russian bratva member's wife—the guy who's equivalent to a *jefe*. I guess Juan and Pablo grew up next door to this woman, and there were some unrequited feelings. Juan overstepped, and now he's not around anymore.

That's as specific as anybody's ever gotten when they've discussed that with me. I don't need any more details from somebody else to fill in the blanks. I guarantee my imagination, which is active and descriptive, probably didn't do the situation justice.

I'm getting ready for work when my phone buzzes. I glance down and see it's a text from my brother, Santiago. This is the last thing I need right now. I gird my loins before opening it. I'm certain I won't like whatever it is.

SANTIAGO

JoJo where you at? You haven't been home
for Sunday dinner in more than a month. It's
been awfully quiet without you here. We all
miss you so much.

To anybody who doesn't know him, that sounds like a sweet
and sincere, brotherly text. It's anything but. I avoid family
dinners whenever I can because it's my brother and his reprobate friends. Most of our family still lives in Mexico. There are
very few of us in the U.S., and no one else in New York. Both
of us moved here after college. I came for grad school, and he
came for work.

I don't enjoy his friends' company. They're too loud and
too gross. They always expect me to cook dinner and clean up.
But I refuse, which usually winds up with all of us in an argument and me leaving before the meal even starts. Sometimes
Santiago orders in, and that diffuses the situation for a couple of
hours.

Without fail, I usually leave fucking pissed off with his
friends laughing as I walk out the door. I'm close to my brother
in some ways, and in others, Santiago's a man I don't recognize
from the boy I once knew. But isn't that the case with so many
adults? We grow into the person we are partly by nature but a
lot by nurture, whether it's for better or for worse.

The environment we grow up in and the circumstances
surrounding it contribute to who we become as adults. That
means he and I don't always like each other as much as we did
as kids. It's unfortunate since I have no other family here in
New York.

There're some extended relatives on the East Coast, but I
don't know them, never even met them. I just know they exist,
but that hardly narrows it down when you don't know names,

and they're not people whose doors I'll be knocking on for Christmas.

I debate how to respond to the text. I decide I'll wait until later.

If Santiago pushes the issue, I'll say I was busy getting ready, or that I was on the subway and didn't get reception when his message came in. Chances are he won't text me again for a few hours. He knows I'll be formulating a response. Sometimes in the past, he'd text right away and try to badger me into a quick answer. He soon discovered that was the surest way for me to say no. It's faster to type two letters than three.

Nowadays, he lets me think about it, as he says, for a few hours before he presses. I really don't want to go, but after seeing that fight on the street yesterday and then nearly being in a shootout three days ago, part of me misses him more than usual. It would be reassuring to see some family. Our dysfunction is our normalcy. When you face danger and unpredictable experiences, even predictably bad is better than nothing.

I don't have any school visits or home visits today, so I'll be at my office most of the day. It'll be quiet and uneventful. Hopefully.

So much for quiet and uneventful, and so much for staying at my office. Today was one of those days that proves why the career expectancy of a social worker is so short. It was one of the hardest I've had in the six years I've been a social worker. It's never easy walking into a situation where you know the child or children are likely to be removed from the home. But today was worse than usual. If I shut my eyes for too long, I can see the inside of the abandoned shed. If I leave my eyes open for too long, it's like I'm there again, except I'm not.

I text three of my girlfriends to see what they're up to tonight.

ME

> Any of you want to go out and grab drinks?

While I wait for their response, I do a little internet research. I don't know why I'm thinking about Cormac again since what happened yesterday scared me. Today was way worse, and for reasons I can't explain, thinking about being near him makes me feel safe in a way I didn't today.

I search his name, but not much comes up except for some court cases where he's the attorney of record. There are some family photos from various high society events. And there are some articles about family members from a few years back. Two of them are obituaries. One's for Donovan O'Rourke, and one's for Declan O'Rourke. The names are vaguely familiar, but I know nothing more about them than I did Cormac when I met him.

The obituaries are so full of bullshit. I don't believe any of it because if these were O'Rourke men, then they were mobsters, too. My digging goes back a little further to a man named Liam O'Rourke who must have been Cormac's grandfather. Apparently, he died in an airplane crash under suspicious circumstances. The articles suggest it might have resulted from someone from one of the other main syndicate families sabotaging the airplane.

I feel a moment of pity for Cormac and the other people in his family because no matter what role his grandfather played in the mob—and it turns out he was the mob boss—it was still his grandfather. Old photos from social events show Cormac and five other guys and an absolutely gorgeous red-headed woman laughing with the men.

But beyond that, there isn't a ton of information about them individually. It's mostly things about mergers and acquisitions or criminal cases where Cormac's brother Seamus represented defendants invariably linked to the mob somehow.

As I search a little more, I come across the name of a bar owned by a Finn O'Rourke. I tap the back button twice on my phone browser and notice Finn is one of Cormac's cousins. Just as I put those two things together, my friends respond to the group text. It's been a shit day, and I really don't want to go home to a whole lot of nothing.

There's a ripple of responses that ping one after the other from my three friends all saying yes and a couple asking where. My thumbs hover over my phone screen for a moment before I go ahead and type McGinty's as my response. I'm an idiot for doing this, but maybe there's a chance I'll run into Cormac while I'm there.

Who knows whether he will be, and for all I know, he could have a girlfriend or even have a wife. He said he doesn't, but mobsters lie for a living. Nonetheless, something draws me to him after such a fucked-up day. Even if we don't talk, I feel like just seeing him would help me feel reassured. I don't know if it's his size and how solid he is or if it's his personality as well. But just thinking about him makes me feel protected. It's something I crave right now.

That sounds good.

We haven't been there in ages.

I've celebrated St. Patrick's Day there a couple of times, but it's been a long time since then. Plus, the previous times I've been there, I didn't know an O'Rourke owned the bar.

I run home to shower and change. It's ridiculous, but I take a couple extra minutes to consider what I'm going to wear. I take extra time with my makeup, applying a bit more than usual. I never wear a lot, but this time around I actually put some foundation on and do a little eyeshadow contouring. My hair's still wet when I leave my place and get into the Uber I ordered.

It doesn't take long to get from my place in Brooklyn to Queens where the bar is. I thank the woman and slide out. I hang around outside just past the bar's windows while I wait for my friends to arrive. I'm being too chicken shit to walk in there by myself just in case he actually is there. I don't want to look like an idiot coming in on my own. Like I'm desperately looking for him. Again, there goes my ego assuming he'd even think I'd be there for him. I only have to wait a couple of minutes before Tracy arrives, and just as we're hugging, Consuela gets there as well.

We head into the bar where we'll wait inside for our last friend to show up. I know they run pretty amazing happy hour specials here, so it's no surprise it's crowded. We ease our way over to the bar and slide in, sharing a spot that really should only fit one person. All three of us are standing sideways to order.

I glance around to see if there are any tables available or even one or two stools. It's standing room only for right now. There's a redheaded guy behind the bar. Immediately, I know he's an O'Rourke, even if he's facing away from me. He's not built like Cormac, and the hair's too dark, so it isn't him. When he turns around, I recognize him as Finn, the owner. I have a heart-stopping moment wondering if he knows who I am, and then I remind myself I'm probably barely a blip on Cormac's radar in the grand scheme of things. I doubt he's mentioned me to anybody. I need to get over myself, but clearly I want him to think about me as much as I've been thinking about him.

When our last friend, Tanya, arrives, I wave her over and

step out of her way, so she can order a drink after I grab mine from the woman standing in front of me.

"I'm going to see if I can snag that booth over there. It looks like they're leaving, and the waitress is going to clear off the table."

I'm in two minds whether to ask the waitress if Cormac might be here today—I don't know if he even comes to the bar— or trying to get Finn's attention to speak to him and pass a message along to Cormac.

What would I even say?

I have nothing specific or anything important or even any reason to pass a message along to him.

Do I say I'm pissed off about what happened yesterday, and I want to let him know?

Hardly.

Do I want to thank him for shielding me from Pablo?

I've already done that.

I have no justifiable reason, so I don't really have a message. I just want him to think of me. That's utterly pathetic and utterly ridiculous since Cormac O'Rourke is the last man I should want paying attention to me. I shouldn't be interested— shouldn't even be attracted—to a mobster.

Most people would say that makes me clinically insane. It's like those women who become pen pals with convicts and fall in love with them and get married—you know—through bullet- proof glass visitation windows.

All right, maybe that's a little overblown, but still, most normal people don't go thinking about how they can get a mobster to ask them out. And that's really what it is. I not only want him to think of me, but I want him to be attracted to me like I am to him. I hope he wants to spend time with me like I want to spend with him. It's all fucking confusing and batshit bonkers.

I ease toward that table, excusing myself as I bump into a couple of people, and a man apologizes when he steps on my toes. He turns toward me, and I get a look at him. There's no way in hell I'm not looking at Cormac's brother. They're not twins, but they sure as fuck practically could be. Even if I didn't know Cormac, this guy looks enough like Finn that he must be an O'Rourke. There's no doubting it.

I stand there with my mouth open, catching flies, just blinking for a moment before I catch myself. His eyes narrow as though he's trying to figure me out. I'm certain I look like the village idiot. I just wasn't prepared to see a mirror image of Cormac right in front of me.

Cormac and Seamus have lighter hair than Finn and the other guys I saw in the photos, and he and Seamus have baby faces. I don't believe they're the youngest in their family.

"Excuse me, sorry about that."

Now I'm apologizing to him when he's the one who stepped on my toes. I feel flustered, and I'm not even sure why. I just want to get to the table and bury my face in my hands and pretend I'm invisible. Seamus watches me as he continues to assess me, and I think I know when he realizes who I am. At least there's some element of recognition, but I don't know why there would be. I'm positive I've never met him, and he's probably never seen me. He wouldn't have had a reason to. Before, a couple of days ago, Cormac didn't know who I was, and I only know who Seamus is because of digging around on the internet.

"Shay, what are you up to?"

I peer around him, and—oh, fuck my life—here comes another one of them. This guy looks almost exactly like Finn, but again, just enough of a difference for them to be brothers or cousins but not twins. I recognize this guy as well, and I'm fucked every which way from Sunday because the New York mob boss is approaching me. Finn's position is equal to Pablo's

—second-in-command—but Dillan O'Rourke is equivalent to Enrique Diaz.

I've met three out of the six who's who of the Irish mob. My gaze darts around the crowded area, wondering if more O'Rourkes will come out of the woodwork. Finn walks over with a tray of drinks I recognize are ones my friends ordered.

I grabbed mine off the bar, but they were still waiting for theirs. The girls are behind him, and he places the tray on the table as he unloads a mixed drink, two bottles of beer, and four glasses of water. My friends thank him and slide into the booth, but I'm still standing there unsure what to do.

A deer caught in the headlights.

I nod and turn toward the table, but I find Finn blocking my way, and now Seamus is to my left, and Dillan is right in front of me. I'm not backed into a corner literally, but I certainly feel like I am figuratively.

Finn examines me, and Dillan's staring at me. I don't know if I should say something or if they're going to say something. If I came here because I hoped to get a message to Cormac, now would be the time to come up with something to fucking say. Nothing's coming to mind.

It's just blank.

I want to ask if they know who I am because the way they're looking at me is creeping me out, but that's a rather conceited thing to assume. Why would they know who I am from Eve? Once again, that would mean Cormac thought about me enough to tell someone.

I look at Seamus, and I take a leap of faith.

"You must be Cormac's brother, right?"

Two sets of russet eyebrows and one set of strawberry blond eyebrows shoot up toward their hairlines. All three sets of emerald eyes that are just like Cormac's narrow at me. I swallow, my throat suddenly parched and scratchy, and say to them the only thing that comes to mind.

"I kept him from getting a bullet through the head."

What the ever-loving fuck is wrong with me?

"I mean, well, I was there the other day when there were some issues in Port Richmond."

All three guys grin as they look me up and down. I noticed they're all wearing wedding rings, so it's not like they're checking me out. It's more like they're assessing me.

"So, you're the linebacker who kept my jolly green giant of a brother alive."

Seamus laughs as his gaze darts to the bar. I follow his line of sight, but I see no one but the woman bartender from earlier.

"Well, I—I suppose so. I played rugby when I was in college."

All of them grin like fucking hyenas. I don't know what I just said that's so funny to them, but it was something. Seamus takes pity on me.

"We never would've guessed rugby would be your thing. There aren't too many Americans who play it, but rugby is our family tradition. We like to play as much as we like to watch. It's the one sport we all have in common."

I wonder if they don't hear my accent as strongly as I assume it is. I didn't grow up speaking English even though I learned it as a child. My Spanish accent isn't like you get from most Spanish speakers in New York. It's a small world after all, I suppose. I sound so lame to my own ears when I speak.

"Maybe if you get a chance, say hi to Cormac for me."

All three gazes turn speculative as they continue to watch me. Do they think I came here to find him or to pass a message along to him? Have they figured out my real motives? I shoot them a smile and turn toward the table, not wanting to be rude and dismissing them, but I can't think of anything else any of us would have to say.

"Shay, I thought you were—"

I hear Cormac before I can see him, but he's so much taller than most of the people in here that he must have easily spotted me. He cuts himself off as he comes to stand beside his brother.

"Jocelyn." He caught himself before he called me Joey, and it disappoints me.

"Hey, Cormac, how are you doing?"

"Fine, and you?"

"Doing well. My friends and I came in for happy hour. I didn't know all you guys would be here."

"Yeah, this is Finn's bar. Have you never been here before?"

"I have, but it's been a while, and I don't think any of you were here the times I was. Or maybe you were, and I just didn't notice."

Cormac's eyes twinkle as he looks at his brother and cousins, then me. He cocks one eyebrow as if to say, you really didn't notice. Four giants with red hair and green eyes. I can practically hear his thoughts, and it makes me feel like a simpleton even more than I did before.

"I come here for the darts and pool. I haven't always paid attention to who else is here."

That's not entirely true. I'm always aware of who's around me, but something flashes in Cormac's eyes, and he doesn't like that response. His brother shifts, so Cormac can stand closer to me. His brother and the three other guys say hi and introduce themselves to my friends. I keep one eye on them, and none of them seem to recognize the O'Rourke last name. They wouldn't have much reason to float in those circles.

"I think you're extremely situationally aware, Joey. That's how you saved me. But if you're telling the truth that you come in bars that get crowded and don't notice who's around you, that's a problem. It means you're not safe."

"I keep an eye on what's going on around me, but it doesn't mean I remember everybody I've seen at every bar I've been to."

Do I sound testy? I don't mean to. He leans over to whisper in my ear.

"Well, if I'd seen you here, I definitely would have remembered you while we rolled around together."

It's my turn to have my eyebrows shoot straight up. The innuendo is definitely there. He seems more relaxed than he has the last two times I've spoken to him. We're in a controlled location—or rather—one controlled by the O'Rourkes as opposed to the Diazes or some other syndicate family.

He's not in one of his three-piece suits like he was the last two times and like he has been in most of the photos I found online. In those images, if he wasn't in a regular suit, he was in a tux.

Instead, he's in a midnight blue shirt with tan slacks. He has the sleeves rolled up to just above his elbows, the throat open to the second button. He looks sexier than sin on a stick. The way his shirt pulls across his biceps and his chest leaves me wanting to drool.

Seamus, Finn, and Dillan are dressed similarly, but they do nothing for me. Even Seamus, who looks so much like Cormac, is ridiculously attractive. I couldn't care less. My attention is strictly on Cormac now. Riveted, you might say.

Chapter Eight

Cormac

I can't believe Joey's standing in front of me at McGinty's, and I can't believe I just insinuated rolling around while fucking her. She might not realize it, but the guys are already giving me shite. They're going to bust my balls as soon as she's gone, but for right now, they've just got their shite eating grins in place. For anyone who doesn't know my family, they appear charming. I could throat punch them all.

My gaze meets Dillan's. My expression doesn't change except my stare gets more intense. He knows they're pissing me off, and they're about a breath away from pushing me too far. He nudges Finn who glances at me. Seamus notices because his gaze darts to me.

"It was nice meeting you, Jocelyn. I need to get back to the bar."

Finn excuses himself with a smile and nod to her friends, who barely keep their drool from puddling on the table. Finn's the pretty one.

"Mair's going to wonder where I went. I came out to get her some 7-Up."

Dillan offers the same smile and nod before he strides to the bar to get his pregnant wife something to settle her afternoon sickness. So much for just mornings. The poor woman's sick around the clock. Seamus appears in no hurry, which might be a blessing in disguise. He's keeping the women occupied while I come up with something to say to Joey. I know that won't last much longer since I see the flush starting at the base of his neck. It matches mine since neither of us enjoy striking up conversations with strangers.

I suddenly feel tongue tied and regret chasing my cousins off. Neither of them is as shy as Seamus and me. We're the most introverted of the cousins, even if our parents are the least introverted of their siblings. I need to come up with something since I already know Joey's been here before. The ball's in my court, and it's rolling out of bounds.

"Did I interrupt a meeting or something?" Joey's gaze sweeps the bar before glancing down at my shirt, which is far more casual than she's seen me in before.

"No. I stopped by to read some documents Finn asked me about. Dillan's wife was going to help out tonight since Finn's short a waitress, but she's not feeling well. Dillan swung by to check on her."

Check on her means he'll insist she go home where he can hover and practically force feed her saltines. He's no better than Finn was a few months ago when his wife, Ally, was going through morning sickness.

"That's sweet. But if she's sick..." Joey watches a bartender deliver a tray of drinks.

"It's morning sickness, nothing contagious."

Her eyes widen as she nods, then she shoots a sympathetic glance toward the hallway Dillan disappeared down.

Sympathy or empathy? Does she know how Mair feels? I didn't think about that before just now.

"Jocelyn, we're going to play darts." One woman stands next to Joey as the other two slide out of the booth.

I know they hid their purses under their jackets. Fortunately for them, no one here would dare steal anything from anyone unless my brother, cousins, or I ordered it. Anywhere else, it would be foolish. As though thieves don't know people hide shite like that.

"Do you play?" Joey watches her friends walk to the corner where the boards are on the wall.

"This bar was my nana's before Finn inherited it. I practically grew up in it since Nana watched all of us after school until our parents could pick us up." I can't believe I shared that.

"But do you play? Or should I ask if you're any good?"

"I can hold my own. Do you play pool?"

"Yeah."

There's a table free, so we walk over. I watch her rack the balls after we flip to see who'll go first, and I wonder if she's a ringer. Good thing we're only playing for the quarters we each put down. She's about to win twenty-five cents.

"Solids."

I nod and speak, having just watched her sink three stripes with the first shot. She moves her way around the table, and it's obvious she's not just a natural. She's had practice. I step back to let her shoot where I just stood. Her arse is directly in front of me, and I'd love nothing more than to grab her hips and sink into her cunt.

It's the first shot she's missed. When she stands and glances over her shoulder, I watch her swallow. Maybe she was more unsettled than she looked. It's crowded enough to justify how my body grazes against hers as I step around her. It's my turn to lean over the table with my cue. I pray I don't make an arse of myself as I inhale. I'm handy with a pool stick, but it's usually not when I'm trying to get a ball in a pocket. I make my target, but only that ball. I breathe a little easier. I move on to the next one and miss. So much for impressing her.

Her eyes narrow as she steps in front of me. "You aren't going to throw this, are you?"

"No. I said I was practically raised here and played darts. I didn't say I played pool or darts well." I grin, but my heart stops as I wait for her to laugh at me, not with me.

I'm excellent at darts because my dad wouldn't teach me how to throw a knife until I could hit the bullseye with precision every time I threw a dart. Not a family story I'm sharing. I'm not as good at pool because I think it's boring and rarely play. But it was the only thing open to give me a chance to stay near Joey.

She chuckles, and I don't feel like it's at my expense so much as appreciating a self-deprecating sense of humor.

"I'll take a win where I can get it. I doubt there's much you don't excel at."

She's on the opposite side of the table from me now as she leans forward. Her top isn't loose, but there's just enough space between the material and her skin for me to have a stellar view of her perfect tits. I almost forget it's my turn when she misses because I'm too busy daydreaming about fucking her.

I pull my head out of my arse and take the shot. I do better than I expected and sink three more, which ties us. Someone bumps into her when she walks past me. It knocks her into me, and my arm goes around her waist. Our gazes lock, and I want nothing more than to kiss her. From the way her gaze darts to my lips, I think she feels the same way. If I don't ease her away from me, she's going to feel my semi-erect cock shoot to full mast.

"Sorry about that."

"Not your fault." I ease my arm away until just my hand rests on her waist.

She pulls away, but the same arselick knocks into her again. He's drunk and being obnoxious. I reach out with the hand holding the cue stick and tap on the guy's shoulder blade with my knuckles. It's a light tap, I swear. But he spins around with plenty to say.

"What the fuck, asshole? Touch me again, and—"

He takes a moment to shift his gaze from Joey to me. When he does, he wants to swallow his tongue. His head jerks back, and his mouth hangs open.

"Sorry. I meant nothing by it." His tongue practically trips over his teeth as he rushes to apologize.

"You're cut off."

He thinks he grew a pair. "Mind your own fucking business. You don't tell me—"

"Yeah, I do." I signal two bouncers already easing their way through the crowd to me.

"What the fu—"

"Stop swearing." If he were my mother's son, he'd already have a bar of Irish Spring between his cheeks.

"Get your motherfucking hands off me."

He tries to pull away from a bouncer and winds up driving his elbow into Joey's shoulder. I barely moved her in time to keep it from nailing her jaw.

"You're going to let Mikey and Tommy escort you outside *after* you pay your tab. You do *not* want me to help you out, and you do *not* want my cousin—who owns this establishment—to help you out."

"It's not my fault the bitch was standing in the way."

The man has a fucking death wish. Mikey and Tommy are my second cousins through my dad. Their parents are just as strict about no swearing in front of women and children as mine are. They each grab an arm, and Mikey's shoulder goes into fuckwad's chest as he pushes him away from Joey and me. It looks more like he's steering the douchebag, but I guarantee it feels like a linebacker's charging into him. The NFL scouted Mikey, but he blew out his knee at the first season opener.

"Are you all right?"

I keep my voice low as I ease Joey's hand from her arm and rub her shoulder. She nods, but she looks anything but fine.

"Joey, answer me. Are you all right?"

I infuse a little command in my voice, and her gaze immediately shifts downward. I feel like an arsehole until her body leans into mine.

"Yes, Cormac." *Yes, sir.*

That's what it sounded like she wanted to say. The way her gaze remains averted. She drank the beer she bought while we played, and I got her a second one she'd just finished before our game got so rudely interrupted. My cue's leaning against the table where I placed it before squaring off with the drunk piece of shite and telling him to leave. My free hand goes to Joey's hip, and I squeeze. She doesn't react, so I squeeze harder.

"Are you telling me the truth, *cailín?*"

She raises her gaze to meet mine for a moment, uncertain what the Irish word means. But she looks down a second later.

"Yes, Cormac."

I test the water a little more when I give her hip a tighter squeeze before snagging her wrist and pressing her good arm behind her back. Her body sways into mine as the hand on her shoulder slides down to capture her other wrist. I barely push it back before she crosses her wrists at the small of her back. She doesn't wince, and she didn't favor her bad arm while playing pool. I'm relieved her injury wasn't as bad as I feared.

"Would you be a good girl and tell me if you weren't?"

"Yes, Cormac." She whispers her answer on an exhale.

Holy fuck.

"Look at me, Joey." I wait for her. "Are you someone's sub?"

She meets my gaze. Is that relief? She shakes her head. I lower my head to whisper in her ear.

"You don't want to find out what happens to naughty little subs who make their master's repeat themselves each time they ask a question."

"I'm sorry, sir."

I don't date. I fuck. I don't have girlfriends, but I did have a long-term sub.

"Are you tipsy, *cailín*?"

"A little. What does that mean, sir?"

"Little girl."

"I'm not a Little, Cormac."

She gets serious fast, snapping out of whatever alcohol haze she'd been in.

"I know you aren't. I wouldn't be interested if you were. You didn't mind me asking if you'd be a good girl a moment ago."

"You didn't say a good *little* girl."

"That word aside, how tipsy are you?"

"Not as tipsy as a second ago." Her clear eyes and sharp gaze tell me she's not exaggerating.

"We're going to finish our game, then you're going to finish having a good time with your friends. If you want more by the time you're ready to leave, tell me."

"I'm ready to leave. I want more." The words fly out of her mouth.

I know who's around me, and I know who's paying attention to us and who's not. Her friends definitely are. My back's broad enough no one can see me holding her hands behind her back, but they can see my extended arms. I let go of her wrists and withdraw my hands. She doesn't move.

"If we do this, you need to know it's not a prelude to me asking you out for dinner and a movie."

"It's a one-night stand?"

"Not absolutely. I don't date, Joey. I'm not a monk, but I don't do attachments. I had a sub until a couple months ago. I was with her for three years, and nothing ever became romantic. If you're looking for more than that, we're not a match."

"Are you looking for a new sub?"

"Yes."

What? No!

I told myself I didn't want a new D/s arrangement right now. I wanted to enjoy being unattached. If I wanted to fuck, I'd go to the club I belong to. I didn't see Joey as a potential sub only a few minutes ago. I never imagined she'd ask if I was in the market for one.

"Sir, test me tonight. If we like it, then we go from there."

"How long ago was your last Dom?"

"Four months. I was with him for a year, but it wasn't fulfilling."

I cock an eyebrow and wait.

"He wanted to make it romantic, and I didn't."

"Was it monogamous?"

"Yes, except for when we went to the club where we met."

As I gaze down at her, I know I don't want to touch another woman. The idea is as off-putting as it gets. The idea of another man touching her in front of me makes me want to tear the imaginary guy's head off. I didn't have this visceral a reaction when I met my last sub or discussed our arrangement.

"Cormac, I don't want to be with or have you see me with another guy. I enjoy threesomes, but I don't need them. Maybe in the future, but right now—I—I don't want the distraction." She rushes to finish her thought.

"I won't share you, Joey. Not now. Not in the future. We're both monogamous, or we're nothing. If I find out you—"

"Cormac, I won't break my promise. If I find someone else I want to fuck, or if I find someone I want to date, I will end this. If you don't want a threesome with a guy, then we won't."

"I don't want a threesome period. If you want a woman to join us—"

"No."

That's as definitive an answer as there ever was one.

"Good. I would have if that's what you want, but I do not."

She shifts to look around the bar and notices her friends are back at their table. I follow her gaze, and the three women watch us. They appear curious about our conversation, but they seem bored at being here.

"I don't bring guys home, Cormac."

"And I don't bring women over."

"The only way out of that impasse is a club. I belong to Cries and Whispers."

We are definitely not going there. It's a bratva owned club as of last year. I sold my silent quarter share because it's one a few other syndicate couples enjoy, so none of my family will step foot in there. We know each other's business and that we're all kinky as fuck. But that doesn't mean I need any of their nasty arses seeing me fuck.

"I belong to Obsidian." And own a quarter.

So does Seamus because all the men my age in my family own significant *silent* shares of the best clubs to have access to their confidential member lists. It pays to know where the rich and powerful go to get their rocks off.

Her eyes widen. It's one of the most exclusive BDSM clubs in the country, and it's one that caters to just about any and every idea. If anything's unavailable, it will be within twelve hours. The wait list is six years long.

She glances at her friends before she nods. I step aside, and she hurries over to the women while I collect our two quarters and return the cues. I know people want the table, but no one dared come over to me and interrupt my conversation. The regulars know better, and after I kicked that dumb fuck out, even the random people aren't interested in approaching me.

ME

I'm headed out with Jocelyn. I'm not available until the morning.

SEAMUS

Don't feck it up.

Trust my brother's immediate response to be words of encouragement.

ME

Bye

SEAMUS

Can you come down to Trenton with me tomorrow morning?

ME

Something come up?

SEAMUS

Yeah. Tiera's mom is having a procedure done. T wants me with her, and I want you guarding her.

Things are still rocky with the Trenton mob. They're our vassals and majorly fucked up with my sister-in-law. We don't trust them, so Seamus won't go down there without an extra bodyguard for Tiernan. It's more of a flex on our part, but just in case any other syndicate thinks the O'Briens are weak and decides this is a good time to target them, I'll be there to help. It wouldn't surprise me if one of our cousins comes too.

ME

What time?

SEAMUS

9

ME

Got it

"They're catching rides in a few minutes. I told them you're taking me out, but we're still making plans."

Joey keeps her voice low as she comes back to where I'm waiting. I look over to Finn, who has the same sixth sense we all do about people watching us. He scans the bar until our gazes meet. I tilt my head slightly toward Joey, then turn my chin toward the door. I can imagine what he'd say if I was close enough to hear.

I put my hand at Joey's lower back and usher her toward the front door. I don't move my hand once we're outside. It's possessive and protective, and we both know it. But we're not a couple, so I don't take her hand or wrap my arm around her. She doesn't ask where we're going, trusting me. I lead her to my car and open her door, but before she gets in, I have this over-whelming need for our first kiss to not be at a sex club.

Chapter Nine

Joey

Cormac watches me as his hand slides up the outside of my hip to my waist and rests there. If I didn't want to touch him so badly, I'd feel trapped standing between the car frame, the door, and him. But I like it. I don't want to go anywhere. I like that I'm confined where he wants me. His fingers flex, pressing me toward him. I step closer, and he lowers his head, his lips only inches from me.

"Any time you want this to stop, you say so. It ends immediately."

And if I never want it to end?

I lied when I said I was fine with this not being romantic. I wish it were. But if he's not interested in that, I'll live with it because I don't think I can live without feeling Cormac inside me. Maybe he's hot, but he's shit in bed. It would make it easier to exorcise him from my mind. But I doubt that man doesn't come in first place for everything he does—except for pool.

"What's your safe word, *cailín*?"

I love the sound of that word so much I nearly forget it's a question. His emerald-colored eyes have me transfixed. My brain stalls, then it comes to me.

"Bodega."

He grins, and tiny lines form around his mouth. I want to run my finger over them, but that's affectionate. That's the opposite of what we agreed to.

"Bodega it is."

His lips brush against mine as I cant my head, so our noses don't smash. He's going tantalizingly slowly. The tip of his tongue traces my lips while his barely touch mine. When he slides it into my mouth, his lips finally press against mine.

Hell.

I feel my nipples tightening. He nudges me back against the car frame, and the hand not on my waist captures my wrist like he did inside. I'm completely malleable once I bring my other hand behind me.

His one hand encircles both of my wrists, and I long to know what it would feel like on my tits. I feel his cock against my pussy, and I long to climb him like a fire pole and slide down on it. I pull away from the car, wanting to be closer, but he doesn't allow it on my terms. He gives me what I need, but he does it by widening his stance to have one foot on each side of mine. He tilts his hips and rubs his dick against me.

The kiss keeps going, and his tongue sweeps around my mouth. I let him explore before I suck on it lightly. I make sure it doesn't feel like I'm going to swallow it. Just enough to hint at what my mouth could do on his cock. The hand on my waist jumps to my ass and squeezes so hard I whimper. Most men would stop at that sound. Cormac understands. He digs his fingers in harder. It'll leave marks, and I want that. I want to see them in the morning and know Cormac left them. It's possessive, and I know it. But it's the only thing I'll have after tonight.

We pull away, breathless. Our gazes lock for a moment before he kisses along my neck to behind my ear.

"That was delicious. I can't wait to taste the rest of you. I plan to lick your cunt and suck your clit until you beg to come. I haven't decided yet if I'll let you."

"Please." I'm begging already.

"Maybe. If you're a good girl."

He adds the second sentence as he pulls away. His gaze drops to where my nipples stick out.

"Mmm. These might distract me. How sensitive are they?"

"Just enough, sir."

His gaze grows even more intense, and I'd drop my panties right now if I could. He shifts away, so I can get in. He closes the door gently before moving around to his side. Once he pulls out of his spot, he explains how things will work.

"When we arrive, there's a back door we're going to use. I'll make sure one of the Dungeon Masters has masks for us. I have recognizable tattoos, Joey. If you want people to watch, then you need to understand I will never be naked, even if you are."

Fuck. That's hot.

"I'll only take my shirt off in a private room. My mask will always be a full hood. My hair is too recognizable too. If you want me to scene with it on, even in private, I will. Otherwise, I'll take that off too when we're alone. What's your middle name?"

"Esmerelda."

"Does Esme work?"

"Yes. Will the mask cover my entire face or just my eyes?"

"Whatever you prefer."

"Can we start in a private room and see how things go?"

"Of course. You lead, Joey. We'll do what scenes you want, but once we start, I expect your obedience. If you can't or don't want to do something, say 'bodega.' I'll never guilt you or argue with you about your limits."

He makes it sound like this really could happen more than once. Like we really might be together after tonight. I want to cross my fingers, toes, eyes, whatever.

"Do I call you sir or master?"

"Either, but I prefer sir."

I test the water since his tone tells me he doesn't like master. I'm fine with that. I don't love it either, but I've said it plenty of times.

"How do you say sir in Irish?"

He glances at me as we turn right. Something flashes in his eyes that makes me think he likes my question.

"It's not one word. It's *a dhuine uasail*."

"Oh." Well, shit.

It's definitely not something I'll master in one try. His hand rests on my thigh for a moment before he shifts gears. Maybe he wouldn't mind master in Irish.

"What's master?"

He scowls, and this time he doesn't look at me.

"Very similar to English. *Máistir*."

"You don't like that term, do you?"

"I don't like you using it."

That stings. Doesn't he want to be a real Dom to me?

"What are your limits, Joey?"

"No marks that can show at work. Either a blindfold or earplugs, but not both."

I struggle with double sensory deprivation. I need one or the other.

"Okay. Anything else?"

"I'm okay with everything else."

"Birching? Caning?"

"That's fine."

I watch his Adam's apple bob. He doesn't love that either, but he'll do it if I specifically ask.

"Is that not your thing?"

"Not always."

For someone who just told me he wants to eat me out, he's suddenly gotten awfully shy. I shift my attention to look out the windshield, but I see his grip loosen on the steering wheel and gear stick.

"Is there anything else I should know about the club's rules?"

"Normally, you wouldn't be within the dress code, but they'll make an exception."

For me.

That's what's silently left dangling. Just how much time does he spend there?

"Will anyone approach us?"

"No. We won't be in the areas where couples can encourage others to join them. We'll find a private room to start."

Tonight, or whatever this is between us? I don't think I want to know the answer, so I keep it to myself.

"Do you expect me to remain silent when we're in the public areas? When we scene?"

"You decide how much you do or don't want to talk, *cailín*. If you're not comfortable talking in the main areas, then I'll do it. When we're scening, you can say whatever you want unless I command you not to. I'll ask questions to check on you. You will answer those."

Or we stop.

Yet another sentence that dangles silently between us.

"What about noise? Do you prefer a moaner, a screamer, or nothing?"

We're at a stoplight. He twists to look at me fully. His hand rests on my thigh again, much closer to my vag. The backs of his fingers graze over my clit before he squeezes.

"I prefer to know you're enjoying what we share. If you prefer being quiet, then I'll ask more questions to ensure you're okay. If you want to moan or scream, do it. This is as much about you as it is me. You might be my sub, but you won't become my slave."

I nod. *You might be my sub, but you won't become my slave.* Again, I wonder if he means just for tonight or for more nights to come. We should get through this one before I ask those kinds of questions. We hinted it would be more, but we might hate this and never want to be together again.

Bull-fucking-shit.

I'm going to love this.

"If I like something, and I want to keep going, but it's too much, how do I let you know? I mean, if I don't want to stop altogether, but I need it lighter?"

He thinks for a moment, then quirks a brow. "Deli?"

Bodega and deli.

I laugh and nod. "Sure."

We grow quiet as he parks. When I reach for the door, he leans across me and stops me.

"Most days aren't like the one when we met or even when I ran into Pablo. Most days are normal by normal people's standards. But when you're with me, there are extra precautions. Never get out of the car before I open the door for you. Part of it is chivalry. My parents would skelp my arse if I didn't. But an equal part is precaution. I want to be outside and surveying the area before you get out of the safety of my car. If I tell you to stay inside, you obey. You lock the doors and stay put. The windows will always be up before I pull into a spot. What I'm willing to risk when I'm alone isn't what I'm willing to risk with you. When we have our masks, I'll park a little farther away because anyone looking for me would recognize my cars. Tonight, I want us closer since we don't have the anonymity."

That definitely sounds like he assumes—expects—there to be more than just tonight. And cars? Just how many does he own? I'm certain he's richer than I can imagine.

"Yes, sir."

"Cormac...Or Cor." He says his nickname softer. "We're not in a scene. I'd rather you say my name."

"Am I only your sub when we scene? Or do you want D/s dynamics whenever we're together?"

"You can always call me by my name, Joey. If we're scening, I'll punish you if you do because you're being careless or flippant. But if you need my attention or we're merely talking, then use my name or sir. Whichever you prefer."

He slides out of the car, and it gives me a moment to breathe as he walks around to my door. This is fucking intense. One moment I was hoping to run into him at his cousin's bar. The next I'm agreeing to go to a sex club with him. Now, I've agreed to be his sub. I feel like we leapt over about sixty steps, but I don't want to go back or slow down.

He stands outside my door for a moment while he taps his phone screen. Perhaps he's requesting the masks be at the door when we get there. He slips his phone into his pants pocket and looks around. He opens my door and offers me his hand. I feel like a princess—at a BDSM club. Not quite what Disney had in mind, but it might be my happiest place on Earth.

I get out, and he closes the door behind me. Once again, his hand is at my lower back. I know not to expect him to hold my hand or wrap his arm around me. But I can still wish he would. He knocks on the door, and an enormous guy opens it. None of us speak as the bouncer gives us the masks.

Mine covers my entire face, but not the rest of my head. Cormac's is like you see in a mocking all-leather BDSM meme.

Except, he doesn't look like a middle-aged potbelly, hairy man. He looks mysterious and intimidating, which only adds to his sex appeal. I know I'm not alone in my opinion because I see men and women watching him as we walk toward the reception desk. It's not mere curiosity. It's lust.

And I'm jealous.

We have to wait for a Dungeon Master to come to us, so while we're alone, he leans in to whisper to me. "Are you comfortable being in your bra and panties or naked? Or would you rather stay in your clothes until we get in a room?"

"I'm fine with any of those. The clothes are getting more attention than I think either of us wants, so it might be best if I just wear my bra and panties."

He sweeps his gaze around the room, lingering on someone, but I don't know who before he looks back at me. It surprises me when he shifts his hand to my waist. From behind, it'll look like his arm is around me.

"We agreed no one is joining us. Stay close to me because I won't be as patient as I was earlier if a guy approaches you. No one is going to think you're available. My former sub is here, and there's a good chance she'll try to embarrass both of us or try to join us. I'm not interested in seeing or speaking to her. Things didn't end well when I broke it off. If I'd known she'd be here, I would have suggested somewhere else."

"Somewhere else? How many clubs do you belong to?" I didn't mean to blurt that.

"One other, but I know enough people to have unlimited guest passes just about anywhere."

I hurry to fill out the forms the DM gives me, then I slip into the restroom to change, putting my clothes in a locker. I step through the door as a woman who looks like a fucking *Sports Illustrated* swimsuit model sidles up to Cormac. She reaches for him, but he shifts away. He crosses his arms, and she tries again. He unfolds them and turns toward me. I don't know how he knew I was here, but he did. The woman's speaking as he walks away. I never imagined he'd be so rude.

"That's Deirdre, and I'm not interested in anything she says. There's a room for us upstairs."

We head toward the stairs, but Deirdre beats us there.

"You won't answer my calls, Cor. I'm pregnant."

Chapter Ten

Cormac

If she were a man, I'd shoot her. Instead, I swallow my sigh.

"Congratulations. Excuse us."

I feel Joey stiffen, shocked at my rudeness. Normally, I wouldn't be, but I'm not in the mood for Deirdre's theatrics. She's trying to fuck things up with Joey, and I won't allow it.

"Cor, don't—"

"I've never allowed you to address me by my name. Just because we're through doesn't mean you get to now. Goodnight."

Both women stare at me agog. If I don't adjust my attitude, I'll ruin things with Joey. I care way more about that than Deirdre's feelings. I didn't think I was bitter. I thought I was indifferent after we ended things. I guess three years of amazing sex with someone I wasted my time and effort with left me more jaded than I realized.

"Sir—"

"I'm not your Dom."

"Then what am I supposed to call you?" Deirdre's getting as testy as I am.

"Nothing. Excuse us."

"How can you be like this when I tell you you're going to be a father?"

Rage. Pure, unadulterated rage.

"Deirdre, I discovered how big a liar you are when we ended things, but this is beyond even what I thought you were capable of. I never once fucked you bareback, and no, you can't claim the condom broke. I always checked, and I never once used one you offered. I knew better than to trust you implicitly. You've proven I was right. I doubt you're pregnant. If you think this'll win me over long enough for you to get pregnant and trap me, you don't know me at all. If you think you can string me along only to be accidentally mistaken or to claim you lost a baby, you're wasting our time. Move, please."

"But—"

"Do you wish to be banned?"

That makes Deirdre freeze, and I didn't think Joey could go more rigid than she already was. I refuse to entertain Deirdre's claims, but the longer we stand here arguing, the worse things will be with Joey when I explain.

"You wouldn't." Deirdre's defiant, but it's only a whisper.

My eyes narrow. It's an expression she knows well. She can be bratty. Sometimes it made our encounters fun. But plenty of times, it annoyed me to where I wouldn't punish her. I'd leave.

"I know you just got a new Dom. Would you like me to talk to him about this stunt?"

She leans toward me, thinking it's seductive. "You asked about me."

It's not a question. It's an assumption.

"No, he asked if I was cool with it. I told him you're not part of my life anymore."

"But—"

Joey steps between us. I flex my fingers, trying to keep her from moving, but she ignores me.

"Back off. *Cormac* and I have plans, and I'd like to enjoy them before dawn. He said the baby isn't his, and I believe him. He'd never be that reckless *with you*. He won't let you touch him, but he is touching *me*. I don't share. Believe me, my bite is far worse than my bark."

She reaches back to take my hand, and I don't hesitate to give it. Deirdre seethes when I don't correct Joey for using my name and for any kind of display of affection—even one as simple as holding hands. I never did that with Deirdre. To me, it implies a level of intimacy and equality in dynamics I never felt. It's a girlfriend thing, not a sub thing to me.

Joey's hand in mine feels perfect.

That's something to consider later. I'm into her, and I wish I could offer her more. But she agreed to being my sub—or at least trying it out. She didn't reject it because she wants something else. After Deirdre's bullshit and how she's acting now, it makes me wary of any kind of relationship.

Liar.

It makes a girlfriend more appealing.

No. It makes something real with Joey more appealing.

Joey steps closer to Deirdre, but she makes sure I can still hear her. My cock twitches at what she says. My hard on died when I saw Deirdre, then jumped back to life when I saw Joey in her bra and panties. It was at a frustrated half-mast with Joey near me, but Deirdre in the way. Now it hurts from how hard it is.

"Move or I will move you. I don't care what you think, and I can't wait for Cormac to punish me. I can't wait to suck him off to make amends. He won't touch you because you're done, and he's not a man to strike a woman in anger. I, on the other hand, have no limits."

The way she says that last part holds even more innuendo than threat. Fuck, I want her alone. Joey looks around and waves to a DM. The woman comes over, and I *know* her. She's scened with Deirdre and me.

"Hi. This member is causing a problem. She's speaking to a Dom who's already made it clear he doesn't want to speak to her. She has her own Dom and is interrupting my time with mine. Could you do something about it, please?"

The woman glances at me before turning toward Deirdre. Neither Joey nor I wait to listen. The moment Deirdre's distracted, we step around the women and rush up the stairs. I point to a room that doesn't have a light shining beneath it. It means it's open. A red light means don't interrupt. A green light means the people are open to voyeurism or having someone join them. We slip into the room, and I flick the red light as the motion sensors turn on the interior lights.

I pull Joey's hand and spin her around. I trap her against the door, my forearms boxing her in. When she doesn't move, my right hand wraps around her throat as I maul her. My kiss is demanding. Savage, even. I haven't asked her about breath play, so my hand rests heavily on her throat, but I don't tighten my hold. I grind my cock against her, and her moan intensifies everything. I sense her arms moving, but she hesitates before she touches me. Then her hands are all over me.

I press her so hard against the door, I doubt she can draw a full breath. My free hand brings her right leg up to my hip, allowing me to press my cock fully against her cunt. I want to fuck her not to get it out of the way in a flippant sense. I want to get it out of the way because I can't think about anything else. Because I can't wait to know what it's like to be inside her.

Because I can't wait to show her my impatience, my need for her.

I reach into my pocket to grab one of the condoms I snagged while she was in the locker room. I wasn't sure if she'd find something else she wanted to try before going to a room, so I wanted to be prepared. I'm not a guy who keeps one in my wallet because I don't do random sex. With it on my palm, I grip the back of her raised thigh long enough for her to feel and recognize it.

She slides her hand under mine and pulls it out. She's tearing the wrapper while I unfasten my pants. By touch, we roll it down my dick, then I'm pulling aside her panties. Her pussy and my dick are magnets. I pull away before I thrust into her.

"If you want to wait, we will."

"If I wanted to wait, I wouldn't have put the condom on you."

"Once we do this, you are mine, Joey. Your body, your pussy. They're mine. I will do what I want, when I want because I can. I will fuck whatever part of you I desire, however I desire it. You will obey. I won't share any part of me with anyone else. My body, my cock are yours."

I told her I want a sub, not a slave. She understands this is dirty talk, but there's more truth in it than I've ever meant before. I want her to be mine, and I want to be hers. I want her obedience when we scene, but I want to hear and know her thoughts or opinions about our sex life and real life. I want something beyond sex, and that scares the ever-loving shite out of me.

I know the wonderful lives my brother and cousins have with their wives, but I'm not convinced I'm ready for that. Just the mere fact I have a nickname for her throws me for enough of a loop.

"Thank you, sir. I am yours."

Am I reading something into her tone? I must be.

I lift her, and she wraps both legs around me before I thrust into her. I rock my hips while I lift her up and down my cock. When she swoops in for a kiss, I let her lead. I want to feel how her desire matches mine on her own accord. Not because I make her respond. Not because I drive her to match my lust.

It's the opposite of making her obey, of claiming her. The opposite of what I just described. If everything I'd said was the God's honest truth, I wouldn't allow this. I would dominate her. But I crave this in a way I didn't know I could.

She cups my jaw, and I wish I'd taken the fucking mask off first. With an arm under her arse, I whip off her mask and toss it aside. We pull apart long enough for me to yank mine off. Then our lips fuse again. I carry her to the examining table—this is a doctor's office themed room, hardly my favorite but was available—and perch her on the edge. I unfasten her bra, and she shimmies out of it, flinging it to the floor like I did our masks.

No longer needing my hands to support her, I sweep them over every part of her. I don't stifle my groan as I savor inch after inch of her. She's short, so it's easy to reach all of her. As my dick surges into her over and over, I kiss her shoulders, her neck, her collar bones. I ease her back to lie down, so I can feast on her tits.

"Sir, may I come?"

"Yes. Don't hold back, *cailín*. I can barely wait, but I'm not coming before you."

"I want to get you off, sir. Tell me how."

"Keep touching me. Let me feel your hands on me."

I lean farther forward to kiss her lips again, and it makes it easier for her to run her hands over my back, shoulders, and neck.

"I'm close, sir. I'm going to come...Fuck!...I'm coming."

"Me too, little one."

I grunt, then shudder. It's the most powerful orgasm I've had in—well, probably ever. I twitch over and over until I have no cum left to spend. But I don't stop moving. I want to get her off again. With each thrust, I grind my pubic bone against her clit until I set her off a second time.

"Cormac!"

I want to hear her scream my name. I want to know I'm the only person she's thinking about. Not some guy from the past.

Me.

I keep going, wanting to draw every orgasm from her she can manage. Even though I've come, my dick's still hard. The tip's sensitive, and I don't love the condom squeezing it. But the feel of being inside her is too sublime.

"Fuck, Joey. I'm going to come again, too."

It's not like I never come twice, but it's not always. I definitely didn't think I could after the first one. But I am. I know she's concentrating, trying for a third. But I know when she grows frustrated because it isn't happening. I pick her up, guiding her head to my chest before walking her to the loveseat. It's here for moments like this. A time for aftercare. But this is cuddling in a unique sense.

At least, it is for me. It's not about—or not just about—supporting her as her endorphins slow. It's not just about reassuring her she pleased her Dom. This is affection that's foreign to me. I wonder if she's used to it with her previous Dom. She said it wasn't romantic, but how did they feel about each other?

I don't recognize this neediness in me.

"Sir, that was—that was—holy fuck is what it was."

I feel her smile through my shirt.

"Are you all right?"

"Do you really need to ask after what I just said?" She giggles, and I love it.

"I enjoyed it too, but I wasn't too rough?"

"Sir, it was perfect. I want it again."

She's more hesitant than a moment ago. Does she fear it wasn't as special to me? That I might not want her again?

"I do too, Joey. Over and over."

"Is there a time limit for the rooms?"

I ease her away from me to gauge her expression. Her gaze meets mine, and it's like she can barely keep her eyes open.

"No. Not for this one. I asked if anyone else reserved it. No one has. We can stay as long as we like. But I didn't just mean tonight."

"Do you mean you want an arrangement?"

For the first time in my adult life, I want to call it an emotional relationship. I want more than just sex.

"Yes. If you want more time together to see if we're a good match, we can take our time. But I'd like something formal."

"With a contract?"

"If that's what you want."

She's slow, but she nods.

"Do you need more time?"

"No. I just haven't had anything that formal before."

That surprises me, but I don't ask about her past. Does she want something more open? Something easier for her to escape? Is it because I'm a mobster? I feel myself retreating. I don't want to push anything on her she doesn't want. I don't want to pressure her. And I don't want to hear her reject me.

"We can take our time."

I said that already, but I don't know what else to say. She has nothing else to offer, so she leans against me again until my dick softens. I stand and carry her back to the examining table. I don't know if this scene interests her to roleplay.

"I think I need a thorough examination after something so taxing, sir."

Her grin is pure seduction. Fucking hell. My gaze sweeps the room as I step back and slip off the condom. I pull my boxer briefs up over my dick, but leave my pants unfastened. I spot the things I want as I toss my condom in the biohazard box kind of like the needle disposal ones in doctor's offices. I spied the doctor's lab coat, but there's no way it'll fit across my back.

Instead, I walk behind the table where different implements hang on the wall. They're purposely there, so a sub can't see what their Dom picks. I grab what I want and a bottle of lube, placing them on the metal wheely table. I adjust the examination table, so Joey's reclining, then I pull out the stirrups. I slip off the ballet flats she's still wearing then the panties.

"You said blindfold or earplugs, but not both. Are you all right with a blindfold right now?"

"Yes, sir."

Her submissive tone calls to me more than any other woman's because I know she's not like this in her everyday life. The contrast heightens the pleasure I'm getting from this evening.

I slide the cover over her eyes, ensuring it's in place, so she can't peek. I watch her until I sense her unease beginning because I've done nothing. I dive in and bite her right nipple just hard enough for her back to arch but not come off the table. I suck hard as she whimpers. I watch her left hand twitch as though she wishes to lift it off the table, but she catches herself.

"If you can't keep your hands down, I will restrain you. Can you be a good girl for me?"

"I'll try, sir."

"Try? You will obey."

"Yes, sir."

My tongue flicks her nipple before sucking again. I skim my fingertips from between her tits to just above her mons. I stop, teasing her with how close they are to her pussy. I rest my hand at the lowest part of her belly. I keep the pressure light, just enough to be dominant without having to prove it. Her knees fall apart in invitation.

"Close your legs."

I know it's a standing invitation to play with her cunt. I don't need her to show me. I want her to ache for my attention there, but I want the frustration of pressing her legs together with no relief. I don't want to ease it by letting her rock her hips with her cunt ready for me. I decide when it's time for her pussy to get what it needs. Closed legs mean I open her at my whim.

I brush a quick kiss against her lips in reassurance, a contrast to my command's harshness. I toy with her other nipple as I whisper close to her ear.

"You are a good girl. Shall I reward you for obeying me immediately?"

She knows it's rhetorical. She remains quiet.

"You said you want me to punish you, then you want to make amends by sucking me off. I'm not upset, and I didn't disapprove of you speaking to her." I don't want to say her name when Joey and I are like this. "But your reward could be wrapping your plump lips around my cock as you take me in your hot little mouth."

She moans her agreement. I cup her breast and massage it as I nip, then tug at her earlobe. I move away, and her head turns toward me as though she might see what I'm doing. I let that impulse go, not correcting her, glad she's curious. I pump alcohol-free, hypoallergenic hand sanitizer and rub it in before positioning myself between her legs. I drop a healthy dollop of lube onto my left index and middle fingers. I run them over her arsehole and pussy until I rub her clit. She's still wet from earlier, so I dip my fingers into her, coating them with more than just the lube.

I rub them over her arsehole and press without entering her. She pushes her heels into the stirrups, wanting to lift and offer her arse to me. But she stops herself. I ease both fingers in to the first knuckle.

"This belongs to me too, Joey. I will fuck you here and leave my cum inside you whenever I want. I'll leave it to dribble onto your thighs to remember I possess all of you."

"Thank you, sir."

I chuckle, but it's not with humor. She shivers, and I love it.

"I haven't done anything yet."

"But you have, sir. You offered something I want."

"You've felt my cock in your pussy. Is it something you can take in your arse, Joey? Do you have experience with it?"

"Yes, sir."

"Do you enjoy it?"

"It's not enough to make me come, but I enjoy knowing my partner enjoys it. It's arousing."

"That knowledge or the feel?"

"Both, sir."

"Are you all right with sanitized implements?"

"At a club, I prefer not to use them. I've brought my own in the past. But I will if you want us to."

"No. I'm fine without. I feel the same way. I know they're clean, but—mmm. Only if you wanted them. I can make do without."

"I'm sure you can, sir." That seductive smile from earlier is even hotter when it's just her mouth.

I press my fingers in farther as I clip nipple clamps to her tits. I grab a feather and trail it over the tips of her nipples then down her belly. She shivers, and her fingers curl. Otherwise, she doesn't move. I see her concentration, and the effort it takes to remain still. I continue to tease her until I see goosebumps rise on her arms. When I grabbed the feather, I also grabbed a crop. She's unprepared for me to bring the leather down on her belly then quickly over her left nipple before snapping it on her right one.

Her body twitches, her back coming off the table. I slap it across her clit, and she moans. I do it twice more, increasing the pressure and sting each time. With the third, I press my fingers all the way into her arse. I spread them as I flick the crop back and forth against her inner thighs.

She screams when I lean forward and suck her clit. I watch her, ensuring I don't cross the threshold into something she doesn't enjoy. I set the feather and crop back on the table, shifting to use the pedals to slowly lower the top of the table until it's flat. Joey reclines, and I ease my fingers out. She crushes my forearm between her legs and moans her disagreement.

"*Cailín.*"

Immediately, her legs fall open again, and her chin tucks. She'd avert her gaze if she could see me.

"I will fuck you there and fuck you often, but I decide. Roll over."

I walk to the sink and wash my hands before sliding the stirrups back into their holder. I help her shimmy up the table until she's comfortable. I push the wheely table away as I pick up the cat o' nine tails. I remove her blindfold, watching for the moment her eyes open. I bring the flogger down across her arse and lower back.

"More, sir."

"More what?"

"Please, sir, more."

"Good girl."

I indulge her request. I set a steady pace of a figure eight with my wrist. She tries to raise her hips to me, but I spank her with my palm.

"Stay still, or I will restrain you."

She wiggles.

"Naughty for the sake of being naughty. Now, I shall deny you."

Instead of following through, I spank her five times on each arse cheek. When her skin moves toward red rather than deep pink, I put the flogger aside and pull another condom from my pocket. I don't want to do too much our first time together, but I can't wait much longer. I strip before sliding the condom on. She watches, enjoying the sight of my body as much as I enjoy hers. I lower the entire table to align her cunt with my dick before grabbing her hips and guiding her onto her hands and knees. I inch the head of my cock between her pussy lips.

"Beg."

Chapter Eleven

Joey

I'm ready to sell my soul to the devil to get what I need next. I've never been this aroused in my life before. I'm ready to do far more than just beg.

"Please, sir, anything you want. Just don't make me wait."

"Is that what you consider begging?"

It's not, but I'm not sure if he wants me to say more or change my tone. So, I go for both.

"Please, sir, don't make me wait. I can't stand it. My pussy aches for you. I can't think about anything besides that."

"Are you supposed to be thinking about anything else? Or is this all you're supposed to think about?"

He's taunting me, and I don't mind. I'm here for that. It's only heightening my need. This entire experience has left me desperate. Not just for what he'll do next tonight, but the next time we can be together. And every time after that.

I didn't have a contract with my last two Doms, and they were pretty solid arrangements. But now I'd love to read a contract he'd prepare that spells out everything he'll offer me. My imagination is the sky's the limit. And from what he's doing tonight, I suspect he's the same.

"No, sir. This is all I'm focused on, but I can't help wondering what will come next each time you make me wait. That's not a distraction, sir, but it certainly makes me more impatient. Please, sir, can I have more?"

I feel like Oliver Twist, but I'm certainly not asking for more gruel.

His fingers dig into my hips. There are mirrors in this room, so as he thrusts into me, I can see the marks he's already placed on me besides what the crop, flogger, and his hands did. The feather was practically a cruel tease, so I was unprepared for the bite that came with the crop.

I loved it.

That balance of pain and pleasure. How it alternates. How it steals my breath. Both good and bad, which makes it even better.

He guides my hips, pushing me away each time he withdraws, then pulling me tight to him whenever he thrusts. I rock on my knees, my hands barely supporting me against the power he demonstrates as he controls my body. He's rough without hurting me. He knows his strength, and he's careful not to hurt me. He gets the difference between pain and harm, and it only makes me trust him more.

Is there something beyond implicit? Implicit compounded? Implicit to infinity and beyond? I don't know, but right now, I'd let him do just about anything to me. Considering he had his fingers in my ass, I'd say I am letting him do anything. I hoped he would restrain me.

Like he said, I should have known it wasn't an empty threat, but a test. He reminded me I can express my wishes, but if they don't align with his, then I won't get what I ask for. I sense he'll always give me what I need, but he won't always give me what I want.

I hang my head as I breathe through each thrust, struggling not to moan. Each time he impales me, he works my pussy like a fucking jackhammer. I know my body well enough to know this won't get me off without something rubbing my clit. I won't orgasm, and even if I try to do it myself or he does it, bracing myself and balancing doggy style will keep me too distracted to come.

As though he's trying to prove my point, his right hand glides along my hip and wraps around to my pussy. His index finger and middle finger rub my aching clit while his ring finger and pinky slip inside me, just enough to add to his cock's girth. There isn't enough room for him to move them deeper. I feel like he's about to split me in half with no help from his fingers. I'm so full, and it's not just this position. It was like that when he held me and when I was sitting.

I've been with guys who have big dicks before. I've been with guys who have big dick energy and disappointing dicks. I've been with guys who have both, but Cormac has it all in spades. The body, the dick, the skills, how he makes me feel. I moan just from thinking about that alone.

He assumes it's from how he's working my pussy. Some of it is as he rubs harder, and I try my best to focus, so he can make me come. I ache to do the same for him. I Kegel each time he presses into me, pulling his cock deeper. I wish I could see his ass flexing, but the mirrors aren't in the right place for that.

When I look to the right, I can see the hollow on the side of his ass deepen, but I can't see the muscles. I really wish I could. He's got the best butt of any guy I've ever been with. He looks like he spends all day and maybe even all night at the gym, but I know he doesn't since I've seen him at "work."

My mind's drifting again, so I force it back to the moment. I can't let it drift just because I know this position won't get me off. He seems to sense I'm not fully focused on this. Maybe he understands I'm doing this for him rather than for me. That by doing this for us, I wish to pleasure him the way he just did for me.

He redoubles his efforts on my clit, leaning forward and kissing between my shoulder blades and up the side of my neck. I tilt my head away so he can run his tongue up to behind my ear. He kisses his way back down.

It's beyond erotic.

When he nips at my ear and then sucks on it, he must hold his breath because there's not the distracting noise that usually comes from somebody with their nose inside my ear. Focusing on that and how arousing it is takes my mind away from anything else, including how I can't come in this position.

"Oh God, sir...Yes, please, sir...Yes!"

Holy fuck. I'm about to explode.

"Please, sir, may I come?"

He doesn't pull his mouth away to grant me permission.

"Mmhmm."

It's barely more than a grunt, but it's all I need to shatter into a million little pieces. My body pulses with the pleasure as I strain to keep going. I don't want this one to end. The three he already gave me were extraordinary, but this is life-changing. Maybe it wouldn't be if it were some position besides doggy style, but there aren't too many firsts I can still offer him. This is certainly one of them.

He continues to thrust, and then his fingers are painful as his teeth nip and tug my ear.

"Yes, *cailín*, yes."

He straightens as he gives one more thrust that's enough to knock me onto my forearms. Knowing he's coming this hard gives me a sense of gratification I haven't needed, wanted, or had before. It's almost as exquisite as the orgasm itself. I couldn't ask for better, but I reach back for him as he starts to pull out. I'm not ready for it to end.

He's quick to pull off the condom, snagging a paper towel by the sink to put it on since he's not close enough to reach the bio box. He picks me up and cradles me bridal style as he walks back to the loveseat, holding me as our hearts continue to pound.

When I rest my head against his upper chest—practically his shoulder—I can hear his heart. It's steady even if it's rapid. I match my breathing to his heart as it slows. Two beats in, three beats out. It calms me, making me feel completely boneless and spent. His cheek rests at the top of my forehead as his hand lies on my hip, and the other strokes the outside of my arm and the side of my back. His hands are large enough to do that. And I don't even have skinny arms.

We remain silent as we just enjoy each other's company, coming down from that rush of endorphins for both of us. I want to confess this was unlike anything I've ever experienced. Unlike anything I've dared to want. Certainly exceeds any expectation. But I feel too vulnerable to tell him something like that if it didn't mean as much to him.

I don't know him well enough to share that thought or to know whether it was significant to him. Despite how big a bitch Deirdre was when I met her, they were together for a while. It must have been special to him if he had a formal arrangement with her. That prompts me to wonder if he had some place for them to go.

He said he doesn't bring women to his home, but did he have a condo or a favorite hotel room? Something that was just for them? I don't like the spike of jealousy I feel. I have no right to it yet. I can't help it. I don't want to be ugly and conniving like Deirdre was.

I don't think I am, and I don't think I ever would be. But I don't want to have the same emotions she did that drove her to do what she did. I can't imagine ever spewing such a lie to trap a guy or humiliate a woman he was with. She did that on purpose. I don't enjoy understanding her because it makes me think I could be capable of the same thing.

I don't expect the affection to continue as he kisses my forehead. I lean away, and he peppers my temple and cheeks with soft pecks. I turn my head toward him. I don't know what's going to happen next. If the evening is over or if he wishes to move on to something else, but I could die a lucky woman after what we've just shared.

It wasn't necessarily the longest or the most elaborate scene, but I've never finished feeling this fulfilled before, even after my best scenes with other Doms or vanilla sex with guys I've dated and been seriously emotionally attached to.

Replete would be the word that comes to mind.

"*Cailín*, how are you doing?"

"I'm well, sir. How about you?"

"If well is the best you can say, then I didn't do it very well."

I laugh and shake my head. "Sir, if you did it any better, I think I might be in heaven by now."

He chuckles along with me and gives me another soft kiss against my lips.

"I agree. If it'd been any more than that, my heart might have given out. What do you want to do, Joey? Do you want to do another scene, or are you done? What would you prefer?"

I just wondered the same thing, and now that he's asking me to decide, I'm a complete blank. I don't know what to say. If I say I'm done, will that be the end of things? Will it disappoint him? Will he think I can't be what he needs and wants as a sub? Or is he done and wants an excuse to leave?

"Joey, this isn't some trick question. If you're tired, or

you've just had enough, then we can leave. If you want to continue, then we can stay in here or go somewhere else, but this isn't the only time I want to see you unless..."

"No, I want to see you again."

I hear the hesitation in his voice, and I can't spit my answer out fast enough. If he wants to see me, then I want to see him. Or rather, I want to see him, regardless. At least I'll admit my thoughts to him if he's brave enough to go first. I feel like complete chicken shit putting him in that position, as though just because he's the guy he should lead the way. That I shouldn't express my opinions unless he has first, but it's a lot less scary if I'm responding to him than me waiting for rejection.

I know it's not fair to expect that of him. Perhaps he fears the same things I do, but he's a hell of a lot braver than I am. That's how he comes across even when he's being the strong silent type.

"I don't know, sir." I remember what the original question was.

"Cormac. We're not scening right now, Joey. We might be in here, and we might be at a club, but this isn't a scene. This is just the two of us deciding what we want together. I don't want to make those decisions on my own."

"I want more tonight, Cormac. But that was so perfect I don't know that I have the energy to match that or top that. I definitely would like to do it again sometime soon."

"Tomorrow?"

He asks so softly I almost don't hear him. It's his turn not to meet my gaze. He looks like he's staring at me, but I can tell he's looking at my nose rather than my eyes. I know because it's a tactic I used with my father and uncles when I was growing up. I did it when I was too scared to look them in the eye.

"I don't have plans, so that would be really nice."

I wonder at what point he might bring up a formal contract and some type of established schedule or routine or whatever it would be for him since my guess is his schedule is even more unpredictable than mine. I often work later than I expect because home visits or hospital visits can take longer than I prepare for.

"Joey, let's try this out for a month or two, and if we like how things are going, then we can draft a contract and make this formal. I don't want to push you into something that might not be right for you after all."

"And I don't want you to feel obligated to offer me something if you realize it's not right for you either."

"Thank you."

Is that relief, or am I reading too much into those two words? Probably reading too much into it, but as the endorphins and dopamine continue to wear off—it's not quite sub drop, but I'm not feeling as blissful as I was a few minutes ago—he can tell. It's obvious he's an experienced Dom because he pulls me closer. The hand that was stroking my arm now strokes my head and my hair down my back. I close my eyes, and I could drift off if we were anywhere other than a play place.

"Joey, how did you get to McGinty's?"

"I took a ride-share."

"Okay. Do you want me to take you home or would you rather a ride-share again?"

I feel his already stone thighs tense beneath me, even though the rest of his body feels relaxed, and his breathing and heart rate haven't changed. I can tell he doesn't like the idea of me getting into an Uber or Lyft.

"I could take a cab or the subway."

I test those ideas, and his arms tighten around me, disliking it even more than the idea of some type of car service.

"Joey, if you don't want me to take you home—you don't want me to know where you live—that's fine. I can call a car from my family's fleet. The guy doesn't have to tell me where you live. I will promise I won't ask, and he won't offer. I really don't like the idea of you going home without someone there to guard you. Not after being with me and possibly being seen and recognized getting out of the car here or even getting into the car near McGinty's. And after everything we just did, I want to make sure you get home safely."

"Thank you, Cor. I'm happy to get a ride from you. I trust you if I'm willing to let you spank me and fuck me. I'm pretty sure I can let you drop me off at the corner."

I try to infuse some lightness in my tone, but he merely nods. I doubt he'll let me out anywhere but my front door. Despite what we just shared, I have a moment's hesitation about him coming to my door. It seems a little foolish to worry about that now, but there's a level of protection here at the club where there are Dungeon Masters if ever I needed them. It'd be different if he came to my apartment.

"Joey, just let me be sure you make it to your place without any trouble. I don't have to come inside with you. I just want to know you're safe. That's all I want."

"All right. Thank you."

It doesn't take us long to dress and put our masks back on before we make our way down to the lower level. I know we're both watching out for Deirdre, but neither of us spies her. I duck into the restroom and grab my clothes from the locker. I hurry in case she's still here. I don't need a repeat of our earlier conversation.

I'm exhausted by the time we arrive at my place, and I'm glad I agreed to him driving me home. I have a moment's worry when he doesn't open my car door immediately when he gets to it. He reassures me everything is fine, but I let him walk me up to my apartment since it made me nervous.

"I'm glad we ran into each other tonight."

We're facing each other outside my unit. He didn't hold my hand or wrap his arm around me as we left Obsidian or as we walked into my building or out of the elevator and to my apartment. But his hand rested at the small of my back, actually touching it rather than merely hovering.

"Me too, sir."

"Cormac. When we're not scening, let's stick to first names."

I nod, but I no longer meet his gaze. He shifts to look me in the eye, but I refuse.

"Look at me, Joey."

He might say we're not roleplaying, but his tone says we are. My gaze snaps to his.

"Yes, Cormac."

"What aren't you saying? What do you need that you don't think you're getting?"

I put on my big girl panties.

"How often do you want to see me? And if I'm allowed to use your first name when we aren't roleplaying, I take it you don't want a twenty-four seven dynamic."

"I'd like to see you as often as we can, but at least once during the week and most of the weekend. I travel a lot for work, so there may be last-minute cancelations, or times I can't make it even though it's a scheduled day."

Scheduled day.

It sounds so sterile, but we're not a romantic couple. It doesn't have to be. But I don't want to just be an appointment. That hurts.

"Do you want a twenty-four seven, Joey? Do you want us to

check in daily? Do you want a D/s dynamic every time we interact?"

If I say yes, how fucking needy does that make me after one night? I hesitate a moment too long before he shifts, forcing me to stand with my back to the wall. He cages me in again, his forearms resting on the wall. He keeps his voice low so none of my neighbors can hear.

"You are going to be a good little subbie and tell your Dom what you want. You are going to tell the entire truth, little one. If you don't, I'll know. Then I'll spank you, right here, right now. If you don't, I'll edge you and make you warm my cock the next time we're together before you get on your knees and swallow my cum."

I'm ready to fall to my knees now.

"Yes, sir. If we run into each other in the neighborhoods where I work, then I want us to be Cormac and Jocelyn. But when we're alone in person or on the phone or via text, then I want to be your sub."

"Do you want me to check on you daily?"

"You don't have to."

"That doesn't answer my question, *cailín*. Do you want me to?"

"It would be nice."

"Are you trying to get a spanking, Joey? Or are you that uncomfortable expressing what you want?"

I shrug, suddenly nervous.

"Joey, what do you *need*?"

You.

Desperate much?

But I can't remain silent when he asks that. It's the question and his tone.

"I need to know you're sticking around, so the calls would make me feel more confident. I want them, sir."

We seem to realize at the same moment we don't even have each other's phone number. Cormac reaches into his pocket and withdraws his phone just as I retrieve mine. We smile at one another, but he hesitates to offer his to me so I can enter my number. He doesn't ask for mine, so he could do it.

As he watches me, I still haven't figured out why Cormac grows shy sometimes. It's as though he thinks I might not give him my number despite what we've already talked about. Despite the fact he's already fucked me. Despite the fact he's had his fingers in my ass.

It's funny to me—perhaps I shouldn't say that because I'm not laughing. It's perplexing to me that he's such a confident man in most situations and so dominant during sex, yet he has these moments where he seems to withdraw, almost too shy to ask for what he wants.

He's never talkative, even when he's conversational. He expresses his thoughts, but he doesn't chatter, and he isn't into small talk. I pluck his phone from his hands and enter my number to text my phone. As soon as I do, I hand it back to him, and when mine pings, I respond to the text.

I save his number and wait to see what he has to say next. But since he's so shy, I realize making plans to see each other again will fall to me. That's one of the scariest propositions I've ever encountered.

What if he rejects me instead? I have no reason to believe that, just like I don't think he has a reason to be shy. However, that's where we're at. I shoot my shot.

"Are you available again this week?"

He smiles even broader than when we both pulled our phones out at the same time.

"I'd like that. Right now, I'm available tomorrow night. Would you be interested in meeting up again?"

"Yes, I'm free tomorrow as well. We could always try my club."

The moment I say those last two words, his entire expression changes. He shakes his head.

"If that's really where you're most comfortable, then we can. But there are members of that club I'd rather not run into, and I'm certain they'd prefer not to see me there, of all places."

It only takes me a moment to deduce what he means. My eyebrows shoot up and my eyes widen.

"Do you mean there are members of other families who go there? Does P—"

I catch myself before I say his entire name, but immediately Cormac's eyes narrow and his expression changes. His jaw hardens.

"Yes. He does happen to be a member there. So is Javier."

I should have known this would come up eventually. I'd hoped to make it through the entire night before it did.

"I've never seen either of them there, Cor. That's why I almost asked if Pablo's a member."

"It's a club now owned entirely by the bratva, and I'd rather not run into them, either. Explain it to me, Joey."

"Explain what? I don't know what you mean."

His eyes narrow even further to slits. They've got to be almost closed, but I doubt he ever closes them longer than to blink if he's somewhere other than his own home. It would mean somebody could approach him without him noticing. Then again, he seems to have a sixth sense for any of that stuff. He could be blindfolded and gagged, and he would still know somebody was approaching. Even ear plugged.

"He made it sound as though you were flirting with him the other day."

"What other day?"

He must mean the day they fought. I only caught snippets

and knew they spoke about a woman, but I didn't realize it was me. I got pissed because of how they acted in public.

"He said you were having a conversation and checking him out throughout it. Then he implied you were in that building to see Javier.

"Why would I ever see Javier at that building?"

"Because he owns an apartment there where he keeps a sub."

Now it's my turn for my eyebrows to shoot straight up. "You think I'm that woman?"

"No, not anymore."

"You ever thought that?" I'm incredulous and insulted.

"I wasn't sure what to think for a while."

"But you don't believe it anymore? Or did you believe it until we fucked and now you don't?"

"I wasn't sure what to believe until somebody in the neighborhood explained Pablo was lying to me. I want to know why he would do it. What did he think to gain by telling me you were checking him out or that you might be involved with his cousin?"

"Obviously, he was trying to piss you off, and in the meantime, probably risking my fucking life. What if somebody heard that and believed I was involved with a Cartel member?"

He shoots me a sardonic smile as though I should realize how stupid it sounds to object when I just spent the night at a sex club with a mobster. But I already know I feel differently about Cormac than I ever could about a Diaz or even somebody in the Mafia or bratva. I'm probably a fool for that, but I just do.

"I don't know, Joey. It sounded like you and Pablo are much more friendly than you claimed."

"Well, then he lied, and you believed him, and that's precisely what he wanted. He wanted to goad you, and he succeeded. I bet you showed no reaction to it, but I also bet he knows you well enough to read you even when you don't want to be read."

"Is that how he is with you?"

"No, Cormac. He's nothing with me because you've seen how I try to avoid him."

"But do you really?"

My anger spikes, and I'm ready to walk in my apartment and slam the door in his face. I don't want to see him at all right now, and I definitely don't want to see him tomorrow night if this is the way he's going to be. He can't trust me even a bit. I know he's known Pablo longer than he has me, but I'd like to think I've been more trustworthy than Pablo Diaz ever could be.

"Cormac, Pablo will say anything and everything to fuck somebody over. If he thinks he can do that to you—someone who's always been his rival—then he'll use any excuse to do it. That's me right now. I resent that he would include me in whatever little vendetta the two of you have against each other. And I resent you believing him at all when I've given you no reason to think I want anything to do with the man."

He watches me for a moment, and it's only giving me more time to stew, and my anger spikes to the roof.

"You know what, Cormac? Never mind. Never mind about any of it. Never mind about tomorrow night. Never mind about me. If it's going to take you this long to even consider believing me, then I want nothing to do with you. I don't want to be with somebody in any capacity who doesn't trust me, especially not when I'm going to submit everything to him and put my well-being in his hands. Why should I trust you if you won't trust me?"

"That's a fair question, Joey, but it's not just about me. Every decision I make will always include my family's well-being. It's never just about me. Anything I choose to do will affect them, so I must always consider that, even if it seems like it should be private between just me and my partner. I can't be with anyone who might jeopardize my family."

"And you believe what? That I'm going to sell secrets to Pablo? That I'm going to have him come over tonight, or leave here as soon as you do and run to him for some pillow talk? You're unbelievable."

I turn around and put my key in the lock.

"Joey, wait. This isn't how I want the evening to end."

"Then you should have thought of that before you started accusing me of things. You just took a perfect night and turned it to shit. I don't appreciate that. I wish we'd ended tonight with wonderful memories, and instead I'm going into my place insulted and pissed off. So, like I said, forget about it. There's nothing else to say to each other. I don't want to see you, and I don't want to hear from you."

"Joey, don't be like this."

I grit my teeth to keep from snapping at him and saying something I can't take back when he's already said way more than he can ever take back.

"Cormac, go home."

Chapter Twelve

Cormac

I have fucked things up every which way from Sunday. I couldn't have made more of a mess if I'd tried. I'm completely unaccustomed to these feelings of jealousy, and I let them get the better of me, which is also something I never do. I don't allow emotion to rule unless it's a sense of calm, which I've cultivated over the years even when situations tempt me to panic.

That's exactly what I just did. I let jealousy make me panic and made me speak without thinking. I'm an utter fool, and now I'm standing by myself looking at Joey's door that didn't even slam in my face. Just the opposite. It closed with cold indifference, or at least that's how I felt because she didn't look at me again after she told me to go home.

Not even a slight glance from the corner of her eye. It's as though she forgot about me before she even got all the way inside. I have no one to blame but myself for this because she's right. I took a perfect evening and sent it to shite. It's not something I can recover even if she forgives me, and I doubt that's possible at this point. But even if she did, it doesn't change how I ruined this. That when she looks back at tonight, she won't just remember what we shared at Obsidian.

To me, it was the most pleasurable, erotic, soul-defining night of my life. I was with Deirdre for three years and never felt about her what I just did with Joey. It wasn't the most structured or planned scene I've ever done, but I felt like she took a part of me tonight, and that's why I got so jealous so fast. It felt like I gave her a piece of me that left a hole that jealousy filled with thoughts of Pablo.

I believed that little boy when he said Pablo lied, yet when she started to mention his name, and it was connected to a sex club, all sound reason flew right out my ear and down the hallway out to the street. She was asking me, not telling me, that Pablo was a member. I'm certain her surprise was genuine, yet I completely ignored that—or overlooked it—or didn't see it until it was too late. I don't know what the fuck I was thinking, but I let envy and hurt rule the day. There's never been a fool greater than me.

I chastise myself the entire way home. There are things in life I've regretted, but I usually tell myself regrets are useless. I can't go back and change the past. I can try to right wrongs and do better in the future. But a fuck load of good that does me when Joey wants nothing to do with me. There won't be a future between us for me to fix, and that's almost the most painful thing I've ever experienced.

Only bullet wounds and a few stabbings have hurt more. I don't know how to fix this, and as I lie in bed, I don't know whether I should even try. It's not Pablo's bullshit that makes me wonder whether it's worth it. I don't want to upset her more by insisting on something she clearly doesn't want. However, if there's even remotely a chance to make this right, I don't want to pass that up.

Should I text her and apologize? Thank her for one of the best nights of my life? Would she even believe me if I included that last part? She might think I'm just saying it to manipulate her.

We don't know each other well enough for her to be confident that's not what I'd do. I'm certain she now believes I'm no better than Pablo since my objection was him being a manipulative little fuck. She probably thinks I'd do the exact same thing, since I'm certain now she believes I'm no better than he is.

I'm not any better than he is.

That rankles, and my doubts and self-loathing are almost all-consuming. I wonder if there's any chance for me to make things up to her. I fall asleep with that on my mind, and I wake to it.

I realize how massive a fool I've been, and what a mistake I've made. But just realizing my stupidity isn't enough. I gave her last night to cool off, but it wouldn't surprise me if not texting her only made it worse. I consider what to say as I brush my teeth. I text her after I get dressed.

ME

> I had an amazing night with you. Then I ruined it by becoming jealous. You've given me no reason to be. I let somebody who's been tormenting me since we were kids get in my head for no reason. I regret that. I'm sorry for ruining the night for you. I should have been a bigger person than that but I wasn't.

I think I've said enough. If I say more, it'll feel like I'm trying too hard. I want it to be sincere. I don't want her to feel as though I'm manipulating her.

I finish getting ready, waiting to see if she'll respond. The minutes tick by as I head into the kitchen and round up the fruits and vegetables I soon blend with ice to make a smoothie. I add in some organic fiber and protein powders to round it out. I'm like a hobbit; this is first breakfast. I'll have something later when I get to Dillan's house where we're all meeting this morning. He'll have something ready for all of us.

We all know I'm the awkward one in the family because I'm entirely organic and practically vegan. I read an article and saw a documentary when I was a kid about processed foods and what they do to you. Ever since then, I haven't been able to dredge up an appetite for anything that started out as pink sludge. No matter how delicious I'm certain it allegedly tastes, it's just not for me.

I head down to my car, and I've still heard nothing back from Joey. I have to respect that she doesn't want to hear from me anymore, and she may not accept my apology. I hope she does, but it's unreasonable for me to expect her to. I look at the passenger seat as I climb in and think about how she rode there just last night. There's still a whiff of her perfume in the air, and it's better than any air freshener I could possibly have.

I doubt that's a romantic thought she'd appreciate, but then again, romance was never supposed to be part of our arrangement. Not being a jackass was. I have no one to blame but myself for fucking things up. And boy, did I ever fuck them up.

It makes me wonder what she's up to this morning and what her routine usually is. We were out pretty late, but I'm certain she got a full night's sleep. I slept like shite. It wasn't for lack of hours. It was lack of a quiet mind. Even when I was asleep, my brain kept ticking over this situation, and I dreamed about all the ways we could be together. I dreamed about all the ways it could end even more spectacularly, horribly than it did last night. I suppose it's a blessing in disguise all she did was close the door in my face.

I shoot off a dictated text to Dillan as I approach the neighborhood everyone but me now lives in. It's funny how, as a teenager, you can't wait to get out on your own and live in your own home and do things your own way and not be like your parents. Yet, as everyone in my generation has married, they've all moved back to the same Queens neighborhood we grew up in.

None of them have moved in with our parents but have purchased homes on the same streets as bratva and Mafia families. Thanks to some gerrymandering and school district lines, we didn't go to elementary or middle school together, but we wound up at the same high school. Many of us played on the same sports teams together all the way from peewee and little league up through high school. It was times like that when we put aside family rivalries to stomp our rival teams. When we were really little kids in those peewee and little league sports, we competed against each other just as often as we were teammates.

In that stupid movie, *Goodfellas*, Ray Liotta's character says Saturdays are for wives and Fridays are for girlfriends. That's hardly the case in any of the Four Families. There isn't a man who would stray from his wife no matter what. He'd take a bullet before he'd ever betray his wife.

So, Friday night lights and Saturdays and Sundays were family days where the leaders of the four major families put aside the loathing and came together to watch their kids compete. The only family that didn't have a dad there was the Kutsenkos.

They had their uncles, but their father was killed in the Second Chechen War before they immigrated to the U.S. The rest of the families all had their patriarchs cutting up orange slices and handing out juice boxes. Massimo Mancinelli even drove a minivan.

Yes, the almighty Mancinelli family's *consigliere* drove a minivan. With that many kids, either he or his wife had to have a vehicle that could ferry all of them around. Four brothers and one sister. Their mom drove a tank of an SUV. But it was Massimo who pulled through the drive-through and got the happy meals for his kids after the games. They were in front or behind my family. My mom and dad always made sure they packed a special snack I could have while my brother and cousins devoured their chicken nuggets and cheeseburgers.

I didn't mind being the odd one out because it was my choice. We're all as healthy as it comes nowadays, but I'm certain all those cholesterol-riddled children's meals will catch up with the guys in our old age. It's not like I want to live forever. I'm happy to be alive today. But I also intend to enjoy my golden years without higher blood pressure than this life already gives us.

I knock loudly on Dillan's door and wait for someone to open it. None of the couples can keep their hands off each other. It's not like we had role models of propriety for that. All our parents are as in love and in lust as they were when they married. None of us have walked in on them, so we still have an open-door policy with our parents. It wouldn't surprise me, though, if we've come pretty fucking close.

Dillan opens the door for me and smirks. I shake my head and his brow furrows. I'm certain he's confused, as will be Seamus and Finn, when I let them know things cooled between Joey and me. I won't go into any details about what she and I did in Obsidian's private room, but I can let them know it didn't work out.

"Hey, what's up? How's Mair feeling?"

"Better by the day, but it's definitely touch and go. She had a fried egg on toast last night and was up most of the night."

"Even something that bland?"

"Yeah. But she's not overly concerned."

"But you are."

Dillan shoots me a remorseful frown before it morphs into a grin. He knows he hovers just as much as Finn does, but no one has been a prouder future papa than my two cousins. Family is everything to us. Before my generation met the women they've fallen in love with, most of us were certain we'd remain perpetual bachelors. None of us wanted to bring yet another generation into the mob. I think most of us hoped the O'Rourke name would die with us. At least the O'Rourkes being the boss and his immediate family.

Life carries on, as do families, so I can't begrudge Dillan and Finn for wanting to have kids with their wives. However, it makes it difficult for all of us when we think about the life we're going to leave behind to the next generation. I'm certain all the members of the Four Families in my generation think about the same thing. And it wouldn't surprise me if our parents' generation didn't think about it too. But I guarantee there was pressure on them to breed more mobsters and Mafiosos.

It's not like any set of parents didn't rejoice with each kid's birth. And it's not like they hatched us rather than birthed us. But every family was encouraged to have at least an heir and a spare. It just so happened the families had so many sons. There are no bratva daughters in my generation, but Maks, Bogdan, and Niko each have little girls.

Maria Mancinelli is my generation. She's the most untouchable woman in New York. She's the daughter of the Mafia's *consigliere*, the don's niece, the underboss's sister, the *capo dei capi's*—the top captain's—sister, and the wife of the

149

capo dei capi's best friend. Her third brother is the accountant, and her cousin is head of intelligence.

Dillan had a sister too, Colleen, but she died almost six years ago when a mercenary mistook her for Aunt Breda. It's a subject we don't avoid or ignore. However, it's not one we discuss often. I don't know how Aunt Siobhan and Uncle Tate survived losing their child. I'm certain Dillan was the reason they carried on. Unbidden, my mind jumps to Joey and what a family with her would look like.

Dillan leads me into the dining room where Shane and Sean are already devouring their breakfast. They're only a couple minutes apart, and most people outside the family can only tell them apart by the freckle on the left side of Sean's throat. They have distinguishing scars, but none of them show unless they're undressed.

Five minutes later, Finn and Seamus show up too. I'm certain they walked over together since they live a couple blocks away from Dillan and a couple streets over from each other. They walk in on their own since Dillan already spoke to my brother and said he could. Márgrég—that's Dillan's wife's full Irish name—is already at work. She went into the office early. She's a lead investigative reporter for New York's largest newspaper.

I grab a plate and pile fruit onto it just as high as the other guys. There's a smaller plate with poached eggs on it. I know those are free-range ones Dillan set aside for me. I read in another article that poached is supposed to be one of the healthiest ways to eat eggs. I won't melt cheese in the scrambled ones the way the other guys like them. I'm not doing some Rocky Balboa shite and eating them raw. That's a good way to kill yourself with salmonella. Though I have been known to sneak a spoonful of raw organic cookie dough. Everything in moderation. I finish getting the rest of my food and join the guys at the table.

"Cormac, where's your head today? You're even quieter than usual."

I shift my attention from my food to Shane as he cocks an eyebrow.

"Are you tired?"

Dillan, Finn, and my brother clearly already filled Sean and Shane in.

"Yeah, I am."

I know that won't suffice, but hopefully my tone tells them not to push too hard. Sean's elbow nudges me as he fixes his stare on me.

"We hung out after we left McGinty's but realized we're not as compatible as we thought. It was an enjoyable night, but I doubt I'll see Jocelyn again."

It feels so strange on my lips to use her full name. However, that's how I should think of her now. She's not Joey to me anymore if she wants nothing to do with me. The guys let it rest. At least for now.

Our attention shifts to work. We don't meet every morning to plan the day, but we do many mornings. We also alternate hosting Sunday family dinners. It's my week to cook, so I'll have everyone over in a few days. With nine households in the family, your turn only comes up once every two or so months. We spend time together out of necessity and by choice.

"What's going on with Matteo? Is he still being a whiny little bitch about the yacht?"

I look over at Shane and grin. Matteo Mancinelli bought Maria the yacht Shane already had his eye on to give his wife as a wedding present. Shite went down between them, and now nobody has the yacht. Shane's already replaced it with another one, and it wouldn't surprise me if Matteo isn't in the process of getting one, too.

But he's been little Mr. Pissy Pants ever since. He was always the little bitch in the family who cried when somebody snagged one of his toys, even if he didn't want it until somebody else had it. I know this because Seamus and I were in the same preschool class as him. We may not have gone to elementary and middle school together, but many of us went to the same Montessori preschool.

When outsiders meet us, they assume we're some type of pro-athlete or trust fund baby. Most people don't believe every member of my generation in the Four Families went to Ivy League or top-tier universities. When they find out, most of them assume our parents bought our way in. Not a damn one of us got in on anything besides merit.

It's all good and well to have somebody buy a spot into an Ivy League, but it's not like an idiot can stay. At least not an idiot who doesn't figure out who to pay to keep their grades up for them. I made a small fortune doing homework and taking tests for those very types of people.

I'd say all of us have had an entrepreneurial spirit since we were young. No lemonade stands in the neighborhood, but we all came up with jobs once we were in high school. There were those our families assigned us, and there were the other independent ventures.

"Cormac, could you fecking pay attention?"

Dillan's staring at me. My mind wandered, and it doesn't even have anything to do with Jocelyn. I don't know that I'll get used to thinking of her that way. I'm just entirely distracted this morning.

"I have plenty on my mind. I've got two cases right now, and neither is turning out to be simple." That's not a lie, and I'll make myself think about that instead.

"Where do we stand with that?" Dillan's not letting me off the hook, which is fine because it's on this morning's unofficial agenda.

"The biotech acquisition stalled because the lawyers aren't willing to present our offer to their clients. They believe they're stonewalling us in their clients' best interest."

"It's hardly in those lawyers' best interest."

I nod to Sean. His observation is correct. It's not like we're going to whack the opposing counsel, especially since two of them are women. But we'll put the screws to them.

"How about you, Seamus? What's going on with the robbery case?"

I breathe easier when Dillan turns his attention to my brother for his update. Seamus swallows the massive bite of pancake he practically inhaled and shrugs.

"We have a continuance until next month. The homicide trial starts in two weeks. Discovery's been a bitch. Prosecution's definitely withholding something. But I'm not worried I won't learn what it is in time. My CIs are working overtime, and info's trickling in. Not as fast as I'd like, but better than nothing."

Finn speaks up with the quarterly audit's results. The man isn't obsessive, but he doesn't sleep well if he can't account down to the last five cents. Even that makes him twitch. Shane looks at me before he speaks.

"I need to go over to Staten Island today to check on the mini mall project. Where do things stand with Pablo?"

"Same as it usually is. We didn't make any progress the other day when I ran into him in Port Richmond. I distracted him while Luke collected the last payments from the shops. They want us to stay out of there. I'm not interested in giving up those deals. However, now that those shop owners know there was never a need to pay us for protection, I'm going to have to find businesses somewhere else on Staten Island."

It won't be Port Richmond anymore, which might be a blessing in disguise since it means I won't see Joey—Jocelyn—by accident. However, that's like a knife to the chest since all I want is to see her again and fix my major fuck-up. Just going to Staten Island today will blow.

"I'll scout out some new neighborhoods and their small businesses today. What's going on with Misha and Pasha? They were bringing in a big shipment."

Sean's the head of our intel gathering, so he's bound to have an update. Finn's a talented hacker because he's a forensic accountant, but his little brother can hack a government site and leave it cleaner than he found it.

"Yeah, it's due to arrive today. I'll have guys go out and watch it come in, see if it's what we think it is, and get a rough appraisal. I'm pretty sure it's going to be worth our efforts to snag it, but one of my CIs says they're expecting us. After all the shite that went down with the Polish, they're being extra cautious with any of their deals. They're going to have this shipment guarded tighter than Fort Knox."

Dillan sweeps his gaze around the table as our cousin finishes. Misha and Pasha own an import/export company—Bear Imports—original name for fucking Russians—and they bring in a shite ton more than just pineapples and guavas and send out a lot more than corn and soybeans.

"We've got buyers lined up, so just let me know when we're ready to move on it." Finn will ensure we know where and when we should make the move once he gets the report from his brother, and we know how much cargo we need to store.

We finish the meeting, and I head back to Staten Island. I rarely spend that much time in this borough. The only thing worse would be this much time in Jersey. At least the red hair keeps anyone from confusing me with some *Cosa Nostra* Guido. Perish the thought.

I'm trying for more inconspicuous today, so I'm not rolling in one of our SUVs or even my Audi. I left my car in the parking garage we own, so we can house our fleet of vehicles. I switched to a nice midsize Lexus sedan. I'd look ridiculous pulling up in a Civic or Corolla when I'm wearing a custom-tailored suit. The Lexus will stand out, but it won't appear as ostentatious as my souped-up sports car.

Fuck my life.

The only parking spot available on the entire block is behind Jocelyn's car. With my luck, we'll walk out of neighboring buildings at the same time. She hasn't responded to my text, which makes me think she won't. I doubt she's stewing over the perfect response since I doubt she's considering answering.

I recognize several Cartel cars along with hers. They've upped their surveillance in the Latino communities, which doesn't surprise me. The Diazes knew I'd be back to conclude my business here. These men won't confront me. They'll react if I go on the offensive, but none are high enough to take on a senior mobster. They'll just tattle-tale to Enrique and Pablo within the next thirty seconds. It means I have little time to work.

I head into the first shop—a bakery—and the owner freezes. I see the guy's gaze dart to the new security camera I immediately noticed as I walked in the door.

"Eduardo, *mi amigo*, you didn't pay on time when my guy stopped in to say hi. I hope you remembered to add the interest."

"O'Rourke, I'm not paying. The Diazes own my ass now."

"They can have the left cheek, and we'll keep the right for now. You've always prided yourself on not reneging on business deals. That means you need to make a final payment. Since you're still in business, it means Pablo didn't throw a tantrum about you paying us. I can't say I'll be as forgiving."

I put my right hand in my pocket, which draws my suit coat back. It's a move we all refined by the time we were twenty. It nonchalantly shows our gun holstered at our hip. If we're wearing shoulder holsters, then we place our hands on our hips. If we're wearing a lower back holster, we aren't looking to advertise we have a weapon.

"I know you made your bank run this morning, so I'll take what's mine and be on my merry way."

"I—"

The door chimes.

Fuck my life.

Joey—fuck it; I'll never think of her as Jocelyn—spins on her heels. I can't chase after her without drawing attention to her. I want to, but I can't. I need to finish here. I put my other hand in my pocket to show Eduardo the matching handgun. I'm certain he knows I have a pocketknife.

"Fine. Fine."

He relents, and pops open the cash register. Anger fills his gaze as he pulls out all the cash and hands it over.

"Be sure to run to the bank at lunch. Pablo'll be back to collect their first installment this afternoon."

"What? I can't afford that."

Eduardo splutters, and his face flushes a deep red. His hand darts under the counter.

"You know what a bad idea that would be. Do you really want to leave your wife a widow and your kids without a father?"

"At least they'd have the life insurance."

I snort. "And that'll provide for what? The funeral? You know you're better off letting me walk out of here, then doing whatever the Diazes want. If you kill me, my family will blame the Diazes. Then they'll blame you. Is that the sort of visit you want from Pablo?"

The man has no soul. None. It seeped out of him sometime during our mid-twenties. His cousins'll rough people up, but Pablo's the one who puts them to the screws—literally.

"I didn't think so. *Vaya con dios*, Eduardo." Go with God.

I tuck the money into my inside coat pocket and saunter out. The moment my head is outside, I scan the area for Joey. I spot her immediately. She's talking to three Cartel guys. She's shaking her head and takes a step back. When one of them leans too far forward, I'm done.

By the time I step behind Joey, the guy's voice rises as he confronts Joey in Spanish. I'm a fluent Spanish speaker, as are most of the guys in my family. We're all multi-lingual. It's necessary for business, and speaking Spanish in New York City is hardly shocking. My Yiddish ain't bad either.

"Does Enrique know you stand on street corners yelling at women, you *pinche pendejo*?" Fucking idiot.

Joey's back straightens, but she does nothing else.

"Back off, O'Rourke. You know better than to come back to this neighborhood."

"What I know rarely stops me from doing what I want. Ms. Bracero, I'm sure you have an appointment you're late for. We'd hate to keep you or the family waiting."

"We're not done talking to—"

"You must be confused, Andres."

I step around Joey and put myself between her and the men rather than beside her. When I slide my left hand into my pocket, they know I just wrapped my palm around my knife. Considering the scar the man has from a confrontation just like this where he thought a little too highly of himself, he won't want a repeat.

"The bit—"

"Finish that word, and I'll dump you on Enrique's doorstep myself."

Despite shite that's gone down among the Four Families in the past few years that's involved women, we're still all old school about how we speak about women. It's not like none of us makes crass comments about sex, but we don't speak that way in front of women and children. Enrique will peel the skin from this guy's bones before handing him over to Pablo if he insults Joey by calling her a bitch.

"You're not doing her any favors by coming to her rescue. We were just asking her about you."

"Now you can ask me about me. Ms. Bracero, I'm certain you're late now. Have a good day."

I hear her walk to the street, and I see her from the corner of my eye as she steps off the curb. She crosses and hurries down the block, crossing another street before taking steps two at a time. She punches in a code and disappears into a building. I shift my attention back to Andres and his buddy.

"If the Diazes want to know shite about me, they know how to find it. Tell Pablo to stay the fuck away from her."

"You fucked up this time, O'Rourke."

"You won't do shite to me on the street, and by the time your dumb-arse can call Pablo to whine about seeing me, I'll be done."

I'm bigger than both arseholes put together. I plow through them, each shoulder shoving into theirs. It forces them to step back like a shite game of Red Rover, except they weren't holding hands. I have four places left, and when I come out of the last, it's in time to watch Joey walk to her car.

She notices me and scowls. We reach our vehicles at the same time, and her brow furrows. I cock an eyebrow, and her eyes narrow to slits. I cock the other eyebrow before opening my door and slipping into my car. Neither of us pulls out of our spot for a couple minutes, then she gives in and inches forward until she can maneuver out. She had more room in front of her than I did. We're on a one-way street, so I have no choice but to follow her. Even if I had a choice, I would.

We take a series of them until we get to a road where I can pull alongside her. I point to a parking lot we're approaching. She shakes her head. We pass it and a second place I point to. I tell my hands-free system to call her. I notice she glances at her screen before hitting a button on her steering wheel. I should keep my eyes on the road. I call her four times before she finally answers.

"Leave me alone, Cormac. I don't want to talk to you."

"I need to talk to you. It has nothing to do with last night and everything to do with what I just saw. This is about your safety, so unless you want me to follow you every minute of every day until you finally talk to me, I'd pull over now."

"You don't dictate what I do."

"Jocelyn, pull over. Don't make me prove I'm not exaggerating." I infuse command into my voice, making me sound like a Dom rather than a man chatting with an acquaintance.

"Cormac, I really don't want to do this." Her voice softens, and I have a moment's regret intimidating her.

"I know, *cailín*. This is because of us, but it's not about us. Pull over." I temper my tone until the last two words.

I hear her sigh and glance over as she nods.

"Drive around back of that church coming up on the left."

I follow her into the parking lot, and she picks a spot that's as far from the building as our cars can get. I pull in alongside her. Her wariness tempts me to park perpendicular to her, so she can't leave until I'm ready for her to, but that won't set a pleasant tone. We get out of our cars, and I walk around to her.

My gaze sweeps over her, then settles on her face. She

watches me as I watch her. She matches my stare, waiting for me to go first since I insisted we talk. I want her to get to where she relents and doesn't hold back. It's manipulative as fuck. I've gotten good at it, though. But I don't have forever.

"Jocelyn—" She flinches. "—what did they say to you?"

"Nothing they haven't said before. They wanted to know about a family I saw today. The rumor spread that I was with Javier, so they wanted to know what you thought about me fucking both of you."

My jaw tightens. It's a good thing I didn't find this out when those motherfuckers were in front of me.

"Why'd he step forward?"

"I told him the only fucking going on was him fucking off. He didn't like that."

"A boy chased me down and told me the rumor wasn't true. Do people believe it?"

"I'm certain some people do, so they have something new to gossip about."

"Was goading me all this was about?"

"I guess. This is why I wanted to stay off Pablo's radar. He's punishing me by ruining my reputation. Everything I do here requires that people trust me. He's turning them against me by making them think I'm with you."

"You were with me last night." She understands the innuendo.

"You said we wouldn't talk about that."

"And we aren't. I'm considering how much danger you're in. I'm assigning you a detail."

"The hell you are!"

"Jocelyn—"

"Don't call me that." She snaps at me, but she's not yelling.

"It's your name. Unless—"

I leave that dangling, letting her decide how she wants to

respond. When her gaze lowers, I have my answer. I step closer, but she doesn't retreat. I rest my right hand on her hip and squeeze. She sucks in a breath, but I feel her relax a moment later.

"Look at me, Joey."

She's reticent, but she looks up. I know she's staring at my ear, even if most people would think she's looking me in the eye. I grasp her chin between my thumb and forefinger, but I only turn her to look at me. She could pull away easily. She doesn't.

"You don't like it when I call you Jocelyn, do you?" I'm back to my Dom voice.

"Not particularly."

"Why?" I demand an answer without raising my voice.

"Because only you call me Joey."

"But you said you didn't want to see or hear from me."

"That didn't stop you from texting me, and I'm standing here with you."

"You want to remain *my* Joey, don't you?"

Her gaze darts away again, and her eyes water. That's my answer. I pull her to me, pressing my fingers deeper into her hip as the hand on her chin drops, so I can wrap my arm around her. I lower my mouth to hers, hesitating, giving her a chance to pull away. Her chin inches up, so our lips touch. Then I lead this kiss.

I press my tongue into her mouth, sweeping it past her teeth. The arm around her waist lowers enough for my hand to grasp her arse. The hand on her hip now grips a handful of hair. I turn us, so her back is against her rear passenger door. She moans, enjoying me crowding her. She runs her hands over my chest and back, and I let her. The feel of her touching me makes my skin tingle, and I can't get enough.

I nudge her feet apart and press my thigh between hers. I

guide her to ride it, starting with a slow rocking motion. When she picks up the rhythm, I skim my hand from her arse up to her breast. I squeeze, eliciting another moan. I tug her shirt out of her skirt waistband and crawl my fingertips up her ribs, making her shiver. I pull her bra out of the way, so I can cup her skin to skin. When I pinch and tug her nipple, she grinds harder. I twist us again, so I have my back to the car. I release her hair in favor of spanking her.

If my Catholic grandmothers knew what I was doing in a church parking lot...Good thing it's Methodist.

There are trees behind Joey, separating the church grounds from whatever business is behind it. I drag her skirt up and out of the way, so I can get to her bare arse, and the only thing between her cunt and my pants is her thong. Since we have as much privacy as we can in a public place, I don't worry about anyone watching us. However, as much as I'm concentrating on her, I'm keeping my ears peeled for any nearby sounds.

I rain down ten spanks that must sting her arse because they sting my hand. Her movements show her growing impatience as I finally end our kiss and pull away. She clutches my shirt, her expression wholly needy.

"Are you going to be a good girl and talk to me after this?"

"Yes, sir."

"Do you know how badly I want to see you come and know I did that for you?"

"A lot, sir?"

"More than you can imagine. Do you know why?"

"No, sir."

"Because you're mine, Joey."

With both hands, I move her against me, pressing her hips down. I flex my already hard thigh, giving her the friction she needs.

"May I come, sir?"

"Yes. You may always come unless I tell you to ask."

"Please, sir, make me come."

I move her as fast and hard as I can. She whimpers with need.

"*More, sir.*"

She begs, and I love it. It feeds my hunger to dominate her. Give her what she needs when I know she needs it. To show her what we shared last night wasn't a fluke. There was something there worth exploring again.

"Come for me, *cailín*. I know you're close. Your nipples are so tight. If I had a condom, I'd be inside you. You'd be fucking my cock instead of my leg. Mmm. You want my cock again, don't you?"

"So much, sir. Fuck, Cormac, I'm close."

Her gaze meets mine, and she used my name on purpose. I pinch her nipple as hard as I dare while I land three jarring spanks. Her head falls forward to my chest as she shudders.

"That's my good girl. Such a good girl coming for me."

I pull her tight against me, so there's no space between us. I pry her hands from my now rumpled shirt and pin them behind her back with one of mine. With the other I stroke her back.

"I love feeling you come, *cailín*. I love knowing I give you pleasure. I want to keep doing that. You deserve someone to take care of you. Who understands what you need and always tries to give you that. You deserve someone who trusts you and listens to you. You deserve someone who'll stand beside you most of the time and in front of you when you need it. I didn't give you that last night, and I'm sorry."

She kisses along my neck, over my jaw, then up until she reaches my mouth as I bend over farther, and she stands on her toes.

"May I kiss you, sir?"

"Yes."

I don't know what to expect from this, but it's languid. She doesn't rush us, instead drawing it out. It feels as possessive as my more aggressive ones. She gazes into my eyes when she pulls away.

"What Pablo said was messed up, and he did it on purpose. I didn't appreciate what you said, and it pissed me off. You understand my needs and try to fulfill them. You've stood beside and in front of me every time we've been around each other. I want us to build that trust if you'll listen to me. I didn't realize my phone died until I got in the car this morning. It was only at five percent when I got to the neighborhood, so I turned it on but didn't check anything. It wasn't until we got to our cars that I read your text. It's why I didn't pull out right away. I was forcing myself not to get out of my car and go to you. I couldn't come up with what I wanted to say and didn't want to reply with something stupid."

"What do you want, Joey?"

"What you said earlier. You said I was yours. I want that."

"You want to be my sub?"

"Yes. Contract and everything. I want to play like we did last night, and I want to submit again like I just did. If we run into each other, then we're equals in front of others. When we're alone or at a club, I'm your sub."

"Do you want a weeknight and most of the weekend?"

"Yes. I get you might have stuff that comes up, but I usually know any plans I'm making with a few days to spare."

"Do you want me to call and check on you throughout the week?"

This makes her blush. She nods.

"Answer me, little one."

"Yes, sir. That would be really nice."

"Did you think I wouldn't offer or that I wouldn't want to?"

"I wasn't sure."

"Give us a month of getting used to each other. If you still want a contract in four weeks, I'll give you one, Joey."

"When can we start?"

"Tonight. I'm going to assign you a security detail, and when you argue, I'm going to punish that delectable derriere of yours."

Chapter Thirteen

Joey

How the hell am I supposed to concentrate now?

I've been thinking that since Cormac gave me another searing kiss and a slap on the ass, before holding my car door open for me to get back in. I thought it the entire way back to the office. I thought it the entire time I sat in a staff meeting. I'm still thinking it as I take a cab to Obsidian.

He offered to pick me up, but I don't want another uncomfortable situation like last night in case things go to shit again. I don't relish being stuck in a car with him if I don't want to see or hear him. I hedge my bets with the cab. I don my mask before I get out of the vehicle and look around. The moment I shut the door, Cormac steps out of a shadow with his mask on. There's no way I could confuse him, even with his entire face and hair covered. I've been with him once, but I already know his body. It's his bearing—his stance and walk. It's captivating and hypnotic in its pure masculinity.

If I had panties on, they'd be soaked. Instead, it's the inside of my thighs. I glance down to ensure my coat covers the parts of me the real world doesn't need to see. He meets me more than halfway while allowing him to remain mostly out of sight of anyone walking down the street. He slides his arm around my waist and fists my hair. Even in the near darkness, his emerald eyes stand out. With holes only for his eyes and mouth, he should be unrecognizable. There's no doubting who he is when he kisses me.

"Cailín—"

"Please, sir, can we just go inside?"

He sweeps his gaze over the surrounding area before looking down at me.

"Sir, I'm too impatient. That's why I want to go in."

"And if I want to make you wait until I'm ready?"

I look below his belt and grin beneath my lacey mask that covers me from mid-forehead to the end of my nose and over my cheeks. I cross my wrists behind my back and lean to whisper to him.

"You might want to make me wait, but I don't think you want to wait."

"Mmm. You might be right."

He cups my jaw, and I wonder what suggestion he read into that somewhat bungled and ambiguous comment. He kisses me again before we turn toward the door. His hand rests at the small of my back like yesterday. There's a coat check near the door, so we stop. He helps me off with my trench coat. His eyes sparkle with approval at my wetlook style dress. The way it hangs on me—gathered in some parts and clingy in others—gives the appearance of the dress being wet and sticking to me.

I've had it for a while, but only pulled the tags off today. It's sheer, so he can see my demi bra, garter belt, and fishnet thigh highs beneath it. The one part that isn't transparent is over my pussy and ass. It leaves something to the imagination, so he can't see that I'm not wearing panties. The way he watches me makes me feel like a million bucks. It's as though no one else exists. Like I'm the only person in the world right now. Even though I'm certain his situational awareness is so keen, he could describe everyone on the first floor.

"Little one, you're stunning. You must have been one of the great Renaissance artists' muses in a past life."

"Sir, you exaggerate. I know the Irish are renowned story-tellers, but that's a 'I caught a fish this big.'"

His gaze hardens as he pauses halfway through unbut-toning his shirt. He leans so close his lips brush my hair when he whispers.

"Are you telling your Dom he's wrong? Are you arguing with me, little girl?"

"No, sir. I appreciate the compliment. It's just over the top."

"I know you think you do, but I will punish you."

"What? Why?"

I jerk away, but a swat to my ass makes me freeze.

"If you don't believe the compliment, then you don't believe me. If you don't believe me, you must be calling me a liar. That's part one. Part two is not being gracious when given something. Downplaying the value of what I say means you can't accept it in the nature I gave it. Next time I give you a compliment, say 'thank you, sir' and leave it at that. Understood?"

"Yes, sir. I'm sorry."

Goosebumps rise on my arms as I fear I've ruined the night by earning a punishment before he's even gotten his shirt off. He slides it off, his pecs and shoulder muscles rippling as he moves. I want to lick him like a lollipop should be licked. His black tank top stretches across his chest. I know the thick straps over his shoulders hide tattoos. I know a large shamrock with an

O in the center sits on his left pec. There are likely other women here—like Deirdre—who know the secrets his shirt hides, but I feel like I'm part of an exclusive club. I want to remain a part of that, but I pissed him off.

He hands the shirt over to the attendant, who puts it on the same hanger as my coat. He pockets the slip before his hand slides around my waist and down to my ass. He squeezes it so hard I squeal.

"You apologized, Esme. You're forgiven. That's unconditional. I'm going to punish you, so you know I'm displeased, and hopefully, it deters you from making the same mistake twice. But I won't hold this against you, and it doesn't change how much I want to be with you."

He remembered to use my middle name rather than my real one. The protected anonymity along with the relief that he's not angry eases my worry about returning to a club I don't know.

"Thank you, sir."

"Liam. It's my middle name. If I use your name, we're not Dom/sub. If you need a break from that, then use my name. During a scene, when we're here, or when we're in this dynamic, I'm sir. Only use Liam here if you need my attention immediately, *cailín*."

He pauses for a moment, and the hand on my ass pulls me against him. His free hand cups my jaw. I don't know what he searches for in my eyes. I don't know if he found what he wanted when he speaks.

"I don't want to—I won't—limit the endearments to scenes. Unless you ask me to, I won't call you a slut or a whore. Cunt refers to your body part, not who you are to me. That means I need something else to call you when we scene, but the same words come to mind even when we're not scening. If you're confused about how things stand, ask. Unless you want continuous roleplay, you speak to me as an equal whenever we're not in this dynamic. When we are, you speak to me with the respect and deference your Dom deserves. Little subbies who don't, will get a hot arse to remind them who leads."

A shiver courses down my spine. I feel no compulsion—or even motivation—to act out to get that kind of reaction from him. No part of me wants to be a brat. But earning a punishment isn't unappealing.

"Come, little one."

He leads me to the dance floor where other couples sway to the music. Unlike a nightclub, the music's quiet. The steady beat is erotic in a way I can't explain, but when a couple moves to it—their bodies pressed together—I don't know. If music were an invitation to sex, I'd RSVP yes.

The way Cormac moves proves there's nothing this man can do to lessen his sex appeal. He could be a stripper between his banging body and how he moves to the rhythm.

"Is there anything you don't do well?"

"Draw."

I grin and shake my head. "You're a superb dancer."

"Because my mom and aunts insisted my brother, cousins, and I learn ballroom dancing. I guess I'm just comfortable."

Comfortable.

The man could put Thunder Down Under AND Chippendales out of business.

He leads me off the dance floor to a dimly lit alcove that I didn't notice until we stepped inside. He takes his hooded mask off, so this must be important.

"*Cailín,* I put together a security detail for you. With Pablo taking any interest in you to get to me and after those guys accosted you today, I won't take chances with your safety. Even if this goes nowhere beyond tonight, I won't risk it."

"What does that mean? I can't have mobsters escorting me into people's homes or kids' schools."

"Unless there's a credible threat of bodily harm, they'll be shadows. You won't know they're there. They'll see you and be close enough to get to you, but you won't notice them."

"But Cartel guys will. They'll know exactly what to look for."

"Exactly. Pablo needs to know you're under my protection. That fecking with me doesn't include using you."

"Fecking?"

He blushes!

"I'm not allowed to use the real F word in front of women and children."

"Not allowed? Is that like some mobster code?"

Even in the low light, I can see his fair skin is close to tomato.

"Sorta. It's the rule in my family, and my parents, aunts, and uncles terrify me enough not to break it."

"That's sweet! Let me guess. Your mom isn't much taller than me, but you wouldn't stand close to her if she had a wooden spoon in her hand."

"Pretty much. She's a few inches taller than you, and she doesn't need the spoon. But she has one. My two aunts do too. By the time my brother, cousins, and I realized they'd never use it on us, they'd scared us into perfect manners. I've also never had Irish Spring soap for dinner, but I wouldn't put it past my mom to give me a full serving if she ever found out I swore in front of a woman or child or at one of my relatives."

I don't think he fakes the shiver. I believe he's truly scared of the women in his family. It's utterly endearing.

"My *abuelita* has a pair of *chanclas*—the wooden soled slippers—she'd wave around. She never spanked me with them or actually threw them at me, but I never pushed her far enough to find out if she would. The woman's the same height as me, but about thirty pounds lighter. She's *muy pequeña* and nearly eighty. Not even a hundred pounds soaking wet, but I'd bet on her in a fight. She's the Mexican Sophia Petrillo. If there were a modern-day *Golden Girls*, she'd be the matriarch. Rather than Sophia's dreaded melon baller, it would be the *chancla*. When I was twenty, I gave her a t-shirt that says *¡Teme a la chancla!* She still wears it with pride thirteen years later. She might be buried in it." Fear the *chancla*.

He chuckles, and I feel the vibration in his chest since my tits are pressed against him. I'm wearing heels like I do most days. Otherwise, they'd be closer to his ribs. At my whopping five-two-and-three-quarters, I look like a kid next to most adults. Even a two-inch heel makes a difference. The deep rumble fits with how he can be a grizzly bear one moment and a panda the next. Manly while easygoing.

I don't know. It's just nice.

"Are you close to your grandparents?" He wants to get to know me better, and I love it.

"Only my mother's parents are alive. My dad's died when he was a kid. He was close to one of his grandfathers. What about you?"

"All of mine have passed away, but I was close to all of them. My grandfathers traveled a lot and worked long hours. But my grandmothers were always soft in the right places and smelled like flowers—you know—the way grandmas are supposed to. It was Nana on my mom's side and Granny on my dad's. Nana used to babysit all of us after school every day."

"All of us?"

"Yeah. My brother, five cousins, and me."

"Holy smokes! Seven kids?"

His gaze softens as he slips into his memories. It makes him even more handsome because it's a moment's reprieve from his usual intensity.

"She owned McGinty's. We'd go there after school. We had to do our homework then help do dishes and wipe down tables. If there was time, we could play darts or pool or watch games on the TVs. Most of the time, though, we had to read. It made sure we were seen and not heard, and it was good for us."

"You grew up really close to your cousins."

"Three sisters married three brothers. We're close because of work and because we want to be. I enjoy my brother's and cousins' company. There's never been a time when I haven't been surrounded by a massive family. What about you?"

I shake my head. The question was inevitable since I sent us down this path.

"My mother had a sister and three brothers, but two of the brothers died. I'm close to my brother and cousins, but all of my cousins are still in Mexico. My brother's here in the city, but we don't see each other that often. Once every few weeks. We keep different schedules. And there was no one on my dad's side. He had a sister, but she died too."

"Did you and your brother get along when you were little?"

"Mostly. We played together when we were little, but by the time he got to middle school, he had his own friends and interests, which was fine by me. What about your brother?"

"He's my best friend. He's only seven months younger than me because he was a preemie. We've always been together."

"An infant and a preemie. That must have been really rough on your parents. Two months early usually means some lasting health challenges."

He chuckles again, and my pussy aches. It's so hot.

"The only health challenge my brother has is a tendency to eat way more chocolate than is healthy. We're the same size and are almost identical. You've met him. People often confuse us.

He has our mom's eye shape more than I do, and my nose is a bit more like our dad's. Our freckles are different. But we have the same eye color as our cousins, which comes from our moms. We get our lighter red hair and build from our dad. He's the biggest of his brothers, and they all have lighter red hair than my mom and aunts."

"You're truly as Irish as it comes in America."

I marvel at that. They're the poster boys of what people picture when they think of the Irish. Red hair, green eyes, and fair skin—though he clearly tans.

"Everyone speaks fluent Irish, too. So yeah, we're pretty Irish even though my family's been here for three and four generations."

Even though we're not on the dance floor, we're in each other's arms and swaying to the music as we chat, and it's comfortable. I haven't talked about my family to previous Doms, even the ones I'd been with for a while. This kind of getting to know you hasn't been a priority. I'm enjoying this. His hands roam over my body while my left hand rests on his chest, and my right arm's around his waist.

We decide simultaneously story time is over. He leans forward as I raise my chin for a kiss. He slides his thigh between my legs again, guiding me to grind my pussy on him. I can feel how hard he is. It's been that way since we came together to dance. But my new position makes it more obvious.

"Sir?"

"Yes, little one. What do you want?"

"Anything you do, just more than this."

His kiss is short and fierce before he slips his hood back on and leads me past the other dancers and to a spanking bench. It's the kind that looks like a gymnastics vault, except it has handles built on each side on a lower platform. My feet will go on the end of the platform, putting me at the right height.

"What's your safe word?"

"Bodega."

"And if you *need* it lighter?"

"Deli."

I can want it lighter all damn day, but I'm agreeing to the pain for pleasure's sake. Before he tells me to pull my dress up to bare my ass, I push the right strap, then the left, down until I slip out of them. I reveal my demi bra, and I know I have his undivided attention. He steps in front of me and runs the back of his fingers over my tits and down the valley between them.

I push the dress down to my hips, and his hand sweeps over my ribs before resting momentarily on my belly. It's possessive with its insinuation, but I get the message. He's laying his claim. I like it. I shimmy my hips enough for the dress to pool on the floor around my feet. His gaze watched the dress fall. Now it snaps back to my face as he cups my pussy.

"You enjoy being watched."

"I don't mind it. It can be hot."

He pulls his hand away, and I nearly grab his wrist to keep it in place. He guides me to the bench, and I step up.

"In what way?"

"Knowing people envy me for the pain and for my Dom. Knowing my partner enjoys seeing me like that and that he wants people to watch. Knowing a person my Dom or I know might want what they see enough to ask to touch."

"That is not happening." He's emphatic.

"And I don't want anyone but you to touch me. I haven't always felt that way before. It would flatter me if someone asked, but I trust you'll say no because that's a hard limit for me."

"It's a hard limit because I won't share you. No one but you touches me."

He skims his fingertips over my leg to the top of my fishnet thigh high. He pulls and snaps the elastic. He walks to the rack affixed to the nearby wall and considers his options. Much like the examining table was in the private room, it's strategically placed behind the spanking bench, so a sub can't see what their Dom chooses. I wiggle my toes in anticipation. I don't know if he chose immediately and is making me wait or if he's still considering the options. I jump when his hand runs down my back between my shoulder blades.

He palms, then squeezes each side of my ass before gliding his hand up my ribs and around to my tits. Only one hand explores, making it hard to concentrate when I wonder what he's holding. His hand trails down my belly again until he gets to my pussy, which he cups. He leaves it there, just a heavy weight pressing against it. I fight not to squirm with impatience. He rewards me by sliding a finger between my pussy lips.

"Is my little girl eager to start?"

"Yes, sir."

"So creamy and wet."

I am. More than I usually am with a guy. It's probably a fucking slip and slide down there. I hope I'm not so wet he gets no friction when he fucks me. He helps me straddle the vault-like bench and lean forward.

"Deep breath."

I do as he commands, and the moment I do, a crop lands across the top of my left thigh. It's far lower than I expected. I lurch forward and Cormac tsks.

"Do I need to strap you in place, or can you stay where you're supposed to?"

"I can stay where I'm supposed to."

I want the restraints, but I know this is a test. Can I master my instinctive reactions? Can I trust what he'll do won't make me fall?

I tighten my hands around the handles and squeeze my

thighs like I'm on horseback. I used to ride all the time on my grandparents' farm. The crop lands in the center of my right ass cheek. He sets a wicked pace, sparing no part of my ass and upper thighs. He nails my horizontal cracks several times. His free hand strokes my back, periodically massaging my shoulders. The contrast between comfort and discomfort is heady. The pain on one end and pleasure on the other.

He pauses for only a moment before I feel the feather swirling over my punished skin. It soothes, but I suspect it's merely the intermission. He doesn't wait until the sting entirely ends, but it's lessened when the next form of torment begins. It's a single tail whip. It's the type that resembles a rose stem with thorns. He's wielding it much, much gentler than he could. His pace is still slower than I expected, but he's not putting nearly as much force into it as he could.

I shift, trying to find a more comfortable position as my thighs are already tiring from how hard I'm squeezing the bench to control my instinct to run from the pain.

"Deli?"

"No, sir. My legs are sticking to the leather. Just repositioning. Keep going, please."

"Do not lie to me, little girl. Do not take more than you can because you think you have something to prove or some standard you must meet. If I harm you rather than this just hurts, we're through. I won't engage in any BDSM if I can't trust you to tell me your limits."

We're through.

As in, there's no reason for us to be around each other. Despite the friendly conversation earlier, we aren't friends. This certainly isn't a romantic relationship...If only it were.

"Yes, sir. I understand. Thank you for looking out for me."

"Always, *cailín.*"

Okay. He was definitely quieter when he said that, but was his tone different? Like—I don't know—kind—or—like sweet?

I don't know because my mind blanks with the whip's next slash. I scream. I'm reaching the tipping point. The crop hurt enough to steal my breath a few times and make my eyes water, but the whip pushes me to where a few tears slide down my cheeks. Cormac knows in an instant.

"Talk to me, little one." He brushes the tear from my cheek.

"I'm all right, sir. I want to keep going, and I can. But it fu—fecking hurts."

He laughs and turns my head enough to peck my lips.

"You're adorable."

He pecks them again before straightening.

If he's uncomfortable swearing in front of me—at least not *that* word—then I can adjust, too. The next three lashes make me shudder and continue to cry. But my mind's slowing as I focus on what's happening rather than trying to guess Cormac's next move. I focus on controlling my breathing. I close my eyes and sigh. I don't react when he pauses, then a paddle lands across both cheeks. He positions me how he wants by pulling my hips back.

"Ooooh."

I moan when two fingers slip inside me as the paddle lands on my right ass cheek.

"*Cailín,* I told you I'm going to punish you. Now it begins."

Chapter Fourteen

Cormac

I watch Joey's reaction to my declaration, and I know she's praying I forgot or that what we already did counts as her punishment. This was just a warm-up. However, I've already put her fine little arse through its paces, so her punishment won't be more spankings. It'll be far more creative than that.

All the men in my family lean into our kinky side. We're all alphas, though I'd like to think none of us are alpha-holes. I can't say as much for the other men in the Four Families. They're just all arseholes to begin with. But we're men who thrive off control because life shites on us when we're not.

Being kinky is, I suppose, a constructive way of living out that need. It also feeds into the protective side of all of us. We have a duty to protect our people, not just within our own family, but within the entire organization. Caring for people is one of our greatest responsibilities and privileges in our role as members of the boss's family.

Caring for a sub is much the same way. Not only do we

need to be mindful of their physical well-being, but there's a deep emotional connection that happens between a Dom and his sub. It's a complicated connection to explain to outsiders, especially since you're not necessarily romantically involved with your sub or Dom, and you're not even necessarily friends. But there's a tremendous amount of trust two must share between them.

As I watch Joey tonight, I'm testing her, and I know she knows it. I need to see whether she has faith in me to protect and leave her unharmed. If anything, better off than when the night started. That's part of the reason it bothered me so much that our first night together ended as such an epic failure because I didn't take care of her properly. We were both on an emotional high until I fucked things over by getting jealous.

I smooth my hand over her back and down to her arse. I could hold on to it for days and never tire of filling my hands with it. I've had enough partners to know what I do and don't like without being a man-whore, and I very much like Joey's body. The corner of my mouth twitches as I think it's a good thing she can't see me. I ease her off the spanking bench and hold her at the elbows while she steadies herself.

"Are you dizzy?"

"No, I'm all right. I just—I need a moment. My ass burns."

"I would think so. You did so well, *cailín*. I definitely wasn't as gentle as I could be."

"I know, sir. Thank you."

I could have been far rougher, but I don't know her tolerance and preference yet. I'm still learning those things, just like she's still learning what I desire and what levels of control and submission we have between us.

I return the tools of my trade to the wall rack and look around as I slip my arm around her waist. I hold her close to me, kissing her temple.

"Do you want the first time you come tonight to be in public or private? How much more exhibitionism are you comfortable with?"

"I don't know that I'm ready to be fully naked in front of all of these people, but I obviously am not that timid."

It shocked the hell out of me to discover she wasn't wearing any panties. I love the demi bra and garter belt with the fishnet thigh highs. She definitely understands the dress codes at these types of play places. The dress she wore made her look like the living embodiment of Venus on a half shell. I'm glad she wore a coat over it, or I might have had to gouge her taxi driver's eyes out. I don't mind other people seeing her in here wearing that.

All the women have similarly revealing and enticing clothing. However, outside of here, I admit a level of possessiveness I've never felt toward any of my previous subs or women I've scened with here and at other clubs.

I watch Joey as her gaze sweeps the open area before glancing up at the mezzanine and second floor. There are more private rooms like the one we were in last time, each with different themes. There's a classroom, a child's nursery, an extreme torture room. Users of that room can indulge their very darkest fantasies in private. Those who are into lesser stuff can still enjoy the room. It's just there for those whose preferences might shock even the most experienced members of this lifestyle.

"Can we try the chain station?"

Joey points toward the wall where there is a set of chains with cuffs on a pulley and chains attached to the wall at floor level.

"If that's what you would like, little one. Is your elbow up to being restrained over your head?"

"Yes, sir. It's almost entirely healed. I only get a twinge once in a while."

I stoop to pick up her dress, and she reaches for it. I cock an eyebrow, and she lowers her gaze, a small smile playing at her lips. As her Dom, even small things like carrying her dress shows taking care of her is important to me. I guide her over to the open station, passing a couple of people I know. They don't know who I am here, but I can recognize them. It pays to be silent owners of the best BDSM clubs in the tri-state area. We know who likes to spank and who likes to be spanked. That's been invaluable information over the years.

Who knows to what extremes people will go to protect their privacy? We do.

A couple just finished here at this chain station. The Domme's cleaning off the cuffs while her sub guzzles a bottle of water.

"It's all yours."

I keep my voice low when I speak to others here. I thank her for switching off with us. Because of some clientele, I don't want people to recognize my voice any more than I want them to recognize my hair. The full-face mask also hides my swath of freckles. While my eye color is pretty unique, it's something I don't worry about as much since the lighting is so dim in most areas. I lay Joey's dress over the back of a chair and lead her to the wall.

"Face me, arms up."

My command is crisp and unemotional, even though part of me is as giddy as a kid on Christmas. It's not like I think of her as a new toy to unwrap, but I am excited we're making progress. That she wants to be part of my life and will allow me to be part of hers.

I attach the cuffs to her wrists, adjusting the pulleys to make sure they're the right height for somebody as petite as her. The last man attached to this was at least a foot taller than her. I test the cuffs once they're on to make sure they won't chafe her wrists or ankles, and she gives me a nod. I remember she told me a blindfold or earplugs but not both.

I pull a satin blindfold from my pocket. I know the ones here are good, but they aren't as soft as I'd like for her. I don't know why I thought of it on the way here, but I did, so I stopped at a salon my cousin used to go to that I knew carries things to pamper yourself with, including sleep masks.

"*Cailín*, I'm going to blindfold you. I want you to remain silent. If you can't do that, then I will gag you. Anytime I do that, make sure you can still snap. If you need me to stop, I know what signal to look for."

"Yes, sir."

I slip the satiny material over her eyes, then back away. Much like I made her wait before, I do the same now. I let a minute, then two minutes tick by before I know she grows restless. She shifts, trying to sense where I am, but I know she can't. Since I checked the blindfold myself, I'm certain she can't see me. I'm not close enough for her to hear me breathing, and I haven't moved enough for her to feel any change in the surrounding air.

I move on silent feet, trained to be undetectable. She's fully unprepared for me to flick one finger at her left nipple and then her clit half a second later. She opens her mouth to cry out but catches herself and stifles it. Her lips are open, so I can see how she grits her teeth. I know how it stings, and that's exactly what I want. I back away yet again, letting her remain confused and needy. Her sheer bra's material does nothing to protect that nipple I now pinch. Her arousal's obvious from her tightened nipples and how wet she is.

I can admit it's always been flattering to know I arouse my partners like this. Whether it's from my looks, my attitude, or my touch. It's always nice to know your sexual partner desires you. But for reasons I don't want to dissect, knowing how turned on Joey is brings me an entire level of satisfaction—smug satisfaction—that's unprecedented for me. I appreciate knowing she wants me as much as I want her.

My fucking cock hurts. It's not just a dull ache or a horny desire to get off. I feel like my balls are going to explode. I've wanted women to the point of distraction in the past. I've enjoyed my past partners and had some mind-blowing sex and some average sex and unfortunately some pretty shitty sex too.

All of this shocks me. It's not just my body that craves her. There's more to it than all of that. It's heightening all of my senses, making every feeling exponentially more intense than it has been. But I'm not in a position to make this anything more than it already is. It's probably not even wise that I enter a new D/s relationship so soon after my last one ended. However, nothing about Joey reminds me of *that* woman. I don't want to even think her name, or it'll piss me off. I don't want her ghostly presence to dampen my mood.

I pull Joey's right bra cup down. I wrap my hand around her breast, and it's the perfect size for my palm and fingers. I squeeze, then massage, then squeeze again before bending forward and flicking the nipple with the tip of my tongue.

I swirl my tongue around it before sucking the very, very tip. Just enough of a hint for what I could do without actually giving in. I move to the other side and repeat the same motions. When I step back, I admire how distended they are. They're like a light milk chocolate against her sun-tanned skin. Since I see no tan lines at all, she must sunbathe topless somewhere. That's another arousing thought. It's both sexually arousing and arouses my jealousy.

Who's looking at her when she's like that? This jealousy will drive me crazy. With my past subs, we agreed to monogamy, but I wasn't overly concerned with who else they were around or what they did away from me. With Joey, I'm interested in her daily life, but thinking of other people seeing her naked bothers me more than I expected.

I walk over to a dresser that's positioned between the chain station and the St. Andrew's Cross. I open the second drawer, knowing what I will find there. I grab the implements of choice and head back to Joey's side. I slide the blindfold up for a moment and hold up a pair of nipple clamps.

"Have you worn these before?"

"Yes, sir."

"Even the kind without the rubber covers?"

"Yes, sir."

I put the blindfold back in place and start with them pretty loose.

"As I tighten them, tell me when to stop. You decide."

"Thank you, sir."

I clip the first one on and slowly tighten it, surprised at how many twists of the small knob it takes before she finally lets me know she wants me to stop. I repeat it on the other side. When I'm certain they're secure and are pinching without harming her, I move around to stand behind her. I brush the hair away from her back and over her left shoulder.

She can't see what else I have in my hand. I kiss along her shoulders, up to her neck, then to behind her ear.

"Do you have any idea how ravishing you look like this? Do you have any idea how envious everyone is that I have you chained and ready to go?"

"Sir, I think that really is an exaggeration. I'm pretty positive plenty of people are way more interested in their partner than in me."

"Maybe a few, *cailín*, but I'm the one who can look around."

It's true. There are several people looking at us. It's likely the drastic difference in our sizes. She's about five-two, and I'm six-three-and-a-half. She weighs possibly a hundred-and-twenty pounds, and I weigh two-hundred-and-forty. We are apples and oranges, or maybe I should say peaches and bananas. Since she's so petite compared to me, I'm even more alert to how much force I use in every contact I make with her. She's athletic, but she's still smaller.

I kiss behind her ear again before I take the Wartenberg pinwheel and graze it down the center of her back along one side of her spine, then up the other. I move it in a zigzag pattern back down to her hips. I bring it from left to right, then over each arse cheek. I'm careful not to pinch her skin when I run it along her horizontal crack. When I bring it up to her right ribs, I drag it over them around to her belly.

I moved slowly before, but now I set an excruciatingly slow pace as I move the tiny, spiked wheel over her tits. I run it around her clamped nipples, then over the tips, before bringing it down to the inside of her hip to where her leg forms the joint. With her pussy bare, I can torment her even more.

It rotates along her pussy lips and around her clit, but I never let it touch where she most wants my attention. Her hips jut forward, begging me to touch her where she's neediest. It's the one place I won't. Yet. Her breathing grows shallow with her growing frustration.

She leans her forehead against the inside of her arm, trembling as I play with her nipples again, running the pinwheel over the exposed parts. The one that isn't getting attention from the tiny implement gets attention from my mouth. I switch back and forth between rolling the sexual tormentor and my mouth over the tightened buds.

My free hand cups her pussy; the heel right above her clit. My fingers spread like I'm making the Star Trek greeting, so I'm not touching her clit. My fingers stroke the outside of her cunt. Her hips rock more insistently, and I observe her every breath and movement. I'm attentive to any sign this might go from pleasure to real pain, either physically or emotionally.

"Little girl, how are you doing?"

"I'm fine, sir. Keep going."

Her voice trembles, but it doesn't sound as though it comes from sadness or fear. It's still frustration. I never want to hear it get to defeat. I move my hand to flick her clit three times before I allow the heel of my hand to finally press against the tiny bundle of nerves. My index finger and pinky continue to move outside of her pussy, and my middle finger taps against her arsehole.

I don't enter her, but I tease her. She can't tell if she wants to press her hips farther forward into the heel of my hand or tip her hips back to my finger. That's a good sign she won't just enjoy anal sex, but other butt stuff, too.

I keep the pressure light as my hand rubs circles over her clit. It's the motion she'll need to get off, but not nearly the pressure to do it. She moans, and it's music to my ears. Between her panting and her moans, I am driving myself crazy. Just as her fingers claw in the air, I step away.

"No!"

"What's that, little one? You issuing me a command?"

"No, sir. I just don't want that to end."

"I know that. That's why it did."

"Is that what my punishment is? You're going to edge me?"

"That's part of it."

"What's the other part?"

"Something else. You'll know when we get to it."

I want to give her something to think about. Not as fear, but as something to focus on when her frustration grows. She knows it'll be some other type of orgasm denial. But she doesn't know whether it'll be harder or easier than what I'm doing now.

She might fear it'll be worse, but there's also the prospect it could be better.

I lower myself onto one knee, flicking my tongue against her clit. She's already soaked, but I've purposely kept her cream away from her clit. Now, I lave it over and over and flick it several times before sucking. Anything to tantalize and torment her. Each of her moans is like a symphony of angels to me.

I love knowing I'm bringing her such pleasure. It may be on my terms and the way I desire it, but she's enjoying it, and that brings me happiness. It's the old cliche, her pleasure is my pleasure.

I purposely only tease that little bud back and forth, even though she tries to widen her legs, hoping I'll thrust my fingers into her. I bet she'd prefer my cock and so would I, but we're not there yet. I continue until her hips rock on their own, insistently wanting to get her clit more pressure.

I pull away and slap her pussy. More music to my ears. I do it again, a little harder.

"Sir!"

"Say your word if you need it."

"Sir, you know that's not why. You know I'm begging."

There's a rasp to her voice that makes it husky and even sexier than usual. I pinch her clit, making her hips buck forward, again inviting me to do more. That's exactly the opposite of my plan. I let go and don't touch her.

Not able to see, she has no way to know whether I have some other implement or I'm just waiting. She whimpers in her need, and I watch her expression. Her brow's furrowed and her hands fist, but she's not shivering. Just when I know she's getting nervous, I put my mouth back to her and suck as hard as I dare.

"Sir!"

That elicits a chuckle from me as I pull away again.

"Is there something that you need, little one?"

"To come, and you know it, sir."

"I do."

"I'm sorry, sir, for what I said earlier. I'll accept your compliments graciously. I won't make that mistake again."

"Oh, I bet you won't, but I need to be sure."

"Can't you just believe me?"

That elicits a full, deep rumble from my chest as I chuckle again. Now she shivers. I know she loves that sound, and I've already noticed how she enjoys having her head against my chest when I do that.

"It's not a question of not believing you, little one. It's a question of your punishment not being over. I suppose you think it should be, but I don't agree. I think there's still plenty more to come."

She blows out an exasperated breath, and that earns her a tweaked nipple. The bit that's free of her clamp is just enough for me to enjoy or to give her a burst of pain. I kiss along the inside of her left thigh until I reach her pussy. I swipe my tongue along the seam, ignoring her clit this time, before kissing my way down her right leg.

When I get to her knee, I wrap my hand around the back and tickle.

"Shit!"

She doesn't expect that type of teasing—a gentleness, a playfulness—and her knee bends as far as the ankle cuffs allow. She tries to shimmy away as my fingers dance along the inside of her thigh. I brush them over the spot I know will arouse her most. I feel her leg tremble. Her head falls back in a sign of supplication. I ease one finger into her and don't move it. That's an even greater torment since I know she desperately wants more.

I do nothing as the seconds tick away. When I'm certain it's been one of the most excruciating minutes of her sexual life, I thrust in a second, again doing nothing else except leaving it there. I let her rock her hips again, trying to move my fingers to rub her g spot. I indulge her twice, my free hand pressing against the outside of her belly.

"Thank you, sir."

But the moment she says that, she realizes her mistake. I withdraw my fingers and slap her clit.

"You're welcome, little one."

She tries to stomp her foot, but the cuff is too tight for her to lift it. She inhales a deep breath that fills her lungs and expands her chest. The temptation to remove the clamps and suck her tits is too great. I stand and ease off the right nipple one.

I know the burst of pain she's receiving as the blood rushes back into the punished little nub. I wait for when the pain begins. I count to five and then latch on, sucking and flicking the distended bud with my tongue. She sighs, the relief immeasurable. This is my own form of torture. I want nothing more than to strip naked and fuck her as hard as I can. My balls ache for release, but we're not there yet. As though she reads my mind, she whispers. I almost miss what she says.

"Sir, why are you punishing yourself? Don't you want to get off?"

I let go of her breast.

"*Cailín*, there's nothing I want more than to please you. My desire to get off is only slightly behind that."

"So, you are punishing yourself."

"Perhaps, but I don't see it that way. I see it as anticipation will make our intimacy even stronger."

At that, she smiles. It's a soft one. It's not a grin. It's gentler than that. Even without seeing her eyes, it lights up her face, and it makes her even more beautiful than she already is to me. I feel a pinch in my chest I haven't felt in a long time. Not since

I gave up dating in college. My life isn't conducive to relationships. I haven't dated anybody seriously since my freshman year. Sometimes I miss the companionship of having a girlfriend.

However, the danger it brings to a woman I know I won't make a life with long-term isn't worth the risk to her. That's part of why getting into D/s relationships works so well for me.

I ignore the emotions threatening to push to the surface. The warmth that spreads through my chest is even more troublesome than the jealousy I've felt since meeting Joey.

I blow cool air over her nipple before releasing the other one from its clamp, only to give it the same treatment as I did the first one. Relieving some of the ache after the pinch, but not enough to satisfy her. Only enough to keep her ready to beg again. Her chin drops as though she would look down to see what I'm doing, but with the blindfold in place, she still doesn't know what'll come next.

I know I'm going to push her beyond her limits if I continue teasing her for too much longer. I want to exert dominance, but I don't want to make her miserable. There's often a fine line between the two, and if I break her trust again, I doubt there's any coming back from it. I can't afford that when things are still so very new.

I rise and slip the blindfold off her head. She blinks several times before she focuses on me. She remains quiet, waiting for my instructions, which is exactly what I expect. It's clear she has experience as a sub, so it reassures me nothing I did tonight would be too unusual. She handled it all very well.

"I'm proud of you, little one. You took everything I gave you, and the sounds you make when you beg are music to my ears. The only thing that would sound better is knowing I'm making you come, my cock deep inside you."

"Yes, please, sir."

She asks so nicely. I can't help but be ready to indulge us both. I release her arms and help move them around, rubbing her shoulders and upper arms now that they're in a different position than they were. I don't want her sore.

There are different types of soreness. Her pussy feeling well-used and aching for more is one thing, but not being able to move her arms over her shoulders is another. I release her ankles as well, rubbing around them to make sure the cuffs didn't chafe. Once again, I wrap my arm around her waist and gather her dress, taking her over to a loveseat where I pull her onto my lap.

She curls into me as her eyelids slide shut, her breathing still heavier than usual. I press her legs apart and ease three fingers into her pussy.

"Are you ready to come, *cailín?*"

"So ready. I've been ready since I saw you outside."

"What makes you think I should let you come now?"

"Because I might combust on the spot if you don't."

She infuses humor into her voice, and I kiss her temple. It's yet another example of unprecedented affection. I like it. I want more of it, which is exactly the opposite of how I should feel. It's the opposite to what she's agreed to. She might want to be my sub, but that doesn't mean she wants to be involved romantically with a mobster. I need to set those thoughts aside and just take this for what it is and appreciate what she offers.

I stroke the inside of her pussy as my thumb rubs slow, deep circles on her clit.

"Look at me, little one."

Her eyes open as she turns to gaze at me.

"You are so incredibly beautiful. You take my breath away."

I bring my lips to hers, brushing them together before I press mine to hers and deepen the kiss. She opens to me immediately, and our tongues duel before she sucks lightly on mine.

My thumb rubs more insistently on her clit as my cock demands relief, but I won't move us to the next spot until I've gotten her off here. We continue to kiss as she squirms on my lap, her arse rubbing against my cock. If I don't get her off soon, she's going to make me come in my pants. There's only so much that I can withstand. She pulls away.

"Sir, may I come?"

"Yes, little one. Come in five...four...three...two. Come for me, little girl."

Her body tenses, and her back arches. Her thighs trap my hand between them. Even though the light's not bright, I can see the flush that builds from the top of her tits, up to her neck, and into her cheeks. She's magnificent. Her body is so responsive to mine. Anything I do, she's been willing to try with an open mind.

"Sir, that was amazing. I—I—thank you."

She laughs, unsure what else to say, and I'm happy with her gratitude. I need nothing else from her.

"Can you stand, *cailín*?"

"I think so."

I ease my fingers out of her, and she watches me lick them. "Mmm."

I waggle my eyebrows at her as I clean my fingers. She laughs and shakes her head.

"If you say so."

I slide her bra back into place and gaze down at her.

"*Cailín*, do you want to go back to a private room, or is there somewhere out here you'd like to fuck me?"

"Whatever you want, sir. I'm happy to go along with that."

"Well, I'd like to strip you bare and have my way with you."

"Okay."

"And I want to feel your naked skin against mine, so that means going to a private room."

"That's fine with me, sir."

I guide her to the stairs, and we make our way to the second floor. There are several rooms open this evening, so I let her peek into each as we pass them.

"Which one appeals to you?"

"Mmm. I'm not really down for the nursery, but the class-room or the extreme room work for me, since we already used the doctor's office."

"All right. If we go to the one with all the equipment, is there anything in particular you do or don't want to use?"

"Um, not that I can think of. To be honest, sir, I trust you with whatever you have in mind, so whatever you would like."

Chapter Fifteen

Joey

As I tell Cormac I trust him, I realize I do. I should have understood his spike of jealousy last night because I felt it too when we encountered Deirdre. We don't know enough about each other's pasts to be completely comfortable yet. I could have lost my shit when another woman came up to my new Dom and announced she was pregnant, or at the very least, wanted to trap the guy into believing he fathered her child.

I worried I'd stepped too far over the line when I spoke up, but it didn't faze Cormac. I said it out of jealousy, and I think he understood. I think his fuck-up was greater than mine, but I could have been more forgiving. I am tonight.

If I'm honest with myself, I've trusted him since the moment he tried to shield me when we fell down the steps. I may have protected him first, but he's tried to keep protecting me ever since. Some of his jealousy comes from fear for my safety, and I get that. He's not the first man in my life to act that way, even if the same thing didn't motivate their jealousy. My brother's been a royal pain in the ass because of it.

"Can we use the tantra chair, please?"

"If that's what you'd like, then that's what we'll do."

"Thank you, sir. May I undress you?"

"Yes."

It's better than unwrapping Christmas and birthday gifts combined. Peeling off each layer of clothes, exposing more of his impressive body, makes my pussy throb. The emptiness aches to the point of a burn. But I refuse to hurry. I relish each moment as I pull his shirt along his arms. The massive shamrock with the O in the center moves every time his pec flexes. The tats across the back of his shoulders—ones I'm certain hold significance—ripple with each movement. He's a masterpiece chiseled from granite.

We remove our masks now that no one else can see us. He removes my lingerie once I've stripped him and slid a condom on. We move to the tantra chair, and I wait for instructions. I wonder what he has in mind, and Deirdre's face flashes before my eyes as I look at the curved piece of furniture. He wraps his arms around me and kisses my shoulder. I sink back into his embrace.

"Don't think about her, and I won't think about your past. We're here together now, and we have time to make fresh memories."

I nod and swallow. I don't like this wave of emotion crushing me. Memories as only his sub and nothing more. That's all he's offered, so that's all I can take. It's a sad refrain that plays through my mind. But I refuse to let it ruin tonight. I want this more than I want to think about what might have been.

He steps around me and reclines on the chair, holding his arms open.

"Face me to start."

I oblige and straddle him as I stroke behind his balls. He needs no coaxing, and neither do I. He guides me to ease down his length, teasing us together. Once I'm seated to the hilt, he rocks my hips as he thrusts. His hands run over my body as I lean forward to brace myself. My swinging tits are the invitation I hope them to be. He latches on and sucks the left one as his eyes drift shut, but only for a moment. Our gazes lock.

Everything else fades away. I don't care about anything else happening—not here, not in the world, not in my life. He consumes every nook and cranny of my mind right now. I'd do anything to keep these sensations going. To keep him looking at me the way he is.

"You test my restraint, *cailín*. I want this to last. There are too many positions to enjoy to finish this fast."

He offers me a lopsided grin, and I can't help but laugh. When I do, my flexing muscles make him groan. He bites my nipple before stopping my rocking motion.

"Turn around."

One benefit of a tantra chair is it's possible to change positions without having the guy pull out or the woman get up. I spin around, placing my feet between his spread legs, his feet on the floor. He guides me to recline onto his chest, arching my back. I watch us in the ceiling mirror, and I can see he's doing the same thing. He lifts and lowers me on his cock until we move at the pace he wants. His hands glide over me once again, then linger over my tits as he massages them. He's kissing my shoulder and neck, moving my hair out of the way before trailing his fingers down my sternum and belly until he reaches my clit. It's tender, but it only heightens my arousal.

"May I come, sir?"

"No. You will not come until we do it together, and I'm not ready for this to end."

He levers me forward, so my forearms rest in front of me, and I bounce on his cock.

"Fuck, little one. You feel better than anything I've ever experienced. Your arse is glorious."

He kneads and spreads it, and I watch in the mirror as he stares at it.

"One of these nights, I'm going to come in your arse. Then I'm going to check in the morning to be sure you haven't spilled a drop."

What the hell does that mean?

Would he come by my place to check? How would I make it home without any leaking? Would we spend the night together?

He rearranges my legs to draw one back over his hip, my shin resting on the upward portion of the chair. I push my other leg forward since it's the only way for me to balance when I'm pretty much doing the splits.

"Are you all right? Or is this position too uncomfortable?"

"It's fine, sir. I do yoga and Pilates, and I was a gymnast when I was younger."

I've remained flexible because of my workouts, but also as a sub to please my Doms. It's benefiting me now.

"Holy shit, sir. You're so deep. I—I—Fuck."

"I know, little one. Keep going."

I push up onto my hands, and my head falls back. He fists my hair and pulls me toward him. He nips my earlobe before biting the crook of my neck.

"Thank you for trusting me, Joey."

Did the roleplay just end?

"You're welcome, s—"

"Cormac."

Nothing prepared me for this sudden shift. Why did he end it?

He eases me back into a position where he can maneuver me. He's said nothing else, and I don't know what to say. He lifts me and turns, so now my back is against the upward curved part of the lounger. He slides his arms under my legs, so the backs of my thighs rest over his upper arms.

"I'm going to fuck you hard, Joey. I need it. You're mine."

"Fuck me as hard as you can because I am yours."

"It doesn't go one way."

As I stare into his gaze, something is different. I feel it in his touch, and I hear it in his voice. I can't name it, but I think I feel it too. I don't know what changed or how he knew.

"You're so damn tight, little girl. You're going to squeeze the cum out of me. Can you be a good girl for me and do that?"

"Yes, sir."

I guess we're back to our roles again.

He shakes his head. Maybe not.

"Joey, we're equals in this. Tell me what you want. Anything."

"Just you."

That's the truth. I want him more than my next breath. He fills every part of me.

He grunts and slams into me over and over as I tilt my hips to him. Our gazes don't waver. Tonight is unlike any I've ever experienced. I've fucked plenty, but this is like a spiritual awakening. Everything we've shared since the moment we arrived. It's all led to this moment.

We built a lot of trust with what we've shared here. I don't know if he feels the same, but it's as though he's imprinted onto me. Maybe I've been reading too many shifter romances or something. I'm romanticizing something that may not exist, but my mind's convinced.

"Are you close, Joey?"

"Yes. So close...I'm almost there...I'm about to come."

"Good. I can't last."

"Come in me, Cor. Fill me with your cum."

I know he has a condom on, but he gets it from the gleam in his eyes. He surges into me two more times before I scream.

"Cor!"

He's right there with me as he screams my name, too. "Joey!"

My body trembles as I pant. I cling to him, frightened by the intensity of what just happened. It was nearly the sensations of breath play, but he wasn't anywhere near my throat. He lifts me and walks to a basket with sub blankets, ones to wrap around subs when they finish a scene. Subs often sweat during scenes from the strain, so when it's done, it can suddenly feel like the room's freezing.

He wraps one around me and another around himself. He takes us back to the tantra lounger and reclines. I nestle against him, my head on his chest, eyes closed. He runs his hand up and down my back while the other pats my ass. It's beyond soothing.

After a couple minutes, I feel more like myself and pull away. But his embrace tightens, and his hand puts my head back against his chest. I'd had my arms folded between us, but I wrap them around him. I feel his shuddering sigh. I tighten my arms and legs, and his entire body relaxes. I hadn't realized it could. It's not like he's gone soft—not even his dick—but I don't feel the tension I didn't realize was there because of his muscular build.

My heart melts as my left hand runs over his ribs, then up to his chest. I tilt my head back and nudge his chin. I pray he'll kiss me, but he doesn't. When I gaze up at him, he nods. I start the kiss, and it's fucking bliss. I wish I knew what he thinks and feels.

"Joey, will you come home with me tonight? Or if you're not comfortable with my place, then a hotel where there's security and a front desk staff. I don't want to let go of you yet."

I push up to look at him without my head being at an awkward angle. "Do you invite women to your place?"

"Never. You're the only one."

"Is this just for tonight?"

"I don't know. I hope not. Can we talk about whatever this is in the morning? If you still want a contract, then we can draft it. If you want to come to my place during the week and weekends, we can do that. Or I have a vacant rental we can use."

My blood freezes.

You stupid idiot.

I rear back and am ready to climb off him until I truly see his expression. He'd practically whispered the offer. I can't describe the way he looks as anything short of anxious. The longer I don't respond, the more I witness him retreat. He nods and moves to sit up.

"Wait. Did you make that offer because you believe it's what I want?"

"Yes. You agreed to be my sub. I'd like to meet somewhere besides here. I want you to be comfortable wherever that is."

"Besides meeting somewhere else, what do you want?"

He won't meet my gaze, looking at my nose instead. I know the difference since I do the same thing when I'm uncomfortable.

"Cormac, you don't want what you're offering, so why are you?"

"It's what we agreed to."

"And if our agreement needs to change?"

He jerks away, lifting me off him and placing me on the chair as he stands.

"If here is all you want, or you don't want this, then I'll understand."

"Stop. Cormac, you've put up a wall so high, I don't even know if there is anything on the other side. Why do you assume I'm rejecting you?"

"Because I'm asking too much of you too soon."

"You know what happens when you assume. Don't be an ass and don't make me into one. If being your sub is all you're comfortable with or all you want, then I still agree to it."

He pulls me from the seat and nearly suffocates me with how tightly he holds me.

"I don't just want you as my sub. I shouldn't be entering any agreement so soon after ending my previous one. But what I thought I could accept even an hour ago isn't what I can handle now. Joey, I want this dynamic with you when we have sex. But I don't want this to be the only thing we have. I don't want one night a week and most of a weekend just to fuck. I want any and every night to be together. Sex isn't my only wish."

"Are you saying you want to date?"

He eases his hold on me and runs his hand over his face.

"I started this here, but it's fecking awkward to discuss in a BDSM club while we're naked."

Fecking.

He's adorable. He'll say fuck when it's an activity, but not when he needs an expletive in conversation. It's sweet.

"Then let's get dressed at least."

"That's not enough. What we need to talk about has to be done in private. I can't risk somewhere so public."

I mouth "mob stuff?"

He nods.

I hurry to dress, which takes me a lot less time than it does him. When we reach the door, he pauses and looks back.

"*Cailín*, it's never been like that before."

"Same."

It was a quiet ride to his place, but we held hands the entire way. I'm in a pair of his sweatpants rolled over five times to keep me from tripping, and a sweatshirt that dwarfs me. I've never worn anything so comfortable in my life. He's in a pair of black track pants, and his ass is delectable. You could bounce a quarter off it. The pants are male lingerie.

"Let's sit, and I'll explain what I can."

I doubt I'm going to like most of what I hear, but I'll listen, nonetheless. He guides me to the sofa and waits for me to sit. He takes a spot in the corner, and I scoot closer. It's all the hint he needs. He lifts me onto his lap and cocoons me again like he did earlier. Like he always does when he embraces me. I feel safer, and I need that right now.

"You know who I am and what I am. You need to understand I choose what I do every day, but I don't choose who I have to be. I was born into this, and I will die in this. My family's been in the mob for three generations on one side and four on the other. My cousin is the mob boss. Our uncle was our boss before him, and our grandfather before that, and so on and so on. Right now, I'm third in line. Dillan and Finn are both older than me, but I'm older than the other guys. Not by much, but I am."

"Cor, I grew up in Mexico. I know what the cartels do. Maybe you do the same things, but if you do, you keep it private. I've seen what the cartels leave on the street. I've seen it happen. There's far less you need to explain than I think you realize. I get this isn't a choice. If you walk away, you're as good as dead. If your family is as close as they seem and as close as the Diazes, then I know they wouldn't let you be a target. It would only endanger you all. Your family can't abdicate without agreeing to their deaths. No new family would let the old one live without fear of them coming back. I know you probably do things you hate. I'm sure you're not proud of them like some syndicate men are. Nothing about you makes me think you find joy in whatever you do. You're too kind, and the men I've met who thrive on what they do are never kind. I've lived my life with a don't ask, don't tell policy. I will never ask you what you do or where you go, and I don't expect you to tell me. Keep me away from that part of your life, and I can accept it."

I've seen shit most people couldn't fathom. I don't want that in my life, but I want Cormac. I can't have one without the other, and I get that.

"I wish it were still that simple, but it's not. My uncle, his cousin a few times removed, and his best friend fecked us all over by going after bratva women. They died for their sins, but it started a tsunami of shite my cousin couldn't stop before the waves came ashore. It was our family or theirs, and ours will come before anything else until kingdom come. Their deaths didn't stop what they started, and now women and children aren't off limits anymore."

"Cor, the Mexican cartels don't discriminate. They target anyone within range. I don't enjoy knowing there were dishonorable men in your family who could endanger me, even after they're dead. As long as you don't use children or target them, then I'll figure out how to accept all of this."

"What kind of life did you have in Mexico?"

"The kind that made me move here. I grew up with plenty of privileges, but I have more opportunities here."

I kiss his cheek and nuzzle his neck. We're wading into dangerous waters—I'm keeping the metaphor going. I don't want to talk about my past. Nothing good can come of it. He covers my hand that was stroking his chest. He looks down at me, and I know he's aware I'm trying to distract him. He observes me for a moment before kissing my forehead and continuing.

"If we move this beyond what we planned, I need you to accept a security detail permanently. It won't be negotiable. I told you they're trained to be unobtrusive, but they'll keep you safe. That's the highest priority to me, Joey. I won't compromise, and I'll punish you if you do things to endanger yourself or my men. It doesn't matter if it's willful or by accident."

"I understand. You know this world here, and I don't. I defer to you because all you've wanted is to protect me and take care of me."

"There will be times when I disappear. I can't tell you where I'm going or how long I'll be away. Many times, I won't know until I leave. If it's for more than three days, I want you to go to my parents. I know you don't know them yet, but they'll know what to do. My mom's the one whose family rules our branch, but my dad's family has been in since the old country. Both sides of the family were once part of the same clan and somehow related about ten or fifteen generations ago. Both sides have had sons to keep passing along the O'Rourke name. I'm one twice over."

"You mean your mom didn't have to change her name when she got married?"

"Yeah. Neither did my two aunts. Three sisters married three brothers."

"Were they arranged or something?"

"No. Not at all. Dillan's parents got together first when they were teenagers. My mom and dad and my other aunt and uncle dated a few years later."

"That's super sweet."

"It is. Nauseatingly sweet."

As I watch Cormac, I wonder if we could ever be that way. When he tips my chin up and presses a gentle kiss to my lips, I think maybe we can.

We're interrupted when my phone rings. I stretch to where I put it on the coffee table. Fuck my life.

Chapter Sixteen

Cormac

"*Hola.*"

I don't know who Santi is when I see Joey's phone screen just before she answers the call. I can't hear the person on the other end.

"*Estoy ocupada en este momento...No. Esto es más importante...Porque no quiero.*" I'm busy at the moment...No. This is more important...Because I don't want to.

Does she know I speak fluent Spanish? I could assume by the man's name that he's a Spanish speaker too, and that's why she's speaking that and not English. But maybe she thinks I won't understand.

"*Mañana.*"

What's happening tomorrow?

She gazes up at me and shoots me an apologetic smile.

"Brother."

She mouths it and points to her phone before she rolls her

eyes. There's something about the way she's downplaying this. He wants something she doesn't.

"Hablaré contigo sobre esto mañana. Necesito irme." I'll talk to you about this tomorrow. I need to go.

I listen as she finishes up the call and puts her phone back on the table. I remain quiet and just offer her a smile. But when she offers nothing to me, I can't help asking before it gets awkward.

"Is everything all right?"

"Yeah. That was just my brother, Santiago, but it wasn't anything important. I can talk to him tomorrow."

"Is there somewhere else you need to be tonight or something else you need to do?"

I pray she says no, and I think she will from what I heard. But I also feel like I should offer her a way out if she needs it.

"No, absolutely not. There's nowhere else I'd rather be than here with you. And it's not anything important. He wanted me to stop by to look at some new furniture he bought. He's proud of his new living room set, but it's hardly something I need to do at this time of night."

"Is he worried about where you are?"

Did she tell him she's entering a D/s relationship with a mobster? She wasn't alone with her phone at any point between when we met at McGinty's and when we got to the club. Did she go there on purpose to find me?

My mind whirls with suspiciousness ingrained in me practically since birth. However, I have no reason to question her, and the last time I did, I nearly fucked it all up. Once bitten, twice shy, so I won't make the same mistake again. I've been cautious about that all evening.

"No, he just wants to brag, and he knows I don't always go to bed early. So, he thought he'd try to catch me, see if he could get me to come over. He was going to bribe me with my favorite *sopa*."

"He thinks soup would get you to go over at nearly one in the morning."

"Yeah, well, he's not always very time conscious. He may not have even realized how late it was."

"Do you do that often? Do you go out to his place, wherever that is, in the middle of the night?"

"No, Cormac, I don't. Usually at this time, I'm tucked away at home, even if I'm not asleep. I'm not out prowling the city in the wee hours of the morning."

I shoot her a scowl that tells her I don't appreciate her being flippant. Her gaze drops, and she places her hands in her lap.

"I'm sorry. I just know my brother, and no, it's not that big a deal. But I get you're trying to watch out for me."

"I am, and I've already told you I want guards for you. If I'm concerned about you during the day, don't you think finding out you go out on your own in the middle of the night in New York would bother me?"

"I suppose so."

"You suppose? Joey, come on."

"I know, but Cormac, you've got to realize this is a new relationship for us. There're plenty of things I've been doing on my own since well before I met you. And it's not that I don't respect your wishes and your concern, but it's going to take me a moment to adjust to making them as high a priority as I want them to be."

"So, what do you want, Joey? Do you want to continue our D/s dynamic and add in being more of a romantic couple? What would that look like to you?"

"I think I want both. I mean, I know I want both, but I think…"

"What do you want? What do you need?"

She hesitates as she considers her explanation.

"I think you're a man who thrives off control, and I think most of the time you have it, but not always. And when you don't, it gets to you even if you don't show it."

She stumbles a little over some of her words, but I won't deny she's right, so I nod.

"I also have a stressful job that often leaves me feeling powerless to help families the way I'd like. That frustrates me with little emotional outlet. If I won't have control over something, then I'd rather it be because I chose to give it up, rather than feeling like someone took it from me or I never had it."

"That makes sense."

"I want to date and do the same things a regular couple would as they get to know each other, but I want more out of our D/s dynamic than just one night a week and part of the weekend."

"What are you suggesting?"

She hesitates again as she looks at her lap, and then sweeps her gaze around my living room before finally looking at me."

"I want to submit twenty-four seven, Cormac."

She bites her bottom lip and looks majorly uncomfortable. I tug her lip free and press a gentle kiss to it as I cup her jaw.

"I'd like that too, as long as you're not suggesting TPE."

I have no interest in total power exchange with Joey. I might want her to submit, but I don't want her subservient. I don't want her to feel like she has no voice, and I want us to slip in and out of the dynamic whenever we need or want to, even if we plan to keep our Dom/sub dynamic daily.

"I don't want that either. I'm not ready to give up that much control. I don't know that I ever would be."

"That's fine, Joey, because I will never ask for it. I don't want that."

"Good. So, what do you think it would look like, sir?"

"No, not yet, Joey. We're equals while we decide what we want."

The look of relief on her face makes me smile.

"Well, little one, I appreciate you want to start as we plan to continue, but not yet."

"All right. I'd like that one night a week and most of the weekend together. I'd like that night and part of the weekend to be time for us to scene, but I don't want..."

She bites her lip again, and I can't tell if she's truly nervous or simply hasn't thought all of this through and is sharing her ideas as they come to her.

"Do you want nights where it's just a regular date, where maybe a Monday night we go out to dinner and a movie, or a Thursday we cook at home and play board games?"

She grins. "If you're willing to take me on in Monopoly, I will absolutely hold you to that, but yes, that's what I'd like. A mix between the two."

"Do you want me to call and check on you each day?"

"Yeah, I would like that a lot. I enjoy talking to you, but we haven't gotten to do much of that."

"You know you can call me anytime you want to check in as well. You don't have to wait."

"Thank you, sir. I mean, Cormac."

She lets out a nervous laugh, and I stroke her back.

"Have you had these kinds of conversations with your past Doms?"

"Sort of, but I've never been in a twenty-four seven, and I've never been in a romantic relationship with my Dom, either. This is all new to me."

"It's the same for me. My previous relationships were never romantic, and they weren't twenty-four seven. My subs were free to do as they wanted when we weren't together, as long as they were monogamous. And most were."

Fucking Deirdre. That was a fun thing to discover at the end. Joey's eyebrows shoot up practically to her hairline.

"So, she really could be pregnant?"

"Maybe. I don't know, and I truly don't care. All she wanted to do was cause problems between us, and I'm not interested in that. She can do as she pleases."

"Okay. It's good to know."

"If this is twenty-four seven, Joey, no more panties, and you wear skirts or dresses when you're with me. When I want to fuck you, I will. When I want your mouth on my cock, that's exactly what I'll get."

She's pushed my sweatshirt's sleeves up to her elbows, and I see the goosebumps rise on her skin.

"That sounds good to me."

She practically whispers her response. Even though we're still conversing as equals, we're slipping into our roles.

"When you're here, you will either be naked, or you will only wear a bra or negligee. If I see you in panties, I will take every pair you have and destroy them. Then I will punish your fine little arse for disobeying me."

"Yes, Cormac."

"I don't know your wardrobe yet to pick out clothes for you. That doesn't really interest me. I trust you to wear what's appropriate. Besides, I'd prefer to be surprised whenever I see you. But I expect you to be punctual whenever we agree to get together, that you obey my men just as you would obey me, and that you share your location with me."

"That's fair. I mean, if I'm with your men, they would know anyway. But you're entitled to that."

"I am, but it's not because I'm your Dom. In case anything should happen to you, I can't protect you if I don't know where you are. What do you want from me, Joey?"

"I want to keep feeling safe with you. I know that's sort of unrealistic. But when I'm with you, in the same place, I've never felt safer. I want to always feel that way when I'm with you."

"I'll always strive to make you feel that way. Do you want me to place limitations on who you can see and when you can go out, how late you can go out?"

"Maybe. I'm not sure yet."

I study her for a moment before my head tilts a little, and I consider the conversation I heard her having with her brother.

"Do you wish you'd had me as an excuse for why you couldn't do what Santiago wanted? I mean, even if you didn't tell him somebody wouldn't allow you to go out, did you want to know I wouldn't allow it?"

She nods. "But I think I already did."

"Well, you were right to think that. There's no way in hell I would have agreed to it unless I was going with you. I don't know that you're ready for me to meet your brother yet."

Something sparks in her gaze akin to fear. It's gone in a flash. If I didn't know what that looked like, I wouldn't see it. I've caused it in enough men to recognize it with ease. I want to know why she would fear her brother for even a moment. Yet if I push too hard on that, it'll derail this conversation. Then I won't have any chance of finding out what's going on.

"I won't police your coming and going, but you will ask me for permission if your schedule deviates from the norm. What else do you want or need from me, little one?"

"This. What we're doing right now. What you keep offering me. The affection. I didn't realize how much I wanted it until you started giving it to me. I didn't think it was missing from my life, but I guess it has been."

"I offer that openly and freely, regardless of our dynamic. Whether we're dating or we're in some type of power exchange. It's genuine."

I kiss the top of her temple when I finish speaking as though to punctuate the sentiment.

"I know it is, and that's why it's so special to me. Can we play it by ear for the rest of the stuff and talk about it as it comes up?"

"Of course. Joey, do you want a contract for all of this?"

"I don't know because I've never mixed romance and submission together. I don't know what that would look like. Should we?"

"I don't know either. I don't think we need it. If either of us changes our minds and thinks we do, then we can revisit it. Does that work for you?"

She considers that for a moment before nodding. "Yeah, completely. Is there more that you feel like we need to talk about tonight?"

"Not that I can think of. You?"

"No, I've enjoyed tonight, and I can't remember a better night than this in a long, long time."

"Same, little one. You ready to go to bed?"

I scoop her into my arms and carry her through to my bedroom. I playfully toss her onto the mattress as I land on top of her, always careful not to press my entire weight on her. We dissolve into a fit of laughter. We tease each other with little pecks here and there until our lips brush. Then everything changes.

The kiss deepens immediately, and we're back to needing each other as though neither of us has had a meal in a week. We strip each other and stretch out on the bed. I love touching her petal-soft skin, but not just with my fingertips. It puckers her nipples, and she arches her back into it. I grab a condom from the bedside table. When we kiss again, I roll us so I'm on my back, and she straddles me. Together, we position her over my cock until she can slide down on it.

216

"*Cailín*, that is beyond a doubt equally satisfying as coming inside you, and nothing tops that."

"I agree. If only I could hold on to that sensation all day."

We move together, and this is completely vanilla. We're equals in this. I'm not trying to exert my will or decide exactly how things go.

I want her to touch me how she wants and move how she wants. I haven't had vanilla sex in years. Just like she hadn't realized how much she missed the affection until I offered it to her, I didn't know I was missing a different type of intimacy.

I don't think I was, or that I needed it until meeting Joey. But if this goes away, it will devastate me.

It's been three weeks since Joey spent the night at my place for the first time. We've spent Wednesday nights scening at the club. She comes over on Friday evenings and stays until midday Sunday. I've had my normal work during the week. Some of it more unsavory than others, but we've also had regular dates.

The first Monday, we went out for dinner at one of Finn's restaurants, and then to a movie before spending the night at her place. The following Thursday, we stayed in and made dinner together here before playing board games. It wound up being a tie in Monopoly—or rather—a stalemate. There wasn't a clear winner, and we'd already played for hours.

I beat her at checkers, but she beat me at chess, which made her laugh when she took my king, and her queen was left. We went out for happy hour with my brother and his wife on Tuesday of this week. None of my family is giving me shite about her, but I know they're thinking it.

It was pointless to deny it, so I've already confessed I had a nickname for her almost as soon as we met. The knowing looks

I got from my brother and cousins made me roll my eyes. I knew I was a goner from the start.

We're at my place now on Friday, and we've both just gotten here from work. However, I had a conversation with one of her guards today that didn't leave me in a good mood. I'll give her time to tell me what happened before I ask questions.

The moment she arrives at my condo, she knows to go straight into the bedroom and strip down to her bra and whatever lingerie she brought or camisole she's wearing. Tonight's the first night I'm not supervising to make sure she isn't wearing panties.

She hasn't yet, not on our nights when we scene and not on our regular dates. I'm staying in the living room to calm down.

"Sir?

"Come here, little one."

We decided earlier this week tonight would be our night to scene, and tomorrow night would be our date night. We've slipped into our roles. She comes and sits on my lap as I fondle her tits.

"How was your day today?"

"It was fine. Long, but just work as usual. How about you, sir? How was your day?"

"The same. I had a couple of meetings and a few phone calls here and there. One that irritated me more than the others. How were your client visits?"

"Good. Unfortunately, one family isn't doing as well as I'd like, so the mom may go back to court soon, but the kids are doing well with their father."

That wasn't the situation I heard about.

"Did you have to go to several schools today? Neighborhoods? Or were you mostly in Port Richmond?"

She knows I don't look at her location services if there's no reason to. I trust her to tell me where she's going or where she's been. She knows even though I can have my men report to me everything she's done, I haven't.

"I was mostly in Port Richmond again today, but I needed to go out to another neighborhood before I finished up my last school visit."

"Oh yeah? How did that go? Was it a family you already know?"

"Sort of, but not very well."

She twists to meet my stare, and I see confusion in her eyes. Then her brow furrows to confirm it.

"What's going on, Cormac? I feel like you're fishing for something. What is it you want me to tell you?"

"I think you know exactly what I want you to tell me. I think you're avoiding it. So not only would I like you to tell me what happened, I'd like you to tell me why you refuse to volunteer this."

"Because it's not that big a deal, Cormac. It wasn't anything that hasn't happened before. It wasn't anything that won't happen again. I don't feel like it's worth talking about."

"Oh, you are so very, very wrong about that, little girl. It is absolutely worth talking about, and that is exactly what we're going to do. You are going to tell me what happened because right now I only have my men's version of it, and it sounds pretty fecking bad."

With a deep inhale, then a beleaguered sigh, she nods.

"I arrived while a couple was arguing over custody, and the mom wasn't supposed to be there. It was the dad's visitation time, and that pissed him off. She was angry because she'd gotten a call from their kid's school saying he'd gone without lunch for a third time that week, which meant all three days their kid was with him. I tried to intervene and de-escalate the situation. I've had to do that with this couple before, and it's worked in the past. But it didn't today."

"And?" I infuse command into that one word; my eyes narrow as my gaze sharpens.

"And the mom lost her shit on me. She tried to slap me. She pushed me, then she grabbed my hair and screamed in my face. The guy supported her and encouraged her to beat the shit out of me."

"And why didn't that happen?"

"Because your men stepped in."

"Would you have been able to defend yourself if they hadn't come?"

"Actually, yeah, Cormac. I could have and would have. I appreciate your men's help, but I didn't need it. I appreciate they were there, but next time, unless I'm bleeding, they don't get involved."

"But you were bleeding. I heard she split your lip, and I can see the cut. That wasn't just a little dribble."

"That doesn't count, and you know it."

"I know somebody—male or female—laid their hands on my woman and hurt you. I know it scared you, so I'm not okay with that happening. I'm not okay with you not telling me that. And I'm not okay with you thinking my men shouldn't intervene when that's why I've given you bodyguards."

"You didn't give me a security detail because of my clients. You gave me a security detail because of your rivals."

"Wasn't it a blessing in disguise?"

"Yes, Cormac, it was. But I've already told you—"

"I know you said you can defend yourself, and I'll believe you once you show me. But you weren't going to tell me about this, were you?"

She ducks her chin and shakes her head. "I didn't want you to make a bigger deal out of it than it needed to be."

"And didn't you tell my men not to tell me?"

She cringes at that.

"I figured they probably would, but I also thought it was worth the chance, hoping they wouldn't."

"You thought hoping it wasn't a big deal—" I hold up a finger. "—*and* me finding out you planned to keep this from me —" I hold up a second finger. "—*and* you tried to get my men to lie to me—" I hold up a third finger. "—wouldn't be a problem? Joey, I am punishing you for this."

"I know, sir."

"I think today freaked you out way more than you want to admit. I think that kind of loss of control really bothers you. A punishment from me gives you back that balance. The control you give up by allowing me to punish you is something you actually have control over. As contradictory as that may sound, I think it's why you didn't volunteer it. You had to have known I already found out."

"Yes, sir. I think it was. At least partially. Or maybe in the back of my mind that was it, but I wasn't thinking about that specifically. Maybe I just knew that's what I needed."

"Maybe it was. What do you think your punishment should look like?"

"Well, at least a spanking."

"Of course, that's a given. What else?"

"Orgasm denial?"

"That's also a given. What else?"

It's obvious she's racking her brain as she tries to figure out what I believe is the right answer.

"Orgasm denial for me, but not for you. That you get off even if I don't."

"That's right, little one. And how do you think that should happen?"

"In my ass?"

"Is that what you want?"

"Yes, sir.

"Then you're going to blow me."

She cringes when she realizes her error. As much as I would love to fuck her in the arse and come right there, I won't indulge any of her requests right now, even if they're made knowing she believes she's offering me something I'd want.

"When's the punishment going to start, sir?"

"I'll leave that up to you. Before or after dinner?"

"I'd rather do it right now, sir."

"Do you just want to get it over with?"

"No, not like the way you make it sound, but I don't want to keep feeling this anxious all evening."

It tempts me to deny that request for the same reason I won't fuck her in the arse. However, this is the first time I'm giving her a true punishment, and I don't want to distress her too much.

"All right, little one. Let's go in the spare bedroom."

We walk into my guest bedroom because I don't want either of us to associate what I'm quickly coming to think of as our bedroom as a place of punishment rather than pleasure.

"Strip all the way and kneel beside the bed."

"Yes, sir."

"I'll get what I need."

The first night she came over here after the night we entered this relationship, we sat together and ordered just about every toy and implement we could think of that might even remotely interest or tempt us. We have an entire collection of them in a bin at the foot of my closet. We certainly have more than what fits in my bedside table drawer. We have some of our favorites there and a box of condoms.

When I've gathered the things I want, I head into my guest bedroom. She's obeyed me perfectly and is kneeling with her wrists crossed behind her back, her chin dropped, and her eyes down. She makes such a beautiful picture.

I know how lucky I am, not just to have her as a sub, but to have her in my life. I think of her as my girlfriend, but we haven't defined the relationship completely.

I show her the earplugs before I step behind her. She offered a few days ago to try out both a blindfold and earplugs, but she grew too nervous. I asked her to explain what bothers her about it and if she knew why.

I've rarely felt like she's keeping things from me, despite the reason for her punishment tonight. But there are things about her past she doesn't openly share with me. I don't love that, but I'm a hypocrite to expect her to share more of herself than I can share about my childhood.

We've spent hours talking to each other on the phone on nights when we aren't together. It's turned into more than just a nightly check-in. I call her during the day simply because I want to hear her voice. So even though I'm her Dom, I'm also a guy totally into her.

On nights we're apart, we video call to just talk about any and everything. Our travels and the things we want in life. What we see retirement looking like. We're both careful not to allude to being a couple or that we're specifically in each other's life that much further down the road.

I bind her hands with Shibari rope, then wrap it around her in a complex set of loops to create a harness that makes her tits stick out beautifully. I know how much she enjoys nipple clamps, but because of that, I won't give them to her today. She'll have to live without, and that's its own form of denial and punishment.

When she glances down at her chest, then turns her head slightly toward me, I know she wants to ask for them or why I'm not using them, but she knows better.

"Snap your fingers."

"Yes, sir."

She snaps both hands, confident she can let me know if she needs me to stop. I place the ball gag in her mouth. With both earplugs in place and her facing away from the mirror, I move on silent feet to stand by the door. I'm directly behind her, so her peripheral vision won't allow her to see me. I keep an eye on my watch as a minute ticks by. I creep forward, making sure she can't hear me and doesn't sense me.

She's unprepared for how stealthily I move when I bring the crop down over her shoulder onto her right breast. I pull back and switch hands, bringing it down onto the left far faster than she expected. She yelps with the pain. Even though I know it hurts, I also know she enjoys this. As long as I keep the fine balance between pain and pleasure, then I know I can offer her what she needs.

Chapter Seventeen

Joey

I knew I was a fool to think I could hide any of this from Cormac, but I didn't want to make a mountain out of a mole-hill, and that's exactly what I've done. He swats my tits five times each before moving to my ass and upper thighs. That feels like it goes on forever, but it was only ten slaps on each cheek and each thigh before he took the gag and earplugs out. He's standing in front of me now, pinching my nipples mercilessly.

"*Cailín*, why are you being punished?"

"Because a lie of omission is just as bad as a lie said aloud, sir."

"What did you omit?"

"Telling you the truth about somebody getting in my face and threatening me today, sir."

"Why would that matter to me?"

"Because you care about me, sir. Because all you've tried to do since we met was take care of me and protect me. And you can't do that if I'm not forthcoming or I only give you selective truths."

"That's right, *cailín*. Do you have any idea how worried I was when my guy told me a woman slapped you and grabbed your hair, and that some man a foot taller than you got in your face? That the only reason they backed down was because my guys walked up to you?"

"I know, sir. I'm sorry I didn't volunteer it. Maybe part of me thought your guys already told you, so I didn't have to.

"Is that really the type of relationship you want us to have?"

"No, not at all. I don't want you to worry I'm going to hide things from you."

The moment those words are out of my mouth, I want to cringe. There're plenty of things I don't want to share with Cormac. I know it'll change things when I do. It's inevitable I'll have to. But all of this is still too new. I need to be sure we're invested enough for it to be worth sharing family secrets. But I know if I wait too long, then he'll feel betrayed.

"Sir, I'm sorry. It's been a long time since I've depended upon anyone to take care of me. But I can't tell you I want that, then not give you the chance to do it."

"That's right, *cailín*."

He releases my nipples, and I moan. He cups my face in both hands as he gazes down at me. Now he's the one who appears remorseful.

"You were right about an omission is as bad as a lie said aloud. I realize the hypocrisy in me saying that because sometimes I will lie to you. I'll omit the truth, or I'll tell you an untruth. But it's always for the same reason. To protect you, to protect my family, and to protect the people who depend upon my family and me. It's never just about me."

"And my omission was just about me. *I* wanted to avoid upsetting you. But I should have known secrecy would do the exact opposite."

"Do you know why I care about you, *cailín*?"

"Because you enjoy my company, and you want us to continue getting to know each other?"

"That's part of it. But do you know why I want us to continue to get to know each other?"

"Sir, I can only guess at this point. I don't know."

He doesn't respond right away. Instead, he steps around me again and brings the crop down across my ass, making me lurch forward. My core tightens, and my thighs flex to maintain my balance. He flicks it again and lands it across the other side. It smarts from where he's already spanked me. With my legs pressed together, I can feel I've already gotten wet for him.

I can't see him easily, but I can picture how his face must appear. The way the muscles in his arms flex each time he brings the crop down. I know my imagination doesn't do it justice, but he's truly the sexiest man I have ever seen.

As much as the pain from the spanking hurts, and as much as I hate this is coming from a punishment, his dominance over me arouses me. It's emotionally fulfilling knowing he cares. It does something to me, submitting myself to his dominance. He could punish me without this conversation, without listening to me, without explaining. He could exert his will over me, but he doesn't.

Even when I cede control to him, he still treats me as a partner, includes me in a conversation about what's happening. Every day my trust in him grows. I'd like to think his trust in me continues to increase, and that today didn't set us back.

"Sir, what can I do to earn your forgiveness?"

He steps before me, so I can see him again. He helps me to my feet and holds my upper arms.

"Joey, I forgave you the moment you admitted what happened, even before you apologized. You told me the truth. It matches what my guys told me. I understand why you did it, even if I don't approve of it. This punishment isn't to earn my forgiveness. It's for you to understand the severity of the situation, so you get that when I give you my word about taking care of you, I mean it. That any threat to you is something I take gravely. I won't tolerate anything or anybody who jeopardizes you, including yourself. That's why you're getting punished. But my forgiveness is always unconditional."

"But how can I make amends, sir?"

"Cormac, and you've made amends by accepting your punishment. You could have refused. You could have argued with me. You could have walked out, but you didn't. You keep placing your trust in me, and I want you to trust me as much as you think you do."

"Thank you, Cormac, but I still feel like there's something I should do, some way to repay you."

"Joey, this isn't a debt. My forgiveness comes with no cost, no stipulations. I forgive you because I care about you and because I know you're a good person. You care about others. You're conscientious and giving. You're kind. You're intelligent. You're resourceful. You're brave. You take risks that'll probably shave years off my life, but I can appreciate why you do. I admire plenty about you. It's not just my physical attraction to you, so I won't hold this against you. You're still getting used to life connected to a syndicate."

This would be the perfect time for me to explain more about my life growing up in Mexico. Instead, I keep my mouth shut.

"You don't have to do anything for me. You don't have to service me to make things right between us. Like I said, you accepted the punishment, and that's all we need for amends between us."

"Thank you, Cor."

He unties the Shibari rope, then moves my arms around and rubs my tits as blood rushes back into them. He draws me over to the edge of the bed and lifts me onto it. It's not like I'm so short I couldn't do it myself. It's not like I would have to climb on like a little kid, but I enjoy being so much smaller than him, and I like how he can do that.

"Cormac, I don't want you ever to think I take for granted that you care and that you take my well-being seriously. I don't want you to think it goes unnoticed because it's not just the security detail. It's not just the punishments that show me you care. It's in the little things, like just now. We both know I could get on that bed just fine—despite how short I am—but you made it just a little easier. In the few weeks we've been together, I've seen you do that repeatedly, and I don't know if you're a nurturer by nature. I don't even know if you're a protector by nature or by nurture, but whatever the reason, I know how fortunate I am to have you treat me like that. I appreciate how you take care of me and not just protect me. You do the small things to help me out, to make me feel important."

"You are important, Joey. More so than anybody else I can think of outside of my family."

We stare at each other for a long moment before we cup each other's faces and lean in for one of our tender kisses. It doesn't turn into anything more for once. It just remains languid.

A word pops to mind that's wholly disconcerting. It's not one I've ever thought of before for a guy I've dated or who's been my Dom. Yet, for some reason, this one word seems to fit Cormac better than just sir."

"Cor...You know—"

I stumble over my words as I try to figure out how to broach this subject and whether he'll run for the hills if I say what I'm thinking.

"Joey, you know you can tell me absolutely anything, especially if it's something to do with us and improving our relationship."

"You know even though I'm short, and I enjoy playing board games, and I enjoy letting you lead, I'm not a Little, right?"

He grins down at me, then tries to smother a chuckle, which sounds like he's choking instead.

"*Cailín*, never in my wildest dreams would I think the woman who tackled me, pushed me down the stairs to protect me, stood in front of two men with guns, and then argued with me over seeing a doctor is a Little. Nothing about that makes me think you believe or want to be any age other than you are. Not when we're scening and not when we're in the regular world."

"But you are protective of me, and you call me little girl and little one. You tell me you want me to be a good girl. Do you see yourself as something other than just a regular Dom?"

He straightens and then leans back slightly as he looks at me.

"Joey, what I'd like to think of myself as is your boyfriend. I'd like to think we're building a relationship that has a future. I wouldn't have brought you anywhere near me or my family if I didn't think there's a strong probability we have a future together. I didn't say this before because I didn't want to freak you out, but I'm in this for the long haul, and I want to be your boyfriend. I'd like you to consider being my girlfriend. On top of that, we have a dynamic where I'm the protector, like you said. But I'm not a Daddy Dom. I don't want age play or anything like that. I do like the idea of you calling me Daddy, if that's what's on your mind. I don't think of myself as a paternal figure. I'm not trying to replace your father. I think of it as much a term of affection as it is when I call you *cailín* or little one or little girl. I think it fits because of our dynamic. Is that what you were thinking, too?"

"Yes, exactly. I couldn't have described it better. I want to think of myself as your girlfriend. I already hoped you're my boyfriend."

"I'm glad we agree about that. Is there anything else you want to talk about?"

"Not right now, Daddy."

The word rolls off my tongue with ease. It's only considering how easy it is to say that makes me think of my father. I never even called him Daddy. It's not the word we use in Spanish, so it conjures no image of him unless I take the moment to draw the comparison now.

"Who am I, little one?"

"Daddy. My daddy."

"That's right."

He leans toward me, boxing me in with a fist on each side of me.

"Scoot back, little one."

That voice. That tone. All of it. It excites me more than I can explain.

"I know you're innocent in the syndicates' way of life. But promise me before we move forward that you'll come to me if you're ever in doubt."

"Cormac, I will. I don't know syndicate life here in New York, but I trust you. I want you to know it wasn't lack of trust today. Just the opposite. I thought I was taking care of you by not upsetting you."

"I get that, little one."

He presses a kiss to my lips before I scoot all the way back to rest against the pillow. He stands up and strips before climbing onto the bed.

"*Cailín*, I'm about to have my way with you just the way I want it. It might be slow and smooth, or it might be fast and rough. You're going to do exactly as you're told because you're mine, and I decide. You will not come until I tell you, you can."

"Daddy, I'm a good girl. A good girl who needs to be fucked."

He thrusts hard enough for me to grip the sheets in both hands. Holy hell. If he were any deeper, he'd be pushing up my throat.

"Yeah, Daddy...Make me a good girl...Daddy, do I make you feel good?"

I don't have a clue what I'm rambling on about, but my dirty talk's making him thrust harder and grunt.

"Daddy, I'll be a good girl for that cock."

The pace he sets steals my breath for a moment, but I'm here for it.

"Ooh, Daddy, you're getting a little rough. Your cock is so big. Holy fuck!"

"And you're so fucking tight, little one. You make it so hard to last."

"I'd say you're perfectly hard."

I grin, but it ends on a moan. Neither of us speaks as we move together, our bodies in sync. I grasp his upper arms as he rocks into me. He lowers himself onto his forearm, and his left hand wraps around my throat. At first, it just rests there. As sweat beads on his brow, he squeezes incrementally. He's observing me, attuned to everything about me. Just as I feel the need to gasp, and things threaten to get fuzzy, he releases me.

"Come!"

I scream as my orgasm rips through me. He tenses above me, his face a picture of concentration. Then he smiles, and it's a ray of sunshine after a thunderstorm. He rolls off me, and that's when we both look down.

Fucking hell.

We forgot the condom.

Cormac's gaze meets mine as we both stare in horrified shock for a moment. I've always been incredibly careful and never had sex without a condom, even with guys I was in committed relationships with or Doms who I was exclusive with. I've also been on birth control since I left for college, so I've been doubly careful practically since I started having sex.

I inhale deeply and wait for Cormac to say something, unsure how pissed he might be. He must see my anxiousness because his hand reaches out and entwines our fingers.

"Little one, I get tested regularly as a member of my clubs. I can show you the results from just after Deirdre and I ended things, but I've never had sex without a condom, not once."

"Same thing, Daddy. I've only ever had sex with condoms and only twice before I went on birth control. I have an IUD, so I'm not overly concerned about that, and I have to get tested for my club too. It's been nearly six months, and I'm due for a new test, but I can show you the results from the old one."

"I believe you, Joey. From the look on your face, I have no reason not to. More like stunned surprise, shall we say?"

"You don't exactly appear unruffled either, Cormac."

We lay looking at each other for another moment, then we roll onto our sides, and he wraps his arm over my waist. I slide my thigh between his, and his hand drifts down to my ass. I love how he cups it and holds onto it.

It's one of the many ways he makes me feel precious. We go back to the gentle kisses from before. I could curl up and fall asleep right now, completely content, but my stomach grumbles and seems to trigger his because we laugh and sit up.

"Did you work up an appetite, little one?"

I glance down at his cock and lick my lips. It's an insatiable appetite. He playfully pushes me toward the edge of the bed, and when I roll over, he gives my ass a playful tap, mindful it's sore from my punishment.

Just like the other times when I've been here, I opt to remain naked after sex. We usually start our evenings when I'm here with me in lingerie I bring or just the bra I was already wearing. But once we've had sex a few times, I see no point to dressing again. If I get chilly, then he'll offer me a shirt. It's always a button down I leave open, allowing him to fondle me whenever he wants. With our around the clock dynamic, he has free use. With how often the man has his dick inside me, I've never felt so desired or desirable in my life.

We head out to the kitchen, and I grab the apron he bought for me—since I'm usually mostly naked—before we make dinner together. Safety first.

Our defining conversation was a week ago. We've been seeing each other for nearly a month now, and this is the happiest I've been in a long time. Even people at work have asked what's different. I don't know whether I'm supposed to tell people about Cormac specifically. I'm evasive, only saying I'm seeing somebody new, and it's too soon to talk about it since I don't want to jinx it, which isn't entirely far from the truth.

Ever since my first punishment and then having sex without a condom, we've admitted how much better it is. I love the feeling of his cum on the inside of my thighs when I wake up in the morning. He orders me not to move after we have sex, so his cum remains in me like a brand. Sometimes he'll command me to flex my pussy, so a bit dribbles out.

"Martha, do you have the file ready for the Horowitz case?"

I'm at work, and I can't daydream any longer, or I'll be late to a mediation.

"Yeah, it's on my desk. Give me a moment, and I'll grab it for you."

Today is one of the few days when I need to head into Manhattan for work. Mostly, I'm able to stay on Staten Island for school and home visits. This is the case with the woman who screamed at me and slapped me. The court that has jurisdiction is in Manhattan. Once I have the file tucked away in my bag, I meet my guys outside.

Both of them and Cormac grumbled this morning when I insisted it would be much easier to take the subway into the city from the outer borough. Where I need to be in Manhattan makes parking even trickier than usual. There aren't many garages in the area that'll be empty at this time of day, and there'll be next to no street parking. It'd be the eighth wonder of the world if there were.

That's means one guy would have to keep circling the block because you can't double park. If he's doing that, then that leaves me with only one bodyguard. Just hinting at that practically sent Cormac into a conniption. He relented and agreed we could take the subway, but he had some very specific protocols he ran through with me, and I had to agree to.

It's easy enough making our way into Manhattan, and fortunately, the mediation was fairly easy, at least until the exchange between the woman and me came up. We almost had a repeat of what happened out on the street. This time her attorney and the court officer convinced her it wouldn't be in her best interest to take a swing at the court-appointed social worker who plays a significant role in determining whether she loses custody of her kid. I meet with two other social workers from different boroughs before I can call the day quits.

"Okay, Malcolm, I'm all done and ready to head out."

I greet one of my guards who's waiting outside the door. That was an interesting explanation I had to give when we arrived. I didn't expect the guys to make it through security since I'm pretty positive they're at least carrying knives if not a gun holstered at their lower backs. One look at their driver's licenses made the security guards at the metal detector turn a blind eye. Once again, my don't ask, don't tell policy was in place. They haven't been inside my office, so I haven't had to explain them there. They've stayed close in the parking lot, but they haven't had to come in with me.

Malcolm, who vaguely resembles Cormac except with dark hair and dark eyes—apparently, he's an O'Rourke on Cormac's dad's side and their third cousin four times removed or something like that. Even Cormac couldn't remember how they're related—speaks into his earpiece, and we wait for Billy to show up.

With Billy in front of me and Malcolm behind me, I'm securely sandwiched between them while my left and right sides are unprotected. I know Billy's hyper aware of what's in front of us, and Malcolm frequently checks over his shoulder behind us. If anything were to happen, Cormac explained Billy would be my shield in front of me, and that if Malcolm pushes me to the ground, I'm not to resist. He'll cover my body with his.

Fortunately, no one's tested that, but I can tell from how vigilant they are and how loyal they are to Cormac, they wouldn't think twice before putting themselves in harm's way for me. It's not the easiest pill to swallow; however, I won't be unappreciative, since it makes me feel a lot more confident now that I'm with Cormac. While I don't speak about him specifically at work, we've been out and seen in public together, so it's no secret we're involved. I don't know who's seen us and who it might matter to, but Cormac's attentiveness to my safety lets me breathe easier.

The sidewalk is extra congested along this block because the opposite side is closed where they're repairing the concrete. People jostle me from each side, and Billy and Malcolm barely allow two inches between us. When we reach a street corner, I'm practically knocked off my feet as a guy pushes me out of the way to avoid a cyclist he stepped in front of. Malcolm catches me and keeps me on my feet.

"Are you all right Ms. Bracero?"

"Yes, thank you. Just another regular day in the city."

"Yeah, but the guy could have at least said excuse me."

I grin at Billy as he looks back over his shoulder to speak.

"True, but not everyone grew up with the O'Rourke etiquette."

It's obvious good manners were drilled into most of these men probably since conception. I'm pretty positive they know they'd lose at least a finger or their tongue if Cormac believed they were anything besides perfectly courteous, professional, and respectful to me.

We make it down to the subway platform. It's almost the evening rush hour, so it's filling up even more than it was when we got off here a few hours ago. Malcolm stands beside me while Billy goes to the other door of the car we're going to enter. Billy steps in quickly and assesses the occupants before looking over at Malcolm and nodding. I'm about to step into the car with Malcolm when a guy getting off slams into my shoulder, pushing me back three steps.

I try to get around him, but we do the stupid dance of each moving in the same direction. After it happens twice, my spidey sense is on alert. This doesn't feel normal.

"Excuse me."

I'm brusque as I point to my right and move to step around him. However, he pretends not to hear me as he pulls his phone from his pocket. The doors to the subway car close with both of my guards on it. I watch in mild panic as the train departs. The guy who was in front of me has now disappeared as I look around. He vanished into the crowd.

How convenient.

Something is massively wrong about this.

I slide my hand into my pocket and wrap my hand around my non-metallic pocketknife—the kind that doesn't set off metal detectors. Cormac isn't the only one who carries a weapon with him, but I'm yet to admit that to him. No doubt I'll be telling him tonight. I sweep my gaze around the platform as it empties. I'm too exposed here to wait for the next car or for the guys to come back for me. I head up the escalator to the street level and make my way toward the building I just came out of.

From the corner of my eye, I recognize the guy who stepped in my way. He's completely nondescript. He's about as average as a man can be. Dirty blond hair, a bland shade of brown eyes, medium height, medium weight. Nothing memorable about him besides being unmemorable. Nothing about his appearance tells me if he might be from another syndicate.

He's walking in the same direction as I am. As I approach the building, I notice a guy who flicks his gaze toward that man then me. My intuition screams to go the other way. I dart across the street, jaywalking and not giving a shit about it. Two cars honk as I weave past them. Luckily, traffic's bad enough nobody's driving that fast.

I spot the public library half a block away. Since I'm so short, I know I easily blend into the crowd. When I get to the library, I check over my shoulder as I run up the steps. Those men are still following me, now much more purposefully. However, they're far enough behind I get into the building and bolt to the children's section, then into the men's restroom. Fortunately, from being here before, I know it's a single. I hope nobody needs the changing station.

I came in here because I pray they assume it's unlikely I would hide in a men's room rather than a ladies' room. I pull out my phone and tap it awake before tapping on Cormac's contact. It rings four times before going to voicemail.

Come on, Cormac, answer.

I hang up and dial again. I go through this two more times before he answers.

"Joey, what's wrong?"

"I got separated from my guards, Cor. I'm in the public library in Manhattan."

"How'd that happen?"

"We were getting on the subway, and everything was fine until this guy getting off bumped into me and knocked me backwards. Then he stood in my way, blocking me each time I tried to get around him until the car doors closed. Billy'd already gotten on to check it out, and Malcolm had just stepped on as I got pushed backwards."

"What did you notice about the guy?"

"That he's perfectly boring. There's nothing that makes me think Russian, Italian or Colombian. He doesn't even make me think of any other type of Latino. He's average, with no distinguishing features. When I was about to turn to go back into the building where I had my meeting to call you, I noticed another man standing at the bottom of the steps, who looked over at the same guy. I don't know what's going on, but I knew I couldn't go past the second guy to get into the building, and I knew I didn't want the first one coming up behind me. I crossed the street and made my way here."

"You blended into the crowd?"

"Yes. But, Daddy, they followed me. I know they must be in here now. I'm hiding in the men's room in the children's section. I've got the door locked, and I'm as far away from it as I can be."

I've whispered this whole time, so I don't think anybody who might stand on the other side of the door can hear me.

"Stay right where you are, little one."

"Yes, Daddy."

"It'll take me a little while to get there because I'm in Queens right now, but my parents aren't that far away. I'm going to send them to you."

"No, Cormac. These guys might be dangerous. I don't want your parents involved. I'll just wait here until you can send other guards or call Billy or Malcolm and let them know where I am."

"I'm doing that anyway, but I'm still sending my parents to you."

"But your mom—"

"Joey, don't argue with me, and heaven help anybody who comes near you while my mom is around. They'd do well to fear her far more than they fear my father."

That makes me smile since it reminds me of my parents. "All right, Cormac."

"I'm going to get off the phone with you just long enough to call my parents and to call the guys, then I'll call you back as soon as I'm done."

"All right, Daddy."

It's only when we hang up I realize I've used the term of affection I've saved either for our scenes or playfully when we're hanging out. I'm scared, and it just slipped out.

It feels like hours as the minutes tick by.

This reminds me of when I was nine, and I got separated

from my parents in a plaza in a town a couple hours away from where I grew up. We were there because *papá* had a business meeting. Since it was on the beach, he brought my mom, Santiago, and me along with him. Santiago was already at the beach with a couple of guys who were sons of men *papá* was meeting with.

It was super crowded that day, and the sun was so bright it reflected off almost every surface, dazzling me when I tried to look around. When I stopped to tie my shoe, I had to let go of my mom's hand. She stayed with me until I stood up, but then a couple of guys stepped between us.

My parents always told me if I ever got lost, I was to stay exactly where I was, and they would come back to find me. However, even at that young an age, I understood the men who separated me from my mom weren't just regular townspeople. I knew they'd done it on purpose, so I ran.

It only took one look for me to know they were *soldados*—cartel soldiers. I didn't know if they planned to take me to a *sicario*—hitman—or a *sanguinario*—"the blood thirsty one"—"the blood drinker"—the butcher who'd hack me to pieces and leave me for the flies and crows. It wasn't like my young mind ran away from me. At nine, I was old enough to understand I was just as likely to wind up with a *timador*—intimidator—someone who'd extort my wealthy parents.

My worst fear, as I ran through those streets, was winding up with an *escopalaminero*. That's a man hired to drug someone with scopolamine. I didn't know the drug's name back then, but I'd heard it would make someone sleepy enough to do whatever their kidnappers said, but it would keep them awake enough to answer questions. It was like a "truth serum." I feared they'd ask me things I didn't know the answer to, or worse things I knew but wasn't supposed to. Then—either way—I'd definitely wind up with a *sicario* or *sanguinario*.

My family had men with us too, but they were too far away for me to get to them. I was too short even then for them to see me in the crowd. I remember weaving among the people and running down side streets to double back until I could get to where I knew we were headed. By the time I got there, two of my dad's security guards were already in place outside the building.

I bolted straight to them. It was Paco, my dad's most trusted security guard, who caught me when I almost tripped up the steps in my rush to get to them. They radioed my dad, and my parents came to get me surrounded by all their bodyguards. My mom wouldn't let go of me for the next three hours even when we sat together safely in our hotel room.

After that, my father insisted I learn to defend myself. Over the years, there were times I got hurt while practicing, so I learned to come up with excuses for my teachers. Admitting I needed to learn to protect myself from would-be kidnappers would've brought far more attention than my periodic bruises and two cases of nursemaid's elbow.

I'm waiting here in the bathroom for Cormac to come and get me, then hold my hand just like my mom did. I refuse to panic until there's a reason to panic, but I'm pretty fucking close. This has unnerved the hell out of me because I can't tell who the guys were. The second one I spotted was just as unremarkable as the first.

I freeze when there's a knock on the door, then I pull my knife from my pocket and flick it open. I don't make a sound until there's another knock. I creep a bit closer to the door.

"Jocelyn, this is Kieran O'Rourke. I'm Cormac's dad."

"*Prátaí*." Potato.

"*Cabáiste*." Cabbage.

The two words are the code Cormac taught me. If I say anything different or I get any other response, it means it's not safe to open the door. I unlock it, keeping the knife down at my side until I can peek through the small opening. I put it behind me and flick it closed, keeping it in my palm. It's small enough to hide easily when I open the door all the way and step out.

"Are you all right, Jocelyn?"

"Yes, Mr. O'Rourke. Thank you."

This man looks like he could be Cormac and Seamus's older brother rather than their father. Their hair is almost the same shade of strawberry blond, but slightly darker. The man has the most piercing blue eyes I've ever seen. They're just as impressive as Cormac's, even if they don't match in color.

A woman moves behind him, and I shift my attention to her. She's positively stunning. Her russet hair falls in thick waves around her shoulders, and the exact hue of emerald-colored eyes as Cormac's stare back at me. While his build, posture, and hair remind me of his dad, that intensity in his gaze definitely comes from his mom. I realize that what I thought was a penetrating stare a moment ago when I looked up at his dad makes the man look like a pussycat compared to the woman in front of me.

"Did they get near you? Did they touch you? Did they say anything to you?"

She rapid fires the questions, and all I can do is shake my head. Immediately, her entire posture relaxes, and she offers me the most maternal smile I've ever seen. I almost burst into tears when she opens her arms just slightly, and Cormac's dad steps out of the way. I fall into her embrace, and she engulfs me in a hug. She's a virtual stranger to me, yet this is almost as comforting as my mom hugging me.

From everything Cormac's told me about his family, I feel like I already know his parents, but I'm definitely a stranger to them.

"Jocelyn, Cormac's almost here. He'll come straight inside,

but I want to move you to another part of the library now that we've arrived. I don't know where these men are or if they saw you come in here."

I turn my head to look at Cormac's dad as he speaks, but I don't leave his mom's embrace until she gives me a quick squeeze and a pat on my back. I step away only to have her wrap her arm around my waist, and Cormac's dad's arm goes around my shoulders. Not only is it a show of solidarity, but I realize they're now functioning as my bodyguards. His mom is just as attentive as his dad, and it dawns on me just how deeply entrenched she's been in the mob.

If her father was once the boss, and so was her brother, and now her nephew is too, this is a woman who's seen some shit.

We head over to one of the study rooms that has a glass wall but solid door. When we get inside, Mr. O'Rourke positions himself to shield both his wife and me through the glass windows. Three guys materialize from the stacks and stand in front of the glass wall as well.

That doesn't look suspicious or intimidating at all.

It's not like they're relaxed and shooting the shit. It's clear they're bodyguards.

"Jocelyn, Cormac told Kieran there was nothing distinguishable about either man. Is that what's so memorable about them?"

Mrs. O'Rourke's voice is quiet, but there's no ignoring the woman when she speaks to you. It's straight up no nonsense.

"Yes. There's nothing that made me think they belong to a particular syndicate. I never heard either of them speak, so I couldn't tell you if there was an accent. None of their facial features made me think of a particular stereotype. Do you think it's possible they're men someone hired to frighten me?"

"That's entirely possible. I don't know." Her honesty is

jarring and completely the opposite of how reassuring her hug was.

"The guy who was in front of me as he got off the train pulled out his phone as if to ignore me when he finally stepped around me. He only glanced at it. He didn't answer it or anything. If he and the other guy spoke as they followed me, I was too far away to hear anything."

Mr. O'Rourke twists to look back at us. "Could you describe anything about their clothing?"

I nod. It's probably going to freak them out just how detailed I can be.

"Yes, I can."

I'm just about to explain when I spot motion over Mr. O'Rourke's shoulder. It's Cormac, and he's clearly on a mission. As much as I want to burst through the door and run to him, I know better than that. It's the best way to make us all easy targets. So, I wait until he comes through the door. Then I'm in his arms. His parents step away, giving us a moment of privacy.

He twists us so his back is to everybody. Once again, shielding me like he always does, which is a good thing because the kiss we share is not anything anybody should watch. It's a good thing he has a suit coat on that's buttoned. Otherwise, the entire world would know just how hard he got in the space of two seconds. The moment he slides his hand up my skirt, he'll know how wet he made me.

"*Cailín*, I'm so glad you're okay. That terrified me."

"You and me both. Daddy, thank you so much for coming for me and for sending your parents."

"Of course, little one, I'll always come for you."

He winks at the double entendre, and it melts the last dregs of fear. I waggle my eyebrows at him, and he relaxes, happy to see I'm not panicked.

"We're going to go to my parents' house. My brother and cousins are going to meet us there."

"All right."

I know it's not like I have a choice, so it wouldn't matter if that wasn't what I wanted. However, I'll go anywhere Cormac goes right now, as long as we stay together.

When he slips his hand into mine and intertwines our fingers, once again, I feel like I can breathe. That same sense of relief I had when I was a little girl and my mom took my hand after getting separated from my parents is back, but it only lasts for a moment before it morphs into something different because it's Cormac I'm with.

As I look up at him, he brushes the pad of his thumb over my cheek and gazes down at me. We're not alone, so neither of us is going to say what we're thinking, but I think it's the same thing. I hope he understands from my expression. He mouths the word "later," and now I'm sure he does.

I dip my chin before he kisses me again, this one just a soft brushing of our lips. We head outside with a swarm of guards around us. Billy and Malcolm are waiting near a car, and Mr. and Mrs. O'Rourke have their own bodyguards, plus men who came with Cormac. It feels like a small army. I'm certainly not going to complain. His parents get into an SUV while Cormac and I climb into a town car.

Any time we've ridden in one, the privacy glass is always up before we even get in. This time is no different. We've fucked in the backseat of them numerous times now, and he's reassured me we're hardly the only couple in his family to do that, and that's part of the reason they keep the fleet so pristine.

That made my nose curl and made him chuckle.

Right now, I know just like every other time we ride together, I should sit in my seat with my belt on. Irrationally, I feel far safer being in Cormac's arms, having him hold on to me as I sit on his lap, than I do being by myself, even just a few inches from him.

We don't say anything, just embrace, and that's what I need right now. I need a respite from this and the opportunity to let my mind rest and my emotions settle because I can only imagine the hell that's about to break loose once Cormac decides what to do next.

Chapter Eighteen

Cormac

When we get to my parents' house and walk in, we find my aunts already there. After a round of introductions, which included properly introducing Joey to my parents, my dad gives my mom a kiss rivaling the one I gave Joey when I got to her in the library, and my mom wasn't even in any danger. He gives me a quick hug and offers Joey one, too.

Then he takes off for a meeting with my uncles that's been on the calendar for weeks. My mom and aunts practically yank Joey from me, and within moments have her laughing hysterically at my expense. You will never find three women more devoted to their family than my mom and aunts, and part of that devotion includes teasing the men in our family ruthlessly and mercilessly.

Even my ears are aflame. I can feel heat radiating from my cheeks, my forehead, even my chin as I listen to them tell stories about me from when I was little. The kindest thing any of them have said about me so far is Aunt Siobhan calling me precocious.

Tears stream down Joey's face as she listens to these stories, and I'd do anything to melt into the floor. It's hardly the best light I'd like my girlfriend to see me in. But hearing her laughter and seeing her smile after I know how scared she was today is everything to me. So, if they want to have a hearty laugh at my expense, I can live with that.

By the time Seamus arrives with Finn and Shane, I'm ready to escape into my dad's study. We wait there for Dillan and Sean to arrive. Then we close the door to the sound of the women clinking wine glasses together.

Lord, that's all I need is my mom and aunts getting my girl-friend sloshed. I should have warned her they can drink all of us under the table. They've been imbibing Irish whiskey since they were old enough to hold their own sippy cups. It almost tempts me to go back and warn Joey, but I know she's in excellent hands with them.

I turn my attention to my brother and cousins.

"I want to know who the feck did this to Joey. I want them at the station in the next thirty minutes." I know that's an unrealistic expectation, but my temper is about to get the better of me.

"I'm already working on it, Cor."

I nod to Dillan, and I believe him, but that doesn't make me any less impatient.

"If I have to scour the streets on my own to find these moth-erfeckers, I will. There's no way this was some accident or some coincidence. They definitely targeted Joey."

"We don't doubt that, Cor. But the little you gave us in the texts isn't enough to really get a solid picture of who we're looking for."

"I know, but it's the best we have right now."

"We're working with what we have. It's just not much."

I turn my attention to Finn, who cocks an eyebrow at me as he asks the sixty-four-thousand-dollar question.

"Do you have any idea who?"

"Of course, I have some thoughts on who it might've been, but I have no proof it was actually them."

"Does that mean you assume it was Pablo?"

"That's certainly the first person who comes to mind, if not one of his fucknut relatives."

"I know you've said Jocelyn was on his radar for a while, and he taunted you by saying she was involved with Javier. But that's a pretty massive jump to make from suggesting she's fecking the guy to actually having two of his guys approach her. Do you really think it's come to that? Is he that pissed about us being in their neighborhoods? Is Jocelyn really of that kind of value to him?"

"I don't know, Finn. I don't have an answer to any of that, but I sure as hell plan to ask and find out."

"And if it wasn't him?"

Seamus quirks a brow just like Finn did. It's one of those nature versus nurture things. We don't even realize when we're doing it. It's an inherited paternal family trait, an expression we all share.

"Well, if it wasn't Pablo or even Javier, who else do you think tops the list?" I sweep my gaze around the table as I look at the guys.

The list of candidates is so long, we could put each name on individual sheets of an entire roll of toilet paper, which is fitting because whoever did this is on my shitlist.

"Well, I suppose we won't know unless we ask." Dillan pulls out his phone as he speaks.

I listen to it ring as he holds it up, so we can see the name on the screen.

"What do you want, *niño?*"

"It's a pleasure to hear your voice, *cucho.*" Old man.

"I'm in the middle of something. What do you want?"

"I can guess what you mean by that. I'd call back at another time if I could, but this is important. Why'd Pablo send guys after her?"

"Who?"

Enrique's clearly not interested in playing guessing games. We all know that tone. We've known the guy since we were infants. Most of us can remember him since we were toddlers. He was the cool uncle who used to bring the unhealthy snacks to soccer games when he was filling in for his brother and sister-in-law.

However, once we each turned twelve and our parents gave us our own pocketknives—that's a fucked-up tradition in all Four Families—things changed. He was no longer the cool uncle, but the guy who issued orders to have the shite beaten out of us by his psychotic, reprobate nephews.

"Get on with it, Dillan. Spit it out, whatever it is you want to know."

"Why'd Pablo send men after Cormac's girlfriend?"

There's a long pause that unnerves me, and it takes a lot to do that. I look around the table, and all the guys shrug before I look down at Dillan's phone where he put it on the table since he has the call on speaker. Just when I'm about to ask Enrique if he's still there, he speaks up.

"Cormac, undoubtedly, you're listening to this call as well. If you're asking me whether it was Pablo or one of my other nephews who did this, then you don't know her nearly well enough. I'd have a conversation with your little girlfriend and get a little more information about her family tree. Don't look to mine as the scapegoats for this."

"I'm not looking for a scapegoat. I'm looking for the perpetrator."

"Well, you can look for whomever the hell you want. You just won't find them in my family."

"So, Port Richmond's not still pissing off you and Pablo?"

"Pablo and I are definitely still pissed about that, but your girlfriend isn't how we'll get our retribution. Remember, our families are not the same."

Seamus grimaces before he chimes in. "Yeah, our family owns up to our transgressions. We don't wallow in hypocrisy. Maybe you haven't fecked over any women recently, but your nephews sure have. So, don't play as though your family is any better than the rest of ours."

That leaves Enrique quiet for a moment because, unless he's going to deny the truth in that or lie, there's nothing he can say to refute my brother. We know how much it irritates the other families when we say feck instead of fuck, so we throw it in for extra measure. They may taunt us about it, but that just means our provocation works.

"Look, Cormac, I'd talk to her about her family because it seems like there's still plenty for you to learn. But in the meantime, I'd ask Niko what he's been up to lately."

"Niko? Why him?"

"From what I understand, your little scheme in court last week cost him two million dollars, so I'd say he's probably pretty pissed right now."

"Do you think he'd take his anger out on my girlfriend?"

"I think they're not as perfect as they want everybody to believe."

"That's true. But I have a hard time believing two million dollars is enough for them to break their cardinal rule since they're the only family who hasn't targeted women and children outright. They may have disturbed the peace and caused some fights, but they've never endangered any of the women."

"Okay, *niño*, if you say so."

I can practically hear Enrique rolling his eyes. I can picture the disdainful look on his face without even seeing him. I've witnessed it enough times over the past three decades.

"If I find out you're lying, Enrique, and your nephews have anything to do with this, you'll discover why everybody believes I have the worst temper in the family."

It's not true. None of us really have a bad temper, but because Seamus and I have always been so much bigger than everyone else and grew taller than most of the kids in our class by second grade, it was easy for us to cultivate a reputation for having the shortest fuse. That, coupled with our size, means people leave us alone when, in fact, we're really the shyest of the family and don't want people picking on us for it.

That reputation stuck with us thanks to our role in the boss's family. Neither Seamus nor I intend to change it anytime soon, so I play upon it to my benefit.

"Simmer down, *niño*. Make your call and speak to Niko, then speak to Jocelyn."

It's one of the few times I've heard anybody say her full name with a Spanish accent yet. The huh sound rather than the juh, and the long vowels sounds seems so fitting when I think of her. Soft to start, but strong to the end. I love her accent. Even though she speaks perfect English, and it's pretty neutral, it's still noticeably there. Pablo and his cousin Alejandro have the New York Spanish speakers' accent, but *Tres J's*—Javier, Joaquin, and Jorge—and Enrique have a similar accent to Joey's.

All four men and Joey grew up speaking Spanish before speaking English somewhere besides America, and the few times I've heard Joey speak Spanish are about the sexiest things I've ever heard. The way she rolls her r's makes me think of what her tongue does when she's sucking me off. That's hardly the direction my mind needs to go in right now.

Dillan hangs up with Enrique, and I sit back in my seat. He asks what everyone's probably thinking.

"Are you going to go talk to her right now?"

"No, not yet. Tonight, when we're at home."

"Home?" Shane's smirk makes me want to slap it right off of his face.

"Don't even give me any shite about this. I was the last man standing until a month ago. How all the mighty have fallen. You've all said and done the exact same things, so don't give me grief when I learned from the rest of you."

I point to each of them as I speak. All five guys grin at me and nod.

"Should we call Niko?"

Shane speaks up, bringing us back to the subject. I noticed him glancing at his watch a few times. Something must be going on with Carys that's making him want to leave because normally he's not so impatient.

"Do you need to go somewhere?"

"Not yet, but I want to be home when Carrie gets back. She got called in for another interview. I think they're going to try to make her testify, even though she gave up her badge."

My cousin-in-law was a former federal agent who had to give up her job in order to be with Shane, considering her agency's sole mission is to crack down on people like us since they run drug interdiction. Things didn't go smoothly when she was leaving her position, but every once in a while she's still getting called back into the office. She goes willingly rather than have a judge compel her to show up. Shane likes to be home when she gets there after days like that because he knows that just like us, she won't show her feelings, but those meetings always upset her.

"Okay, let's call him now and get this over with."

I pull out my phone, but Dillan shakes his head.

"No, we'll call from mine again."

It's not just to avoid being obvious we're calling about Joey if he has anything to do with it. I know some of it is the weight that comes from him being the mob boss. The guys from the other families are more likely to answer when it's him. He's right. I don't need to play my hand quite yet by Niko seeing my number on his caller ID.

That's part of how fucked-up this world is. We've had each other's numbers in our phones since we were kids. Not only that, we've had each other on speed dial, and we were among each other's first non-family contacts. When we all got cell phones, we were young enough to still get along well and were naive enough to think there was a possibility we could be friends. All of us got phones younger than most people would think was appropriate, but considering the danger in which we all grew up, our parents knew just having us wear trackers wasn't enough. We needed a way to call for help just like Joey did today.

"What do you want, Dillan?"

"Top of the afternoon to you too, Niko."

"Cut the crap. What do you want?"

There's a time and a place for bullshitting, and most of the time it's not when we're dealing with other syndicates. I'm used to Niko's brusqueness, and so is Dillan. He ignores it as he carries on.

"I hear you've taken a bit of an interest in the newest addition to our family."

"Why the hell would I care about the dog Shane got his wife?"

"That's not who I meant."

"What other recent addition to the family do you have?"

"Niko, as dumb as you look, nobody here thinks you're stupid, so don't act like it. You know just as well as everybody else in the other families that Cormac has a girlfriend. So, what's the deal?"

"What do you mean, what's the deal? Shouldn't you ask your cousin what the deal is? I don't know what he's been up to with her—at least I don't want to—even though I can guess."

"Yeah, the same thing you're always up to with your wife. But why is Jocelyn important enough to you to pay attention?"

"I don't know what the hell you're talking about, Dillan. You make no sense, even less than usual. It's a bit early for you to have been dipping into the whiskey."

"Two guys followed her today, Niko, and I have it on good authority you're still pissed at my cousin. Scaring his girlfriend would be a great way to get back at him."

"What would I be pissed at Cormac about?"

"Don't be obtuse, Niko. The two million you guys just lost in litigation."

"If anybody's pissed about that, it's Laura. That was her case. Despite that, you know she won't go after another woman. And as I recall, you might have gotten the two-million-dollar settlement, but you forfeited far more in property value. I'd say the win goes to my sister-in-law, not you or your deadbeat cousin."

He's not entirely wrong. His sister-in-law, Laura, is married to his oldest brother, the *pakhan*—the bratva's leader. She's a legal shark—ruthless and vicious. She worked in corporate law for years before meeting and marrying Maksim. Now she represents all the bratva's legal enterprises. If she were married to anybody other than that arsehole, I'd fully respect her. She and I have gone back and forth in court before.

I handle our corporate cases, and Seamus handles our criminal. He has his own equivalent to Laura, but she's *Cosa Nostra*. Sinead Scotto is Gabriele's wife. He's their chief enforcer. She and Laura went to law school together along with Lorenzo Mancinelli's wife. Sinead can smell blood in the water from a mile away. She's not somebody to underestimate any more than anyone should underestimate Laura Kutsenko.

Dillan senses I'm getting impatient. He holds his right hand up and pats the air, telling me to hang on. I take a breath before I dive in.

"Niko, if you're not pissed at me, and I'm not pissed at Laura, then why follow Jocelyn?"

"I didn't have anybody follow her. I don't know what you're talking about, and I resent the accusation. There are plenty of other people who loathe you just as much as I do. There are plenty of other candidates for who would want to fuck around with your girlfriend. Remember my family isn't your family. We still have boundaries."

"Sure, you do."

"Whatever, Cormac. I'm about to have dinner with my wife, and she's far more interesting than you are. I gotta go."

Before I can say anything, he hangs up, and I'm more than fine ending the call that way. However, we're back to square one as I look around the table.

"Well, that leaves the Mancinellis. Which one of those dickwads do you think it was?"

Sean's been typing away at his computer, so he doesn't look up as he speaks. I know he's had street camera footage pulled up on his screen while we've been on the phone. He spins his laptop toward me and points to Joey on the steps up to the library. Then he points to two figures half a block away. He zooms in, but the picture gets too grainy to recognize faces. At least we have an idea of what they look like.

Finn leans forward to peer more closely at the pictures. "Sean, send me those files. I'll see what I can do to clean them up a bit."

Sean's grad degree in national security means he can find a country's nuclear codes and keep them a secret from even the devil. But Finn is the one with the degree in computer science. Between his forensic hacking skills, regular programming skills, and overall computer knowledge, and Sean's high-level international organization hacking skills, there's not much we can't find out. Sean nods to his older brother.

Dillan slips his phone back into his pocket and rests his forearms on the table as our gazes meet. "What do you want to do now, Cormac?"

"I guess there isn't much to do until I speak to Joey and find out what Enrique meant about her family tree."

"What're you going to do if you don't like what you find? You know I ran the background check on her, but there wasn't a whole lot to know beyond where she grew up and what universities she went to until she got here a few years ago. Not all the record keeping is that great in the part of Mexico she's from."

"I know there were no red flags with her, and I don't think there are any now, but I'll talk to her when we're alone. Then we'll go from there. Thank you guys for coming so fast."

I know my thanks aren't necessary for my brother and cousins, but good manners dictate I say as much, and my appreciation is always genuine. People may say Seamus and I have the best manners—even if we supposedly have the shortest temper—but we had the same manners drilled into us as everybody else. We were just the ones no one ever had to tell to write and send thank you cards.

We were also the ones who stayed out of trouble the longest, but that's because we're the shyest in the group and never felt the need to lead the charge. We're not followers, but we're also smart enough to survey the scene before diving in.

"Do you guys want to stay for dinner? Shane, I know you need to get home to Carys, but what about the rest of you? I'm sure Mom'll have enough for everybody. Do you want to have the girls come over too?"

Since our three sets of parents still have open-door policies, it would be no surprise if everybody showed up even though it's not my parents' night to host Sunday dinner.

"You don't think meeting the entire family in one day won't be too much for Jocelyn after the scare she had?"

"Maybe. I'll ask her what she wants. We can go from there."

We stayed for dinner, and the wives came over just before my dad and uncles returned. Joey took everything in stride, but she's nearly asleep as we drive home.

Home.

My place.

Our place.

That's how I'd like to think of it. I've gone over to her apartment a few times, but we mostly wind up at my house in Boerum Hills. It's a quiet area in Brooklyn; hardly what most people would expect for a mobster bachelor. Only Finn lived in the city—Soho—for the urban life. Seamus and Shane lived in East Harlem, but that neighborhood's vibe isn't the same as the main part of Manhattan. Shane was already in Queens, and Dillan was in Brooklyn, too.

We prefer the relative solitude rather than the constant noise and lights in Manhattan. Members of the other families lived in Manhattan before marrying and moving back to the two neighborhoods we grew up in. Dillan's house sits on the corner where they meet. From the outside looking in, it probably appears like a massive syndicate compound with that many individual residences all next door to each other.

"*Cailín*, we're home."

Her eyes flutter open, and she offers me a sleepy smile. It's sexy as fuck, but she's exhausted. As much as I want to discuss her family now that we're at the house, it won't be productive. She knows to wait for me to open her door, so I walk around to her side. Even though we're in my garage, she knows I won't take any chances.

"Do you want to go straight to bed, little one?"

She nods, but she perks up. I know that expression. We haven't spent a night together without having sex before we fall asleep. We're yanking each other's clothes off before we even make it to the bedroom. It won't be the first time we have to pick up a trail of clothes in the morning. Our foreplay is the kissing we share as I back her into the room.

Tonight, we go slow. It's entirely vanilla. I've discovered I enjoy it as much as our kinky sex. It'd been years—college—since I had vanilla. Once I discovered what I was into, I looked for partners who wanted the same. No woman I was with once I got into BDSM tempted me. Even when things weren't fully kinky, there was always an element of power exchange. Right now, Joey and I are equals, and it's erotic as hell.

We're breathless and spent when we're done—with this round. We haven't made it through the night without a couple rounds. Joey snuggles into my chest as I spoon her. We're both asleep within minutes, but my last thought before I doze off is that my cum is inside her. It brands her as mine.

MINE.

God help anyone who takes her from me.

Chapter Nineteen

Joey

Yesterday was a day I could've lived without. I'm not loving the conversation Cormac and I are having right now any more than I did my terrified sprint into the public library. I have to tread lightly because I don't know how much I can share.

"Why would Enrique tell me to ask you about your family tree?"

I knew that question was coming once he told me he spoke to Enrique at his parents' house. I fight the urge to fidget. This is when I should admit everything. But I don't know where things are going with Cormac. I want to tell him I love him, and I think that's what he wanted to say yesterday, but we weren't alone. Love isn't enough to convince me to share my family tree or history. If Cormac and I aren't planning a definite future together, then it isn't worth saying anything. But if we are planning a future together, and I don't tell him, it'll all go up in a roaring blaze. It'd be way worse than a puff of smoke.

"I'm certain he knows what part of Mexico I'm from. It's

impossible not to know how the cartels work there. Some of my mom's side of the family has been there for six generations, and my dad's side has been there even longer."

I'm hedging, and I'm certain he knows it. He observes me, and I know he's giving me the chance to come clean. I offer him nothing, and I keep my expression neutral. I want to give nothing away. But maybe not being more expressive tells him more than my silence.

"Cormac, my family's wealthy. It's inevitable they've had contact with the cartels. Enrique's fishing."

I'm certain of the last part. The first part isn't untrue either.

"What does your father do?"

"He's the CEO of an investment firm." My parents trained me to say that as soon as I was old enough to understand that question.

"And your mom?"

"She owns an art gallery."

"Did you and your brother move here at the same time?"

I shake my head. "I came a couple years before him. He came for work, then his MBA. He's in his last year at Columbia. I left Mexico and went straight into grad school here. He took a few years off between undergrad and grad school."

My heart's racing even though I keep my breathing steady. I need to change the topic fast.

"What does your mom do?"

"She's an orthodontist."

That surprises me. I don't know why, but it does.

"No wonder everyone's teeth are perfect in your family."

It's true. They could all be on a toothpaste or teeth whitening commercial.

"Yeah, well, we all had braces around the same time, so I

don't think anyone ate a potato chip in our family for three years. It wasn't worth facing her with a broken bracket."

"Is—is—"

"Yes, my dad and uncles are in, but they're as retired as one can be. With six sons among them, the three of them stepped back once all of us were in our positions."

He only offers that, so I don't ask. It's one thing for me to know his family is mob. It's another to poke around.

This is the first time we've been at a loss for what to say next. We've talked about our families before, but we've studiously stayed away from his dad's occupation, so he hasn't asked me about my parents'. Because I didn't think I should ask about his dad, I didn't ask about his mom either.

"What would you like to do today, little one?"

My heart slows now that we're moving on. "I don't know. It's a nice day out. Do you want to go for a run?"

"Sure."

I've started keeping some clothes here since I come over at least twice a week, and I spend most of the weekend here. I have a toothbrush, a bottle of perfume, and a contact case and saline in his bathroom. He has my favorite kind of cereal on top of his fridge and my preferred flavors of Greek yogurt inside. I've kept a toothbrush at a few guys' places, but I've never arrived one day and found foods I like in their fridge. It makes me think Cormac wants something long term, but we still haven't defined our relationship beyond we're dating exclusively and are sexually monogamous.

We change and head out. The sun's bright and warm with a light breeze. It's perfect. I know it has to be hot for Cormac since he's wearing a sweatshirt. I know he has his gun holstered at his lower back. I don't know how that's comfortable. Maybe he's just so used to it he doesn't think about it.

When we get to the end of the first block, we have to stop

for the light. I glance back and recognize Finn jogging toward us.

"Cor, Finn's coming."

"I know. I texted him while you were in the bathroom. He's joining us on the run. I don't feel comfortable not having guards with us even though we're in my neighborhood. I want to make sure we're extra cautious."

"And you need your cousin to do that?"

"Absolutely."

"Don't you have regular guards for this kind of thing?"

"I do if I were by myself. Joey, your security detail will always be somebody from my family now. I can't always be there, and it wouldn't be good for us if I were always attached to you. After yesterday, I only trust the members of my family. There are only five other guys besides my dad and my uncles I trust to protect you to my standard."

I gaze at him for a long time, and I'm sure he's wondering what's going through my head. The longer I stare at him saying nothing, the more anxious I sense he becomes. I'm quiet for so long Finn catches up with us.

"Good morning, Jocelyn."

"Morning, Finn."

I hope they can tell from my tone I'm not pissed. Just surprised. I don't love this, but I don't want either of them to think I don't agree with it.

"Cormac, will I have a guard everywhere I go until—"

I don't finish that sentence, and I know he's speculating what I was about to say. From his expression now, I know he assumes I mean until we break up. I have no intention of ending this with him. If I weren't in this for the long haul, I never would've gone anywhere near him. I certainly wouldn't have accepted a nickname so easily so soon, but I doubt he's ready to hear that from me, so I'll keep that thought to myself for now.

"How far do you want to run today, Joey?"

"Not too long. Can we do three miles? Would that be good? I know that's probably shorter than you're used to."

"No, that's perfect. Neither Finn nor I love running as much as some of the other guys, so that's usually how far we go."

I think my expression must say I don't quite believe him. I don't think he's lying, but neither is he a hundred percent. I bet plenty of days three miles is all any of them have time for, but my guess is most of them put in a good six to ten. I assume some of it is slow and steady, and some is wind sprints. I hate thinking it, but they don't know when they might have to get away from someone. They wouldn't know ahead of time how far they'd need to run to do that.

We set off again at an even pace. It's not quite a challenge for me, but it's certainly faster than I normally would do. Neither Finn nor Cormac look uncomfortable, either. The thought that I could run from Finn flashes in my mind, but I don't want to run from Cormac.

We do a long loop around Cormac's neighborhood, since we agree we don't love out-and-back runs. One, because it's boring, but two, it reminds us of just how much farther we have to go before we get to the end. A few days ago, I shared I would rather swim, but I don't have access to a pool. Turns out I do now because he has one, and he'll turn the heater on for me.

He added it when he bought the place, so he could swim laps in summer when it feels too hot to run, and he doesn't want to go to a gym to run on the treadmill. He told me all the men in his family are strong swimmers. My guess is it's for the same reason they're endurance runners. They never know when they might find themselves in a situation where running isn't an option, but they still need to get away. Those are things I pray I never learn are true. I only want to hear he enjoys swimming; not that it's a necessity. However, I suspect there've been a few occasions where it came in handy.

We're almost back to his place. We only have two blocks left to go. We're just stepping off the curb when a car comes careening around the corner with no turn signal, no warning. We have the right of way, not just because we're pedestrians, but because the car has a red light, and we have the walk sign. Cormac barely pushes, and Finn barely pulls me out of the way. I'd stepped just ahead of Cormac, coming off the curb.

Cormac moves like he's ready to pull his gun when I sense he recognizes the driver.

Fucking hell.

I'm sure I was the target—not Finn or Cormac—because there's no way that woman would ever be foolish enough to target a member of one of the leading families in such a public place. I'm not only a target, but someone's following me if the woman knew how to find me. There's no denying that after the two men following me yesterday.

Cormac pulls me against his chest, and I feel his heart pounding. I don't think it's from having just been running. I can tell he's looking over my head at Finn because his cousin's eyebrows furrow before they rise almost to his hairline. He must have just realized who that driver was. I know Cormac thinks I can't feel him shake his head because it's subtle. Does he not want Finn to say anything or do anything right now? Does he want to make sure Finn doesn't say something to scare all the living shit out of me?

I keep my embrace tight. I'm not ready to let go. But I have to tap him on the back. He eases his hold. I don't let go, but I draw a deep breath. He was virtually suffocating me. I try not to let my mind run away from me with all the possibilities of how that woman could've hurt me, and what she'll do next because I guarantee she won't stop. Not if Cormac and Finn recognized her. It wasn't Deirdre, so it wasn't some crazy ex. At least, I don't think so.

A mercenary?

That's my guess because this might've been intimidation, but next time could be far worse. From how Cormac's heart rate slows, I know he doesn't want me to sense how upset this makes him.

"Are you all right, *cailín?*"

He must shoot Finn another look. Finn rolls his eyes but nods his head. This time, it must've been a warning glare.

"I'm all right, Cormac. Shaken, but not hurt. You guys protected me in time."

When I tilt my head and finally look him in the eye, he knows I understand that wasn't an accident. All I do is nod my head. Something flashes in Cormac's eyes, and I think he feels even worse because I'm already resigned to being in danger this soon. I'd hoped we could've gone a little longer before anyone posed any serious risks, but clearly that's not the case.

"Martha, what do you mean I'm being written up? For what?"

"Your behavior yesterday."

"My behavior? What did I *allegedly* do?"

"You deny using profanity in front of the children?"

"Of course, I do. Which kids, and what did I *allegedly* say?"

"You don't need to keep stressing allegedly."

"Apparently, I do because I did nothing wrong. I've never even said damn in front of a kid."

"That's not what was conveyed to me. Past incidents were shared but not previously reported."

"Past incidents?"

This is some motherfucking bullshit.

"Yes. It's come to light that you have a habit of swearing in front of kids."

"Since when? Martha, I've worked for you since I came to America. You were my supervisor while I did my clinical hours during grad school. How can you believe this is congruent with what you know about me?"

"It isn't. That's why it's such a shock and disappointment."

"Who's accusing me?"

"I can't disclose that."

"Don't I have a right to face my accuser under American law?"

"This isn't a court case."

Yet. I'll go after whoever this is for libel if they wrote this accusation down and defamation if they only said it. This could ruin me.

"Can I read the accusations in full?"

"No. That's confidential."

Convenient.

I extend my arm to take the papers my supervisor holds. I want to see what the reprimand says. She hesitates before giving them to me. Did she think I would sign them blind?

I skim the allegations before reading the document more closely. This is some motherfucking bullshit. It claims during a home visit yesterday, I became frustrated by uncooperative parents and lost my temper. It states I not only argued with the parents but swore at them in front of their children. I can't believe this family would report me for something I didn't do. It's out of character for them. I reread a paragraph and realize it wasn't the parents. Someone supposedly overheard me. I can't believe this.

I know this is a ridiculous claim because the neighbor to the right of this family's apartment wasn't there. They're traveling out of town right now, and the household to the left only speaks Spanish; whereas, the family I was with only speaks English. There was nobody close enough to hear me to report me.

"This is entirely made-up, Martha. Whoever is doing this is doing it on purpose to ruin my reputation. Do you know who it was? Is it somebody you're familiar with? Are they a reliable source?"

I feel my temper on the verge of exploding. After what happened a few days ago in the subway and on the street, then on my run with Cormac and Finn, I've been hyper vigilant about anybody who might be out to harm me. This feels as premeditated as almost being hit by a car. I wonder who this could be and what the purpose is.

Is this something connected to Cormac? Could this be Pablo finally getting his retribution? That doesn't sit well with me because the more I finally think about the situation with Pablo, the less I think he could possibly care about me and what happened all those years ago. Anything he says about me now is a way to antagonize Cormac, so I pretty much rule him out. Not entirely. But most of the way. That leaves me wondering if this has to do with my family.

I hoped I wouldn't have to admit any connections to them yet, but it's becoming unavoidable. I'm certain Santiago will have plenty to say when I see him this evening. He's been nagging me to come over, and I've been putting it off for days. I suspect he knows about Cormac, and if he knows, then so do other members of our family.

"Martha, do you have any other witnesses to substantiate this? Have you reached out to the family? Do they corroborate this story?"

She hesitates before responding. "They're too scared to admit what they heard."

"Scared? What on earth could they be scared about with me? I've known them for years, and there's never been an inkling of trouble between them and me."

"Yes, well, you stayed out of the Cartel's crosshairs until now, but your boyfriend certainly is causing a stir. The person who reported this mentioned they heard you on the phone arguing with your boyfriend before you went inside, that you were already short-tempered."

"What? This is going from the ridiculous to the insane. Martha, my boyfriend and I didn't speak yesterday while I was outside my client's home. And even if we had, we've never had an argument, so there was nothing to report. This is entirely fabricated. Someone is trying to cause problems for me."

"And who or why could that be?"

"If you know who my boyfriend is, perhaps you can imagine why someone would wish to cause problems for either him or me."

"Then that's its own problem. Jocelyn, if your relationship is going to affect your work, then I can't send you out in good faith to these neighborhoods."

"Are you serious right now, Martha, or is this your own way of handling your concerns or prejudices against who I'm dating?"

"I'd be careful with those accusations, Jocelyn."

"Shouldn't I say that to you? This isn't something that'll just go away if you're putting it in my personnel file. You need to prove this isn't a false accusation before you put in a formal reprimand. If it's just one person, and even the alleged victims don't corroborate this person's story, then it's their word against mine. What makes their word more valuable when you've known me for years? I've received commendations for my work. Never once has anybody claimed otherwise."

"You weren't dating a mobster before this."

"That's what it's really about. It's about who I'm dating."

That makes me think it's somebody connected to the Cartel who wants to punish my boyfriend through me or wants to punish me for dating somebody who's not Latino, somebody who's a rival.

"That's not my issue to determine."

"Martha, that's ridiculous. Of course it is. If somebody's filing a false claim against me, then you have a responsibility to find out why that's happening."

"I'd be careful, Jocelyn, about telling me what I do and don't have to do. You're skating on thin ice. If you argue any further, I'll write you up for insubordination."

I cannot believe she's doing this. Yeah, she's my boss, and I don't consider her a friend, but I thought we had mutual professional respect, and we were friendly.

"I don't have to sign my agreement to that reprimand. I'm going to exert that right, and I will not sign that as an admission of fault."

"But you must sign it as proof of receipt."

"I read the entire document, Martha. I can see the way this one's written means signing is an admission of fault. It's not a recognition of receipt. I won't sign it. If I'm forced to, I will file a complaint for coercion and a hostile work environment."

Two can play this game, and I won't allow Martha to back me into a corner since my annual review is coming up in a month. I refuse to have this as a fresh strike against me. This is so utterly unreal to me. I can't believe this is happening.

My gut keeps screaming to get out of this conversation and call Cormac. Not necessarily because I believe he can fix this or that I even expect him to fix this. We've built a tremendous trust through our physical relationship, and he's who I want to go to when I'm in doubt or something goes wrong. Not as my Dom, but as my boyfriend.

Perhaps tonight things will play out with him as my Dom taking control of this in the privacy of what I'm now considering our home because that's what he keeps calling it. I moved in with him after the near miss with the car. He didn't have to insist that hard to convince me because that scared me shitless, and this is doing the same. Tonight, my Dom might console me, but for right now, I want my boyfriend who I trust above anyone else. I don't know what to make of all of this, but I certainly don't like it.

I hand the report back to Martha, who glowers at me. I won't be cowed. Unless she grabs my hand, shoves a pen in it, and forces it to the paper, I won't sign. In fact, she can shove this and the pen she's holding up her ass.

"I need to be at the middle school in twenty minutes. I have to go."

"I sent Amelia instead. I said you weren't available today."

"You replaced me?"

"While this pending investigation is underway—"

"Pending investigation? You believe I may not have done this. You're going to look into it?"

"I'm going to investigate why you're lying."

I grit my teeth to keep my mouth from hanging open like I'm catching flies.

"I'm taking a sick day."

"No."

"I have the days on the books, and you can't prove I'm not sick."

I'm ready to puke on her shoes. I'm growing more upset by the moment, and I'm fighting not to show it. It's taking all the lessons my parents drilled into me to keep from showing my emotions.

I turn around, leaving Martha staring at me, and I don't care. I gather my bag and head to the door.

"If you walk out, I'll write you up for insubordination and dereliction."

"I'll get a doctor's note."

Maybe Meredith would go along with that. I don't stop walking toward the door as I speak. The elevator can't get here fast enough. I practically run across the parking lot until Dillan steps in front of me.

"What happened?"

It's not friendly concern. It's a demand.

"I need to speak to Cormac. If I call, is he available?"

"I believe so. What happened?"

"I'm safe, Dillan. I'd rather speak to Cormac first."

Dillan stares for a moment, then nods.

"I want to call him from my car. This is private."

Dillan's gaze jumps to my office building, and his eyes narrow as he stares at it before returning his attention to me.

"Did someone threaten you?"

"I'm safe. I won't discuss this until I speak to Cormac."

I'm testy, and I don't want to snap at Cormac's cousin, especially since he's the boss. It's not like I fear Dillan because of his position, but my upbringing insists I show deference to him.

"All right."

He walks me to my car and opens the door for me. I slide in, and he closes it. He stands by the front quarter panel and pulls out his phone. He puts it to his ear, but his lips never move. He's pretending to be on a call in case someone sees him standing around.

I hit Cormac's contact and wiggle my toes in my shoes as I wait for him to answer.

"Joey?"

I burst into tears.

"Joey!"

"Daddy."

I feel like my throat's closing as the lump rises. I inhale and swallow.

"Daddy, are you busy?"

"No. What happened? Finn, I'm on the phone. That'll wait."

Fuck. He isn't alone.

"I didn't know you were in a meeting. I didn't mean to interrupt."

"I know you didn't, but you have five seconds to explain before I call Dillan and demand an answer."

"He doesn't know. I mean, he knows I'm safe, but I refused to tell him. I wanted to talk to you first."

"Then you better explain, little one. My girlfriend calls me crying. You can guess how little patience I have to find out who upset my *cailín*."

I pray Finn can't hear him call me that again.

"I don't know why I'm crying over this. I'm overreacting."

"I'll decide that."

His tone is getting more brittle by the word, but as controlling as that is, it calms me. He's going to take care of me. I knew that, and that's why I called. But it's like the weight of the world just lifted with those three words. He won't let me feel guilty about my feelings.

"Martha wrote me up for allegedly arguing with a family and swearing in front of them. She said the person who reported me heard me arguing with you on the phone before I went into the apartment building. I refused to sign and asked who filed the report. It's a lie."

Tears still stream down my cheeks, but I'm not sobbing, and my throat is clear.

"Of course it's a lie. You'd never behave that way. Do you know who filed the complaint?"

"No. Martha said it was someone who heard the conversation in the apartment. If I'd yelled, only the people on each side would've heard. One family is out of town, and the other doesn't speak English. I've been in that home enough times to know sound doesn't travel through the ceiling or the floor."

"Can you think of anyone who might hold a grudge? Is there anyone who wishes to take your place? Someone who doesn't like your assessments?"

"I can't think of anyone who'd want to take my position as a social worker. Period. Especially not a social worker on Staten Island. But there are plenty of families who don't like my assessments or recommendations. The list is longer than you are tall. Do you think it could be Pablo?"

I ask, hoping my earlier assumption is right.

"No. Even if he wanted to get to me, he wouldn't go through you to do it. He knows how I'd react."

"Then I don't know who. Could it be the woman in the car? Or whoever she's connected to?"

"I'll have Sean investigate. He'll discover who did this, and I'll discuss it with you before I address it."

"You'll address it?"

Oh, fuck.

"If it's someone from my world, then it will be me. That's not negotiable. If it's someone from your work, I'll support what you decide to do. If it's someone from the neighborhood, then I'll intervene if I believe I need to. But I will not agree to anyone escalating this threat."

I know he's right that it's a threat, but it makes it worse to hear it said aloud. I need to tell him what he doesn't know, but I won't until after I speak to my brother. If he's involved, then I want this to remain private family business. I want to find Cormac, fall into his arms, and forget the rest of the world exists. But I can't until I see Santiago.

"Do you want me to come and get you? Dillan or one of our men can drive your car home."

"I need to see my brother today. I'm fine now. I'm not as upset as I was before talking to you. Thank you, Daddy."

I don't think Finn can hear us. I believe Cormac's keeping our conversation private, but it would be embarrassing if Finn heard me call his cousin that. I know I've done it a few times during this call, but it keeps coming out. I don't think I'm a child. I don't feel younger than I am. But he's comforted me, and I feel cared for like he's promised. That's why the name fits.

"Shane will meet you and Dillan at your brother's place. Dillan's got plans with his wife, so Shane will take over."

"I feel guilty pulling Shane away from his wife. I'm certain he could—would—be doing something better."

"Something else? Yes. Better? No."

"Okay. I don't agree, but thank you for making me feel better."

"Always, little one."

"Santi, enough already."

I'm ready to leave, and I've been here five minutes. He's infuriating.

"You've ignored my request that you come over for nearly two weeks."

"Request? You commanded me, but I'm not one of your lackeys. I don't have to obey."

"You're my sister. I shouldn't have to do anything but let you know I'd like to see you."

I stare at a guy who's the spitting image of our dad. Except our dad has never been an arrogant ass to me.

"You've been avoiding me, and I know why."

I refuse to respond. We're back to where we started—for the third time. He thinks he can wear me down. How easily he forgets I'm the more stubborn of the two of us.

"How can you be fucking that—"

"Finish that thought, Santi."

I issue the dare even though I interrupted him. He recognizes my expression, and I can practically hear him gulp. It's taking him even longer than usual to notice he's pushing me too far. For someone as intelligent as him, he's so fucking stupid. I'd throat punch him if I could.

"I don't need to. You know what I'm thinking. You're making a colossal fucking mistake. What the hell am I supposed to tell *papí*?" Daddy.

That word has a different connotation from when I use it in English with Cormac.

"Nothing. If he has something to say, then he can call me."

I definitely don't think of *papá* and Cormac the same way. Santi and I have always called our father *papí*, but I think of him as *papá*.

"He's too pissed. That's why I'm talking to you."

"You're talking to me because you're a *chismoso*."

"I'm not a gossip, Jo-Jo. I'm not spreading rumors."

"If *papí* were as angry as you claim, he wouldn't hesitate to call me. Hell, he'd fly me home or show up on my doorstep. You're trying to make something out of nothing to be relevant."

I fight the urge to cringe. That went way, way, *way* too far.

My brother steps closer. Not exactly in my face and not to intimidate me with his size. But he wants me to know I just pissed him off more than he's pissed me off. It's one of those thoughts I should have kept to myself.

"You know I'd be well within my rights to send you home."

"You'd have to have one of your men bind and gag me to get

me on that plane. How do you think that would go over? Santi, I had a shit day today. I don't want to do this."

"What did he do to you?"

"Made me feel better because of that shit day."

"Gross."

"Not like that. I haven't seen him since this morning. Just shit at work."

"Did someone hurt you?"

We might fight like two wet cats in a bag, but the moment there's even a hint of a problem with someone outside the family, we're both ready to go apeshit on whoever hurt the other.

"No. Just some issues to work out with my boss. It's nothing I can't handle, but it wasn't a good day."

When he engulfs me in a hug, I don't hesitate to rest my head against him and wrap my arms around his waist. He's still my big brother, and I know there's nothing he wouldn't do to protect me.

"Jo-Jo, I'm here for you. But I still don't approve. You know *papi* will have something to say about this. Is he really worth the trouble this'll cause?"

The trouble it might already be causing.

"He really is, Santi."

"You moved here to be safe from the cartels. Now, you're putting yourself right in front of them and the other syndicates. That makes no sense. You don't even like going out with me and my friends because of who might see us together."

"I know. I get how hypocritical it makes me. But it's still safer to be romantically involved with the mob's head enforcer than it is to be a Mexican *jefe's* daughter."

Chapter Twenty

Cormac

I'm ready to crawl out of my skin by the time Joey walks through the door. I couldn't focus on the brief I was drafting. I kept rewriting paragraphs, and I'll still have to revise it tomorrow. I couldn't concentrate for shite.

I stick my fingers in the water and decide the bath is the right temperature. If I fill it any further, the water'll slosh over the side when we settle into it. We haven't started talking yet. We shared a kiss that tempted me to fuck her against the wall. I barely found the restraint not to. Instead, I led her into our bathroom.

I think of this house as ours, not mine now that she's here. It's felt incredibly natural to share this space with her. I haven't lived with anyone else since I moved into this house at the beginning of my junior year of college. I was already wealthy in my own right, just like my brother and cousins. Yeah, we have money thanks to our mob ties. But just like our fathers, we funnel most of that back into the organization. The bulk of our incomes come from our legal ventures. Not only do we feel like it's the right thing to do—keep mob money in the mob—it also means our tax filings are clean as a whistle.

Waking up to Joey in our bed, making meals with her in our kitchen, and sharing this space makes me happier than I imagined. I think she feels the same, but I haven't asked whether she sees this as a temporary remedy to the threat—threats—or whether she could see this being permanent. I don't want to rush her, but I'm dying to know.

"Daddy, just being near you makes me feel better. But this is divine."

She leans back against my chest, my thighs bracketing her hips. I lap water over her shoulders and tits before I rub her shoulders. Her sigh sounds soul deep.

"*Cailín*, I've never looked forward to anything as much as I do being near you."

She twists to look over her shoulder at me. She's hesitant to share her thoughts, so I don't rush her. Instead, I press a soft kiss to her lips.

"Is this where I belong?"

"Yes."

My answer is immediate, but I don't like how she's too nervous to make that a statement. She was unsure I'd agree if she told me that's what she wants. I don't think it's just the stress from today that makes her hesitate.

"Turn around, little one."

"Yes, Daddy."

She pushes up, and I slide forward. Her legs come over my mine and now bracket my hips like mine do hers. My hands go to her waist, and I pull her closer. Her pussy rubs against my cock. I've been hard as a fucking plank since I tasted her during that first kiss tonight.

"Do you know where you really belong, little girl?"

"Where, Daddy?"

I lift her, and her hands shoot out to my shoulders to brace herself. I give her a displeased look, and her hands lower. She smiles, knowing I'd never drop her. Her instinct doesn't need to be to protect herself, even if that's a natural reaction to suddenly changing positions. I slide her down my cock.

"This is where you belong, Joey. As a part of me, just like I belong as a part of you. I don't want there to be an end and a beginning to us. I want us to be one."

"Cor, I want the same thing. When you come in me, you leave a part of you with me. I still feel connected to you. But there's nothing I can do to make it the same for you."

"That's not true. Knowing my cum is inside you and nowhere else makes me feel still connected to you. I hope one day that connection becomes more. That the connection is something that permanently binds us as one."

Does she understand what I'm getting at? Or do I make no sense at all?

"Do you mean a child?"

"Yes."

She stares at me dumbfounded. Is it shock? Or is it rejection?

I tug her hips, pulling her body entirely flush with mine before my right hand cups the base of her skull, and my left hand cups her jaw.

"Joey, I love you. You're my future."

I'm unprepared for how she throws her arms around my neck or the kiss that nearly knocks me backwards. She's led our kisses before, and she's been passionate when she does. She's also been so tender it makes my heart ache.

But this kiss.

It's intoxicating. It's drugging. It's all-consuming.

It's everything.

When we pull apart, she leans to whisper in my ear.

"I don't know whether you're going to fuck a baby into me, or you're going to make love to me to do it. But the only children I'll ever carry, the only children you'll ever father are the ones we make together."

She leans back and cups my jaw with both hands.

"I love you, Cor."

"I'm completely yours now and forever. I'll never want anyone else, Joey. We belong to and with each other. Whether it's this place or your place or somewhere new, I don't want to change our living arrangement. Ever."

"I don't care where the roof over *our* heads is, as long as it's the same one."

Her gaze drops, and it feels as though she remembered something the moment she finished speaking.

"*Cailín?*"

When she looks up at me, I know she regrets what she said.

"Cormac, I meant what I said. But I shouldn't have said it yet."

She closes her eyes and inhales so deeply her shoulders rise, and her chest expands. She tries to move off me, but my fingers dig into her arse. Whatever she has to say makes her fear I'll reject her. Whatever she has to say means we need to stay connected because it's going to challenge our relationship. I won't allow any distance to grow between us.

"You're scared to tell me what's on your mind. You know I won't like it. But that doesn't mean I won't listen, and it doesn't mean I'll want you any less. Whatever it is, we deal with it together."

"You say that now...Cormac, Bracero isn't my full last name. It's Espinoza Bracero. I've told you I grew up near Chihuahua."

NO! FUCK!

It's my turn to close my eyes and compose myself. I take too long because she tries to get up again. When I tighten my hold on her arse, I know it hurts. She can barely shift, let alone get off me.

"I told you, you're where you belong. You're not going anywhere, *cailín*, until after we talk. Then, you aren't going anywhere after that except to our bed with your pretty little pussy filled with my cum. Do you know why you're going to keep every drop inside you?"

She shakes her head, tears welling in her eyes.

"Because you have been mine since the moment we met, and you will be mine until my last breath. You think I'm going to reject you because you're Jesus Espinoza's daughter? Because your father is *El Cazador*. Because he heads the Culiacán Cartel, the most powerful Mexican cartel. Do you fear he'll live up to his moniker? Will the hunter come after me?"

"I haven't told him, but I believe my brother has."

Double fuck me.

"Santiago? As in the newest member of the *Junta Directiva*?" Board of Directors.

She nods.

Wonderful, her brother joined the *El Corredor*. The corridor or board of directors is the senior most leadership in a cartel. Her brother rose another rank in their hierarchy two years ago. He's officially equivalent to Finn, who's our second-in-command. He became a *lugarteniente*—lieutenant—or plaza boss while in college because he carried out a hit on an LA rival visiting NYC. He organized his own team of informants, then spent his spring break junior year tormenting the guy until he put the muzzle of his gun between the guy's eyes and shot the back of his rival's skull across the room. That cemented him as their cartel's top official in New York, and he hadn't even moved here from Mexico yet.

We met when my fist broke his nose during a fight that got men killed on both sides. His rival was one of our tornadoes—a liaison between cartels, or in our case, his cartel and our mob. He was a *cameleo*—camel—an OG member of a Baja cartel. The guy was nearly sixty and survived countless attempts on his life. Those types of members are named for the animal since they have the same lifespan. Santiago cost us six million dollars. I couldn't kill him, and he couldn't kill me without starting a war. I had to settle for the broken nose. He tried to stab me in return. I now have a beautiful pearl-encrusted switchblade.

"If Santiago knows we're together, did he tell you he and I have met?"

Her face blanches so fast it scares me.

"Joey?"

I rub my hands up and down her arms before I pull her chest against mine. I'm gentle when I press her head against my shoulder.

"Joey?"

"Santi didn't mention that."

I barely hear her and have to strain to catch what she said.

"What did he say?"

"He was pissed. He said our father already knew, but I'm not convinced he does. I think Santi was giving me the chance to promise to break things off with you. I'm certain our father knows now if he hadn't heard some other way. Maybe *papá* gave Santi the chance to talk to me before he intervenes. How do you know my brother?"

"We met during a business meeting."

She sits back, her gaze sweeping over my chest and abs.

"Are any of those scars from him?"

"No."

"Are any of his scars from you?"

"No."

She'd curled her arms between us a moment ago, but this time she wraps her arms around me when she leans forward. I run my hand up and down her back.

"Cor, you say I still belong to you...Is that so you—are you—"

She hesitated, then stumbled over her words. But I can guess what she meant.

"I won't use you against them. You're still mine because I've given you my heart. I hope I still have yours."

"You know you do. I gave it to you, knowing I'd have to reveal this."

"Why didn't you tell me sooner?"

"Because I didn't know if you felt the same way about me. If you didn't, and this was going to end at some point, I didn't think it was a good idea to say too much about my family."

I feel like I should be enraged she kept such a massive secret. One that endangers my family. But I'm not because I understand. If we hadn't met the way we did, I would have kept my position a secret as long as possible. I wouldn't have rushed to admit my family is *the* New York mob. We come from the most fucked-up, twisted world.

"Cormac, can you forgive me for this? Or will you realize in the morning this is going to burn a hole through us?"

"It's hardly ideal."

She snorts but says nothing.

"I wish you'd told me sooner because I would have organized a different safety protocol. But considering my position and all the shite I'll never tell you to keep you, my family, and the people who depend upon me safe, I understand your decision."

"Are you silently angry?"

She was monumentally uncomfortable a moment ago. Now I hear the fear. Most people wouldn't, but I've spent years causing that emotion in others and detecting when people try their best to hide it.

"No, little one. Worried. Resentful life put us in this position. But I'm not angry. Joey, I'll never begrudge you keeping that secret. But I need you to promise me something, and it's not negotiable. If you won't, then we might meet an insurmountable problem. I won't ask for your pledge until you hear me out."

She sits up, so we can look at each other.

"I will never expect you to narc on your family. I will never demand—never ask—you to share family secrets about your father and brother's business arrangements or how they lead their syndicate. But I expect you to tell me immediately anything and everything that happens that could endanger you and the family we'll have."

"You still want a family with me?"

I tip her chin up.

"I want a family with my wife."

Her eyes open so wide I think I can see every inch of them.

"That isn't a proposal, but I wouldn't have brought you this close to my family and me if I haven't seen a future with you since the beginning. Knowing your family connection now, you've felt the same way."

"I have. I wouldn't have risked so much if my heart didn't know my future's with you. Daddy, I feel guilty for not telling you earlier. You're handling all of this with kindness and patience. I should have trusted you. I'm sorry."

Tears well in her eyes again, and it breaks my heart. I hate knowing she fears anything, but it shreds me that she's scared about our relationship.

"You've trusted me since the moment we met. I respect your decision because I would have made the same one. But I don't think you're forgiving yourself for what *you* believe you did wrong. I don't want you to hold on to that. I'm going to make love to you or fuck you—whichever you need—then I'm going to spank you. Hard. I don't believe you need a punishment, but you believe you do. Once I'm done, this is done. You don't need to feel guilty about something you didn't do, and you certainly won't need to feel guilty after your act of contrition. You will not punish yourself any further."

I know I sound controlling as fuck. I know I'm commanding her feelings. But the relief on her face tells me I was right. I'd rather dole out a punishment I don't think she needs than let her punish herself far more severely than a paddle across her arse. I'd normally deny her any orgasms before or after a punishment, but I want her to know I love her. That I'll do anything for her, not only to keep her safe but to make her happy. That I'll share any and all of her burdens.

"Thank you, Daddy. Thank you for not making me feel guilty about this and thank you for not making me feel bad about my twisted emotions. Today's been a lot, and I don't feel like I'm thinking straight. I need to clear my mind, and letting you be in control allows me to do that."

She reaches back and pulls both of my hands from where they've settled, cupping her arse. She entwines our fingers.

"What do you need, Cormac? You're giving without taking. I don't want to take without giving."

"I need that control. I need to know you feel loved and cherished. I need to know you're okay."

"Those are all things that come from you taking care of me. I want to know what I can do for you. How can I take care of you?"

"Love me."

✳

We finished our bath while I edged her. She's so aroused as I carry her to our bed, she's practically vibrating with need. She's kissing along my neck, and I can barely focus enough to put one foot in front of the other. Since she's so short, and I'm so tall, sometimes it's difficult to kiss when we're standing. But she's wrapped around me, and it's like having a feather resting on me. I'd easily carry her around with me all day, every day.

Fucking hell.

She's tugging on my earlobe, and I'm ready to come as I walk. I'm as on edge as I made her. Denying her is one pleasure while in another way, torment. I don't think I've ever needed to come as badly as I do now.

I pull back the covers and climb onto the bed, laying her back against the pillows before settling over her. We watch each other for a long time, then we move together as our lips meet. It's another explosive kiss like the one she gave me, but we're taking turns leading. I rock my hips, and she lifts hers to meet mine. But we're slow, and I'm keeping it light.

"Do I make love to you, or do I fuck you?"

"Both?"

I smile because that's what I want too, but I'd have done whatever she asked.

"Hold on to the headboard. If you let go, I risk hurting you. I don't want to push your head into it."

This isn't about being kinky or me deciding how everything's going to go.

"It'll be rough, but I'm not your Dom, Joey. I'm your boyfriend who loves you more than anything."

"I know, Cor. I'm not submitting to you, but I want it rough too. I need that."

"So do I."

She needs to know I still want her as much as I always have. That I'd devour her whole if I could. I need the same thing from her. Once she's gripping the headboard, I draw back, almost pulling out, then slam my cock into her cunt as hard as I dare. She screams, her head tipping back into the pillow.

"Yes!"

I do the same thing two more times before I shift to kneel. I raise her hips and hold them in place as I hammer my cock into her. She lifts and lowers her hips as much as I allow while holding her in place. She lets go with her right hand and scores her nails along my abs. Her fingers curl while she does it, as though she'd sink claws into me if she could. Her legs wrap around my arse and push, egging me on to do more.

I feel the sweat beading on my forehead, but I do nothing about it. Perspiration glistens on her neck, and her cheeks flush. We're in a trance together. I watch her abs clench, and I know she's about to come.

"I'm so close, Cor. Don't stop...I'm almost there...Yes... Fuck. I'm coming, Daddy."

When I see her abs relax, the flutter near her cunt done, I ease her hips to the mattress. The tone changes. I lower my body as I rest on my forearms, mine pressed against hers. Our hands roam over each other, and I draw her left leg over my hip as her right foot pushes into the mattress for leverage. I circle my hips each time I sink to the hilt. We kiss throughout.

"Cor, I never knew just how momentous sex could be until I started having it with you."

Her eyes drift closed as she concentrates. I want to watch every moment, revel in our connection. She's right.

"It's because we're soulmates."

Her eyes fly open as she nods. I settle more of my weight onto her, just like I know she loves. We come together before I roll us, so she lies sprawled across me. I never relax like I do around Joey. I never have any sense of peace unless I'm with her. The world ends at our door, and this is what I need. I need the escape, and only she gives me that.

As I gaze into her eyes, I see her mood shift. Forgiveness. Acceptance. She's made her own peace with not telling me about her family.

"I don't think you need the spanking anymore, do you?"

"No, Daddy."

I stroke my hand up and down the outside of her arm as we bask in the afterglow.

We're all on edge. These gatherings with all Four Families are only enjoyable for the family hosting it. The Irish, Russians, Italians, and Colombians never used to get together this often. But in the past five—almost six years—it's been every few months. One wedding reception after another.

Everyone's dressed to the nines, and we're in a ballroom of one of the most exclusive hotels in the world. We're rubbing elbows with the highest echelons of international business-people and aristocracy, but there's not a single syndicate man in here who doesn't have at least one knife at the ready. Since there are women and children present, none of us have guns. We leave those in our limos and town cars.

Dillan's and Finn's wives are pregnant and showing, so that has my cousins coiled tighter than a jack-in-the-box. Sean's wife's connections to the Boston and Montreal mobs make everyone wary of her, and the same is true for my sister-in-law with her connections to the Trenton mob. Shane's wife's protracted connection to law enforcement practically makes her a pariah. And our hosts watch Joey like she's about to draw her own gun on them.

"*Felicidades Enrique y señora Díaz.*" Congratulations, Enrique and Mrs. Diaz.

No one expected Enrique to remarry.

He hasn't exactly been MIA lately, but he's been less visible the last few months. With the way he looks at his bride, it's no surprise he's delegated more duties to his nephews. Enrique loves his wife as much as all the already-married syndicate men. This isn't an arrangement like last time.

"Thank you, Cormac. Ms. Bracero, it's a pleasure to see you again."

"*Gracias, jefe.* It's nice to meet you, *la patrona.*"

Joey keeps her voice low, but understanding her position makes it obvious why she addresses Enrique as boss and his wife as "the boss lady." The newest member to syndicate life doesn't flinch, but it's obvious she's not used to the title yet. Perhaps Joey's the first one to call her that.

"You as well, Ms. Bracero."

Enrique looks past my shoulder, and I recognize his expression. I doubt either woman sees the disgust register, but I've been the recipient of that look enough times to know it.

"Santiago."

Joey's hand squeezes mine before we twist to see her brother standing behind us. He's a handsome man, even if his nose still has a slight bump along the bridge.

You're welcome, you little pissant.

The way he stares at his sister puts me on edge until he shifts his attention back to the newlyweds. It's clear he's displeased to see Joey and me together, especially since we're holding hands. The Colombian Cartel didn't invite nor welcome anyone outside their organization at the ceremony, so I didn't know we'd see Santiago here. From the warning look Joey shoots me, she didn't expect to see him either. She releases my hand and hugs her brother.

"Hi, Santi."

"*Manita.*" Little sister.

I hear the warmth in the endearment, and I relax. The embrace is genuine, and I can tell Joey's relieved. When they step apart, Santiago and I shake hands. There's a challenge, and I accept. He's no weakling, but he's not as strong as me. I practically crush his hand, and I'm certain he'd love to shake it out when we let go. He's forced to shake Enrique's now, and the *jefe* isn't much gentler than me.

"*Hola, jefe, la patrona.*" Santiago's tone is deferential. Barely.

"Espinoza."

Enrique's mocking the younger man the same way he often does me. He did Joey a favor by using her preferred last name rather than the one she should go by and the one he uses to address Santiago.

Throughout this exchange, his wife remains unflappable. Either she's naturally the most perfectly matched woman to her groom, or Enrique's trained her not to react to anything or anyone tonight. Either way, I'll warn my family she's possibly even more formidable than Laura Kutsenko.

"Ms. Bracero, there's someone I think you should meet this evening."

Enrique points to Olivia Mancinelli, the Mafia underboss's wife. She and her husband, Luca, just walked in with the rest of the Mancinellis.

Meet?

Why would he say that? Joey and Santiago are Olivia's cousins.

Joey and I were the last of my family to move through the receiving line, so we're still standing with Enrique and his wife when Salvatore, the don, and his wife, Sylvia, walk up. Salvatore's gaze meets Joey's as I introduce them. I can tell he's girding his loins for something. He has that expression where he looks like he needs half a bottle of fiber.

Joey's and Olivia's matching gasps tell me why he looks so uncomfortable. I swing my attention to Enrique, who doesn't bother to hide his smirk. Seeing the two women together makes me question how I didn't guess Joey's family connection immediately.

They're near mirrors of each other, except for their hair and eye color. Olivia's blonde, and Joey's a dark brunette. Olivia's got a unique shade of brown hazel she inherited from her father while Joey's are deepening bands of brown. Otherwise, they could be sisters. The same height. Same build. Same shocked expressions.

Joey looks up at me, panicked, before looking at Santiago. He's as stunned as his sister. She turns back to me, and I wrap my arm around her waist. Luca does the same to his wife as Olivia stares up at him. Luca doesn't appear surprised by Joey but rather his wife's reaction.

"Joey, has it been a while since you've seen Olivia?"

She doesn't answer me, instead speaking to Olivia. "Who are you?"

"Who're you?"

Olivia's expression hardens into a look becoming the future *la madrona*—Godmother. It's suspicious and superior. It takes only a second for Joey to revert to the haughtiness only a woman from as much wealth and status as Joey grew up with can command.

They stare at each other, and the tension crackles in the air. Clearly, they don't know each other, and clearly, neither wants to get to know the other. Their suspiciousness is understandable given their respective positions in two of the world's most powerful syndicates.

It's Santiago who broaches the truth, and it surprises me

how gently he speaks to both women. But only after shooting Enrique a glare that promises retribution for putting his sister in such an uncomfortable position on purpose. The older man did it for sport. His wife finally looks confused.

"Mrs. Mancinelli, you must be our cousin. I can't think of any way you and my sister could look more alike unless you were our sibling, which I know you aren't."

"I don't have any cousins."

"But you have an uncle, Jesus Espinoza, don't you?"

Olivia's face drains of all color, and she sags against Luca. He pulls his wife closer, twisting to shield her from Santiago and Joey. He barely spares my girlfriend a glance before fixing Santiago with a menacing glare. The scar that runs from his cheekbone to below his collar only accentuates the harshness. I've known the man since we were in preschool. He means every bit of his silent threat.

"Did your father send you?"

Before Santiago can answer, Joey speaks up. Her voice trembles, but her expression doesn't waver as she watches Olivia.

"Our father had a sister, but she died decades ago. She wasn't old enough to have had children, and you aren't old enough to be his sister."

"My mother is alive and well. Your father's a liar."

"And your husband and every man in your family aren't?"

Joey's confidence is back as she pulls away from me. She casts her gaze over Luca, then Salvatore before sweeping it over the other Mancinellis who strain to hear what's happening. I know the men in my family have conveniently crept closer. The Kutsenkos and their Andreyev cousins are keeping a close eye on this situation as they sip their cocktails.

"What the men in my family are, is no concern of yours. You should call your *papi* and ask him your questions. Let him know my opinion of him is even lower than it was when we had the misfortune of meeting."

Joey shifts to square her shoulders, and Olivia does the same. If they were men, I'd expect them to pull guns on each other. I watch both women place their hands on their purses. I already know Joey has a knife in hers, and I expect Olivia has one too. This is escalating too fast. I dart my gaze to Luca at the same time he looks at me. We put our hands at our women's lower back, but neither responds to us.

"You didn't know about me, but it's obvious your husband did. Maybe you should find out why he kept that secret."

"Just like your boyfriend should explain it to you."

"Yes. Except his family didn't put a hit on you like yours did to me."

"What?"

Santiago grasps Joey's arm and twists her. I can tell he isn't rough, so he's still breathing.

"A couple men followed me from the subway. Then someone tried to run me over a few days ago, and someone's causing trouble at work for me. Now it makes sense."

She fixes her glare on Luca, who narrows his eyes. The accusation surprises him. I shift my focus to Salvatore, who looks pissed as he glares at Enrique, who looks ready to laugh. This tableau is attracting too much attention from outsiders.

"Enrique, this wasn't cool. Joey, people are staring. We'll finish this later."

"We finish this now, Cormac. We can all step out of the ballroom."

"That won't work. You know my family won't let us go alone, and neither will Olivia and Luca's. Between the Mancinellis and O'Rourkes, we make up at least a third of the guests."

"You and one of your men come with me, and Luca picks a man to go with him and his wife."

"You go nowhere without me, *manita*."

Santiago wraps her arm around his, and I think it's anchoring her in place as much as it is to show support. He's prepared for the stubbornness I discovered when Joey and I met, and she refused to get her arm checked out.

I shift my attention to Luca and lift my chin. He dips his. He's agreed to step outside the ballroom, but it presents a challenge for me. I don't trust Santiago enough for him to be the man who leaves with me, but I know he won't leave Joey.

"Salvatore, you come with us, and so does Dillan."

I look at my cousin, who's the closest family member to us. I tilt my head toward the door. He looks to Finn and Shane, who're standing with their wives and Dillan's. Our silent communication tells them to stay put.

I escort Joey out to the hotel lobby, followed by Santiago and Dillan, then the Mancinellis, who now includes Marco, Luca's next younger brother. This isn't where we can have our conversation. I steer Joey down the hall to where I know there's an empty ballroom. The Diazes will have rented all the spaces in the hotel, so no other event can take place here. No one wants an enemy sneaking into the reception, looking like they belong at another gathering. I try the door and find it unlocked.

All of us slip inside and spread out, so no one from opposite families is within arm's reach of one another. Joey and Olivia take a step forward at the same time. They both brush off the arm Luca and I attempt to wrap around our respective woman. I sense Santiago wants to stand beside her, but that'd only antagonize Luca, Marco, and Salvatore. That'd amplify the protectiveness I feel now.

"If your mother isn't dead, then why don't we know her or you?"

"Because my mother left that life behind."

Joey cocks an eyebrow at Olivia's response. Her gaze darts to Luca before she smirks. In turn, Olivia shoots me a disgusted look. Joey takes another dig, and while I don't disagree, I want to cringe.

"She ran away to hide in America and look who she wound up with as in-laws."

"And you're not hiding here?"

"No. We can't hide any more than you can when you married a man who's clearly senior Mafia. Have you met our father?"

"Unfortunately, yes. It was when he tried to kill me."

Joey's only reaction is not to react. Fucking hell. What kind of training did she go through as a child? I hope it didn't fucking match half of mine.

"Did you deserve it?"

Fucking hell, Joey.

"Do you deserve the hit on you?"

Joey casts a speculative gaze at Luca. "What do you think? How much did you pay for whatever revenge you seek against my father?"

"We're not responsible for whatever you're talking about. We're on good terms with Jesus."

"Does your wife know that? Are you that good an actress? Did you know about me and decide to get revenge for whatever my father did to you?"

She doesn't deny Jesus likely did something. He did. At least his men nearly did, which made the Mancinellis hold him responsible.

Jesus and Enrique can't stand each other. I don't know if Joey knows that. It makes me wonder if Pablo or Javier have anything to do with this. Was Enrique merely enjoying toying with the Mancinellis and me? Or was he crowing "dance, monkeys, dance" to himself?

"I knew nothing about you. Are you with Cormac, feeding him information to sabotage my family?"

"No. Until tonight, I didn't think about your family because I didn't know any of you existed."

The women stare at one another, and the rest of us stare at them. Joey's tone softens a smidge.

"Does my father know who you are now?"

"Yes."

"Does he know his sister's alive?"

"Yes."

"My father carries a photo with him everywhere. He's done things I'll never know to get it back when someone's taken it. It's your mom and my dad when they were kids. He's handing her a toy, and she's handing him a ball. He thought it was the only thing left. Our grandfather did this, not your mom or my dad."

Olivia's gaze isn't as piercing as she shifts her gaze to Santiago for a moment before returning it to Joey.

"I know. My mom thought he was dead, too. Our grandfather took him and trained him. By the time he came back from wherever, my mom was already here."

"Do they talk?"

"I don't know. I think once in a while."

Joey nods. I think it bothers her that Olivia knows more about their family's past than she does. That sparked her anger and defensiveness. It sparked Olivia's resentment and distrust from what happened before Jesus learned who she was.

"No one I know in our family has your eyes. Did you get them from your dad?"

"Yes, and the blonde hair's from his side, too."

Olivia's lips flatten as she realizes she just told Joey something she must already know. They stand in silence, and it's

Luca's and my cue to wrap our arm around our women and pull them into our embrace. We move with a synchronicity that would normally make us snarl. But neither of us cares about the other more than we do the women we love.

Joey gazes up at me, and I can tell she wishes to say something for my ears only. I kiss her forehead, bringing my head closer to hers.

"Would your family allow me to get to know her better? Would they worry if Santi did, too?"

"Of course you can."

We both see Olivia whispering to Luca, and my guess is it's the same thing Joey asked because both women turn to each other.

"I'm sorry."

They speak together, then smile. Joey tries again.

"I'm sorry for my harshness. I never imagined I'd meet my mirror image. I'm protective of my family, just like you are yours. But we're also each other's family, and three of us live in the same city." She glances at Santiago. "I'd like to get to know you better."

"I'd like that too."

Both women turn their focus to Santiago, who's remained quiet, only observing.

"Me too."

Salvatore and Luca position themselves in front of Olivia, who tries to peer between their arms. Santiago casts them a disdainful glare as he speaks.

"I know your history, Luca. Don't assume I'm like you because of what men do in Mexico or because of my father's past. I don't hurt women and children. I wouldn't survive my sister if I did. I fear Jocelyn far more than anyone else. You'd do well to do the same."

The women in syndicate families grow up resilient and

protective. They have no choice; it's in their genes. But women who marry into syndicates are no less fierce. Joey will be both a syndicate daughter and wife before the end of the month.

Chapter Twenty-One

Joey

To say meeting Olivia blindsided me is the understatement of the year. Our resemblance is uncanny. It made my hackles go up immediately. I know there are miles upon miles of lies and secrets my father'll never share. But this...

If Olivia knows, then why couldn't Santi and I? It's not like I expect my parents to invite Olivia and her family to Christmas, but this is a big fucking deal to keep hidden.

It makes me wonder if *papá* really doesn't know I'm with Cormac. If he did, he'd know I'm likely to meet members of the other syndicates, and that means I'd likely meet Olivia. I've been thinking about that for the last three days. We ended our conversation far better than it started. My combativeness shocked me, but instinct told me to protect my family and Cormac's. It made me defensive and untrusting to an extreme. I know my behavior displeased Cormac, but he's said nothing about it nor treated me any differently. But it put him in an awkward position during the conversation.

Santiago let me have it, though. He texted me like every five minutes until I relented and answered the phone the next day. He chewed me out in English, Spanish, and Spanglish for fifteen minutes. It tempted me to put the phone down and walk away. Instead, I folded laundry. He defended Olivia a lot more than I expected, but nothing he said was untrue. I was a royal bitch. I don't know if her attitude was a response to mine or the other way around, but neither of us was nice during most of the exchange. However, we're meeting for lunch today.

I need to get a few things from my place before I head to the office then the restaurant. I seem to be progressively moving my stuff into Cormac's place. All of this season's clothes are there, but I need some more as the weather transitions and keeps getting cooler.

"Sean, I'll be five minutes. I just want to grab a few things."

Cormac's cousin reaches for my keys as I insert them into the lock. I turn it and push the door open an inch as he steps in front of me. The moment he opens it wider, heat and sound combined with the force that launches us backwards keep me from understanding what's happening. Immediately, fire detectors go off in my apartment. I hear people screaming, but I can make no sense of it.

"Jocelyn? Jocelyn?"

"Sean?"

"Yeah. Where are you hurt?"

"I don't know. You?"

I force my eyes open and see a deep cut on his forehead and cheek. His suit coat is off and smoldering beside him. The front of his shirt's ripped and shows cuts and likely burns, but nothing anywhere near as bad as I expected. How long was I out of it?

I look down at myself and realize I'm sprawled on the floor of the apartment across the hall from mine. The blast burst open that door. I hurt, but I think it's from landing so hard. I feel some cuts on my arms, and I spy a wood shard in my thigh. I don't think it's done any serious damage, so I reach for it.

"No."

Sean pushes my hand away and scoops me up. How the hell can he carry me when he just took the brunt of the explosion? I don't understand what's happening, but he's running toward the fire exit. So are my neighbors. Everything's been in slow motion, but now it whips back into real time. I feel the heat as we rush away from my fiery apartment.

"Sean, my head hurts more than anything else."

"I know, Jocelyn. We're going to get you to a doctor. You took a nasty blow to the back of your head."

I try to lift my hand to feel for an injury, but Sean has my arms pinned to my sides. I struggle, but he tightens his hold. He's keeping me from reaching, so it makes me think it must be bad.

"How're you carrying me down four flights of stairs?"

Are my words slurred? They feel like it.

"Because Cormac will kill me if anything else happens to you."

"But—"

"Jocelyn, save your energy."

That's a nice way to tell me to shut up.

Sirens greet us as we reach the street. Mobsters push through the crowd until they get to us. I don't know them, but Sean's issuing orders. They bundle me into an SUV. I don't understand why it's not an ambulance if it's severe enough we need to leave.

"We need to make a statement to the police and fire department."

Everyone ignores my comment. Sean's kneeling beside me in the back of the vehicle. The second and third row seats are down, so I'm stretched out. My vision's blurry now, but I know I recognize automatic rifles in the back. There's one laying on the floor beside Sean. I twist my head and wince, but I see men beside the passenger windows with rifles at the ready.

It's only now that it sinks in.

That was a bomb.

A bomb in my apartment.

A bomb in my apartment meant to kill me.

"Cormac."

"I'm calling him right now, Jocelyn. He'll meet us."

"Our place. He calls it ours."

I hear one side as Sean explains what happened. It helps me to understand because I don't have a clear memory.

"Cor, Jocelyn's safe, but you need to meet us at Meredith's. There was an explosion at her place. Opening the door triggered it...Yes, I was in front of her. Yes, I'm all right...I'm sure I'm fine. A few singed hairs, and my suit coat is worthless."

I lift my hand to point to his forehead. Blood's streaming down it. I know head wounds bleed profusely, but he should be unconscious.

"I'm going to talk to Seamus and see if Tiernan can get in there once it's safe. She'll know what happened."

Tiernan?

My future sister-in-law. A fire inspector.

I feel like my brain's slogging through mud, but it still works.

"Yeah. She's awake. Here you go."

"Daddy?"

"Yes, *cailín*. I'll be at Meredith's as soon as I can. I'm already in the car."

"This is a lot worse than my shoulder and elbow."

"I know, little one. But Sean doesn't think it's serious

enough for the hospital if he's taking you to Meredith. What do you think?"

"I ache all over. My head's killing me, and my thigh's—"

I look down and realize someone's wrapped a bandage around the wound, but the piece of wood's still protruding from it. I don't remember that. Did I pass out for a while?

"What about your thigh, Joey?"

"Don't panic, Da—"

"I'm not, Joey. Tell me what's wrong."

"I'm trying to, but you interrupted me, Da—"

"I'm getting impatient, Jocelyn."

"Fine, Cormac."

Oh fuck!

Saying his full name makes me realize what I almost called him twice. I cringe. I already said it once loud enough for the men in this SUV to hear.

I look up at Sean, and he's shooting glares at his men that promise retribution if they repeat what they heard. He leans forward as though checking my pupils. Maybe he is.

"My wife calls me that, too."

"Joey?"

"Sorry. I have a piece of wood in it. But I didn't see bone or anything earlier, and it must not have hit a major artery if I'm still alive and talking. Mered—"

"Joey!"

I hear Cormac bellow my name, but everything's already fading to black.

"Joey? Little one, can you hear me?"

"Da—Cor?"

"Yes. I'm here."

I catch myself this time. I'm coming round from whatever Meredith must have given me. I'm not in pain anymore, which is a plus. I look around, but I don't recognize where I am. When I look down, I'm under the covers on one of the comfiest mattresses I've ever felt. Cormac and I are alone.

"Daddy, where are we?"

"My parents' house. This is my bedroom."

"Was this your childhood bed? It's enormous."

"I've been a big guy for as long as anyone remembers."

"Yeah, you are."

I grin, then giggle. Okay. This medicine's made me a little loopy.

"I thought we were going to Meredith's."

"I decided here would be better since it's going to be awhile before I'm comfortable moving you."

I shift my uninjured leg and feel the sheet against my bare skin.

"I'm naked."

"I know. Meredith and I got your dress off, so she could stitch up your leg with nothing dirty around it."

"Oh, God. She saw I didn't have any panties on."

"I draped the sheet over you while she lifted the dress up. I held you up so she could get it over your head. She saw nothing."

"She probably guessed."

"Does it bother you that much?"

"Considering your men and cousin heard me call you Daddy, I suppose not." I can add Finn to that list thanks to the call after my argument with Martha.

"They won't dare say anything, *cailín*."

I nod as I shift to find a more comfortable position. I'm propped up with pillows half under my back. I'm not entirely on my side, but it means the back of my head isn't pressing too heavily into the pillow. When I move it, blinding pain reverberates through my skull.

I moan, and Cormac's immediately hovering. I pat his cheek before trying to lift my head. He cradles it as though he's holding something as fragile as a Fabergé egg. He presses his lips to mine, knowing what I need. He's so gentle, it makes my heart swell. When we pull apart, he strokes my temple with the back of his fingers.

"Little one, you're going to get fed up with me hovering. But I may never leave your side. I never want to be that terrified again. I doubt Seamus ever wants to be in a car with me when I'm that terrified. I'm pretty sure he was reciting the rosary—in Latin."

"Is Sean okay? His head was bleeding really badly."

"Yeah. He has a row of stitches. Fortunately, we're all so fair his singed eyebrows don't look odd."

"Will you hold me?"

He looks skeptical for a moment, judging whether he can get on the bed without jostling me.

"Cor, I really need you right now. It's coming back to me, and I'm about to lose it."

It hit me like a tsunami when I asked about Sean. How he stepped in front of me because he would have done a sweep of my apartment before letting me in all the way. I was rushing because I needed to get back to work before I could meet Olivia for lunch. I wasn't thinking about the protocols I've known since I was a child. It was inevitable he went ahead of me, but it should have been me who was closer to the blast.

Cormac hurries to shed his clothes but leaves his boxer briefs on. We've had a couple heated—dialogues—about those wretched things. He insists he has to wear them to keep the entire world from knowing he gets hard the moment he thinks about me, which is, apparently, about every thirty seconds. I told him if I have to go without panties because he wants free access to my pussy whenever he wants, then I should get the same for his dick. He only wins when he points out it would draw anyone's attention who's into dicks.

He eases onto the bed as he pulls the covers over him. He lies on his side, resting his head on the fist of his bent arm. He reaches for me, and his thumb brushes my cheek. He sprinkles kisses over my cheeks, my nose, and my forehead before leaning farther to kiss along my neck. He lays his head beside mine, and his arm drapes over my stomach. He's careful not to drop the full weight on me. I press down with both hands until he relents. I sigh.

"I should have had better security at your place. Finn's combing through the footage to find the breach. I want to know who did this."

"How did Sean and I come away with so few injuries? It was so loud, and the fireball felt scorching."

"We won't know until Tiernan investigates. But while Meredith had you out to stitch up your leg and head—"

"My head?"

No wonder it hurts like a motherfucker.

"Yes. You had a cut near your crown, likely from the edge of the door across the hall when you hit it as you fell backward. Tiernan thinks the trigger was on the door handle or hinge, but the actual explosives were somewhere across the apartment or in the bedroom. The blast was big enough to cause a serious fire and hurt you, but it didn't explode your entire place. She thinks whoever designed it made it big enough that you'd get hurt but not killed opening the door, and it wouldn't endanger the entire building. Apparently, your sprinkler system and some of our guys with fire extinguishers got it under control before the fire department arrived."

"Your guys? I thought there were only two staking out my place, plus the one who's Sean's guard."

"There were only ever two you saw. I had more around your block. I didn't want anyone else to see them, and I didn't want to worry you. They got there within minutes."

"Has it always been like that?"

"No. Only since the car incident. I was going to ease off, but then you had issues at work almost immediately after. This confirms I was right to assign the team."

"Who do you think it was?"

"I have suspicions, but nothing confirmed."

"Who, Cor?"

"If this is about your dad, then any of the Culiacán's rivals."

"The Diazes?"

"They're certainly on the list."

"But not at the top."

"For now, no. If this is about my family and me, then the list gets a lot longer."

"I was supposed to meet Olivia today."

"I know."

"Could meeting me have been a distraction to keep me from my place? Could the bomb have been on a timer, and it was just bad luck Sean and I stopped by?"

"Both're definitely possible. The *Cosa Nostra* doesn't do much business with your dad, but they do some. I thought they were on peaceful terms, but maybe I'm missing something. Sean'll look into it tomorrow."

"Shouldn't he rest for a few days?"

"He has a wife to hover over and spoil him, but he can work from bed. We'll know more soon, but we don't know much now."

"And when you find out?"

He says nothing, and I knew better than to ask. He won't

speak lies when he doesn't have to, which means I get lies of omission instead. In this case, I'd rather guess since I'm certain it's far less graphic than what Cormac will do to whoever's responsible for this.

"How long will I be on bed rest?"

"A couple days."

"Can we go home today?"

Cormac pauses before he shakes his head.

"Do you not want me at your place?"

"Our place, Joey. I feared *you* wouldn't think of it as home anymore."

"Daddy, that's why I said we. My home is wherever we lay our heads together. I don't think I can sleep anymore without being in your arms. You're definitely the comfiest pillow I've ever had. Who'd think sleeping on marble could be so restful?"

"I'm like marble?"

"Yeah. Exquisite to look at. Smooth but hard." I run my fingers down his abs, which flex since I know he's ticklish.

"I don't want you to sleep anywhere but with me in our bed. You're officially moving to the Brooklyn house for now, but I'd like us to consider a home in this neighborhood or the one adjacent. In a twisted bit of fate, all the married syndicate families live here. They're the neighborhoods we all grew up in. It's Switzerland, so it's the only place I know you're safe."

A month ago, I would have bristled at a command like that. Now I revel in it.

"We're safe, Cor. The explosion could've hurt you just as easily as Sean since you offered to go with me after work."

"Speaking of that. I'm going to punish you once you're well enough to take it."

"Punish me? For what?"

"You were going to enter your apartment before Sean

swept it. You know better than that. That bomb could've hurt you so much worse if he hadn't shielded you."

My mouth drops open, and I blink. That's all I can do as shock steals my words for a moment. Then they tumble out.

"How can you say that about your cousin? How can you so flippantly be fine with him getting injured because of me? How—"

"Because he was your bodyguard. Because we all know and accept the risk when we guard the people we love most in this family. Because he's one of the few men I trust implicitly with your wellbeing. I didn't want what happened. I definitely didn't want to be petrified I'd lose either of you. I'll never wish harm upon him or any of our relatives. But we guard each other because these things happen."

I insulted him. My mouth's run away from me twice in a week. I need to get my head out of my ass and think more before I react.

"Daddy, I'm sorry for what I said and for not obeying protocols I've known since I was a kid. I've had guards enter before me, but I realize it was different with them. I didn't think of them the same way I do your brother and cousins." Something else registers with me. "You said 'our relatives.'"

"You're going to be my wife soon. You're already accepted as the newest O'Rourke. They're your family now, too. When we talk amongst us, we don't use qualifiers like in-law. We're just parents, siblings, aunts and uncles, and cousins."

"Are you proposing while I have a head wound? Do you think being concussed guarantees a yes?" I tease him, smiling to let him know my questions are jokes, not accusations.

"No, that isn't a proposal. It's fact."

I release a puff of air, which isn't quite a sigh. It's more resignation that things aren't that simple.

"I have to tell my father about us. He'll expect you to ask

for my hand. Not just because it's traditional, but because he could have arranged a marriage for me I don't know about."

"Would he do that?"

"I don't think so. He's sworn he wouldn't. But you know arranged syndicate marriages happen for many reasons, and one of them is safety for the leader's family. I don't know if he'll agree."

"You wouldn't marry me if he disapproves?"

"Of course I'm marrying you. It'll just complicate things. I'd understand if you don't want to."

I yelp as his hand wraps around my throat. There's no pressure. I just didn't expect it.

"You just doubled your punishment, little girl. I'm going to heat your arse until you can't sit for a week. Never suggest I don't want you or a life with you. You'll remember that every time I fuck a baby into your belly, which I might do every year for the next forty if that's what it takes to remind you, you belong to me just like I belong to you. Every inch of you is mine. Mine to protect. Mine to love. Mine to do whatever the feck I want. And what I want is our life together."

"I like how you won't say fuck in front of me unless we're talking about sex. It's endearing. You say the most wonderful things."

I smile as I tug his hand from my throat. He releases me, but he resists moving his hand down my body at first. I draw his palm over my right breast, then down to my cunt. I spread my uninjured leg, so I can guide his fingers into my pussy. I'm soaked after what he said.

"Daddy, I wish your cum was inside me right now. I wish you could paint my ass red right now."

"Because they'd brand you as mine?"

"Exactly. But I want to leave my cream all over your cock. I want your palm to be sore. Only I get that because you're mine."

He pushes back the covers and shifts down the bed. My gaze darts to the closed door.

"Daddy, you can't—"

"What's the rule?"

"Whenever, wherever, however."

He's my Dom right now, along with my boyfriend. The angle's a little weird because of how I'm lying against the pillows, but he makes it work. He kneels before leaning forward, resting on one forearm. I watch him push down his boxer briefs enough for his cock to spring free. His lips latch onto my clit and suck so hard I cover my mouth with both hands to smother my scream. He grazes his teeth over it as he fists himself.

My right hand reaches for him even though I know my arm's not long enough. He knows I hate it when he deprives me of pleasuring him. He's starting my punishment now. It's divine torture. He gets me close, then pulls away. Through it all—four rounds of it—he strokes himself. My left hand continues to cover my mouth while my right hand clutches the sheets.

"Open your mouth. You're going to take every drop. It's going to brand you from the inside, but it won't be where you want. Why?"

"Because you decide, Daddy."

"That's right, and your needy little cunt will wait until I'm ready for you to take my cum. It won't be until after I fuck you in the arse, and that won't be until you're healed."

"That could be weeks!"

"And I could have gone the rest of my life without you. A few weeks is nothing compared to several decades."

I open my mouth as wide as I can. Any protests I could make evaporate with his words and the distress I see on his face. He shifts to straddle my ribs as best he can. His cock slides down my throat, and I wrap my lips around him. I suck as hard as I can as I watch his head fall back, the cords in his neck straining. I swallow his load, my tongue licking him clean when I feel no more cum slide down my throat.

He stretches out beside me, his touch feather soft as he caresses my chest and tits. When he toys with my nipples, it makes me think of the babies I want to nurse. If I'd rushed into the apartment the way I'd planned, I'd probably be dead. I pushed the door open an inch or two. Sean was slower, so he could peek into my place first. That's likely what saved us. The door wasn't open all the way.

"I'm sorry, Daddy."

"I know you are, *cailín*. You're forgiven because I love you unconditionally. But your punishment stands, so you remember I won't accept any risk to you, even if it comes from your mistakes."

I can't fight the yawn that escapes. He's extremely careful as he rolls onto his back and brings me with him. He ensures his legs don't bump my injured one as I settle my head against his chest.

"Sleep, little one. Then we'll call your father."

Chapter Twenty-Two

Cormac

I don't exactly dread speaking with Jesus. I just didn't plan for him to be the man I ask permission from. I'd always thought I'd ask Joey's dad before proposing because I know she comes from as traditional a family as I do. This isn't only about tradition. It's not even about Joey in many ways. Even though I'd thought it would be a nice sentiment, now I'll be asking if we can link our syndicates. With ties to the Mancinellis, there's a strong chance he'll say no.

Then, how will I elope?

And by elope, I mean have twenty-one people discreetly at our wedding because I know my family will be there come hell or high water, if for no other reason than the men protecting Joey and me during the ceremony. There's no way all the men would leave all the women behind because they wouldn't be guarded to our standards, and only we meet our own standards.

Hell in a hand basket as my granny would say—a far less

colorful idiom than what my nana would've used. As though life wasn't already complicated enough.

Joey's in a deep sleep beside me, and it tempts me to call her dad now. But that would upset her, even though it might be better if she can't hear what's said. As though her family's manifested just from a thought, my phone pings.

UNKNOWN NUMBER

This is Santi. Answer my call.

Fecking hell in the devil's arse—that was a Nana phrase.

I answer on the first ring, girding my loins for whatever's coming.

"Hello."

"Where the fuck is my sister? I went to see her, and her apartment's taped off. All I can get from anyone is there was an explosion. Who the fuck set off a bomb in my sister's apartment? What the fuck happened?"

"She's sleeping next to me. She has stitches in her thigh from a piece of wood imbedding in it, and she has some stitches from where her head hit the door across the hall. We don't have any details beyond speculation. We haven't dealt with the police yet and won't until my family investigates."

"Investigates? You mean tampers with evidence."

"Depends on what we find. The bomb was either rigged to go off when the front door opened, or she was there by chance when the timer went off. I know her living room blinds were closed, so I don't think it was a remote detonator since no one could see in."

"This is all because of you. She was safe until she started dating you. Stay the fuck away from my sister. I'm coming to get her. Where are you?"

"Santi, I can hear you yelling. It was loud enough to wake me."

I look down and find Joey staring up at me. She reaches for my phone, and I hand it to her. She hits the speaker button.

"Where are you, *manita?* You aren't staying with that *pinche pendejo catire hijo de tu puta madre.*" Fucking stupid, fair-haired and fair-skinned son of a motherfucker.

He *really* can't stand me.

"Don't speak that way to your sister."

"*¡Chinga tu madre!*" Fuck off!

"Santiago, unless you want me to say the same thing to you and hang up, you'll stop swearing. We don't know why it happened. It could have just as easily been about our family. Maybe someone knows our connection to the Mancinellis now and went after me for that. Maybe someone already knew our connection and is pissed we found out. Until we know what's happening, I'm safest with Cormac."

"The hell you are. You're coming to one of *my* safe houses. *My* men are guarding you since it's obvious the O'Rourkes are useless. How'd someone get into your place to set it? This wouldn't have happened if you'd accepted my detail years ago."

"I won't argue with you, Santi. My head already hurts."

I stiffen beneath her, not pleased to hear she's in pain. She holds up her right index finger and shakes it. Then she makes the talking gesture with her fingers and thumb and rolls her eyes. I relax, but just barely.

"It'll hurt a hell of a lot more when you speak to *papí*. He knows."

"I suppose you called and told him everything."

"He called me. He told me shit I didn't even know about the two of you. Said he has video. I doubt he watched them with popcorn. I sure as fuck wouldn't."

He must have someone in with the Colombians. I suspected as much when I learned who Joey's family is. Hell,

Luca probably told him before the door shut to his limo the other night.

"Don't be gross. Nothing anyone could've recorded between Cormac and me would be anything more explicit than kissing."

Only because all of our vehicles have windows tinted as dark as they can get while still street legal. My cars technically aren't, but no cops give me a ticket when they realize who I am. Just a friendly suggestion to lighten them. I'm not friends with any cops, so I ignore them. When we've been at my place and the few times we've stopped at hers, we've always made sure the blinds and curtains are closed for this reason.

"You'll find out in fifteen minutes when he lands."

Joder.

Fuck. Now I'm the one swearing in Spanish.

Joey pinches between her eyes, and her shoulders droop.

"He'll know I spoke to you, but I better call and leave a message before he turns his phone back on."

"He isn't flying some piece of shit commercial plane. You know that. His phone is on."

"Wishful thinking."

"I'm calling and putting it on three-way. Take yours off speaker. This is a family matter. We don't need Cormac panting in the background."

I haven't made a sound, but it didn't take a genius to know Joey would ensure I can hear. She shakes her head at me. She won't take it off speaker. We listen to it ring three times before a thick Spanish accent answers.

"*Hola, osito.*"

Little bear? Cute.

"*Jocelyn también está al teléfono con su inútil novio.*" Jocelyn's on the phone too along with her worthless boyfriend.

"*Monita?*" Little monkey?

"*Sí, papá.*" Yes, Dad.

The situation feels a little too fraught to call my father Daddy, especially when Cormac is right next to me.

"Mr. O'Rourke."

"*Hola, jefe.*"

I don't make my accent as accurate as I could. I hope they continue in Spanish, and Jesus believes I can't understand all of it. He'll speak more freely.

I get my wish as the conversation carries on in Spanish.

"Where are you, little monkey?"

"Safe."

"I find out my daughter's almost blown up today. Don't play games."

"I am safe, but I don't want you storming over. It won't go well for anyone."

"Does that mean you're well-guarded?"

"By a small army."

All our homes are like mini compounds with armed guards patrolling. The neighbors don't ask questions about why there's a guard shack at every private gate in an already gated community. The walls are all brick, and high enough that people can't see how many guards are on duty around the clock. I'm certain the neighbors would rather the top echelon syndicates didn't swarm the communities, but who's going to tell us no? Especially when we pay cash for each home. Millions in cash.

"Tell me what happened."

"I went to my place with my guard. He's Cormac's cousin. No one outside his immediate family is my personal guard. It's always his brother or cousins. It'd be his dad or uncles if any of the other guys weren't available. I put the key in the lock and pushed it open an inch or two before his cousin stepped in front of me. I knew better, but I didn't wait. The moment he opened it wider, there was a blast of heat and the loudest noise I've ever heard. It blew me backwards into my neighbor across the hall's door, which the blast burst open. I must have hit the corner because I have stitches. A piece of wood from my door got stuck in my thigh, so I have stitches there, too."

Each time I hear the events recited—and now in a second language—I feel rage unlike anything I've mustered before. I want to tear everyone connected to this to shreds. But I'll do it slowly. I'll draw out their agony over days—weeks if I can. I'm outwardly calm for Joey's sake, but I'm ready to combust on the inside. The bomb that went off today will be nothing compared to when I explode. I'll leave nothing but ash.

Joey might not know the extent of my anger, but she senses it. She places my hand over her heart before she puts hers over my heart.

"Which hospital are you at if you got stitches in your head? You probably have a concussion."

"You know I didn't go to one. Nothing I described is serious enough for that."

"This isn't home. You don't need to fear dying and organ harvesting."

"I hadn't thought about that until you mentioned it. Besides, no one'd steal any part of me in Mexico to satisfy American medical tourism. No one who does that would touch me because I look too much like you. Speaking of which, why didn't you tell Santi or me about Olivia?"

"To protect you."

"From our cousin who's my size but grew up in America."

"With a father connected to the *Cosa Nostra*, and a mother connected to the Culiacán."

"Her father?"

"Yeah. She didn't just marry into the Mafia. Apparently, she had ties she didn't know about."

"Like Santi and me. She had no clue we existed. We didn't know about her. You let us believe our aunt was dead. You didn't tell us when you found out she wasn't."

"Because it was safer for everyone."

Jesus snaps at Joey, but her expression tells me she knows he's right. As hurt as she is by the secret, she gets why her father kept it. It protected both women from exposure to other syndicates. But that protection ended when Olivia married Luca, and it'll be nonexistent when Joey and I marry.

"The Mancinellis said you're on good terms with them now. Is that true?"

"We do some business here and there."

All of our homes have cell phone jammers. No one from the government is listening in—not in English, or in Spanish like now—but it still pays to be vague.

"Did something go wrong here?"

"No. They aren't using you to get to me. What's your boyfriend done to screw them lately? It's more likely because of him. You've lived in New York for years with no problems. You take up with that blue-eyed foreigner and look what happens."

Zarca gringo. Better than what Santiago called me.

"He has green eyes, *papá*. And he's not the foreigner here."

"Americans—"

"We're in New York. The French didn't steal this land from us and sell it to the Americans."

"No, but they still stole it."

El ruco. Old geezer.

No, not quite.

El chavoruco.

I've seen photos of him. A middle-aged man who dresses

like he's some suave twenty-something when he's got gray hair and wrinkles.

Being a dick—even in my head—toward my future father-in-law won't get me anywhere. I set aside my annoyance because I've got to play nice for Joey's sake.

Joey's phone is on the bedside table and buzzes. I reach over her and grab it. I show her the screen. She grits her teeth before mouthing, "work." I hit ignore. She can call them back later.

"Don't pretend not to get the point, little monkey. You were fine here before him. You might have done your studies at Universidad Nacional Autónoma de México, but you did your grad school and clinical hours at CUNY-Hunter. You've been in America for years. A few days with the gringo, and you're almost dead. Don't think I don't know about the mercenary who almost ran you over. I let that slide because it was just to scare you. This I won't ignore. O'Rourke, you had your chance and failed. Stay away from my daughter or else."

I don't take the bait. I let Joey speak, even though it might kill me.

"I decide, *papá*. Cormac and I are permanent. You will *not* convince me otherwise. He was probably going to call and ask your permission to marry me before he found out who I was. I kept that from him until I knew he's as serious about me as I am about him. He didn't know my father heads one of the biggest cartels in Mexico. He fell in love with me for me. If I wanted a man just because he's in organized crime, I could have found a man back home. I'm with him for him. If today hadn't happened, he probably would have extended an olive branch and still asked your permission."

"He isn't getting it."

"Then you'll lose another woman in your life."

I shake my head. Vigorously.

Jesus Espinoza isn't a man to issue idle threats to. I don't want to break up their family. That's the one thing that would make me walk away from Joey. Her hand's still over my heart. She fists my shirt and tugs. Her expression warns me not to argue.

"Don't issue me ultimatums, Jocelyn. It didn't work when you were a child."

"But it did, so I'm giving you one now. Either accept Cormac and support us, or I only speak to you on Christmas and Easter. You and Santi don't have the men here to take me, so you know it would be a death trap for anyone you send. Your niece grew up not knowing you. Do you want any grandkids to do the same? Would you do that to *mami*?"

"Jocelyn—" Santiago tries to intervene, but it's as though he said nothing.

"Enrique won't be pleased to know you're here. Do you want to rely on the Mafia to protect you when you have a flimsy relationship at best with your niece and only do business with them here and there? Or would your future son-in-law make a better ally against the *jefe de jefes*?"

Boss of bosses.

Enrique Diaz is the most powerful cartel king in the world. Nothing happens in Latin America he doesn't allow, unless it's the NYC *Cosa Nostra*, bratva, or us. We're the only three syndicates he can't control because our international reach is too far.

Joey nails the coffin shut.

"I doubt the O'Rourkes would help you if I'm not even speaking to you."

My future fiancée's dragging me into shite that isn't my decision. It's Dillan's. She's not wrong, but I'm not the one who makes that call. She's banking on a lot right now, and I don't know that it's a check she can cash. Jesus isn't without connections here in the city. There are plenty of Mexican gangs tied to him, and there are some other Latin American ones who wouldn't mind taking some shots at the Colombians. It'll be a domino effect if that happens because the Diazes will aim straight for my family.

"Jo-Jo, you can't speak for Cormac's family. Don't do this."

Santiago finally gets a word in edgewise. He never struck me as a voice of reason. I suppose there's a first time for everything. I'm either going to smother the fire or toss oil on it. I switch the conversation to English because I still don't want them to know how well I speak Spanish.

"Jocelyn's right, though. We'll stand by you if you accept Jocelyn and me. If you don't, then my family has no reason to help you when Enrique loses his shite. He's still pissed about the deal you screwed up for him, and that was nearly three years ago."

"He was a whiny kid, and he's a whiny old man now."

They're about the same age, but I never guessed they've known each other that long. Joey gestures for me to lean forward so she can whisper in my ear.

"Their fathers hated each other, but they hated my grandfather's rivals even more. Enrique's father helped secure my father's position just before Enrique's uncle killed his own brother. My father said he'd take care of Enrique's uncle to repay the favor, but the man disappeared into the Amazon only to resurface as the head of the major cartel in Colombia. He lives because Enrique dealt with him and made his uncle his bitch. Enrique's pissed because he believes *papá* still owes him a favor."

She fired off the story so fast, I almost missed parts. I knew about Enrique's uncle committing fratricide and disappearing, then becoming Enrique's vassal. I didn't know the stuff that happened before that.

I can acknowledge Jesus and Enrique's past without giving Jesus an inch.

"He might be a whiny old man, but you came to his home. I doubt you plan to say hello."

"I'm here to make sure my daughter is safe. With a new wife and a chance for kids, he'll understand."

Kids? Nope. Not a chance. Enrique's wife could probably still have them, but she's not going back to that stage again. I'll put money on that.

Joey's not buying that either. "And now you know I'm safe, so what're you going to do when Enrique gets angry at you?"

"You're not safe until I see that for myself."

There's a quiet but insistent knock on the bedroom door. I pull away from Joey and climb off the bed. I'm silent as I cross the room and ease the door open enough to stick my head out. My dad can see my bare chest, but I don't care.

"Jesus is on the phone."

I more mouth it than whisper. His gaze darts over my shoulder, but he can't see the bed from that angle. He nods before he leans close to my ear.

"You stay here, but the rest of us have to go."

Something went wrong.

I lean back, my brow furrowed. What the fuck else could happen today?

"Whoever this is, hit your house with a drone strike. Cor, there's next to nothing left. This was full scale destruction."

"Who the feck did it?"

He glances over my shoulder again before his gaze meets mine. It prompts me to ask what I really don't want to.

"Jesus?"

"Or Santiago. They knew you and Jocelyn weren't there."

"How do you know?"

My dad pulls a piece of folded paper from his pocket and

hands it to me. I don't have to open it all the way to recognize the Culiacán's brand. I look up at my dad before I nod. I step back and close the door. He'll wait for me on the other side.

I grab my pants and slip them on before walking to Joey's side of the bed. I hold out my empty hand. I folded the paper before I turned around. Joey can't see it.

"Jocelyn, give me—"

"Stop calling me that. You never do, and you know I don't like it."

Next to never. Only when I'm scolding her, I suppose.

"What's wrong with your name?"

That's what finally pushes Jesus into losing his shite?

"Santi's always called me Jo-Jo. Cormac calls me Joey."

"But I use your name too, and you never get pissed about it." Santiago sounds as mulish as his father now.

"You're not Cormac."

"Joey, give me the phone, please. The rest of the call is between your father and me. Santiago, go back to the children's table. Jesus, you and I are *not* good."

That's as much as I dare say right now. I tap the phone and put it on mute. I show Joey they can no longer hear us.

"I have to go. Your apartment was just a test. They went after our place."

"What do you mean 'went after our place?'"

"There's nothing left."

"Who did it?"

I look down at the phone in my hand, then back up at her.

"No." She shakes her head in disbelief.

"I have evidence that says it is. I'm going to speak to your dad on the way. I'll find out whether he's lying one way or another."

"Cor, don't underestimate him or Santi. And they can mobilize more men than you probably know. They have

Guatemalans, Hondurans, and Salvadorians working for them, too."

"We know. I love you."

"I love you, too."

I pull on the rest of my clothes after unmuting the call.

"Jesus, we're having a sit down before I blow up something of yours in retaliation."

"What retaliation?"

That's the last Joey hears as I walk into the hallway where my dad's still waiting. He points to my bedroom, but I shake my head. Instead, I point to him, then point down. I want him to stay. I can hear my uncles downstairs with the other guys. They'll stay with him and the men patrolling today.

"I have a piece of your artwork from what's left of my home with Joey. She could've been there."

"What the fuck are you talking about? Jocelyn?"

"I'm not with her anymore. It's you and me. Santiago, you're the one panting into the phone. Hang up, *niño.*"

He's younger than me, but not by much. He has less experience, though. I won't discount his training, so I don't want him hearing all of this at the same time as his father. I don't need them plotting simultaneously. Mexican cartels recruit young boys because once they turn eighteen, their juvenile records basically get expunged. Law enforcement can't enforce or go after them for anything they did as a minor. It means once they're adults, they're fully trained and battle-tested with no legal past to shadow them.

I tap the phone screen and hang up on Santiago.

"It's just you and me, Jesus. Blowing up my house and leaving a calling card wasn't wise."

"I didn't do shit to your house."

"That's not what your brand on a piece of paper that landed in my yard from the drone that blew up my house says."

"Drone? What the fuck are you talking about?"

"Someone just used a drone to bomb my house. Along with it, they dropped a calling card. It's your brand stamped on a sheet of paper."

"You think I'd leave proof?"

"It's not like I'm going to the police with it. My house has had an unfortunate gas leak."

That's the excuse we'll use. That or I left something on the stove.

"That's irrelevant. You think I'd confess to you if I did it?"

"Yes. It's a warning to stay away from Joey."

"That's not her fucking name."

I'm not fighting over that right now. I've just walked into my dad's office where the others are waiting for me. They remain silent while I put the call back on speaker. We've continued in English, but speaking Spanish wouldn't be a problem because my brother, cousins, uncles, and dad are all fluent, too. I know none of us want him to know that yet.

"You don't deny it's a warning."

"I have no reason to deny that because I didn't bomb your house."

"Santiago likes expensive toys."

"So do you, but I don't believe you destroyed your own home."

"You and Santiago admit you've been watching Joey and me. You've known we're together. Why shouldn't I think you're interfering? You might not have bombed her place, but it's not impossible to believe you bombed my place as retaliation for being with her or putting her in danger."

"Cormac, when I retaliate, I look the man in the eye. You'll know it's me. You won't be guessing."

El Corridor. The Hunter.

Fits.

"Then who?"

"I don't know. Believe it or not, I'm too busy to keep track of who you're bickering with."

"Bullshit. You made that your business the moment you found out about Joey and me."

"I still don't know."

We're not getting anywhere. Jesus must feel the same because he offers a compromise. Who knew hell froze over?

"You need me as much as I need you if we're going to keep Jocelyn safe. Whoever the fuck this is has the *huevos* to attack a cartel daughter and mob girlfriend. I've heard the stories about your family. I may as well call her your wife."

"You should."

Huevos may mean eggs, but I like it better than balls. Much more accurate. I look at my dad, then Seamus. My dad nods, and my brother rolls his eyes. It's not like that was a secret. Seamus holds out his phone, so I can see the notes app.

Tiernan and I will head over there now. We'll see what we can learn from your place. Tonight we'll go to J's.

They'll wait until it's dark, so people aren't as curious. Seamus may have loathed cross-examining Tiernan when they met during a trial because he poked holes in her qualifications, but we all know she's the best at what she does. We don't involve her often, but this isn't the first time we've needed her to tell us what happened with a fire or tell us how to make sure no one pins a fire on us.

"I have some calls I need to make. Joey's safe where she is. If I have to go out, four men from my family will be where she is."

"You still won't tell me. She's my daughter, O'Rourke."

"And until I know who did this, I trust no one who didn't

331

give me or doesn't share my DNA. She might be your daughter, but she's mine."

Let him decide what I'm claiming. As far as I'm concerned, she's my everything. More than my house will burn if anyone threatens her again. I'll burn all this motherfucker down.

Chapter Twenty-Three

Joey

That wasn't exactly a disaster, but it didn't go well. It's not like I thought we'd all be sitting together, having *café y pan dulce*—coffee and sweet bread. Maybe if we were at my parents' house, and my mom was there. Definitely not over the phone or even in NYC. I wouldn't have invited my father, brother, and Cormac to my place. It's—it was—a far too enclosed space for the three of them. It seems we won't be having them over to Cormac's house. I can't imagine *papá* or Santi wanting to come here, either. I doubt Cormac's parents want to play host to them. That'd be like hanging steaks on themselves and walking into a lion's den.

If my head hadn't started hurting at the beginning of the call, it certainly would be by now. I glance at the bottle on the bedside table and see it's a powerful painkiller. Not quite narcotic, but pretty damn close. I reach for it and the glass of water. I've just swallowed when my phone rings again.

Work.

Fuck my life.

"Hello."

"Jocelyn, you better have a good excuse for why you aren't back here. You had two meetings this morning you missed without permission."

"I had a gas leak at my apartment that started a fire. It nearly killed me. Can I have the afternoon off?"

Things have been practically hostile between Martha and me for the last few days. Sarcasm won't win me any friends, but she's been riding me like a fucking pony at a fair.

"Are you all right?" Some genuine concern.

"I have stitches in my leg and my head."

"*Dios mio!*" My God!

"I was too out of it to remember the meetings. Please pass along my apologies."

"Jocelyn, I know you wouldn't lie about something that serious, especially since you'll need a doctor's note to miss more work."

Puta.

Bitch.

"But this claim of a fire makes no sense, since we had another complaint against you an hour ago."

"Someone filed the complaint an hour ago, or my alleged misconduct was an hour ago?"

"Both."

"I was unconscious an hour ago while a doctor sewed me up. Unless I was talking in my sleep, and somebody on Staten Island heard me all the way in Queens, that's not possible."

"Which hospital are you at?"

"They won't release whether or not I'm a patient."

Motherfucker. Guess she's over her miniscule concern.

"You can tell me."

"I'll bring the doctor's note."

"Why're you being awkward, Jocelyn?"

"Because something isn't right. I've worked for you for years and had nothing but glowing reviews. Now someone's lying about me. I don't feel comfortable giving out anything personal right now."

"You've been an excellent employee until the past month. Ever since you started dating a mobster. You of all people. I never thought you'd lower yourself to—"

"Martha, I'd stop while you're ahead. You're one of the few people who knows about my family because of my background check. I wouldn't speak ill of anyone in my life."

No one's going to whack her. No one's even going to become a second shadow. But a healthy dose of fear will shut her up.

"I want you to be safe, but I need you to be less disruptive at work. I have to shift cases around, so people can cover for you."

Keep your big girl panties on—if you were wearing them.

Don't quit. Don't quit. Don't quit.

It's thoroughly tempting, but that doesn't resolve my problems. I won't give in to Martha or whoever this is. They can suck it.

"Pass along my apologies to them, too. It's Tuesday now. I should be back to work by Monday. That's no longer than I'd be out for the flu."

That's assuming Cormac lets me go back. He won't let me see how shaken he is unless he wants to. But I can tell. Hover will be an understatement. Until he resolves this, he'll take away almost all my freedom to go anywhere. Frankly, I'm glad. The idea of going out and about, just like everything's still normal, makes me want to heave. I don't want to go anywhere without him. I'll stay put if he can't be with me. Taking command of this and asserting control is the only way Cormac can handle this unpredictability. I know it's his worst nightmare. Me relinquishing control will make both of us feel better.

I feel like shit, so why wouldn't I want to be taken care of? I wish he were back here, holding me again. If the pain meds are kicking in, I can't tell. This conversation's making me want to hurl—that was a strange phrase to learn when I came to America, but the word fits the feeling.

"I'm sorry you're injured, but this disruptive behavior means I need to write you up again. I'll investigate today's accusation further, but just not showing up and causing other people to cover your work is unacceptable."

"I've called out unexpectedly before when I've gotten sick. I did it three months ago when I got food poisoning from the menudo I ate only to be polite."

I hate the soup. I don't like hominy, and I can't stand tripe. I only had some because I felt backed into a corner and didn't want to offend the family. I barely choked it down, and I knew something was off. The tripe wasn't prepared properly. My stomach hurts just thinking about it.

"You didn't give me a hard time about that."

"You threw up at your desk. I had to let you go home."

Those gastro pyrotechnics were quite spectacular. I barely got to the trash can in time.

"If you persist with these unsubstantiated claims and reprimands, I'll file a grievance with the Department of Social Services commissioner and HRA. I'm certain Human Resources will understand my concern about a hostile work environment."

"Don't threaten me, Jocelyn."

"No threat. Just a promise."

My phone beeps in my ear. I look at it and see it's an incoming call from a number I don't know. I don't care. It's the perfect excuse. It beeps again.

"Martha, do what you want. I have another call. Bye."

I don't wait for her to respond, instead hanging up and switching to the new call.

"Hello."

"*Hola, señorita Espinoza.*"

"Who is this?"

I know that voice, but I'll pretend I don't. I won't give Pablo Diaz the satisfaction of controlling the conversation from the start. We'll speak English.

"*Es Pablo Díaz.*"

At least, I will.

"What do you want, Mr. Diaz?"

"I heard what happened today."

I remain silent. It was an observation, not a question. I have nothing I want to offer either, though I have plenty of questions. I won't give that away.

"Are you all right?"

"Yes."

"Are you with Cormac?"

"Why'd you call?"

"Avoiding the question doesn't mean you didn't answer. Since he hasn't snatched the phone from you, he must not be in the same room."

Astute.

"I called because you've done a lot of good for our neighborhoods. You can't pick your family, and there's no accounting for taste. But the people in our neighborhoods respect you and like you. I don't want anything to happen to you because it would upset the children."

Our neighborhoods.

We aren't neighbors. He means the Colombian Cartel.

I pray Cormac didn't leave without saying goodbye.

Pablo's on the phone with me. He called.

"Your concern is noted."

"Ms. Espinoza, you avoid me like the plague. I don't think it's because my uncle knows your father breaks promises. Why do you hide from me? Do you assume the worst because of my uncle's and your father's strained relationship?"

Strained?

I catch myself before snorting. Enrique swore he'd kill my father if he laid eyes on him again. The last time they were together, Enrique beat my father so badly, he nearly killed him. In return, when my father got back to Mexico, he arranged a car accident that nearly killed Enrique's other nephew, Alejandro. He also found two of Enrique's labs in Colombia. Around the same time, there were mysterious fires at both.

"It has nothing to do with our relatives. At least, not my father or your uncle."

There's a prolonged pause before he responds. His tone could freeze ice.

"Juan. You mean when he had to intervene. Back then, you made an honest mistake because you were newly assigned to the neighborhood. You're a first responder and did what you believed was your duty. What you believed was right. You didn't know better."

That last bit. That's a lesson I learned young. The outside world believes syndicates are morally void. Within this world, morals are situational, but ethics are absolute. Someone's idea of what's right and wrong might change by circumstance, but the organizations' ethics are unwavering. The codes of conduct don't differ that much across the organizations. The one thing that's never contestable is you *don't* call the police, and you *never* help the government.

Given that, I think it's pretty understandable why I avoided Pablo like herpes—you're far more likely to catch that these days than the plague.

Since he's figured it out, I see no reason to respond. Even if I wanted to, I don't get the chance because Cormac bursts into the room. He practically rips the phone from my hand.

"What the—" He glances down at me. "—feck do you want with my woman, *caremonda*?" Slang for *cara de monda*—face of a penis.

I stifle my laugh. That's definitely more Colombian than Mexican. They swear a lot more, and the curses they have are definitely more—colorful. It might equate to dickhead, but Cormac means nothing that benign.

He doesn't put it on speaker, but the volume's loud enough for me to hear most of what Pablo says.

"I was checking on your girlfriend."

"Why?"

"People in the neighborhood will worry."

"How thoughtful. What do you want?"

"I told you to speak to Niko. Did you?"

"Yeah."

"And?"

"He told me to talk to Gabriele."

"Did you?"

"Nothing good ever comes from you being a nosy little fecker. *Eres peor que una abuela chismosa.*" You're worse than a gossipy old grandma.

"It's not gossip when it's true. The families will want to know Ms. Bracero is all right."

He's not using my father's last name anymore. Traditional Spanish last names place the mother's maiden name at the end. Espinoza Bracero. He used Espinoza earlier to make a point. One he won't antagonize Cormac with.

"Thank you for your concern. Goodb—"

"Cor, don't be a douche. Put her on the phone. I have one last thing to say, and I promise it won't insult her."

I nod, but Cormac looks like he's about to sit down for a root canal. He hits the speaker button.

"I'm here, Mr. Diaz."

"You've feared I would retaliate for your mistake years ago. It cost us some money, but no damage was done. I regret you feared I'd come after you for it. My uncle can't stand your father, and I detest your—boyfriend. But I didn't exaggerate about the good you've done in our neighborhoods. I already heard what happened today. If you're ever threatened, and you can't get to the O'Rourkes, you come to me or my family."

"Why should I believe you? You implied to Cormac I was fucking your cousin. You used me."

"I did. But I've also had a security detail on you for years. You go nowhere in any Latino neighborhood in New York without someone making sure you're safe. I don't think you realize how much the families value you. My uncle would have a mutiny if anything happened to you."

Can he whack my boss?

I shouldn't think shit like that, but I'm pissed at Martha. Extremely pissed.

"Thank you." I suppose I can be gracious.

"*De nada, señorita.*" You're welcome, miss.

I watch Cormac while all three of us remain silent. What else is there to say?

"Cor, take me off speaker. There's more to discuss."

I nod. Not that it matters.

"What do you want?"

Cormac walks away from the bed, so I can't hear. I only get his side of the conversation.

"Why would he do that?...He'll never pay that...They're

out of their fecking minds...If you're lying...No...I'm telling you right now, if you're lying, even *señora* Margherita won't recognize you."

That's Pablo's mother. She's a kind woman you'd never imagine is married to a senior Cartel member who pops in and out of Colombian prisons like people pop in and out of a bodega. He's more than his older brother's messenger. He's the fucking Colombian Holy Spirit. See him, and you know your soul's leaving your body.

"Fine...Maybe I'll let you know...Feck off. Bye."

I forced myself up to sit while I spoke to Pablo. I rest back against the pillows now. Cormac perches on the edge of the bed.

"What did he say before I came in here?"

"Not much. Just that I was wrong to fear him. He understood what happened, and he didn't blame me for it. He said the families in their neighborhoods appreciate me, so he never wanted revenge."

Cormac's expression relaxes, and I breathe a little easier. His hand wraps around mine, covering it entirely.

"He's right that the families value you. You can see it when they talk to you and about you. It makes no sense that Martha's giving you a hard time."

"I thought the Cartel might be leaning on her, but now I don't know."

"I wondered the same. I have some more calls to make, but they can wait."

"I thought you needed to go."

"We're staying here until later tonight. Once I know more about both explosions..."

He doesn't need to finish the sentence. Either he can't tell me what they'll do, or I won't want the details to avoid nightmares.

"I told Martha it was a gas leak that sparked it."

"Did she believe you?"

"Maybe. I doubt it. She's going to write me up for not going back to work this morning, despite me telling her I was injured. She claims I'm causing problems because she has to reassign my cases."

"For one day? Even the rest of the week wouldn't be that bad. Couldn't you reschedule things or ask someone to cover for you rather than have them reassigned?"

"One would think. I don't know why she's being like this unless someone's forcing her hand. But her voice sounds like she sincerely means it all. I warned her if she persisted in writing me up for unsubstantiated claims and blatant lies—apparently, someone filed another conduct complaint for me today, but it was while I was unconscious—then I'll go to the DSS commissioner and the HRA. Cormac, she knows who my family is from my background check. She can't know the extent, but she knows they're cartel. She knows you're mob. She claims my connection to you is the reason for these problems."

"They could be."

"Maybe. I suspect it's more personal than that. Something changed within her when you and I got together. It's like she's the one punishing me for being with you. I think she's the one making shit up."

"I suspected that, and I asked Sean to look into it. So far, nothing is turning up from anyone besides her. The IP address for the first claim doesn't match your office, her house, or her phone. But that doesn't mean it isn't her. She could have a VPN."

"She does. It makes it cheaper for her to speak to her family in Mexico and Guatemala."

"I'll have Sean check that out. Are you hungry or thirsty?"

I don't expect the sudden shift, but we've discussed everything I can know. If there's more, he's decided it isn't safe for me to know. I won't press the issue because I don't want to keep talking about it. The painkillers have only taken the edge off my headache.

"No. At least not for food or drinks."

I waggle my eyebrows, then shoot him what I hope are bedroom eyes. Another term that made little sense when I first learned it. His hand wraps around my throat, this time squeezing enough to make me lift my head higher.

"You have a concussion, stitches in your head, and a sutured hole in your leg. I'm not fucking you, little girl, so stop tempting me."

"I proved my mouth still works." I open wide.

He squeezes as he pounces. His mouth commands mine, and I submit. My hands clasp around his neck as his kiss drugs me. We're breathless when we pull away.

"Sean and Shane are paramedics. Do you really want Shane to guess why I drag him up here to see if you still have a concussion?"

My cheeks are roasting as I shake my head.

"Then be a good girl and don't tempt me."

"Fine, Daddy." I sound anything but agreeable.

He looks at his right palm before scratching it.

"My palm's getting awfully itchy to land across your soft arse. Maybe I will get Shane up here after all."

Chapter Twenty-Four

Cormac

As much as we both would've loved me doling out a spanking, we both know Joey's not up to that. She yawned right after I threatened to get Shane, so I crawled back into bed with her until she fell asleep. She's in a deep sleep because she didn't react to me climbing out of bed. I watched her from the door for a good two minutes before shutting it silently. I'm back in my dad's office with the others. There are nine of us now because my dad and uncles are here, too.

Three brothers married three sisters and wound up with six sons. Seamus and I are just bigger enough than our cousins to be noticeable. We inherited our dad's size and that side of the family's hair, which is lighter than the red some of my cousins got from our moms. But it's like being in a hall of mirrors when we're all in one room.

I texted them when Joey fell asleep, so they know about Pablo's call. But we couldn't discuss it on the phone, and no one wanted to text back and forth. So, now we're where we can talk about it. I recognized my mom's and aunts' expression when I walked past the living room from the stairs. If our retaliation doesn't live up to their fiercely protective expectations, they'll strike back at whoever hurt Joey and Sean and whoever blew up my home.

Each of them was a mob daughter and mob sister. All three are mob wives and mob mothers. Two are the boss's aunts and one is his mother. No three women better exemplify the phrase "mobbed-up" than Saoirse, Siobhan, and Breda O'Rourke. Hell, they didn't even have to change their last names when they married. The O'Rourke clan division into separate families happened a few hundred years ago, but both sides keep having sons to carry on the name.

When Uncle Donovan was boss, they terrified the pish out of him. When he thought about getting some of us involved too young, Aunt Breda—Finn, Sean, and Shane's mother—put a hit on one of Uncle Donovan's men. The guy lived—barely and only because she let him—but my aunts and mom made sure Uncle Donovan understood he might've been the head of our branch, but they were the neck that held it in place.

The men in the Four Families might be physically bigger and stronger than the women in our families, but the world would do well to understand *nothing* we could come up with will ever match the lengths these women will go to when they're protecting their family. They say hell hath no fury like a woman scorned. Whoever said that first hadn't met a syndicate mother. Hell hath no fury like a mother. Period. Full stop.

"What do you want to do, Cor?"

Dillan and the others will defer to me. Dillan might lead our branch now, but whoever this is, went after my soon-to-be wife. It means I'll lead whatever mission we go on, but I won't plan alone.

"Niko told us to speak to Gabriele, but we never did. That

was before Joey and Olivia met. They were supposed to have lunch today. Shite. Did anyone let them know?"

"Yeah. Thea saw Maria at work, so she passed along the message."

Finn's wife is a neonatologist at the same hospital where Maria Mancinelli—who's Salvatore's niece and Olivia's sister-in-law—is a radiologist. If my mom and aunts are mobbed-up, then Maria Mancinelli is the most unassailable woman anywhere. She's currently—by birth and by marriage—a Mafia niece, daughter, sister, wife, aunt, and soon-to-be mother.

"Thanks. I figured someone let her know since Luca isn't pishing vinegar at me, but I wasn't sure. Luca wouldn't go to this extreme because my girlfriend stood up his wife, and both explosions happened before Joey and Olivia's lunch date. Then again, is he secretly pissed he's about to be related to us? That now Jesus might do business with both of us?"

"None of that explains Gabriele's involvement if Niko told the truth."

We all snort at Shane's comment. Nikolai Kutsenko could look God in the eye and lie. That's the level of chutzpah—audacity—the man has. He and his family rival the Diazes for being the most psychopathic.

We're all a little touched, as Granny would say. Not quite right in the head. I don't believe any of the men in my family are natural sociopaths, but no one does what we—the men in all Four Families—do without having some trained sociopathic tendencies. The bratva and Cartel are depraved. Considering what I've done, that's saying something about those mother-fuckers.

It's not like the *Cosa Nostra* men are any better. Gabriele Scotto's relationship with the truth is even more distant than any of ours. He's a lawyer too, so he can bend the truth so far an angel would believe they're a demon. Fuck. He could turn an angel into a demon. His name has *never* fit.

If it's Gabriele, I'll never let this go. We all helped him when his wife—back then, girlfriend—was in danger. I helped more than the others in my family. If he went after my girlfriend, after I gave him information against one of our men to protect her...His next murder trial won't go the same way as his first. His arse will be someone's bitch in federal prison.

"I'll call him."

I wake my phone and pull up my contacts. Yup. He's saved in my phone too. He's the tallest and broadest in that family—he's basically Salvatore's adopted nephew since he's practically joined at the hip to Salvatore's actual nephew, Carmine—so he and I have faced off plenty of times in fights. It takes two Mancinelli men to rival Seamus or me, but Gabriele's pretty equal to my brother or me.

"What do you want, *faccia de cazzo*?" Testicle face.

We have such endearing names for each other.

"What the feck did my girlfriend do to you, *abhlóir*."

That roughly translates to a special kind of idiot who complains too much and thinks he's far more intelligent than he is.

"I don't even know who your girlfriend is."

"Liar, liar, pants on fire."

That might sound childish if I hadn't once set his pants on fire...With him in them...On accident...Sorta.

"Fucking get on with it. Sinead and I are about to have dinner."

Sinead O'Malley. You can't get a much more Irish name than that short of Márgrég MacDonnell, Dillan's wife.

"You might have gotten off for the last bombing, but you won't get away with what you did today."

"What the hell are you talking about?"

Gabriele and Sinead met when he was on trial for killing two teens when he allegedly set a bomb off at his lumberyard. The charges were plausible since he also owns a hardware store and has plenty of demolition supplies.

"The bomb that went off at my girlfriend's place this morning as she and Sean were going inside. The bomb your bestie's drone dropped on my house today that eviscerated it."

Carmine's always been a nosy fucker. Worse than Pablo. Now he has high-end, practically government grade drones that spy on shite. Fortunately for us, Sean has the same ones. Could this be the *Cosa Nostra's* retribution for the drone strike Shane ordered on a Mancinelli house after shite went sideways for Carys? When you're in families as tightly knit as the Four Families, a strike on one is a strike on all of them. Retribution isn't a straight line. It's a spider's web. Could Gabriele be punishing Joey and me for something Shane did to retaliate against a Mancinelli?

Fucking tangled web, indeed. Maybe Shakespeare knew what he was talking about.

"Neither Carmine nor I did shit to your shitty family. I'm telling you right now, Cormac, leave our family out of it. We have more important shit going on."

The call's on speaker, so everyone can hear. I look at Finn, who shrugs.

"I thought Maria was fine. Finn said Ally spoke to her at work today."

Just like Jocelyn is only Joey to me, Althea is only Thea to Finn. Everyone else calls her Ally.

"Yeah, well, you know Maria."

The woman could be on her deathbed and be more worried about helping others than herself. Considering the fucked-up family she's from, she's shockingly unjaded. She's also midway through a high-risk pregnancy. I know Ally's felt guilty for how easy her pregnancy is since they're due around the same time.

"Does she need anything?"

Dillan leans in to be sure Gabriele can hear him. We might not give a shite what happens to the men in that family, but Maria doesn't deserve any ill will. We'd all give her the shirt off our backs, and not just because our parents would kill us if we didn't. She can't stand any of us because of who we are and what we do, but we all like her. We've known each other since we were in diapers.

"No. She just needs to keep her stress level down. Finding out one of us bombed a woman's home wouldn't do that, so none of us are going to risk her health for your pathetic ass. But thanks for the offer."

That's how we roll. We loathe each other, but we can be gracious. Normally, I'd stab her husband's eye out without a second thought, but no one will touch a hair on Matteo's head if it'll harm Maria. We have consciences. And if we didn't, our parents would skelp us to within an inch of our lives until we found them.

"This is the worst that's happened, but it wasn't the first attack. Someone tried to run her over as she stepped off a sidewalk while she and I were on a run with Finn. Before that, two men followed her from the subway."

After today's fucktastrophe, I consider those incidents as attacks now, rather than mere threats.

"Who'd you piss off more than us? Who'd her father piss off more than Enrique? Or was it one of his little psychopath minions?"

He means Enrique's nephews. There's nearly as many of them as there are the rest of us in each family. Pablo, Alejandro, Jorge, Javier, and Joaquin. *"Este pequeño cerdito."* Any of them could be the little piggy who cried wee, wee, wee all the way home. Did one of them bitch to Enrique about something besides who Joey's father is?

"I don't know. You sound awfully certain while you point the finger at them."

"Because the most obvious answer is usually the right one. I knew you didn't learn shit in law school."

Not all of us went to Yale for law school. I *only* went to NYU, but I know my fucking bar exam score was higher than his. I fucking bribed someone to check.

"Don't deflect."

"Whatever. I did nothing, and neither did anyone in my family. We couldn't give two shits from Sunday about any of you right now."

"Give Maria our best."

"Thanks." Actual sincerity—that doesn't last. "*Vaffanculo a chi t'è morto.*"

I have my own response to his go fuck the souls of your dead family members.

"*D'anam don diabhal.*" Your soul to the devil.

Basically, I hope you eat shite and die. The difference between Gabriele and me—one of many differences—is my family's bothered to learn more Italian than we'll ever let on. No one in the *Cosa Nostra*—or any syndicate—has bothered to learn Irish.

We hang up, and I'm left just as fucked as I was before. Seamus meets my gaze, and I know he's mulling something over before he speaks.

"Besides three of the Four Families, who hates the Diazes most right now? Who'd want us or Jesus to accuse Enrique?"

"How much time do we have?"

I glare at Sean, who I don't find funny. "Shouldn't you be home with a wife kissing your boo-boo?"

I want answers, not smartass quips. I inhale before I say

something I can't take back. It's not my family's fault, and considering what Sean did to protect Joey, I'm being an arse for not showing more appreciation. I open my mouth to apologize, but Sean nods. He gets how I feel, so he apologizes first. I shoot him a tight smile of thanks, dipping my chin to reciprocate the apology.

"Joey told me her father has other Mexicans plus Hondurans, Guatemalans, and Salvadorians to back him. They might want to feck Enrique over."

We're not allowed to say fuck to each other, and especially not at each other. Certainly not with our dads in the room. We're not even supposed to use it amongst us in casual conversation.

"If they side with Jesus, I don't see them going after his daughter. What about the Dominicans and Ecuadorians we squeezed in Port Richmond? Are they pissed at me for enforcing? Pissed at me for dating her? Maybe pissed at Enrique for not protecting them?"

I'm just thinking aloud right now.

"Aren't those families Jocelyn helps?" Seamus's brow furrows as he watches me crack my knuckles.

"I haven't seen her out there enough to know. I can ask when she wakes up. She's also having problems with her boss. The woman keeps claiming people are filing complaints against Joey. She gave her shite about not coming back into work today even though Joey said she had a fire at her place and got injured. I've heard parts of their conversations before. Joey says the woman's completely different toward her now that she's dating me."

"I'll look her up."

Finn's in front of his computer and starts typing. He's not just our CPA. He's like one of those hackers on TV shows with the black and green or white screens with all the mumbo jumbo scrolling. If there's anything worth knowing about Martha, he'll find it. He doesn't even need her last name to get started.

My dad and uncles sit quietly, letting the rest of us hash this out and plan. They're semi-retired, if there is such a thing in the mob. They don't go out on many missions anymore, but they've come out of retirement a few times lately. If we need extra hands or they want to scream a message that no one touches their children—by blood or by marriage—they suit up. We all follow Dillan's orders, but even he still defers to their experience and wisdom.

"Da, what do you think?"

"I think someone in the other families hired low-rung gang members to scout, so they'd go unnoticed. But you recognized the mercenary, and some no-name off the street won't know how to make those kinds of bombs or have drones. Find the woman driving that car. Make her tell you."

Uncle Donovan and Declan shattered the cardinal rule we don't target women and children. It was a downhill fall from grace after that. My family's slowly—like at a fucking snail's pace—rebuilding our reputation for not targeting them anymore. But they opened the floodgates, which means people have targeted most of the new wives.

However, a female mercenary is entirely different. If you hire out your sword arm, you give up any protection. We treat all mercenaries the same: a threat to extinguish or an asset to pay well, but never trust.

Uncle Tate—Dillan's dad—purses his lips and moves them side to side. I don't know if it's nature or nurture, but Dillan's always done the same thing. They only do it when they're thinking among family. In public, you don't know what's going through either of their minds until they want you to know.

"Do you remember who she was?"

"Yeah. Lilly Schneider."

Such a misnomer. There's nothing sweet or fragile about that bitch. She'd hack her mother to pieces for ten bucks. She'll hire herself out to the lowest bidder because a dollar to her is always better than nothing, no matter the job or the boss.

"She used to do a lot of work for your grandda when she was young. That's how she got her start."

"I know. It's why I recognized her."

She's close to my parents' age, so mid to late fifties. She used to work for my grandfather whenever he needed a honeypot. But time's not aged her gracefully. She looks like a haggard old prune. Fuck her.

"I've heard she's been hustling at Declan's."

It's a skeezy hole in the wall pool hall my mom's second cousin owned before he got himself killed. The bratva didn't like how he led for the millisecond he was in charge. The big bag of arse thought to seize power after Uncle Donovan died. Dillan was so pissed Uncle Don wouldn't listen to him as his chief strategist, he went out of town for an unexpected vacation.

While he was gone, Uncle Don died. Declan put a hit on our moms and took over. He died for his crimes—largely because we made sure he couldn't run from the bratva. Before he could call off the hit, a mercenary confused Dillan's little sister, Colleen, for my mom and killed her. A single shot to the forehead while Dillan stood beside her. She was a veterinarian who specialized in rescuing abused animals like in those depressing ASPA commercial. She'd just adopted a puppy, and she and Dillan were taking it home. The woman who shot my cousin is dead, but her sister—Lilly—isn't. Yet.

"I want her at the station."

The abandoned railway station in the Bronx. It's been unused for public transportation in at least a decade. We did some excavating and renovating. It has a second subterranean level now where we have a full kitchen, full bathroom, and bunk rooms plus an office. We take people there who need a lengthy reminder of who we are.

Dillan steps away from the table to make the call. No one who comes as our guest leaves as anything besides ash or toxic ooze. Either way, they wind up in the Long Island Sound. I'll get out every secret she has. I'll sell any worthwhile info to whoever it's about or whoever'll find it most useful to screw over the subject. I'll discover who's behind this, and they'll have no one to hide behind. Whoever did this has no idea what's coming their way.

"Cor?"

Finn's voice floats through the door, and his knock is as quiet as my dad's was. I'm back in my old bedroom, dozing beside Joey. I'm too anxious to let myself fall into a deep sleep, but I'm exhausted. She's barely stirred since I came back after meeting with the others. That was three hours ago. I texted my mom and aunts to ask if I should be concerned. They threatened me on pains of death that I better not disturb her. Not for love nor money. More Granny phrases.

They said if she slept this deeply, it's because she needs it. So, I do my best not to move her as I slip off the bed and walk to the door. I have sweatpants on now since I still have a few pieces of clothing here. I step into the hallway after glancing back at Joey.

"I found some shite on Martha. It's not good."

"Have you told the others?"

"No. I wanted to tell you first."

"It's that bad?"

"Maybe, maybe not. But she's your girlfriend, so you have

to decide what you do or don't tell her. I'd rather you get to decide that without an audience or anyone else's suggestions."

"Thanks."

All our homes are large enough for everyone to have their own bedroom. Cousins and sons alike. My aunts and uncles have theirs too. Missions can start or end anywhere, so it's convenient to have somewhere to crash at all our homes. Plus—really—we're just that close a family. Everyone is welcome in one another's homes, so there's always a place for each of us to lay our head.

Finn gestures toward his room. We sit on the end of the bed together, and he opens his laptop. I'm looking at several incognito browser windows open with emails. I skim the one on top and realize immediately it's about Joey. I glance at the date. It shocks the shite out of me to realize it's probably from a month or two after Joey started working for the city. I scan the next one, then the next one, then the next. There're hundreds of them with nearly weekly or biweekly reports from Martha to an unnamed contact that go back years. They're basically run downs of Joey's schedule. Where she was, when she was there, and who she was with.

The responses are vague, and there's no explanation for why Martha sent them. But as I read more, I piece together the reason for them. Whoever's behind this counts Joey as a valuable asset. They're keeping tabs on her for when—not if—they kidnap her and hold her for ransom. They nearly took her when Jesus tried to fuck Enrique over for a major deal with rival narcos.

That was when Olivia and Luca were dating. There was a shootout one night that involved the Colombians, the Italians, and NYPD—dirty NYPD. It got messy fast. From what I can tell, if things hadn't come out about Olivia's connections to

Jesus, these people were going to use the distraction to grab Joey.

I keep skimming since there are so many. When I'm only a quarter of the way through, I look over at Finn. He looks wiped.

"Did you read all these?"

"Yeah. I found them ten minutes after you came back up here. I wanted to be sure I knew what I'd found before sharing it, just in case."

He doesn't need to fill in the rest. There are way too many possible just in cases.

"Did you track these payments they allude to? How much has Martha collected?"

"Several thousand over the years. But as many times as they've paid her, they've threatened her. They have something on her. From what I've pieced together by searching newspapers and government documents, the *Federales* went after her family in Mexico. It started with her brother committing some legit crime when he was fourteen. It caught the Rumorosa cartel's attention, and they recruited him. Martha tried to get him across the border and into America. She had all the paperwork to sponsor him properly since she's twelve years older than him. She'd already worked for the city for five years."

"Something went wrong?"

"Yeah. When the kid got to Border Control, he sang like a fecking canary. Told every secret he probably didn't even tell his priest. By morning, he was gone. Three days later, his body's hanging from a bridge in Rosarito. His head wound up on a street in Tijuana's worst neighborhood. Apparently, the info the kid gave caused a major crackdown on mules running drugs from Baja into California. Needless to say, it pissed off the Rumorosa cartel. They went after Martha's family. When they discovered she has a solid job here and makes a good living since she's single, they started extorting her. She was sending money to them. One month she didn't send enough, so they cut off her mother's left ear and right hand."

"Fecking hell."

In New York, we don't leave people alive to tell the tale. In Latin America, the cartels make examples of people. I doubt the ear and hand are all they did to the woman.

"Yeah, well, it gets worse. Martha went home to see her mother. She tried sneaking into the house, but the cartel watched it. They snagged her up, and that's when the terms changed. She had to spy on Jocelyn. I think one of three things is happening. It's the Rumorosa who're squeezing Martha and targeting Jocelyn. The Rumorosa are selling this information to someone here in NYC. Or someone here's forcing the Rumorosa to share the information."

I look at all the open browser windows with emails I haven't read yet. If Finn's already read them all, he'll let me know if there are any I still need to see. I think about what Joey told me after she met Olivia.

"The Rumorosa are Jesus's mother's people. Total Romeo and Juliet. There was supposed to be an alliance between the Culiacán and the Rumorosa, but it went to shite despite his parents being in love. Both of them died. If that was his maternal grandparents' side of the family, why are they intent upon watching Joey? Why would they plan to kidnap and ransom her?"

"That was never clear in the emails, but I got the impression someone more powerful is pulling their strings. Someone who wants more of Mexico than they have."

"A rival cartel?"

The Rumorosa are powerful and control the entire length of the Baja peninsula.

Finn shakes his head and shrugs with a sigh. Not at all reassuring.

"I don't know that, but I'm certain it's not the Colombians. Pablo and *Tres J's* come up several times. Whoever this is, warned Martha not to piss them off by being obvious if she fecks with Joey. Until recently, Martha just observed. These people pushed her to act despite their years of threatening to tell Alejandro and letting him deal with her if she fecked up."

"Was this before or after Joey and I met?"

"Before. About two months, but Martha claimed the time wasn't right. When Jocelyn started dating you, Martha decided she'd start her campaign against Jocelyn. To make sure she didn't back down, the Rumorosa killed her younger sister's dog. It was already fifteen years old, but in good shape. Nowhere near dying."

I run my hand through my hair. The Ruiz family—Joey's paternal grandmother's family—runs the cartel. Before them, Baja and Baja Sud—both parts of the peninsula—were contested territory. The Culiacán—the cartel Joey's paternal great-grandfather ran before her father—oversaw it for a long time, but they lost interest because they could grow way more products in Chihuahua. When the Ruizes stepped in, the Espinozas didn't like the competition. It was one of those I don't want it, but you can't have it.

"You know who's felt pushed out of Mexico, don't you?"

I thought the same thing as Finn.

"Yeah. The *Cosa Nostra* was already doing more deals out there, even before they linked up with Jesus. They weren't feeling the pinch. But we've expanded way more than anyone noticed. At least, until now. Someone else definitely found out. Motherfecker."

I know who it is.

※

"You're certain Heather's out of town?"

"Yes, Cormac. For the tenth time. She and her sister went on a girls' trip."

Finn's ready to punch me, but we can't go through with this mission if there's a woman in the house. We won't risk her life.

We're sitting in our SUV a block and a half from our target. Sean's on his computer, hacking what's supposedly an impenetrable security system. Won't it surprise my target and his bag of shite cousins—on both sides of his fucking shitbag family—when they discover we aren't the knuckle draggers we let them always think we are?

"Time to go. We have three minutes before his guards realize the cameras aren't swiveling and the security feed isn't updating."

Sean puts aside his laptop as he speaks, one hand setting it aside while the other pulls down his beanie. Even in the dead of summer, we all wear beanies because our red hair is too fucking recognizable. Three sisters married three brothers and gave birth to six fucking lighthouses. Our hair fucking announces our presence no matter the weather.

I press my earpiece and give the order. Men in vehicles on each street surrounding our target pour forth. We could have gone on foot from my parents' house, but passing all the other syndicate houses on the way was too great a risk. Very convenient we were only five streets over, though.

The thirty men we have work with precision this motherfucker's family would envy. They're not the only ones who can move like a paramilitary unit. Fuck them and their egos. I'm taking them down a peg or two. This fucknut's about to remember why he has a scar that wraps around his right ribs. He fucked with my brother in college, and he paid for it. Now he's fucked with my woman, and I'm going to bring him to the edge of death. It's a shame he's too high ranking for me to kill.

I signal for teams of six to spread out and cover the property. It takes no time to disarm his security patrol. His property wall is high enough that we leave the bodies as reminders they failed. Our men stand outside to ensure our safety after we breach the house. We fan out to check each room. We use only one word in our earpieces.

Glan. Clear.

With three men posted at the doors leading outside, my family and I creep up to the main bedroom. I'm certain the piece of shite's awake by now. We've been silent, but every man in the Four Families has a sixth sense. It's how we've lived into our thirties. It's how all our parents have lived into their fifties. He's probably already texted his brothers and cousins.

I'm behind Dillan when we separate, so three of us stand on each side of the door. I tap my cousin's shoulder, and he kicks open the door. I enter first, my rifle pointed right at him. The other guys stream in, taking positions by the windows, the closet, the bathroom, and the door.

"Aleks, you went too far this time."

Aleksei Kutsenko—Niko's older brother—shrugs. Motherfucking shrugs. He sits in bed like he hasn't a care in the world. We all see the pistol on the mattress beside his left hand, and the knife in his right. He won't do shite to us, but I'm about to fuck his world up.

"Cormac, don't be so dramatic. You and Niko act like you're still in the high school drama club." His Russian drawl makes me want to ram my fist into my throat and crush his voice box.

"You blew up my fiancée's apartment when she was there."

"*Pozdravlyayu s pomolvkoy.*"

"I don't need your congratulations on my engagement."

He shrugs again, but I see the surprise that I understood

him. He probably thought I'd struggle to Google Translate it later. Fuck him with knobs on.

"Why?"

"Why what? Target you? I can't stand you. Use Joey? Because she was there."

It doesn't surprise me he knows my pet name for her. He's baiting me. Seamus and I developed reputations as the hot heads because we're almost always bigger than everyone else. I'm bigger than Aleks, even if not by much. He's an inch and a bit taller than me, but I weigh at least fifteen pounds of muscle more than him. I'm about to let him see the reputation I culti-vated, but I'm shockingly calm. If I fuck this up, it's my broth-er's and cousins' lives, and it's my future with Joey.

I put a bullet into the headboard precariously close to Aleks's left ear. If he'd flinched—which I knew he wouldn't—fucking psychopath—I would have hit him. I point the muzzle to a few inches past his feet and fire again.

"Explain the holes to your wife and tell her how lucky I only put them in the furniture and not you."

I shoot the knife blade beside him, not caring if the ricochet actually hits him. The ping of metal on metal shifts his attitude. He gets serious mighty fast.

"Don't act all holier than thou, Cormac. You're just as shitty as the rest of your ragtag family. Don't come into my house accusing me of shit, or none of you will leave alive."

"Did you have to call your big brother and cousins to come help you?"

My sing-song voice is fucking obnoxious even to my ears.

"Or will it be your baby brothers to the rescue? Let them come. We're ready. You have no men left here, and your family won't take any away from guarding their wives. They definitely won't leave kids unprotected. They won't wait around for extra men to get here. Sergei and Anton definitely won't make it in time. That leaves Maks, Niko, Bogdan, Misha, and Pasha. Five against the six of us, plus the thirty men we have scattered around your property. Call your brothers and tell them false alarm. You and I deal with this just the two of us."

"You know that's not happening."

"Fine."

I nudge my chin toward Aleks, and Sean and Shane rush forward. They have his gun and knife away from him in a heartbeat, then Aleks is pinned to the mattress. I wrap my hand around his throat. There's no erotic pleasure to this like when I hold Joey in place this way. My hand tightens until he grunts, and his chin comes up. It gives me space to drive my fist into it and snap his head even farther back. I slam my fist into his left cheekbone, making sure to nail his nose too. My next punch breaks his nose. Neither Shane nor Sean recoil from the blood. I bet they don't even notice.

I lean into my hand around Aleks's throat, pushing a good portion of my weight onto him. My fist is indiscriminate where it lands now. It just rains down on his face five or six times. When I release his throat, I seize that chance for the throat punch.

"You could have taken away my chance for a family with Joey. Maybe now I'll take away your chance with Heather."

I ram my rifle's stock into his junk. I catch him entirely unprepared because he tries to howl in pain, but no sound comes out.

The bratva leaders were conditioned to never show any reaction to pain. Their leader before Maks beat any reaction out of them, nearly killing them in the process. None of them know we found our way into the old bratva warehouse where they trained. When we were all teens, we spied on Aleks, his brothers, and his cousins. My brother, cousins, and I wanted to know what we were up against since we suspected their old *pakhan* tortured them during their training. He did.

I spy a wedding photo on the dresser. I saunter over to it while Sean and Shane keep holding Aleks down. I pick up the frame, turn to him, and grin.

"I bet this is one of Heather's favorites. You don't look like a bear's arsehole in it."

I bring it down over his now bent knee; the glass contacting the bare skin. It shatters and some shards cut him. I look at the photo, curl my nose in disgust, then toss it on the bed beside him. I won't damage the photo because I'm punishing him, not Heather. Shane steps away, and I pull back my arm.

"Sweet dreams, motherfucker."

I put as much force into the punch as I dare. I don't need to kill him, just knock him out. It lands against his right temple, and it's night, night for him. I mangled his face, and it'll take weeks for the bruises to heal. He can't stay home that entire time, so let the world know he got the shite beaten out of him. That public humiliation'll be worse than the physical pain. That's the point.

With his knife, I find his clothes in the closet and slash through most of his suits. He's rich, and his family's like mine. They can swap clothes interchangeably. This'll be inconvenient though. We rush from his bedroom after I toss the knife on the bed.

Tempting as it is to fuck up more of his house, we won't because we're here to punish him, not Heather. We make a beeline for his office, though. Three shots, and the door's open. We clear it out. We grab his laptops—the one on his desk, and the one we know he hides. It took us a moment to find it, but we all think alike. Behind three loose stones in the fireplace.

Dillan starts a fire as soon as we clean out the safe with the computer and an array of fake passports and thousands in foreign currency. Finn and his brothers sort through papers they pull out of drawers and off shelves. Once there's a blaze, they toss things into the flames. Seamus and I work together to break the massive wood furniture he favors. We smash table legs and rip apart cushions. Together, we hoist his desk and toss it onto the sofa, breaking both.

"We gotta go."

I've been glancing at my watch. We've been inside nearly ten minutes, so we've been on the property nearly fifteen. If his family's gotten any alerts, they'll be here any second. This can't spill onto the street, so we can't afford to get trapped in the house. Tempted as I am to risk the house going up in a fireball, I put the grate in front of the hearth as Aleks's shite burns.

We're climbing into the SUV as we see Maks and the others arrive in their personal vehicles. They knew better than to come on foot, but they couldn't get any of their SUVs in time. All Four Families get aftermarket parts at the same place. If the two neighborhoods where all the married couples live are Switzerland, then that body shop is the fucking Vatican. We all pray at the altar of vehicle customization. The wheels on our SUVs still roll, even if they're punctured. There are metal plates covering the chassis to protect against any street bombs or grenades. All the windows are bulletproof.

The only way to tell the families' SUVs apart are the hub caps. We have emblems that distinguish them. None of them are what people would expect, and the designs are tiny. They're discreet, but we all know what to look for that way we never get in the wrong one if we're all leaving in a hurry.

Shane's driving, so he pulls onto the street as the rest of us fasten our seatbelts. I look back over my shoulder to see Misha stick his head past the gate. He aims a gun at us, but he won't shoot. We're not close enough.

We have another job to do before we're done for the night.

We stay in Queens but head toward the Flushing River. We have a railway station in the Bronx as our secret lair. The bratva, *Costa Nostra*, and Cartel didn't venture far from home and stayed in Queens. Too fucking obvious.

The bratva has a warehouse, the *Cosa Nostra* has a garage, and the Cartel uses an abandoned bodega. We know exactly where each place is. It's not hard to figure out since we all turn our phones off about ten miles from our bat caves. We track where the other families do that. From there we draw a ten-mile radius inward and can pinpoint the abandoned buildings because they don't appear on any city records. No one's bothered to figure out where ours is. We don't think they've bothered to find each other's.

We drive directly to the bratva warehouse, ramming through the fence that encircles the property. I wind down my window as my brother hands me my preferred weapon of mass destruction. At three feet long and fifteen pounds, the rocket-propelled grenade launcher fits in the SUV.

"Around the south side. That bay door is open."

Shane heads to where I can see the perfect target. If our tires could squeal, they would as he makes a fast turn and brakes. Seamus and Dillan scramble out of the SUV after me, their rifles raised to provide me cover. Walking in lockstep, we advanced away from the vehicle. Shane, Sean, and Finn get out and guard the SUV. If we lose that, then we're fucked. We'll have no means to escape.

There's poetic justice here the bratva will likely guess. This is an RPG-7. It and the version before it were designed by the Soviet Union and are still made in Russia. Mother Russia's about to fuck over six of her sons.

I load the first missile. For the havoc they create, they're shockingly light. Only a few pounds.

"Here we go!" I sound like a kid about to go on their first rollercoaster.

We watch the blue-white smoke tail as I launch the first one. It sails beneath the half open bay door. I'm loading the second one before the first one explodes. I aim for where we suspect the office is and fire. Within seconds, flames consume the building. I'm certain my house looked much like this, but on a far smaller scale.

"Let this be a lesson to those motherfucking pieces of shite. Come for me and my house, and I'll barge the fuck into yours and fuck it all up. We might not have fully trashed Aleks's place, but we did some damage."

Now...

Now, they're royally fucked. They're going to need a new place to take their captives and will have to build a new torture chamber. That takes time to get just right, and it's not cheap nor inconspicuous to buy industrial size vats of acid.

An abandoned building isn't hard to find in New York City. One that isn't on any city maps or plans that has no deeds in a neighborhood where no one asks questions is entirely another story.

Seamus's thoughts run along the same line as mine and probably all the other guys' as we watch the destruction.

"The bratva once struck us where it hurts most. This won't cut as deep, but it sure as fuck will sting."

Our ancestral home of sorts. The first home the O'Rourkes had in America. We'd kept it in our family until the Kutsenkos came along. They went on a rampage thanks to Declan's lasting shitstorm and took out a few of our businesses too. Fortunately, no one lived in the old family house.

My brother and I have always thought alike, so I know what I'm about to say matches what's going through his head.

"They didn't come into our homes like we went into

Aleks's. I've made sure they know there's nowhere safe to hide. Losing a couple businesses was inconvenient, but it was nowhere near as personal as taking out one place that was supposed to be impenetrable to them."

Dillan shakes his head, his expression smugger than it was a moment ago.

"This—this fucked them over to a level that'll take time to recover from."

"We've let the other families underestimate us for years. We've let them think we're stereotypical undereducated— though we all went to Ivy Leagues or top tier universities—pipe wielding, dock working, poor—relatively speaking, of course— Irishmen. It's suited us. That shite ended today when I discovered they've targeted my woman *for years*."

We turn back to our cousins and head to the vehicle. When we join Finn, Sean, and Shane, I say what I'm certain we've all thought since we realized they were behind all of this.

"The bratva swears up and down they'll never target women and children because of what their moms faced while in Russia. They swear they'd never be like the men their fathers ruthlessly protected their moms from when the women faced sex trafficking. They might not have planned to sell Joey to a brothel, but they still planned to sell her back to her father. That's what a ransom is. It's selling a person."

Not today, Satan. Not today.

"Too bad those fuckers won't get to see this burn." Dillan gives me an unrepentant shrug as he speaks, and I just grin.

By the time they get here, some of their men who live closer will have put the fire out. There'll just be ash and rubble. It'll take them a while to figure out how we did it. Let them stew on it.

"Are you satisfied?" Finn's looking past my shoulder.

"As satisfied as I'm going to get while they're still breathing."

Seamus bumps shoulders with me. "Let's go home to our women."

⚔

We go straight back to my parents' house, parking in the garage.

Mair, Ally, Nikki, Tiernan, Carys, and Joey jump out of their seats in the living room as soon as we file into the house. Our parents hang back, letting us greet our wives. Joey's as good as my wife after tonight.

"*Cailín*, it's done. No one's coming near you again."

"Are you hurt?"

"No. Not even a hair out of place."

Reassured I'm hale and hearty, Joey dives in for a kiss that makes my toes curl in my boots. If I didn't know all the other couples were sharing kisses like this, I might worry it was indecent. None of the guys worry about our parents seeing us with our women like this. Who else did we learn it from? We all remember what it was like after our dads hugged each of us. The way they kissed our moms was just as scandalous.

The moment each couple pulls apart, the wives hurry to step aside. It's our parents turn. There will never be a day in my life when a hug from my parents doesn't make the world better. Joey's arms are home now, but my parents' embraces will always remind me *nothing ever* comes before family.

Epilogue

Joey

Cormac's a never-ending wealth of surprises. The creative ways he found for us to make love when he got back from the mission left me speechless because I was breathless. The engagement ring he gave me a week later while we were on vacation in Malta blew me away. The speed at which we closed on our new house—five days after a cash offer was accepted—shocked me.

But nothing tops today.

Martha abruptly quit her job. She never officially reported me. She just threatened to. Since I still have an immaculate record with plenty of commendations, the Department of Social Services promoted me. I had a last-minute chance to attend a ribbon cutting ceremony in Queens, so I'm here to represent the Staten Island social workers.

I'd know that red hair in my sleep. The pair of emerald eyes watching me widen as I walk toward him.

What is my fiancé doing here?

"Joey, what're you doing here?"

"I was about to ask you the same. I—"

"Mr. Cormac, did you know the new building has a jungle gym *inside*?"

A little boy of around seven grabs one of Cormac's hands and tugs him toward the door that's still blocked by the ribbon.

Mr. Cormac?

"Hi, Mr. Cormac."

If that girl were over eighteen, she and I would have problems. She's looking at my man like he's her next meal. Cormac barely glances at her and nods as the little boy keeps tugging on his hand.

"Remy, we can't go inside yet."

"But I heard there's a music room—with *drums*."

"Whose bright idea was that?"

I mutter the question to no one in particular, but when Cormac's face flushes, my eyebrows shoot up to my hair. A little girl of about five runs up and grabs Cormac's other hand and tugs down on it while Remy keeps pulling him toward the door.

"*Señor Cormac, ¿puede darme un perdedor más tarde?*"

Perdedor? Can he give her a loser later?

Now my brow furrows, and Cormac laughs. I'm the native Spanish speaker, but I don't know what the little girl means. Is it New York Spanish?

"An underdog as in push her on the swing and run under it."

"Oh."

I wrack my brain for the right phrase. It's been years since I've thought about that game. There isn't a Spanish equivalent.

"*Dar un empujón por debajo.*" Give a push from below.

The girl looks up at me as if I interrupted a private conversation. It's the same offended look the teenage girl gave me when Cormac basically ignored her. I can't win with a five- or fifteen-year-old. Girls at neither age like me when I'm with Cormac.

"*No lo sé. ¿Puedo?*" I don't know. Can I?

"*¿Puedes por favor?*" Can you, please?

He grins as he corrects the girl's manners, and it's about the sweetest thing I've ever seen.

"*Está bien.*" All right.

"*Gracias, señor Cormac!*" Thank you, Mr. Cormac.

"You're very popular among the kindergarten crowd. I had no idea. What're you doing here?"

"I—um—I—"

He's beet red. What on Earth?

"Mr. O'Rourke?"

I turn toward a voice I recognize. Five, fifteen, and now thirty-five. Fucking women flock to Cormac.

"Jocelyn?"

"Hi, Courtney. How're you?"

"Fine. I didn't know you knew Mr. O'Rourke. I got the email you were coming."

"I'm Ms. Bracero's fiancé."

There's something about the way he words that. He's acknowledging my claim to him rather than the other way around. That he belongs to me and no one else. If Courtney was in doubt, he wraps his arm around my waist, his hand resting low on my hip. It's an intimate gesture that's possessive. I know—because he's done it many times, and I've pointed it out—he doesn't even notice what he's doing. He always says that's just where his hand belongs. There and between my thighs.

"I didn't know you were involved with someone."

Bitch, what the fuck is that supposed to mean?

Cormac's chin rises, and the look he casts her is one only a billionaire or royalty can carry off. I discovered he's *WAY* richer than I imagined when we talked about our finances and our future. Like he makes my family look impoverished in comparison, and we're one of the wealthiest families in Latin America. Since he's part of the family that leads *the* mob—*the* Irish—not just in NYC, but pretty much all of North America—he's syndicate royalty.

"Why should you?"

Ouch.

I fight my face to keep from smirking. She and I have a past that involves us dating the same guy in grad school and not knowing it. I dumped the douche when I found out. He dumped her a week later when he no longer had the thrill of dating and fucking two girls. I'm glad I made him bag his dick up.

Courtney turns her nose up at me, and Cormac pulls me closer. I nearly lose my balance, so my hand flies up to his chest to brace myself. The sun catches my ring, which is almost obscenely large, and practically blinds her. He did that on purpose. I don't mind and lean my head against his chest.

"The kids want to play. We should get started, Ms. Luciano."

"Did you want to be part of the ceremony?"

For a moment, I think she's speaking to me. I'm already supposed to be, but I realize she means Cormac, whose gaze hardens. Courtney nods and turns away.

"Cor?"

"*Cailín*, I've been volunteering at the old center for six years. She figured out I was the silent benefactor of this new center about three months ago. She knows the terms of my donation were strict anonymity. She shouldn't have asked that. It wasn't out of politeness."

"No, it wasn't. She wants the hottest man alive standing next to her while she beams at the camera."

"Hottest man alive, am I?"

"Yes, Daddy. The only ribbon you'll be cutting is the one I might wrap myself in tonight."

"I definitely can't stand in front of a crowd now. I give in to the no boxer briefs this morning, and now you say shite that makes me hard as a plank."

"I know."

I try to dance away from him, but he pulls me in for a quick and appropriate peck on the cheek. But I feel his cock against my pussy. Fucking-a.

"Wait. You said you've been volunteering here for six years. Every year for the past six, a new center has opened in one of the outer boroughs, and it's always been an anonymous donor."

"I can't take my money to the grave, and even with you to spoil and any kids we have, there will always be enough to give back to our communities. We both come from a world that's all about taking. Sure, we give things to the people who depend on the organization. But that's our duty. You give to families because you care about those people and believe they all deserve a chance for a stable life that provides for their kids. That generous heart made me fall in love with you. That and your iron will. Your banging body's delicious, too. I want these families to have what we did. My parents didn't use ill-gotten gains to provide for us. It's always come from their legit businesses. My donations come solely from my legit ones. My time costs me nothing, so I volunteer whenever I can. I like kids."

I hear someone call my name, but I ignore them. I wrap my arms around Cormac's waist and stretch onto my toes. I can still only reach his jaw, which I kiss.

"You already have my whole heart, but you just made it

grow. You fill every bit. I never imagined the mobster I pushed down a flight of stairs would be my knight in shining armor."

"I knew that day I would marry you. I love you, *cailín*."

"I've always been yours, Daddy. I love you."

Would you like to discover how Joey and Cormac celebrate a very special day in a very kinky way?

Subscribe to my newsletter to find out!

Silver fox Enrique Diaz doesn't take no for an answer, so when he decides divorcée Elodie McCann needs help cleaning out her rain gutters, he orders her off her ladder. Little do either of them know how Elodie's lifetime of secrets will impact them when she finally relents to Enrique's attentions. Both have been unlucky in love with their past spouses. Discover these soulmates' bumpy road to their HEA in *Cartel King*.

Get a bonus epilogue

Enjoy this free bonus epilogue with a scene from *Mob Knight* where Cormac and Joey celebrate the anniversary of the day they met. You know they can't keep their hands off each other and now have a special play room. Join them for a celebration with a special kinky scene just for my newsletter subscribers.

Check out this extra sexy scene with Cormac and Joey. Get your Copy here.

Don't miss the next installment

Meet Enrique and Elodie in *Cartel King*

Enrique—I control everything in criminal empire. I was born into this life and know no other. Men cower when I look in their direction. That's why it surprises me when a woman ready to fall off a ladder catches my attention. I don't need a second chance at love. I bring too much darkness. I definitely don't need a woman to complicate my life with a list of secrets nearly as long as mine. But something draws me to her. Despite my family's warnings, I'll pursue the woman I can't control. I'm the man she never knew she wanted.

Elodie—I left an unhappy marriage to start a new life in a new state. I don't need a man any more than I need a root canal. My second chance is freedom. I'm middle-aged and happy to be on my own. Besides my past isn't one I can share with someone outside my family. No one can know who I was. But the man who walks up my driveway and insists upon helping me is unlike any I know. Others might fear him, but I don't. He's a different man with me. I see the many he wants to be, but only with me.

Only fools think they can stand in our way, but they learn the same thing others have before.

I'll burn it all to the ground before I let go.

Meet Enrique and Elodie in *Cartel King*, coming March 2025.

Thank you for reading Mob Knight

Sabine Barclay, a nom de plume also writing Historical Romance as Celeste Barclay, lives near the Southern California coast with her husband and sons. She loves her days at the beach soaking up way too much sun, a good Netflix binge, and a strong hot chai. Her heroines are independent women who can defend themselves but love their Alpha heroes who want nothing more than to protect their soulmates in her Mafia Romances. She's Gen Y/Oregon Trail and loves creating engrossing contemporary romances that will make your toes curl and your granny blush.

Subscribe to Sabine's bimonthly newsletter to receive exclusive insider perks.
www.sabinebarclay.com

Join the fun and get exclusive insider giveaways, sneak peeks, and new release announcements in
Sabine Barclay's Facebook Dubious Dames Group

Do you also enjoy steamy Historical Romance? Discover Sabine's books written as Celeste Barclay.

The O'Rourke Brotherhood

Mob Boss
BOOK ONE SNEAK PEEK

DILLAN

I hate meetings like this. I don't need to wear pants from some shitty off-the-rack suit that are too tight to *try* to make my dick look bigger. I'm secure in my cock size, and I don't need to show how big my balls are for people to know I run this part of the city. I loathe strip clubs too. I'm past the point where naked women make my jimmy do jumping jacks. I can appreciate a hot bod and gymnast level strength, but it does nothing for me. These douchebags? They're practically ready to come in those cheap arse pants. Why am I here? I keep asking myself that. Seamus and Shane are doing just fine with these negotiations. I'm just here to look good. I'm the muscle today. Or rather my name and my position. Who the fuck thought— way, way back in the day —that giving the mob hierarchy nautical names was a good idea? Fucking Skipper. This isn't motherfucking Gilligan's Island. None of these numb nuts are the Professor, even if they think they're fucking Mr. Howell.

But who is that? If this is *Gilligan's Island*, then she's Mary Ann.

I glance at Seamus, but he's focused on the Albanian he's trying not to lose his shite at. Shane smirks at me when I dart my gaze to him. I cock an eyebrow as the waitress walks over. She's definitely not a dancer. She has too many clothes on. But you can barely call the pieces of thread she's wearing clothes. She's got on a bikini top that's barely more than pasties, and the skirt she's wearing would make my Catholic grandmother do somersaults in her grave.

It's the standard uniform for this place, but somehow it doesn't look right on her. Not because she doesn't have a banging body because she does. Not because she's a butter face— but-her-face —as in great bod, not so great face. She's beautiful in a super understated way. That's part of what makes her look out of place. She has next to no makeup on. I think those are even her real eyelashes. The natural beauty is drawing way too much attention.

"'Scuse me."

She tries to step around Zef Hoxha, the *kyre* of the Albanian mafia here in New York. When he reaches out to grab her wrist, I'm out of my seat with my hand around his. He never gets a chance to touch her because my hold is so tight he can't bend his fingers. I keep squeezing until it must feel like I'll snap the bones.

"No touching."

Zef drops his arm as much as my hold allows. I let go and stare at him before I tilt my head toward the waitress. I narrow my eyes, and he knows what I expect.

"I apologize, miss."

"That's all right, sir. Here's your drink."

She's polite as she hands him his glass. Unfortunately, to put down the rest, she has to bend forward, giving everyone a view of her glorious cleavage. Tits and arse are what sell here, and she has them in spades. I'm certain it's why my cousin hired her. If I sit down, everyone will know I'm just as guilty as these fuck nuts because she's made my dick do something that hasn't happened in a strip club since I was like twenty-three. I'm now thirty-three.

Mob Star
Mob Princess
Mob Saint
Mob Bride
Mob Knight

Do you also enjoy steamy Historical Romance? Discover Sabine's books written as Celeste Barclay.

The Ivankov Brotherhood

Bratva Darling
BOOK ONE SNEAK PEEK

LAURA

As I sit across from the four Kutsenko brothers, I press my lips
together to keep from drooling. No four men should be so strik-
ingly handsome. Not all from the same family, anyway. I fight a
valiant battle against letting my gaze drift toward the eldest,
Maksim, whose ice-blue eyes bore into me. After years of negotiating billion-dollar investment contracts while facing countless ruthless businessmen, I've learned to keep my expression
studiously blank. But it's a true struggle today. Instead, I focus
my attention on the squirrelly lawyer sitting across the confer-
ence table. While he's disingenuous with each comment, he's a
good negotiator. But I'm better. How cliché am I?

While I feel Maksim watching me, I focus on Dmitry Yakovitch
as he continues to argue the merits of the venture capitalist
company I represent, RK Capital Group, merging with

Kutsenko Partners. What he means is the merits of Kutsenko
Partners acquiring RK Capital Group, then stripping it and
making it another money-laundering shell corporation. While
most people in New York have little awareness of the Russian
mafia, I do. The Kutsenko brothers' names appear on no titles
or deeds anywhere in New York City, but it wasn't difficult to
determine which shell companies likely belong to them. Their
assumption that I'm unfamiliar with them is proving beneficial
to me as they continue to whisper amongst themselves in Russian. I think they may even believe they're convincing me that
they don't speak much English.

The senior partners of RK Capital Group know who I'm negotiating with, though they may not know I'm aware of these
Russians' more nefarious operations. They've given me the go-
ahead to agree to a merger with an eventual acquisition, but
only for the right price. A price to the tune of twenty billion
dollars. Considering an investment firm like Goldman Sachs is
worth nearly one-hundred-and-twenty billion dollars, my
clients' asking price appears reasonable.

"Mr. Yakovitch, I shall stop you now." I raise my left hand, pen
caught between my index and middle fingers. When I have his
attention, I lean back in my chair and casually twirl the pen
over my index finger and thumb. "Fifty billion is my clients'
asking price. You know that. Your clients know that. RK doesn't
oppose the merger. What they oppose is the insulting offer
you've made. It's nearly noon, and I'm hungry, Mr. Yakovitch. I
have a delicious ham sandwich waiting for me. I even have
three chocolate chip cookies waiting for me. If we aren't going
to make any progress, I shall let you go, so I can move onto my
eagerly anticipated lunch."

I cant my head just enough for me to appear as though my gaze
rests solely on the opposing attorney's face, but I can see each

Kutsenko brothers' reaction. My face battles yet again against showing my emotions as I fight not to smirk. Their muted but surprised expressions confirm what I already know.

"Please tell your clients to make a reasonable counteroffer, or I will conclude this meeting and enjoy my ham sandwich and cookies."

Dmitry glares at me before turning to Maksim and his three brothers. In rapid Russian, he doesn't interpret my suggestion. Oh no. There's no need for that. I can't catch every word because his voice is too low. But I catch something along the lines of "The bitch refuses to budge. What now? A fucking ham sandwich. More like a stick up her ass."

Maksim swivels his chair to look at his brothers. In Russian, he says, "Fifty billion is ridiculous. She's not so stupid or naïve not to know that. My guess is they'll settle for twenty billion. We offer fifteen."

"That's barely better than what we already offered," Aleksei, the second-oldest brother, argues. "She'll be eating the fucking sandwich and dipping her cookies in milk before we walk out the door. We need the buildings."

"We offer twenty, Maks," Bogdan, the youngest, insists.

As I watch the brothers discuss, their voices barely lowered, I pull my lunch sack from the black leather satchel by my feet and set it beside my laptop. It's a ridiculously pink floral bag with an embroidered monogram, the L and D overlapping. It's an empty prop, but they don't know that. I watch as five sets of eyes narrow. I offer a smile that would appear innocent in any setting other than this meeting. It's patronizing, and I know it.

Bratva Sweetheart
Bratva Treasure
Bratva Beauty

Sabine Barclay

Bratva Angel
Bratva Jewel

Do you also enjoy steamy Historical Romance? Discover
Sabine's books written as Celeste Barclay.

The Mancinelli Brotherhood

Mafia Heir
BOOK ONE SNEAK PEEK

LUCA

This asshole is pissing me off. We've been going around in circles for five minutes, and the longer we stand out here, the greater the likelihood someone will spot us. I have a sixth sense about these things. It's why I'm still alive at the ripe old age of thirty-one.

"Espinoza, enough already. Either sell to us or don't, but we set the price. Your tequila is good, but it isn't nectar from the gods." I'm watching Carlos Espinoza, some lackey for the Mexican Culiacán Cartel, try to maneuver me into paying more than the agreed upon price. I know it's so he can skim off the top.

"It's as close as you're going to get. You've upped the order, so the price per case goes up."

My uncle, Salvatore Mancinelli, is the New York don. He negotiated this deal, and I warned him it was a bad idea. But what do I know as his underboss and heir? I'm not backing down.

"Haven't you ever heard of a bulk discount? The more I order the better the price should be. No one else around here is buying from you. You know we're your only choice in three out of five boroughs. You aren't going to the Bronx because you won't get more than pennies there. You aren't going to Queens because you don't want to run into the Colombians. You aren't going to Manhattan because then you face the bratva along with us. And what are you going to do in Staten Island? Sell to us anyway? We control Staten Island and Brooklyn when it comes to liquor stores, so take the money and go."

"Luca, there are plenty of liquor stores in Brooklyn that aren't owned by Italians. I'll go there."

We aren't friends. He's patronizing me by using my first name. Fuck him and the horse he rode in on. I have other solutions for this shit.

"And I'll just take what I want from them for free. That's not a half bad idea. The deal's over. Take your shit with the worm in it and go."

"Motherfucking racist. Not all tequila has a worm in it."

"You're selling Mezcal. It's known for the fucking worm. I wouldn't start calling me names, you *penche hijo de puta*."

Fucking son of a bitch.

He has twenty-five crates of stolen tequila that he's trying to offload because he knows he can't sell it at his own liquor store.

"What did you call me?"

Carlos takes what he thinks is a menacing step forward, and his two bodyguards do the same. Not smart. Neither of my two bodyguards nor I react, but the three men in each of my cars open their doors. They won't do more than that. It's just a reminder that the Culiacán can try, but the *Cosa Nostra* still run New York City.

"This is the third and final time I say this. Sell or leave."
Every head turns toward the liquor store's back door as it opens.
A gorgeous blonde steps out, and I wish I had the time to
appreciate her beauty, but she's about to die. Carlos and his
men draw their guns and pivot toward her. My men pull their
weapons too, but we keep them pointed at the Mexicans. The
woman stands like a deer in the headlights for a second before
ducking behind the industrial garbage dumpster like a frightened rabbit. Three shots hit the metal almost at the same
moment. That's all it takes for my men and me. The two bodyguards standing with me aim for a guard each, and I set my
sights on Carlos. We squeeze our triggers, and the men fall.
Screeching tires tell me Carlos's driver takes off. I hear more
gunshots as at least one soldier in my cars tries to shoot the
escaping vehicle. Glass shatters, but the sedan keeps going. I
hear more tires squeal as one of my SUVs takes off and chases
the guy. I holster my gun and wave my men to do the same.
I inch forward toward the trash can, but I see the shadow shift.
The woman bolts from the other side. She's still the frightened
rabbit, but I'm the fox pursuing her. She's fast, I'll give her that.
But she has to be at least a foot shorter than me. My legs are a
lot longer and cover a lot more ground with each stride.
She weaves among the cars, most likely believing it's harder to
hit a moving object. She isn't wrong, but I have no intention of
shooting her. I push myself harder and pounce as she darts out
and tries to cross the last stretch of parking lot to reach a better
lit area near a bus stop. I lunge.
"Stop running, *piccolina*. I won't hurt you."
I wrap my arms around her and pull her back against my chest,
but I'm quick to spin her around and put space between us as I
grasp her arms. Of course, she fights me.
"If I wanted you dead, I would have shot at you, too."
"It doesn't mean you won't kill me after."

She's breathless as she continues to struggle. I almost let go to take a step back, insulted at what she implied. But I can't blame her. If I were a woman, I'd be terrified of the same thing.

"I'm not going to rape you. I'm going to talk to you."

"Talk? You are not a man who talks if you just killed a guy."

"To keep him and his men from killing you. I told you, if I wanted you dead, I would have shot at you too. And I wouldn't have missed."

She stops struggling against me, but her eyes continue to dart from one place to another, trying to find somewhere to flee. I know I can keep her in place with only one hand, so I release her left arm. I still have a firm hold on her right one, but I haven't held it nearly as tightly as I could.

"I'm Luca. I know you figured out you interrupted something you shouldn't have. Did that man know who you are?"

"Yes."

"What about his driver? Would he know you?"

"Yes."

"Do you have a name?"

"Yes."

"*Piccolina*, we won't get very far if yes is all you can say. Are you willing to answer me with more than one word?"

"No."

I knew that was coming, and I grin. I can't help it. I wasn't wrong about her being gorgeous, but I doubt she wants to know that's what I think. At least, not if I want her to know I won't assault her.

"Fine. I have more than twenty questions I can ask that you can answer with one word. Do you work at the store?"

"Sometimes."

Ah, an improvement.

"Did Carlos know you were still working?"

"No."

"Do you have a car, or do you take the subway or bus?"

She raises her chin and remains silent. Smart but counterproductive.

"The subway or the bus will get you killed. You're too easy to find and follow. Do you have a car?"

"Yes."

"Can you stay with someone instead of going home?"

She refuses to answer.

"If that man knew you and you sometimes work in the store, then he knew where you live. If he found that out, so will someone in his cartel."

"I know. Let me go. The longer I stand here, the more likely someone is to come back for me."

"No one will touch you while I'm here."

"Arrogant. If he shot at me, he would have shot at you."

"And he would have died, anyway. What's your name?"

"Jane."

"Look, I know you won't get in one of my cars and let me drive you somewhere. In most cases, I would say that's a smart move. But you did nothing wrong tonight except for leave work at the wrong time. I know that, and you know that. But the Culiacán won't see it that way, *piccolina*."

She freezes for no more than five seconds before she trembles so much that I can see it. I don't know what drives me next, but it's the same instinct that's made me call her little girl three times. I pull her to my chest and tuck her head against it. I stroke her hair down to her shoulders, rubbing my hand up and down her back. This is the most inopportune moment to notice she isn't wearing a bra. I will my body not to react.

"What does that mean?"

Her voice is barely more than a whisper, but I know what she's asking.

"It means little girl."

"I should be insulted, but the way you say it..."

"It has nothing to do with your height. I know you're not a child."

God, do I know she's not. She feels amazing. Her tits are soft as they press against me, and I can see she has the most delectable ass. I'd love nothing more than to cup it and squeeze until she goes up on her toes and begs for me to wrap her legs around my waist and fuck her. For fuck's sake. Stop, you disgusting asshole. That is not what you need to be thinking about.

"Why didn't you shoot me? Whatever you were talking about, if it was with a Cartel member, then it wasn't completely legal. Carlos didn't want me alive to talk about seeing you together. Why are you letting me live?"

"I told you. You did nothing wrong but try to leave work. He should have checked the building before starting the meeting. That was on him. The only thing I take issue with is you leaving by yourself and walking into a dimly lit parking lot. I suspect you do that often, and that's too dangerous. Jane Doe, I don't hurt women."

Mafia Sinner
Mafia Beauty
Mafia Angel
Mafia Redeemer
Mafia Star

Do you also enjoy steamy Historical Romance? Discover Sabine's books written as Celeste Barclay.

www.ingramcontent.com/pod-product-compliance
Lightning Source LLC
Chambersburg PA
CBHW020525110726
47899CB00004B/1253